Born in Paris in 1947, Christian Jacq first visited Egypt when he was seventeen, went on to study Egyptology and archaeology at the Sorbonne, and is now one of the world's leading Egyptologists. He is the author of the internationally bestselling RAMSES series, THE QUEEN OF FREEDOM trilogy and many other novels on Ancient Egypt. Christian Jacq lives in Switzerland.

Also by Christian Jacq

The Ramses Series
Volume 1: The Son of the Light
Volume 2: The Temple of a Million Years
Volume 3: The Battle of Kadesh
Volume 4: The Lady of Abu Simbel
Volume 5: Under the Western Acacia

The Stone of Light Series
Volume 1: Nefer the Silent
Volume 2: The Wise Woman
Volume 3: Paneb the Ardent
Volume 4: The Place of Truth

The Queen of Freedom Trilogy
Volume 1: The Empire of Darkness
Volume 2: The War of the Crowns
Volume 3: The Flaming Sword

The Judge of Egypt Trilogy
Volume 1: Beneath the Pyramid
Volume 2: Secrets of the Desert
Volume 3: Shadow of the Sphinx

The Black Pharoah
The Tutankhamun Affair
For the Love of Philae
Champollion the Egyptian
Master Hiram & King Solomon
The Living Wisdom of Ancient Egypt

Ramses
The Temple of a Million Years

Christian Jacq

Translated by

Mary Feeney

POCKET
BOOKS

LONDON · NEW YORK · SYDNEY · TORONTO

First published in Great Britain by Simon & Schuster UK Ltd, 1997
This edition first published by Pocket Books, 2004
An imprint of Simon & Schuster UK Ltd.
A Viacom Company

Copyright © Éditions Robert Laffont, S.A., Paris, 1995
English Translation © Warner Books, Inc., 1997

1 3 5 7 9 10 8 6 4 2

Simon & Schuster UK Ltd
Africa House
64-78 Kingsway
London WC2B 6AH

Simon & Schuster Australia
Sydney

A CIP catalogue record for this book is available
from the British Library.

ISBN 0-671-01021-2

Printed and bound in Great Britain by
Cox & Wyman Ltd, Reading, Berkshire

MAP OF
ANCIENT NEAR EAST
AT NEW EMPIRE

1

Ramses was alone, awaiting a sign from the Invisible.

Alone, facing the vast scorched stretches of desert. Alone, facing the destiny still just beyond his grasp.

At twenty-three, Prince Ramses was tall and athletic, with well-defined, powerful muscles and a magnificent head of red-gold hair. A broad, high forehead, thick brows arching over small, bright eyes, a long, slightly hooked nose, rounded, delicately lobed ears, full lips and a strong chin added up to a commanding, attractive countenance.

He had already been through so much – younger son of Pharaoh Seti, royal scribe, army officer, finally named co-regent by his father and initiated into the mysteries of Abydos.

Seti had been a great ruler, an irreplaceable sovereign whose reign had brought peace and prosperity. But now Seti was dead after fifteen remarkable years on the throne, fifteen all-too-brief years which had flown like an ibis in the summer twilight.

Ramses had at first not even been aware that his distant, demanding, awe-inspiring father was gradually grooming him for kingship. Seti had put him through several demanding tests, beginning with a face-to-face encounter with a wild bull, the symbol of pharaonic power. At fourteen, Ramses had had the courage to confront the beast, but not the strength to overcome it. He would have been gored to death if Seti hadn't roped the charging bull, leaving Ramses indelibly impressed with the understanding of a pharaoh's first duty: protecting the weak.

The king alone held the key to true power. Through the magic of experience, he communicated it to Ramses, stage by stage, without revealing his master plan. Over the years, father and son had grown closer, united in faith and purpose. Reserved, unbending, Seti was a man of few words, but he had granted Ramses the unique privilege of long conversations, in the course of which he did all he could to pass on to Ramses a thorough grounding in the skills of the kingship of Upper and Lower Egypt.

Those golden hours, those blessed moments, had now vanished into the silence of death.

Pharaoh's words had poured like a blessed elixir into Ramses' heart, where they were stored as precious treasure, infusing his thoughts and actions. But Seti had departed, gone to commune with his fellow gods, and Ramses was alone, bereft of his father's guiding presence.

He felt defenceless, unable to bear the weight thrust upon his young shoulders. To govern Egypt . . . at thirteen it had been his dream, a childish longing for a prize that could never be his. Convinced that his elder brother, Shaanar, was his father's chosen successor, he had finally surrendered the foolish notion.

But Pharaoh Seti and Tuya, the Great Royal Wife, had decided otherwise. After observing the conduct of their two sons, their choice had fallen on Ramses. Why hadn't they found someone stronger and abler, someone as great as Seti? Ramses felt prepared to meet any challenger face to face, but not to steer the ship of state through the uncertain waters of the future. He had proven himself in combat, campaigning with Seti in Nubia; his boundless energy would see him through a war in defence of his country, if the need arose; but he had no idea how to command an army of bureaucrats, dignitaries and priests, all of whom could outmanoeuvre him.

The founder of their dynasty, the first Ramses, had been an elderly vizier, who had become pharaoh only reluctantly. When Seti inherited the throne, he was mature and experienced. Ramses had been content to live in his father's shadow, following his directives and responding to the least of his demands. It had been wonderful to have a trusted guide. To work under Seti's orders, to serve Egypt by obeying the pharaoh, to have him available with the answer to every question – a paradise now lost.

Now fate had unfairly dictated that Ramses, a spirited, even rash, young man, should take Seti's place. It might be better if he fled, laughing, so far into the desert that no one would ever find him.

Of course, he could count on his supporters: his mother, Tuya, an exacting and faithful ally; Nefertari, his beautiful, calm young wife; and his four boyhood friends. Moses, the Hebrew, now supervised royal construction projects; Ahsha was in the diplomatic corps; Setau was a snake-charmer; Ahmeni had devoted his life to Ramses as his private secretary and sandal-bearer.

However, he could count far more enemies. Shaanar had still not given up on claiming the throne for himself. It was anyone's guess what plots he was currently hatching. If Shaanar appeared before him this very instant, Ramses would offer no resistance. His brother might as well wear the double crown if he coveted it so desperately.

But did Ramses have the right to betray his father and abdicate the responsibility with which he had been entrusted? It would be so simple to conclude that Seti had been mistaken, that in the end he might have changed his mind. Ramses would not lie to himself. His fate depended on the answer he received from the Invisible.

It was here, in the desert, the heart of this 'red land'

charged with a dangerous energy, that the answer would come to him.

Sitting cross-legged in the classic scribe's pose, Ramses waited. The vast and solitary desert was the place for a pharaoh. The rocks and sand harboured a fire that would either strengthen his soul or break him. Let the fire pass judgment!

The sun approached its zenith, the wind died down. A gazelle leaped from dune to dune. Danger was near.

It came out of nowhere: an enormous lion, twice as big as a normal specimen. Its blazing mane gave it the air of a triumphant warrior; its sleek dark-brown body rippled with muscles.

At the sight of Ramses, it loosed a fearful roar that echoed far into the distance. Teeth flashing, claws bared, the big cat studied its prey.

Seti's son had no way to escape him.

The lion came closer, then stopped a few yards from Ramses, who noted its golden eyes. For a few seconds, they stared challengingly at each other.

Flicking its tail at a fly, the lion loped forward, suddenly tense.

Ramses rose to his feet, still staring hard.

'Invincible, it's you. Come, boy. I saved your life. What do you intend to do to me?'

Forgetting the danger, Ramses remembered plucking the baby lion from the brush as his army left Nubia. His remarkable constitution had allowed him to survive a snakebite. Cured by Setau's remedies, the cub grew to colossal proportions as Ramses' pet.

For the first time, Invincible had escaped from the pen where he was kept in his master's absence. Reverting to the wild, he was ready to pounce on the man who had raised him.

'It's up to you, boy. Fight at my side for life, or kill me now.'

The Temple of a Million Years

The lion reared on his hind legs and set his paws on Ramses' shoulders, nearly knocking him over. The prince held steady. Invincible's claws retracted. He sniffed Ramses' face. There was friendship, trust and respect between them.

'You've sealed my fate, boy.'

There was no longer any choice for the young man Seti had named 'Son of the Light'.

He would fight like a lion.

2

In Memphis, the palace was deep in mourning. Men stopped shaving, women wore their hair down. The mummification process took seventy days, and during that time the country was in limbo. The king was dead. The throne remained vacant until his successor was officially proclaimed, which could happen only after Seti was entombed and his mummy united with the heavenly light.

The frontier posts were on alert, troops ready to check any attempted invasion, at the order of the Regent and the Great Royal Wife, Tuya. The principal threat was from the Hittites, to the north in Asia Minor. While there appeared to be no imminent danger, a surprise attack was always possible. For centuries, the rich agricultural provinces of Egypt's Delta had been tempting prey for the 'sand-runners', the nomadic Bedu of the Sinai desert, as well as Asian princes who occasionally managed to form coalitions and storm the north-eastern border.

Seti's departure for the Land of the West was cause for alarm. Whenever a pharaoh passed away, the forces of chaos threatened to engulf Egypt, destroying a civilization that had lasted through eighteen dynasties. Would young Ramses be able to keep the Two Lands safe from danger? Some of the notables were less than sure he could and wished he would step aside in favour of Shaanar, his less rash and craftier brother.

The Temple of a Million Years

The Great Royal Wife, Tuya, had not changed her habits since Seti's death. She was forty-two years old, slender and regal, with a fine, straight nose, piercing almond eyes, and a nearly square jaw – and her moral authority was unquestionable. She had always been Seti's full partner; when he was forced to leave the country on state business, it was she who ruled Egypt, and ruled it firmly.

At daybreak, Tuya liked to stroll briefly in her garden, among the tamarisk and sycamore trees, organizing her working day as she walked. Her time was divided between secular and religious duties.

With Seti gone, all her activity seemed devoid of meaning. Tuya's sole desire was to join her husband in a world without conflict, far from the vanity of men; yet she was resigned to serving out her time on earth. Great happiness had been hers. She must repay her country by serving until she drew her last breath.

Nefertari's elegant silhouette emerged from the morning mist. 'More beautiful than the palace beauties', as the common folk said, Ramses' wife had shiny black hair and sublime blue-green eyes. An accomplished musician who played at the goddess Hathor's temple in Memphis, a gifted weaver, educated in literature (including her husband's favourite, the sage Ptah-hotep), Nefertari was not of noble birth; but Ramses had fallen madly in love with her, with her beauty, intelligence and unusual maturity for her age. Nefertari never sought to charm, yet she was charm itself. Tuya had recruited the girl to oversee her household, a position Nefertari continued to fill even after her marriage to the Regent. The two women were very close, almost reading each other's thoughts.

'The dew is thick this morning, Majesty. A blessing on our fair land.'

'Why are you up so early, Nefertari?'

'You're the one who needs rest, don't you think?'

'I can't sleep any more.'

'What can we do to ease your pain, Majesty?'

A sad smile fluttered on Tuya's lips. 'Seti is irreplaceable. The rest of my life will be bearable only if Ramses prospers in his reign. The thought of it is all that keeps me going.'

'I'm worried, Majesty.'

'Tell me what you fear.'

'That Seti's wishes will not be respected.'

'Who would dare go against them?'

Nefertari remained silent.

'You're thinking of Shaanar aren't you? I know he's vain and ambitious, but he would never be so foolish as to defy his father's will.' The soft gold of dawn began to light the queen's garden. 'Do you think I'm naive, Nefertari? You don't seem to share my opinion.'

'Majesty . . .'

'Has something happened to . . . ?'

'No, it's only a feeling.'

'Daughter, you're intuitive and quick as lightning. I know you never speak ill of others. But at this point nothing can stop Ramses from being crowned, short of killing him.'

'That's exactly what I fear, Majesty.'

Tuya stroked the branch of a tamarisk. 'Would Shaanar resort to murder as his stepping stone to power?'

'I hate the idea as much as you do, but I can't get it out of my mind. You may think I'm a fool and tell me it's all in my imagination. Even so, I had to say something.'

'What security measures has Ramses taken?'

'His lion and watchdog are always on duty, along with Serramanna, the head of his personal bodyguard. Since he came back from the desert, I've managed to convince him of the need for constant protection.'

'We're only ten days into the mourning period. In two months, Seti's body will be placed in his tomb, preserved for eternity. Then Ramses will be crowned and you will become Queen of Egypt.'

Ramses bowed to his mother, then pressed her tenderly to him. Seemingly so fragile, she was a lesson in dignity and nobility.

'Why has God put us to such a cruel test?' he asked.

'Seti's spirit lives on in you, my son. His time is over, yours is beginning. He will never die if you continue his work.'

'His shadow dwarfs me.'

'You, the Son of the Light? You must dispel the darkness around us, overcome the chaos that looms around us.'

The young man pulled away from his mother. 'My lion was loose in the desert. He approached me as a friend.'

'That's the sign you were hoping for, isn't it?'

'Definitely, but may I ask you a favour?'

Tuya inclined her head in acquiescence.

'Whenever my father went abroad, it was you who ruled.'

'Yes, according to tradition.'

'You have experience. You have everyone's respect and admiration. What keeps you from succeeding him now?'

'You know that was not Seti's wish. He embodied the law we must all try to follow. *You* are the one he chose, my son, and you must succeed him. I'll help all I can and advise when you ask.'

Ramses did not press her. His mother was the only person who could alter his destiny and lift this burden from him, but she would never swerve from the course her late husband had set. Despite his misgivings, Ramses would have to make his own way.

Serramanna, Ramses' Sardinian bodyguard, stuck close to the king-to-be, never leaving his wing of the royal palace. Naming the former pirate to this prestigious position had been a controversial move. Some were convinced that sooner or later the mustachioed giant would turn on Seti's son.

For the time being, no one entered the palace without his permission. The Great Royal Wife had urged him to send unauthorised visitors packing and to feel free to use his sword if danger threatened.

Hearing distant shouts, Serramanna hurried towards the entry.

'What's going on here?'

'This one was trying to force his way in,' replied a guard, gesturing towards a tall, broad-shouldered man with flowing hair.

'Who are you?' challenged Serramanna.

'Moses the Hebrew, royal construction supervisor and friend of the prince.'

'What do you want?'

'Ramses never refuses to see me.'

'Today I'm the one who'll decide.'

'Is he in seclusion?'

'Security measures. State the reason for your visit.'

'None of your business.'

'Then you'd better leave and stay away from here, or I'll have you thrown in jail.'

It took no fewer than four guards to restrain Moses.

'Tell Ramses I'm here, or he'll have your hide!'

'Your threats don't scare me.'

'Listen, you idiot! My friend is expecting me. Go and ask Ramses.'

Years as a pirate captain and scores of fierce battles had honed Serramanna's ability to read situations. Despite this Hebrew's muscle and swagger, he seemed to be genuine.

Ramses and Moses embraced.

'Is this a palace or a fortress?' Moses asked.

'My mother, my wife, Ahmeni and Serramanna all fear the worst.'

'What is that supposed to mean?'

'An attempt on my life.'

The Regent's audience chamber looked out on the gardens. In the doorway, his huge pet lion dozed, with Wideawake, the golden-yellow dog, curled between his front paws.

'With them to guard you, you ought to feel safe enough.'

'Nefertari is convinced that Shaanar still thinks he should be king.'

'A coup before your father's laid to rest? Hardly his style. He likes to work away in the background and bank on making his move at the right time.'

'He's running out of time.'

'You're right. But he won't risk a confrontation.'

'God forbid! It would only bring harm to Egypt. What do you hear at Karnak?'

'Opinion is running against you.'

Moses had been running Seti's vast construction site at Karnak, where the royal architects had been instructed to add a huge Hall of Pillars to the temple. The pharaoh's death had brought the work to a halt.

'Whose opinion?'

'The priesthood of Amon, some nobles, the Vizier of the South . . . Your sister Dolora and her husband Sary have stirred them up. They didn't take kindly to being exiled from Memphis.'

'Sary tried to have me and Ahmeni killed. He and my sister could have faced a much stiffer punishment than being sent to Thebes.'

'The southern sun did nothing to dry up their poison. You should have banished them from Egypt once and for all.'

'Dolora is my sister. Sary practically raised me.'

'Should a king have different standards for his relatives?'

Ramses was cut to the quick. 'I'm not king yet, Moses.'

'I still think you should have let justice take its course.'

'If the two of them pull any more tricks, I'll show no mercy.'

'I wish I believed you. You don't realize how ruthless your enemies can be.'

'Right now I'm grieving for my father.'

'And forgetting your duty to your country. If Seti is looking down from heaven, do you think he approves of your feebleness?'

If Moses hadn't been his best friend, Ramses would have hit him.

'You want me to be hard and impersonal?'

'You've suffered a great loss, but keep your eyes open. Shaanar approached me, even knowing how close to you I am. He tried to turn me against you. Does that give you some sense of the danger you're in?'

Ramses was speechless.

'You're facing a tough opponent,' Moses continued. 'Wake up, my friend.'

3

Memphis, situated where the Nile Valley began branching out into the Delta, was the country's economic capital. Now it slumbered. In the harbour, called 'Safe Journey', merchant ships stayed in their moorings. For the seventy-day mourning period, trade was suspended, and the nobles stopped entertaining.

Seti's death had sent the town into a state of shock. His reign had brought increased prosperity, but the most prominent businessmen feared that the trend would be reversed under an irresolute pharaoh who made Egypt vulnerable and weak. And who could be strong as Seti? Shaanar, his elder son, would run the country capably, but the ailing Seti had favoured the young and fiery Ramses, who seemed more like a wastrel than a head of state. The most clear-sighted of leaders could make mistakes, the businessmen reasoned, and Memphis quietly agreed with Thebes that Seti might have chosen the wrong son to succeed him.

Shaanar restlessly paced Meba's receiving-room. A fit-looking man of sixty with a broad, calm face, Meba was Seti's long-time minister for foreign affairs. He had secretly worked against Ramses, supporting Shaanar, whose political and economic views more closely resembled his own. Opening the Mediterranean and Asian markets, strengthening commercial ties, was the way to a healthy economic future, even if it meant forgetting a few traditional principles. After all, he felt, the arms trade was preferable to armed conflict.

'Will he come?' asked Shaanar.

'He's on our side, rest assured.'

'That could change at any moment. You can't trust a bully.'

Seti's elder son was short, stocky and overweight, with a round face and plump cheeks. His thick, sensual lips betrayed his love of good food, while his dark, beady eyes were perpetually nervous. He avoided the sun and all forms of exertion. A cultivated voice failed to mask his uneven temper.

Shaanar was a pacifist for financial reasons. Egypt's economic isolationism was folly, in his opinion. 'Treason' was a term for moralizers without a nose for profit. Ramses, brought up in the old ways, didn't deserve to be king – and was unfit to be. Shaanar had no compunction about fomenting the plot that would bring him to power: Egypt would thank him for it.

But he still needed his most important ally.

'A drink,' Shaanar demanded. Meba served his illustrious guest a cup of cool beer. 'We never should have trusted him,' said the prince.

'I'm sure he'll come. Don't forget how eager he is to get home.'

At last, the minister's door-keeper announced the long-awaited caller.

Blond, sharp-eyed Menelaus, son of Atreus and King of Sparta, was lucky in war. He wore a double cuirasse and a wide belt with golden buckles that had served him well in the victory over Troy. With his fleet in tatters, he had sought refuge in Egypt. Now his wife, Helen, refused to leave the land of the pharaohs, fearing bitter treatment from her husband once they reached home. Since Queen Tuya had taken Helen under her wing, Menelaus was unable to coerce his wife. Fortunately, Shaanar had stepped in to enlist his cooperation in overthrowing Ramses, promising to hand over Helen in return. The moment Shaanar became pharaoh, Menelaus would be able to leave for Greece with Helen.

For several months, his troops had settled in, the officers joining the Egyptian army, the soldiers and sailors finding ways to make a living, all seeming content with their good fortune. In reality, they anxiously awaited their commander's order to spring into action, like a new and improved Trojan Horse.

The Greek eyed Meba suspiciously. 'Tell him to leave,' he ordered Shaanar. 'You and I talk, no one else.'

'The minister is one of us.'

'Don't make me repeat myself.'

Shaanar waved the older man out of the room.

'Where do we stand?' asked Menelaus.

'It's time to act.'

'Are you sure? This infernal mummy-making takes so long I'm beginning to wonder about you people.'

'We need to act before my father's mummy is laid in his tomb.'

'My men are ready.'

'I don't want any unnecessary violence or . . .' Shaanar hesitated.

'Out with it, man! You Egyptians are afraid of a good fight. We Greeks kept after the Trojans for years until we destroyed them. If you want Ramses dead, say so. My sword will do the rest.'

'Ramses is my brother, and sometimes deceit is more effective than brute force.'

'They go hand in hand. And who are you to be lecturing me, a hero of the Trojan wars, on strategy?'

'You need to win Helen back.'

'Helen!' he spat. 'The woman makes me sick, but I can't go home without her.'

'Then let's try my plan.'

'What is your plan?'

Shaanar smiled. Luck was with him this time. With the Greek's help, it would work. 'Only two things stand in our way: the lion and Serramanna. We'll poison the first and cut down the second. Then we capture Ramses and you carry him off to Greece.'

'Why not just kill him?'

'I don't want blood on my hands when I take the throne. The official story will be that Ramses renounced his claim and decided to see the world. Unfortunately, a tragic accident will occur during his travels.'

'What about Helen?'

'Once I'm crowned, my mother will have to obey my orders and stop protecting her. If Tuya resists, she'll be placed under house arrest in a temple.'

Menelaus nodded. 'Not bad, for an Egyptian. Do you have the poison to hand?'

'Of course.'

'Our man in Ramses' guard is one of my best officers. He'll have no trouble slitting Serramanna's throat while he sleeps. When do we act?'

'It won't be long. I have business in Thebes. As soon as I'm back, we'll strike.'

Helen relished every moment of a happiness she had thought lost for ever. In a light, nectar-scented dress, with a veil on her head to protect her from the sun, she reflected that her life in Tuya's household was a wonderful dream. She had managed to escape from that vicious, cowardly tyrant Menelaus, whose greatest pleasure was to humiliate her; even his men called her 'evil bitch'.

Tuya and her daughter-in-law, Nefertari, had given Helen friendship and employment. It was a pleasure to live in a country where women were not forced to live as prisoners in their homes, even if that home was a palace.

Was Helen truly to blame for the deaths of thousands of

Greeks and Trojans? She had never wanted the long years of frenzied killing, yet somehow she had been tried and convicted without ever having had the chance to defend herself. Here in Memphis no one condemned her. She wove, she listened to music and played it, she swam in the palace pools, strolled in the endlessly delightful gardens. The clash of weapons grew distant, yielding to birdsong.

Several times a day, white-armed Helen prayed to the gods that her dream might continue. Her only wish was to leave the past, her country, her husband, behind her.

On a sandy path lined by persea trees, she spotted a dead crane. Walking closer, she saw that the bird's handsome body had been torn open. Helen knelt and examined the entrails; her gift for prophecy had been acknowledged by both the Greeks and the Trojans.

It was a long while before she struggled to her feet.

What she read in the crane's entrails appalled her.

4

Thebes, the southern capital, was home to the cult of Amon, the god credited with helping to drive out the Hyskos, a cruel, barbarian Asiatic people who had occupied the country several centuries earlier. Since Egypt's liberation, every pharaoh for generations had paid tribute to Amon and further embellished his temple at Karnak until it became the greatest and richest of temples, a sort of state within the state. The High Priest of Amon was now more a powerful administrator than a man of prayer.

Upon his arrival in Thebes, Shaanar immediately requested an audience with the High Priest. The two men talked in the shade of an arbour dripping with wisteria and honeysuckle. A cooling breeze blew from the sacred lake nearby.

'You came without an entourage?' the High Priest asked in wonder.

'Very few people are aware I'm here.'

'I see. I'll be discreet then.'

'Are you still opposed to Ramses?'

'More firmly than ever. He's too young and hot-headed to be pharaoh. His reign would be disastrous. Seti made a mistake designating him.'

'Will you take me into your confidence?'

'What rank would you grant the Temple of Amon, if you wore the crown?'

18

'The first, naturally.'

'Your father favoured other priesthoods like those of Heliopolis and Memphis. Karnak must no longer be second best; that's all I ask.'

'That's Ramses' intention, not mine.'

'What do you have in mind, Shaanar?'

'We must act, and act quickly.'

'In other words, before Seti's funeral rites.'

'Yes. It's our last chance.'

What Shaanar did not know was that the High Priest of Amon was seriously ill. His doctor had told him he had only months, perhaps weeks, to live. A speedy resolution would be a final blessing from the gods. Before he died, he would see Ramses deposed and Karnak saved.

'I cannot condone violence,' the High Priest decreed. 'Amon gave us peace, which must be preserved.'

'I agree completely. Unfit as he may be to rule, Ramses is my brother, and I hold him dear. I have never for one second intended him any harm.'

'What are your plans for him?'

'He's an energetic man, in love with adventure and wide-open spaces. An extended trip abroad will be a welcome prospect once he's freed from his crushing responsibilities. When he returns, his first-hand observations will be extremely valuable.'

'I would also like to see your mother remain as your close adviser.'

'That goes without saying.'

'Be faithful to Amon, my son, and your future will be assured.'

Shaanar bowed deferentially. This old priest's gullibility was a wonderful stroke of luck.

Dolora, Ramses' elder sister, rubbed soothing unguents into her oily skin. Plain, lanky, always tired, she hated Thebes, hated the South. A princess belonged in Memphis, in the thick of court gossip.

Thebes was boring. High society had welcomed her with open arms, of course, and showered her with invitations; she was, after all, a member of the royal family. But fashionable life lagged behind that of Memphis and, besides, her husband was slowly sinking into a deep depression. Affable, paunchy Sary had been Ramses' tutor, then head of the Kap, the royal school where Egypt's top students were sent. His talents were wasted here, and it was all her brother's fault.

Yes, Sary had come up with a feeble plot to have Ramses killed. And yes, she, Dolora, had thrown in her lot with Shaanar. Yes, they had both made mistakes. Even so, shouldn't Ramses grant them his pardon, considering Seti had died?

Revenge was the only possible response to his cruelty. Ramses' luck would turn eventually, and when it did, she and Sary would be ready. Meanwhile, she attended to her skin while her husband read or dozed.

Shaanar's unannounced arrival shook them out of their torpor.

'My dear brother!' exclaimed Dolora, kissing him. 'Bearing glad tidings, I hope!'

'Possibly.'

'Don't keep us in suspense!' Sary demanded.

'I'm going to be king.'

'Our day is coming soon, then?'

'Come back to Memphis with me. I'll find a place for you until we can dispose of Ramses.'

Dolora blanched. 'Dispose of him, you say?'

'Don't worry, little sister. I'm only sending him on a grand tour.'

'Will you have a job for me?' asked Sary. 'Something important?'

'You've made it just a bit awkward,' replied Shaanar. 'But

I can use a man of your intelligence. Be loyal to me and the rewards will be great.'

'You have my word, Shaanar.'

Iset the Fair was biding her time. Before she gave birth to their son, Ramses had sent her to Thebes; now she was raising her beloved Kha in the royal palace. A striking young woman with green eyes, a small, straight nose and finely drawn lips, she was energetic, vivacious, Ramses' first lover and now his lesser wife.

Lesser wife – hard to accept the title and the status it implied. Yet Iset found it impossible to be envious of Nefertari, so lovely, gentle and serious, with the bearing of a queen, though quite devoid of worldly ambition.

It would have been easier if she were consumed with hate, if she could lash out at the two of them, but she still loved the man who had given her so much happiness and pleasure, the man to whom she had given his firstborn son.

Iset cared nothing for power and prestige. She loved Ramses for himself, his intensity and verve. But the pain of living apart from him was sometimes unbearable. Why didn't he realize how much it hurt her?

Soon Ramses would be king and come to see her only rarely. Each time, she knew, she would give in to her love for him. If only she could meet someone else – but other men paled in comparison to Ramses.

When her steward announced Shaanar, Iset was amazed. What was Seti's elder son doing in Thebes before the funeral?

She received him in a room with narrow slits of windows high in the walls, letting in fresh air but little direct sunlight.

'You look magnificent, Iset.'

'What do you want?'

'I know you don't care for me,' he said, 'but I also know you're intelligent enough to look out for your own

21

best interests. I think you have the makings of a Great Royal Wife.'

'Ramses doesn't share your opinion.'

'What if it weren't up to him?'

'What do you mean?'

'My brother isn't a complete fool. He finally sees that he's not fit to govern Egypt.'

'Meaning . . . ?'

'Meaning that for the good of our country I'll take over and you can be Lady of the Two Lands.'

'Ramses would never step down. You're lying.'

'It's the truth, dear lady. He's planning to leave the country with Menelaus and has asked me to be Seti's successor, out of respect for the memory of our father. When he's done travelling, he'll be treated with all the respect due to a member of the royal family.'

'Has he said anything about me?'

'I'm afraid he's forgotten you and his little son. All he can think of is seeing the world.'

'Is he taking Nefertari?'

'No, no . . . too many fish in the sea,' laughed Shaanar. 'When it comes to pleasure, he's insatiable.'

Iset seemed distraught. Shaanar would have liked to take her hand, but it was too soon. He mustn't frighten her away. First he needed to offer comfort, then slowly begin to woo her.

'Kha will have the finest education,' he promised. 'You won't have to worry. After Seti is laid to rest, we'll go back to Memphis together.'

'Ramses . . . Will Ramses be gone by then?'

'Of course.'

'He's not attending the funeral rites?'

'It's a shame, but there's nothing to be done about it. Menelaus refuses to wait any longer. Forget Ramses, Iset. Concentrate on becoming queen.'

5

Iset spent a sleepless night.

Shaanar was lying. Ramses would never leave Egypt to numb his grief in foreign travels. If he missed Seti's funeral, it would be against his will.

Ramses had treated her badly, true, but she would never betray him by throwing herself into Shaanar's arms. Iset had no desire to be queen, no matter what Shaanar thought. The moon-faced, smooth-talking, ambitious, conceited fool! She hated him.

She knew what she had to do: warn Ramses of the plot being hatched against him and of his elder brother's plans for him.

On fresh papyrus, she composed a long letter relating her conversation with Shaanar. Then she summoned the local head of the royal courier service.

'This needs to reach Memphis as soon as possible.'

'I'll see to it personally,' he assured her.

River traffic at Thebes had slowed considerably, as in Memphis, while the country was in mourning. Guards dozed at the river landing where boats for the North customarily docked. Iset's messenger hailed a sailor.

'Weigh anchor – we're leaving for Memphis.'

'Sorry, can't leave port.'

'Why?'

'The High Priest of Amon at Karnak has the boat reserved.'

'Without going through my office?'

'Just got the order.'

'Well, weigh anchor anyway. I've got an urgent message for the royal palace at Memphis.'

A man appeared on the bridge of the boat in question.

'Orders are orders, my good man and you must obey them.'

'Keep your nose out of this, whoever you are.'

'I'm Shaanar, Seti's elder son.'

The official bowed. 'Forgive my insolence, Your Highness.'

'All right, if you give me the message Iset the Fair wants delivered.'

'But—'

'It goes to the royal palace in Memphis, correct?'

'Yes, to your brother Ramses.'

'That's where I'm heading tonight. Or don't I meet your standards as a courier?'

The official handed the letter to Shaanar.

As soon as the boat pulled away from Thebes, Shaanar tore Iset's letter to shreds and scattered them in the wind.

The night was warm and fragrant. It didn't seem possible that Seti had left his people and that the very soul of Egypt mourned the death of a king as great as those of the Old Kingdom. Usually the evenings were cheerful and lively. In village squares and city streets, people danced, sang and told stories – often fables of animals taking the place of humans and acting more wisely than humans. But, during the time of mourning and mummification, laughter and games had disappeared.

Wideawake, Ramses's yellow dog, slept with his head against Invincible, the huge lion that patrolled the Regent's private garden. After the gardeners finished the evening watering, the two pets liked to stretch out on the cool grass.

Among the gardeners was a Greek, one of Menelaus' men. Before leaving for the night, he had tucked poisoned chunks of meat into one of the lily beds, where the greedy beasts would surely find them. Even if the lion took hours to die, no treatment could save him.

Wideawake was the first to pick up the unfamiliar scent. Yawning, he stretched, sniffed the air, and trotted over to the lilies. His snout quickly led him to the meat; he nosed and pawed it thoroughly, then backtracked. This was too good a find not to share with his friend.

The three soldiers perched on the garden wall smiled as the lion sleepily trailed the yellow dog back to the flower bed. Just a little longer and the coast would be clear. They could slip into Ramses's bedchamber, take him by surprise while he slept, and carry him off to Menelaus's waiting ship.

The lion and dog lay with their heads in the foliage. Before long they seemed to go limp. Ten minutes later one of the Greeks jumped down from the wall. Given how deadly the poison was and how much had been put in the meat, the big cat must already be paralysed.

The scout motioned to his companions, who followed him down the path towards the Regent's suite. They were about to go inside when a growl made them wheel round.

Invincible and Wideawake stood behind them, staring at them. Among the trampled lilies lay the tainted meat, which the lion had shredded after confirming his friend's suspicions.

The three Greek soldiers huddled together, daggers raised.

Claws extended and fangs bared, Invincible sprang at them.

The Greek officer who had infiltrated Ramses's royal bodyguard crept through the silent palace towards the Regent's room. He was assigned to patrol the hallways and warn of any intruders, so the other soldiers on duty, who knew him well, let him pass and thought nothing of it.

He headed towards the granite threshold where Serramanna slept. The Sard always boasted that anyone coming after Ramses would have to slit his throat first. Once he was dead, the Regent would have lost his principal protector, and all his bodyguards would be won over to Shaanar, the new ruler of Egypt.

The Greek stopped and listened. Not a sound, except for the steady breathing of deep sleep. Even a giant had to sleep sometimes. But he might have a cat's reflexes and suddenly wake, sensing danger. The Greek must move swiftly and surely, allowing the Sard no time to react.

Cautiously, he listened a while longer. There could be no doubt: Serramanna was at his mercy. Holding his breath, he unsheathed his dagger, then struck furiously at the sleeping figure's throat.

'Nice try, for a sneaking coward,' a deep voice snarled from behind him. He whirled round.

'You've just killed a dummy,' said Serramanna. 'The breathing was real, though. I had a hunch that something was up tonight.'

Menelaus' man gripped the handle of his dagger.

'Drop it.'

'I'm still going to slit your throat.'

'Try it.' The Sard loomed over him. The Greek's dagger connected with air. For his size, Serramanna was surprisingly quick on his feet.

'You don't even know how to fight,' he jeered.

The Greek tried a feint, stepping aside, then rushed forward, blade pointing at his opponent's stomach.

The Sard's right hand chopped at his wrist, breaking it, as his left hand slammed into the Greek's temple. Tongue dangling, eyes glazed, he collapsed and was dead before he even hit the floor.

'One coward fewer to deal with,' muttered Serramanna.

Ramses considered the two-pronged attack. In the garden, three Greeks had died under the lion's claws; in the corridor lay another dead Greek, a member of his personal body-guard.

'They were after you,' Serramanna said flatly.

'Did the one you killed say anything?'

'I didn't have time to ask questions. No great loss – he wasn't much of a soldier.'

'Weren't they Menelaus' men?'

'Just let me at that bully! I'll send him off to meet all the heroes he's always lamenting.'

'For the moment, just double the watch.'

'Defence is a bad strategy, Prince. Only attacking leads to victory.'

'First we need to know who the enemy is.'

'Menelaus and his Greeks. They're liars and cheats. Send them all packing before they try again!'

Ramses laid a hand on Serramanna's right shoulder.

'With you on my side, I don't have to worry.'

Ramses spent the rest of the night in the garden with his pets. Invincible was fast asleep; Wideawake dozed fitfully. The prince contemplated human folly. The struggle for power had begun even before Seti's mummy could be laid in his tomb.

Moses was right. Lenience towards his enemies had only made them more likely to keep up their attacks, convinced he would not retaliate.

With the dawn, the prince's spirits rose. No one could take Seti's place, but it was time for Ramses to start acting like a pharaoh.

6

In Seti's Egypt, temples were responsible for redistributing excess donations, as well as the food produced on their extensive domains. As long as there had been pharaohs, the law of Ma'at, the fragile goddess of truth and justice, maintained that each child of this blessed land of plenty should be free from want. What god could bless a feast day if even the humblest soul went hungry?

As head of state, the pharaoh was both the rudder that steered a steady course and the captain who held his crew together. He must inspire the cooperation essential to any lasting society.

A key government department maintained strict control over the redistribution of goods. However, the temples were allowed to commission a few independent merchants to travel the length of the country, trading freely.

One such trader was Raia, a Syrian who had lived in Egypt for over ten years. With his cargo ship and herd of donkeys, he was constantly on the move, selling wine, preserved meat, and vases imported from Asia. He was of average height and build, sporting a small pointed beard and dressed in a striped tunic. Polite, discreet and honest, he attracted a faithful clientele with quality merchandise at reasonable prices. His work permit was renewed year after year in recognition of his service to his adopted country. Like many other immigrants, the Syrian had become practically indistinguishable from the natives.

No one knew that Raia was a spy in the pay of the Hittites.

They had ordered him to gather all the information he could and send it to them as quickly as possible. The warlike Anatolians would then decide when to attack Pharaoh's foreign dominions, seize their land, then invade Egypt itself. Raia had cultivated contacts in the military, the customs department, the police. Titbits from their dinner conversation ended up in Hattusa, the Hittite capital, by way of coded messages inserted into the alabaster vases Raia exported to southern Syria, Egypt's official ally. Customs had searched his shipments more than once, finding only what appeared to be routine business letters and invoices. The importer, who belonged to the spy ring, made a profit selling the vases and a bonus for delivering the messages to an agent in Hittite-controlled northern Syria, who relayed them directly to Hattusa.

It was a simple way for the Near East's greatest military power to receive monthly briefings on Egyptian politics from a primary source.

Seti's death and the subsequent mourning period would be the perfect opportunity to attack Egypt, but Raia had argued forcefully against it, telling the Hittite generals it would be madness. If they thought the Egyptian army had been demobilized, they were sadly mistaken. Fearing a possible invasion before the ascension of Seti's successor, the Egyptians had reinforced their border patrols.

Furthermore, the king's loose-tongued daughter had made it plain that Shaanar, elder brother of the future king, was not resigned to being relegated to the second rank. In other words, he was planning to seize power before the coronation.

Raia had made a thorough study of the disgruntled

29

prince. Ambitious, clever, devious – and ruthless when his self-interest was at stake – he was altogether different from his father and brother. That he should become pharaoh was devoutly to be wished, for he seemed to have fallen into the Hittite's trap, believing their claims to want closer diplomatic and trade relations, which would bring an end to the old hostilities. Even Seti had failed to take the key fortress of Kadesh when he had the chance, suing for peace instead. The King of the Hittites had announced that he was abandoning his expansionist plans. He hoped the new pharaoh would believe him and let down the country's defences.

Raia next began to identify Shaanar's co-conspirators and determine how he planned to proceed. His unerring instinct led him to the Greeks who had recently settled in Memphis. Menelaus was no more than a cruel mercenary whose most cherished memories were of the slaughter at Troy. Rumour had it that the bloodthirsty Greek was restless, eager to sail home to Sparta as a conquering hero with his wife, Helen, in tow. Shaanar had paid the Greek contingent handsomely to eliminate Ramses and help him reclaim his rightful place as Seti's successor.

Raia had become convinced that Ramses would mean trouble for the Hittites. Unafraid to fight, he had inherited his father's determination. He was young, hot-blooded, unpredictable. Shaanar, on the other hand, was a known quantity, reasonable, open-minded: clearly the better choice.

Unfortunately, a palace servant in Raia's employ had just brought the information that several Greek mercenaries had been killed while attempting to enter Ramses' bedchamber. The attempted coup had apparently failed.

The next few hours would be telling. If Shaanar managed to avoid being implicated, he still had a future. If not, he'd have to be crossed off the list.

Menelaus stamped on the shield that had warded off so many

blows on the battlefield. He broke one of the spears that had dispatched many a Trojan, then grabbed a vase and threw it against the wall of his antechamber.

Still fuming, he turned to face Shaanar.

'A complete failure! How can it be? My men never fail. It took us ten years to beat the Trojans, but we did it.'

'I sympathize, but the fact is that Ramses' lion got your three soldiers and Serramanna killed the fourth.'

'They were betrayed.'

'No, simply not up to the job you gave them. Ramses suspects you now. He'll probably order you out of the country.

'Without Helen.'

'Yes. You have failed, Menelaus.'

'Your plan was stupid.'

'You seemed to think it would work.'

'Get out!'

'You'd better be prepared to leave soon.'

'I know what I have to do.'

Ahmeni was Ramses's sandal-bearer and private secretary, but first and foremost his lifelong friend. He had sworn allegiance to the Regent and linked his own destiny to his – whatever it might be. Short, slight, with thinning hair, his frail physique did not prevent him from being a tireless worker and peerless scribe, forever studying official documents and briefing Ramses – as he was doing now – on their contents. Devoid of personal ambition, Ahmeni was nevertheless a strict taskmaster, holding his administrative staff of twenty to the highest standards, prizing accuracy and discipline above all else.

Although he had little use for a brute like Serramanna, Ahmeni admitted that the bodyguard had dealt effectively with the Greek assassin. Ramses' reaction to the attack was surprising. The future pharaoh had simply asked his secretary for a thorough description of the main branches of government, how they worked, how they related to one another.

When Serramanna came in to announce Shaanar, Ahmeni was irritated. He did not want to be interrupted as he pored over documents concerning the reform of outdated laws regulating public ferries.

'Don't let him in,' Ahmeni urged Ramses.

'Shaanar is my brother.'

'He's a self-centred schemer.'

'I think I should hear what he has to say.'

Ramses had his brother shown into the garden, where Invincible lazed in the shade of a sycamore tree and Wideawake gnawed on a bone.

'Your security is much tighter than Seti's!' exclaimed Shaanar. 'It's almost impossible to get near you.'

'Haven't you heard that some Greeks broke in here last night? They were after me.'

'I heard. I've come to tell you who was behind it.'

'How do you know that?'

'Menelaus tried to bribe me.'

'What did he offer?'

'To put me on the throne.'

'And you turned him down?'

'I do love power, Ramses, but I know my limitations. No one but you can be the next pharaoh. Our father's wishes were clear; they must be respected.'

'Why would Menelaus risk his neck?'

'He's dying to go home to Sparta as a conquering hero, but to do that he needs to take Helen with him. He's convinced that you're holding her against her will. In exchange for making me king, he wanted me to banish you to the desert, hand over Helen, and clear him for departure.'

'Helen is free to do whatever she chooses.'

'To a Greek that's inconceivable – she must be being controlled by a man.'

'Is he really that stupid?'

'Menelaus is stubborn and dangerous. He's acting like a Greek hero.'

'What would you advise?'

'He's violated our hospitality. It's time that he left for good.'

7

The poet Homer lived in a fine new residence not far from the palace. Ramses had also provided a cook, maid and gardener to look after him. The cellar was stocked with Delta wine which Homer spiced with anise and coriander. There was also a supply of the fragrant olive oil he liked to rub on his skin. The old poet was so comfortable that he rarely left his garden, seeking inspiration in the shade of his beloved lemon tree.

He would smoke crushed sage leaves in a pipe fashioned from a giant snail shell and a hollow reed. Hector, his black and white cat, purred in his lap as he dictated verse after verse of his *Iliad* to Ahmeni or one of the scribe's assistants.

Ramses' visit was an added pleasure. The cook brought a Cretan wine jug with a very thin spout, pouring just a trickle of cool spiced wine. The garden pavilion – four acacia columns with a palm-frond roof – gave some relief from the summer heat.

'This nice hot weather helps my aching bones,' said Homer, stroking the flowing white beard that was such a contrast to his lined and craggy face. 'Do you have storms like we do in Greece?'

'Tremendous ones,' answered Ramses. 'When our god Set unleashes his fury, dark clouds fill the sky, lightning flashes, thunder rumbles, and bolts crash to the ground. The rain floods dry riverbeds, sweeping rocks through the wadis. People are terrified, and some think it's the end of the world.'

'Wasn't your father named after Set?'

'For a long time I couldn't understand why a pharaoh would place himself under the protection of the god who murdered Osiris, his own brother. Then I realized that Seti wanted to harness the powers of darkness and use them to do good.'

'What a strange country Egypt is! And it seems you've been having your own stormy weather.'

'I didn't know you could see from your garden to mine.'

'My eyesight is failing, but my hearing is excellent.'

'So you heard that your countrymen tried to kill me.'

'The other day I wrote these lines: "I greatly fear that you will be caught tight in the enemy's net, that you will all become their prey and spoils of war. They will sack your cities. Think on it night and day, fight on, if you wish to hold your heads high."'

'Are you a seer?'

'I can guess why the future pharaoh should take time from his official duties to seek the opinion of an obscure old poet – not that I don't appreciate your visits.'

Ramses smiled. He liked the way Homer spoke his mind.

'All right. Do you think the soldiers who came after me were acting alone or on orders from Menelaus?'

'Beware of Greeks, my friend! Hatching plots is their favourite pastime. Menelaus wants Helen, and you're standing in his way: violence is the only answer.'

'But I'm still here.'

'Menelaus is as single-minded as he is unprincipled. He'll keep trying, attack you in your own back yard, without a thought for the consequences.'

'What do you recommend?'

'Pack him off to Greece with Helen.'

'She won't go.'

'Through no fault of her own, that woman sows death and destruction in her wake. If you think you can alter the course of her destiny, you're sadly mistaken.'

'She's free to choose where she lives.'

'Don't say I didn't warn you. By the way, I could use some new papyrus and more of that wonderful olive oil.'

Some might have said the white-bearded poet should be less brusque with his royal patron. Ramses, however, valued the old man's frankness. There were yes-men to spare in the royal court.

The moment Ramses walked through the gate to his wing of the palace, Ahmeni came running, in a most uncharacteristic state of agitation.

'What's happening?'

'Menelaus,' Ahmeni panted.

'What now?'

'He's taken hostages down at the harbour – dock workers, women and children. Says he'll kill them unless you deliver Helen to him today.'

'Where is he?'

'On his ship, with the hostages. His whole fleet is ready to sail. Not one of his mercenaries is left in town.'

'And where were our naval police when all this happened?'

'Don't be too hard on them. Menelaus took the guards on duty by surprise.'

'Has anyone told my mother?'

'She's waiting for you, with Nefertari and Helen.'

Seti's widow, Ramses' wife, and Menelaus' reluctant spouse were all looking anxious. Tuya sat on a low gilded chair, Nefertari on a folding stool. Helen stood, her back against a light-green column with a lotus capital.

The Great Royal Wife's audience chamber was cool and

restful, with subtle, pleasing scents in the air. On Pharaoh's throne, a bouquet of flowers marked the temporary absence of a monarch.

Ramses bowed to his mother, kissed his wife gently, and greeted Helen.

'How much do you know?' asked Tuya.

'Only that it's serious. How many hostages?'

'Around fifty.'

'Even one life is more than I'm willing to sacrifice.'

Ramses turned to Helen. 'If we attack, will Menelaus really kill the hostages?'

'He'll slit their throats with his own dagger.'

'How could he live with innocent blood on his hands?'

'He wants me back. If he can't have me, he'll kill before he gets killed.'

'It's barbaric.'

'Menelaus is a warrior. To him, everyone is either friend or foe.'

'And his own men – doesn't he realize none of them will survive if the hostages are executed?'

'They'll die as heroes, with their honour intact.'

'Heroes? Murderers of defenceless bystanders?'

'Menelaus knows only one law: kill or be killed.'

'There must be a special hell reserved for Greek heroes.'

'Frightening as that may be, the need to fight is more intense than the simple desire to survive.'

Nefertari drew closer to Ramses. 'What will you do?'

'I'll board Menelaus' ship alone and unarmed and try to reason with him.'

'You must be joking,' Helen said with a bitter laugh.

'The least I can do is try.'

'He'll take you hostage too!' Nefertari interjected.

'You have no right to put yourself in such danger,' Tuya told him. 'Won't you just be falling into his trap?'

'He'll take you away to Greece,' Nefertari prophesied, 'and

37

someone else will be pharaoh – someone who'll use Helen as a pawn in trade negotiations.'

Ramses shot a questioning look at his mother. She seemed to agree with Nefertari.

'If persuasion won't work with Menelaus, we'll have to resort to violence.'

Helen approached the Regent.

'No,' he said, 'we won't let you sacrifice yourself. Protecting a guest is a sacred duty.'

'Ramses is right,' the Great Royal Wife agreed. 'Giving in to your husband's blackmail would be in violation of the law of Ma'at. It could only bring unhappiness to Egypt.'

'But I'm the one who's responsible for all this and it's—'

'Don't, Helen. Since you've chosen to live among us, we're bound to help you stay free.'

'I'll think of something,' Seti's son concluded.

Trembling and sweating, Meba, the late pharaoh's minister for foreign affairs, stood on the pier shouting back and forth with Menelaus and fearing that a Greek archer's arrow would pierce him at any moment. However, he did win one concession from the King of Sparta: Ramses would be allowed one night to host a farewell banquet in Helen's honour.

Menelaus stipulated that the hostages would be given no food whatsoever until Helen boarded the ship. He would release them once he had sailed clear and was sure no Egyptian warships were trailing his fleet.

Unharmed, Meba walked briskly away from the flagship, not minding the Greek soldiers' taunts. Ramses' praise for his able negotiating was some consolation.

The prince now had one night to find a way of freeing the hostages.

8

Average in height, strong as an ox, dark-haired, swarthy Setau the snake-charmer was making love to his lissome Nubian wife, Lotus, whose slender curves kept him constantly on the brink of arousal. Their large home on the edge of the desert, far from the centre of Memphis, also served as their laboratory and workshop. Several rooms were filled with flasks and vials of various sizes and the strange contraptions they used to process the venom and prepare the medicines the doctors needed.

Lotus was an amazingly agile and willing participant in her husband's seemingly endless variations on a theme. Since he had brought her to Egypt after marrying her, she had never ceased to amaze him with her deep, subtle knowledge of reptiles. Their shared passion for snakes led to important discoveries and the creation of new remedies, after a great deal of experimentation.

As Setau caressed his wife's breasts, tender as flower buds, their pet cobra which lay coiled in the doorway, suddenly lifted its head.

'We have a visitor,' said Setau.

Lotus glanced at the splendid reptile. Its swaying told her whether their visitor was a friend or a stranger. Tonight it did not seem alarmed.

Setau slid off the cosy bed and grabbed a club. Though he

trusted the cobra's judgment, at this time of night it was best to be careful.

A galloping horse pulled up in front of the house. The rider jumped off.

'Ramses! What are you doing here in the middle of the night?'

'Hope I'm not disturbing you.'

'As a matter of fact, Lotus and I were just—'

'Sorry, but I need your help.'

The two had attended the Royal Academy together, but Setau had shunned the traditional administrative career to devote himself to the study of snakes, unlocking the secrets of life and death. When they were still in their teens, he had dared Ramses to face the master of the desert, a lethal species of cobra. Setau was immunized against the cobra's bite, but the prince was not. Their friendship survived the challenge, and Setau belonged to the limited circle of Ramses' closest confidants.

'Is the kingdom in danger?'

'Menelaus has taken hostages and threatens to kill them unless we hand Helen back to him.'

'A fine mess. But why not let her go? The woman did cause the destruction of an entire city.'

'Violating the laws of hospitality would make us no better than barbarians.'

'Let the barbarians sort it out between them.'

'Helen is a queen. She wants to stay in Egypt. It's my duty to keep her out of Menelaus' clutches.'

'You really sound like a pharaoh. It must be your destiny. But then it's a job only a madman or a fool would want.'

'I need to storm Menelaus' ship without harming the hostages.'

'You've always liked beating impossible odds.'

'The commanding officers of the regiments stationed in

Memphis haven't come up with one worthwhile idea. Every plan they suggest would end in a massacre.'

'Does that surprise you?'

'No. That's why I thought of you.'

'You think I'm going to storm Greek warships?'

'Not you – your snakes.'

'Let's hear it.'

'Before dawn, we'll send swimmers to climb up the sides of the ship, carrying bags with snakes in them. When they reach the bridge, they'll release the snakes and throw them at the soldiers guarding the hostages. A few of the guards will be bitten, and in the confusion our men can free the hostages.'

'Original, but awfully risky. What makes you think the cobras will be selective about their victims?'

'I'm fully aware of the enormous risk we'll be taking.'

'We?'

'You and I will be leading the raid, of course.'

'You expect me to risk my life for some Greek woman I've never met?'

'No, for Egyptian hostages.'

'What will happen to my wife and my snakes if I die in the process?'

'They'll be taken care of.'

'No, it's too dangerous. And how many snakes would you expect me to sacrifice to fighting these bloodthirsty foreigners?'

'You'll be paid triple their value, and I'll designate your laboratory as an official research centre.'

Setau looked back towards Lotus, so appealing in the warm summer darkness.

'Enough talk. We'd better start bagging the snakes.'

Menelaus paced the bridge of his flagship. The lookouts had noted no unusual activity on the riverbanks. Just as he supposed, the Egyptians were too afraid of bloodshed to make a move, the cowards. Taking hostages was hardly honourable, but it had worked. There was no other way to pry Helen loose from Tuya and Nefertari.

The hostages had stopped their crying and moaning. Hands tied behind their backs, they huddled on the poop deck, guarded by ten soldiers who were relieved every two hours.

One of Menelaus' officers came up to the bridge.

'Do you think they'll attack?' he asked.

'It would be counterproductive. We'd have to slaughter the hostages.'

'In that case, we'd have no buffer.'

'We'd kill a lot of Egyptians before we were back at sea. But don't worry, they won't endanger their countrymen's lives. I'll get Helen back at dawn and we'll sail home.'

'I'll miss this place.'

'Have you lost your mind?'

'Didn't you think life was good in Memphis? Peace at last.'

'We were born to fight, not for idleness.'

'How safe will you be when you do get home? By now there must be plenty of pretenders to your throne.'

'I can still handle a sword. When they see Helen under my thumb, they'll realize who's in charge.'

Ramses had selected thirty of his best soldiers, all strong swimmers. Setau showed them how to avoid being bitten when they released their snakes. The volunteers' faces were tense. The Regent made a rousing speech. His strength of conviction, along with Setau's obvious competence, convinced the raiding party they would win the day.

Ramses hated keeping secrets from his wife and mother, but neither of them would have wanted him to take part in the raid, thinking it put him in too much danger. He assumed full responsibility for the surprise attack. If he was truly meant to be pharaoh, fate would see him through.

Setau talked to the snakes inside their sacks and chanted spells to calm them. Lotus had taught him the sounds which, though meaningless to humans, had a magical effect on snakes.

Once the secret weapon was ready, the raiders moved quietly down to the far end of the harbour, out of the Greek lookouts' sight.

Setau touched Ramses' wrist.

'Wait. Am I seeing things, or is Menelaus casting off ?'

Setau was right.

'Stay here,' Ramses said, dropping his sack, which contained a sand viper, and running towards the Greek flagship. In the silvery moonlight, he saw the King of Sparta standing on the prow, holding Helen in front of him.

'Menelaus!' Ramses shouted.

The Greek, who was wearing his double cuirasse and belt with golden clasps, recognized the prince's voice immediately.

'Ramses! You came to see me off. It will be a second honeymoon for me and Helen. She'll be glad she decided to come. Believe me, in Sparta she'll be the happiest woman alive!' Menelaus snorted with laughter.

'Free the hostages!'

'Never fear, you'll get them back alive.'

Ramses trailed behind the Greek fleet in a small boat with two sails. When the sun rose, Menelaus's soldiers raised a racket, beating on their shields with swords and spears.

Under orders from the Regent and the Great Royal Wife, the Egyptian Navy made no move, giving the Greeks free passage to the Mediterranean. Menelaus could start his northward crossing.

For a second, Ramses thought he had been fooled, and that the King of Sparta was about to slit his prisoners' throats. But then a boat was lowered and the hostages climbed down a rope ladder to board it. The able-bodied men among them took the oars and rowed away from their floating prison as fast as they could.

On the prow of her husband's ship, white-armed Helen, wearing a purple cloak, a white veil, and a golden necklace, gazed at the coast of Egypt, the country where she had known a few months of happiness hoping that she was free of Menelaus.

Once the hostages were beyond the Greek archers' range, Helen twisted the amethyst in the ring on her right hand and drank the contents of the minuscule vial it concealed: poison stolen from a Memphis laboratory. She had sworn never again to become her husband's slave; she refused to end her days beaten and humiliated in the palace gynoecium, the women's apartments. Returning with nothing but her corpse, the black-hearted conqueror of Troy would be a laughing stock.

She gloried in the touch of the summer sun, wishing her fair skin would turn a warm Egyptian copper, that she could be like her new-found friends, free to love, satisfied body and soul.

Helen quietly slumped, her head rolling on to her shoulder, her eyes wide open and fixed on the bright blue sky.

9

By the time the young diplomat Ahsha returned from a brief information-gathering mission in southern Syria, Memphis had already been in mourning for forty days. The next day, Tuya, Ramses, Nefertari and key government figures were set to depart for Thebes, where Seti's mummy would be laid to rest and the new king and queen would be crowned.

The only son of a wealthy family, well-bred, elegant, with a long, fine-featured face, a pencil moustache, lively, intelligent eyes and a spellbinding, sometimes haughty, manner of speaking, Ahsha had also been a fellow student of Ramses. Somewhat distant and dispassionate, he was both friend and critic. Ahsha knew several languages and from an early age had loved to travel and study other cultures. A diplomatic career was a natural choice for him. Thanks to some notable successes, which had surprised diplomats of greater experience, his professional advancement was assured. At twenty-three, he was considered one of the leading specialists on Asia. He was brilliant in the field and a gifted analyst as well, qualities rarely combined in one man. Some of his colleagues even suspected he was clairvoyant. Be that as it may, Egypt's security hinged on correctly assessing the intentions of Egypt's main enemy, the Hittite Empire.

When he reported to Meba, Ahsha found the minister on the defensive, offering little comment and recommending only that he try to see Ramses as soon as possible, since the pharaoh-to-be was asking to meet all high-level diplomats.

Ahsha was admitted by Ahmeni, the Regent's private secretary. The two old schoolfriends greeted each other warmly.

'Still thin as a reed,' Ahsha noted.

'And you're wearing the latest fashion, as usual.'

'One of my many vices. It's a long time since we were students . . . It's good to see that your talents are appreciated, Ahmeni.'

'I pledged my loyalty to Ramses and I've kept my oath.'

'Wise choice. It won't be long before Ramses is crowned, if the gods are willing.'

'They are. Did you hear he's already survived one assassination attempt? Our Greek visitor, Menelaus, sent his henchmen after Ramses.'

'Menelaus is a minor king and a scoundrel.'

'To put it mildly. He took hostages and threatened to kill them unless we handed Helen over.'

'What did Ramses do?'

'He refused to violate the laws of hospitality and planned a counterattack.'

'Risky.'

'What else could he have done?'

'Negotiate, then negotiate some more. Though I admit it would be almost impossible to get through to a ruffian like Menelaus. His plan worked, then?'

'No, Helen gave herself up without his knowledge. She felt responsible for the hostages. As soon as they were free and Menelaus' ship headed out to sea, she took her life.'

'A grand gesture, but rather final.'

'Ironic as ever, I see.'

'I find that making fun of everything, including oneself, helps keep things in perspective.'

'Helen's death doesn't seem to affect you.'

'Getting rid of Menelaus and his crew is to Egypt's benefit.

If we're looking for allies in Greece, we'll have to do better than that.'

'Homer stayed behind, though.'

'Ramses' charming old poet,' Ahsha said with a smile. 'Still writing his account of the Trojan War?'

'I've had the honour of taking it down for him. His verse is tragic, but not lacking in nobility.'

'Literature will be your downfall, Ahmeni! Do you know what plans Ramses has for you once he's pharaoh?'

'No. I like what I'm doing now.'

'You deserve better.'

'What about you? What are you hoping for?'

'My first concern is to meet Ramses.'

'Urgent business?'

'Do you mind if I save it for him?'

Ahmeni blushed. 'Sorry. You'll find him in the stables. No matter what he's doing, he'll want to see you.'

Ramses seemed strikingly different. The prince was regal and sure of himself, driving his chariot with consummate skill, leading his horses through incredibly complex manoeuvres that left the old stable-hands gaping.

The tall adolescent had become a powerfully built athlete with the incontestable authority of a monarch. However, Ahsha noted a rashness and over-excitement that might lead to errors in judgment. But what use would it be recommending moderation to someone burning with so much energy?

As soon as he caught sight of Ahsha, the prince drove towards him. The horses pulled up short only a length or two from the young diplomat, splattering his spotless tunic.

'Sorry, Ahsha! These young warhorses can be a bit hard to handle.'

Ramses jumped down, called two grooms to look after the horses, and took Ahsha by the shoulders.

'More trouble brewing in Asia?'

'I'm afraid so, Majesty.'

'Wait, I'm not pharaoh yet!'

'A good diplomat always looks towards the future. As it happens, your future is fairly easy to predict.'

'You're the only one who thinks so.'

'Does that bother you?'

'Asia, my friend – I asked you about Asia.'

'Outwardly, all is calm. Our protectorates are ready to welcome you as pharaoh. The Hittites are making no move to expand their territory.'

'Outwardly, you say.'

'That's what the official reports will tell you.'

'But you don't see it that way.'

'There's always a calm before the storm – but how long before?'

'Come, have a drink with me.'

Ramses checked on his horses, then sat down with Ahsha under a sloping roof with a view of the desert. A servant instantly appeared with cool beer and scented towels.

'Do you believe that the Hittites really want peace?'

Ahsha considered this, enjoying the delicious brew. 'The Hittites are fighters and conquerors. To them, the word "peace" is a sort of poetic image with no concrete meaning attached.'

'So they're lying.'

'They hope that a young, peace-loving leader will place less emphasis on defence, gradually weakening the country.'

'Like Akhenaton.'

'A prime example.'

'Are they still manufacturing arms?'

'In fact, they've stepped up production.'

'Do you think war is inevitable?'

'A diplomat's job is to make sure it isn't.'

'How would you go about stopping them?'

'I can't answer that question. My current duties don't

afford me a broad enough view to suggest effective counter-measures.'

'You'd like to take on other duties?'

'It's not up to me.'

Ramses looked out at the desert.

'When I was a boy, Ahsha, I dreamed of becoming pharaoh like my father, because I thought power was the best game of all. Then Seti had me face the wild bull – the traditional test of will, you know. He opened my eyes to the perils of ultimate power. Then I found another dream world: living in my father's shadow, relying on his strength. Now his death has brought reality crashing in on me. I prayed to the Invisible to be relieved of the burden of power I no longer sought, and I looked for a sign from the gods. Menelaus sent his men to kill me; my lion, my dog, and my bodyguard saved me as I communed with my father's soul. Since then I have decided not to try to fight against my destiny. What Seti has ordained will come to pass.'

'Do you remember that night just before graduation, when we discussed true power with Setau, Moses, and Ahmeni?'

'Of course. Ahmeni found it in serving his country, Moses in building monuments, Setau in studying snakes, and you in the diplomatic secretariat.'

'You're still the only one who will have true power.'

'No, Ahsha, it will pass through me, come to life in my heart, my sword arm, but leave me if I misuse it.'

'Living only for Egypt – it's a terrible price to pay.'

'I'm no longer free to choose my destiny.'

'Your words are almost frightening, Ramses.'

'Do you think I'm never afraid? No matter what stands in my way, I shall rule and continue my father's work. I need to leave Egypt stronger and more beautiful than ever. Will you help me, Ahsha?'

'Yes, Majesty.'

10

Shaanar was dejected.

The Greeks had failed him miserably; Menelaus, obsessed with getting Helen back, had lost sight of their goal of eliminating Ramses. The only consolation, which was not inconsiderable, was being able to convince his brother he was not involved in the coup. Now that Menelaus and his men were gone, no one would dare point a finger at Shaanar.

But Ramses would ascend to the throne and rule Egypt single-handedly – and he, Seti's elder son, would be forced to bow and scrape to his brother. No, he refused to accept this reversal of fortune.

That was why he had arranged a meeting with his one remaining ally, a friend of Ramses, a man above suspicion, who might help him fight his brother from within and undermine his authority.

At dusk, business was still brisk at the pottery stands. Strollers and serious shoppers passed the displays, eyeing vases of all different sizes and prices. At the end of an alley-way, a water-bearer hawked his thirst-quenching product.

That was where Ahsha waited, almost unrecognizable in an ordinary kilt and common wig. Shaanar, too, was carefully disguised. The two men bought a water-skin and shared a bunch of grapes like simple peasants, sitting side by side against a wall.

'Have you been to see Ramses again?' asked Shaanar.

'I no longer work for the Foreign Affairs secretariat. I report directly to our future pharaoh.'

'What does that mean?'

'A promotion.'

'To what?'

'I'm not sure yet. Ramses is forming his government. Since he's a loyal friend, Moses, Ahmeni and I should be given high-level positions.'

'Who else?'

'His only other close friend is Setau, but he's so devoted to his beloved snakes that he refuses to take on public duties.'

'Did Ramses seem determined to rule?' asked Shaanar.

'He realizes that it's a crushing responsibility and admits he's not fully prepared, but he won't give up now. Don't expect him to change his mind.'

'Did he mention the High Priest of Amon?'

'No.'

'Good. Then he underestimates the man's influence and potential to do him harm.'

'I heard the old fellow was rather intimidated by royalty,' said Ahsha.

'He was afraid of Seti – but Ramses is young, with little experience of power struggles. Now, as far as getting help from Ahmeni is concerned, it's hopeless. That damned little scribe is as devoted to Ramses as a dog to its master. On the other hand, I think I may be able to inveigle Moses into our camp.'

'Have you tried?'

'He wouldn't have anything to do with me, but it was only my first try. That Hebrew's a tortured soul, seeking some personal truth that may end up clashing with Ramses' views. If we offer him what he needs, he'll switch sides.'

'That makes sense.'

'Do you have any influence with Moses, Ahsha?'

'I don't think so, but give me long enough and I'll find his weak spot.'

'And Ahmeni?'

'He seems incorruptible,' Ahsha commented, 'but one never knows. In time, he may develop weaknesses. If he does, we'll be there to exploit them.'

'I don't intend to wait until Ramses has his network firmly in place.'

'Nor do I, Shaanar, nor do I. But we must be patient. Your experience with Menelaus should teach you that a successful strategy leaves no room for guesswork.'

'How long do I have to wait?'

'Let Ramses get settled on the throne. Power and his own rashness will turn his head. What's more, I'll be one of his advisers on Asia, the one he'll listen to most closely.'

'What's your plan, Ahsha?'

'You want the throne, don't you?'

'It's my birthright. I know how to lead.'

'Therefore, Ramses must be overthrown or killed.'

'I see no other way.'

'Two avenues are open to us: a coup or a foreign war. For the first, we would need to enlist a number of influential people. The onus would fall largely on you. The second would depend on determining the Hittites' true intentions and preparing a conflict that would ruin Ramses, but not Egypt. If the country is devastated, a Hittite king will take over the Two Lands.'

Shaanar's displeasure was obvious. 'It sounds too risky.'

'Ramses is no mean adversary. You won't find it easy to take power.'

'If the Hittites win, they'll invade Egypt.'

'That's not certain.'

'Do you have a miracle up your sleeve?'

'Not a miracle, but a trap that we'll set for Ramses, without our country being involved. Either he'll be killed or else he'll be blamed for the defeat, in which case, he'll no longer be a credible ruler. Then you can step in to save the day.'

'It sounds too easy.'

'I've built my reputation on accurate predictions. When I know exactly what my role in the government will be, I'll set things in motion. Unless you'd rather stop before we begin.'

'Never! I want Ramses out of my way, dead or alive.'

'If our plan works, I hope you won't prove ungrateful.'

'Don't worry. My right-hand man will be richly rewarded.'

'Can I really be sure?'

Shaanar was taken aback. 'Don't you trust me?'

'Not in the least.'

'But . . .'

'Don't pretend you're surprised. If I were that naive, you'd have got rid of me long ago. When a man is ambitious like you, no one ought to believe his promises. The sole basis for his behaviour is personal interest.'

'Are you a cynic, Ahsha?'

'I'm a realist. When you become pharaoh, you'll form a government based on your needs at the time. There may be no room for those who, like me, have paved your way to the throne.'

Shaanar smiled. 'Your intelligence is exceptional, Ahsha.'

'In my travels, I've encountered a great many cultures and all sorts of different people, but wherever I've been it comes down to the survival of the fittest.'

'Not in Seti's Egypt.'

'Seti is dead now, and Ramses can't wait to flex his military muscle. We must find him the right war.'

'In exchange for your research, I suppose you want immediate compensation.'

'Your own intelligence is pretty good, Shaanar.'

'Tell me exactly what you expect.'

'My family is well off, of course, but who's ever rich

enough? Since I'm constantly on the move, having several residences would be both a help and a pleasure. I'd like villas in Upper and Lower Egypt. Three houses in the Delta, two in Memphis, two in Middle Egypt, two near Thebes and one in Aswan ought to meet my needs when I'm here at home.'

'That would cost me a small fortune.'

'A trifle, Shaanar, a mere trifle when you consider what I'll be doing for you.'

'I suppose you want precious metals and gemstones as well.'

'It goes without saying.'

'I wouldn't have thought you so venal, Ahsha.'

'I like luxury – great luxury. A collector of fine vases like you must understand what I mean.'

'Yes, but so many houses . . .'

'Beautifully decorated houses, serving as a background for fine furniture! They'll be my earthly paradise, pleasure palaces where I'll be the absolute master while you climb the steps to the throne of Egypt.'

'When do we get under way?'

'Immediately.'

'You haven't been appointed yet.'

'When I am, I'm certain to have considerable responsibilities. Encourage me to serve you well, Shaanar.'

'Where do we start?'

'With a villa in the north-eastern Delta, near the border. A sizeable estate, a small lake, a vineyard and attentive servants. Even if I spend only a few days a year there, I want to be treated like a prince.'

'Anything else?'

'Well, women. When I'm on a mission, the pickings can be rather slim. I have to make up for that here in Egypt. Yes, a good supply of women. As long as they're attractive and willing, I'm not particular about where they come from.'

'I agree to your conditions.'

'I won't disappoint you, Shaanar. Just one more thing: we'll continue to meet in the strictest secrecy and you will mention it to no one. If Ramses were to learn of our dealings, my career would be finished.'

'Your best interest is my best interest, Ahsha.'

'There's no better guarantee of friendship. Farewell, Shaanar.'

As he watched the young diplomat merge into the crowd, Ramses' elder brother mused that luck was still with him. Ahsha made a first-rate partner. The day he had to be done away with would be a sad one.

11

Tuya, the late pharaoh's Great Royal Wife, sailed at the head of the fleet leaving Memphis for Thebes and the Valley of the Kings, where Seti's mummy would be entombed. Nefertari never left Tuya's side, sensing the pain beneath her usual serenity. Simply spending time with the great king's widow taught Nefertari how a queen should behave when faced with the cruellest of losses. The young woman's quiet presence was a tremendous comfort. Neither of them felt a need to express her sorrow, but their unspoken communion was deep and intense.

All through the voyage, Ramses worked.

Ahmeni, though highly susceptible to the heat, had prepared an impressive stack of dossiers on foreign policy, the safety of the kingdom, public health, public works (including dykes and canals), food management and a host of other more or less complex subjects.

Ramses was fully aware of the magnitude of his responsibilities. An army of civil servants would be helping him, but he needed detailed knowledge of how each department worked, in order to keep the government under his control. Otherwise Egypt was likely to pitch and sink like a rudderless boat. Time was against the pharaoh-to-be; the moment he assumed power, he would be expected to make informed decisions and function as the Lord of the Two Lands. The prospect of serious mistakes plagued him.

His mood lifted at the thought of his mother, a precious ally who would help him to avoid many errors and teach him how to deal with the tricks the notables would use to preserve their status. So many officials had already called on him to plead for their departments!

After long hours of work with the incomparably thorough and meticulous Ahmeni, Ramses liked to stand in the prow of the boat, contemplating the Nile, source of Egypt's prosperity, and enjoying the brisk wind – the breath of the Divine. In these stolen moments Ramses had the feeling that all Egypt belonged to him, from the mouth of the Nile to the desert reaches of Nubia. Would he be able to satisfy her needs?

At dinner his guests of honour were Moses, Setau, Ahsha, and Ahmeni. It was like the old days when they studied together at the Kap, the country's elite school. Even then they'd thirsted for power as well as knowledge. The pleasant reunion did not disperse the melancholy caused by Seti's death. Each of them sensed that difficult days might lie in store for Egypt.

'This time,' Moses told Ramses, 'your dream is about to come true.'

'It's not a dream any more, but a frightening obligation.'

'What?' objected Ahsha. 'You're not afraid of anything!'

'It's the last job you'd ever get *me* to take,' muttered Setau.

'I hesitated for a long time. But what would you have thought if I'd betrayed my father's wishes.'

'That you'd come to your senses. Your father's funeral may not be the only one we end up attending on this trip.'

'Have you got wind of another plot?' asked Ahmeni worriedly.

'A plot? There'll be ten of them, or twenty, or a hundred!' said Setau. 'That's why I'm here – with a few of my trusted assistants.'

'Setau a bodyguard,' said Ahsha ironically. 'Who'd have thought it.'

'At least I have something concrete to contribute.'

'Criticizing diplomacy, are we?'

'It complicates everything, when life is basically simple: good on one side, evil on the other, and nothing in between.'

'Your simplistic outlook is the problem,' retorted Ahsha.

'It suits me,' Ahmeni chimed in. 'People are either for Ramses or against him.'

'And what if the balance tips the wrong way?' asked Moses.

'My position will never change.'

'Soon Ramses will no longer be our friend but Pharaoh of Egypt. He'll see us differently.'

Moses' words were disturbing. Everyone waited to hear how Ramses would answer.

'Moses is right. Since this burden has fallen to me, I accept it. And since you're my friends, I'll call on you for help.'

'What will you have us do?' asked the Hebrew.

'The four of you have already gone far. I'll ask you to join me on a new journey, seeking the greater good of Egypt.'

'You know where I stand,' declared Setau. 'The minute you're safe on the throne, I shall go back to my snakes.'

'I still plan to try to persuade you to work with me.'

'A waste of time. When this security mission is over, I leave. Moses can be your masterbuilder, Ahsha can be head of Foreign Affairs, and more power to them!'

'Are you forming my government for me?'

Setau shrugged.

'Why don't we try the wine?' suggested Ahsha.

'I propose a toast,' said Ahmeni. 'To Ramses' health, and a long, full life in which to enjoy it, by the grace of the gods.'

Shaanar had sailed not with the Regent, but on his own ship, a splendid vessel with a crew of forty. As Head of Protocol, he had invited a party of notables, most of whom were no friends of Ramses. Seti's elder son carefully refrained from joining in their criticism, merely compiling a mental list of future supporters. The courtiers thought Ramses' youth and inexperience were insurmountable handicaps.

He smugly noted that his own excellent reputation remained intact, while his brother would continue to suffer from the comparison to Seti. The breach already open, the trick would be to widen it, taking every opportunity to weaken the young pharaoh's power.

Shaanar's guests sampled jojoba fruit and cool beer. His easy manner and moderate opinions made him a favourite with the courtiers, who enjoyed basking in the public gaze with a great man, whose brother would have to award him a prominent role.

For more than an hour, a man of average stature, with a neat pointed beard and a brightly striped tunic, had been waiting for an audience. He looked humble, almost submissive, yet calm and collected.

When he had a free moment, Shaanar motioned the man forward. He approached, bowing deferentially.

'Who are you?'

'My name is Raia. I come from Syria, but I've been a travelling merchant in Egypt for a number of years now.'

'Dealing in what?'

'Preserved meats and the finest Asian vases.'

Shaanar lifted an eyebrow. 'Vases?'

'Yes, Prince, I'm the exclusive distributor for some very fine manufacturers.'

'Do you know that I'm a collector?'

'So I was told just recently. I came here in hope of arranging a private showing for you.'

'Are your prices high?'

'That depends.'

Shaanar was curious. 'On what?'

From a sturdy cloth sack, Raia extracted a small, thin-lipped vase of solid silver, with a palmetto design. 'What do you think of this, Prince?'

Shaanar's eyes widened. Beads of sweat broke out on his forehead, his hands grew damp. 'A masterpiece . . . an unbelievable masterpiece. How much?'

'Is it permitted to offer a gift to the future Pharaoh of Egypt.'

Could he be hearing things? 'My brother Ramses is the future pharaoh, not me. You're mistaken, merchant. So name your price.'

'I never make mistakes, Prince. In my profession, there's no room for mistakes.'

Shaanar tore his eyes away from the stunning vase. 'What are you trying to tell me?'

'That many people don't want Ramses for king.'

'He'll be crowned in a matter of days.'

'Perhaps, but will that end the dissatisfaction?'

'Who are you, really, Raia?'

'A man who believes in your future and wants to see you on the throne of Egypt.'

'What do you know of my intentions?'

'That you clearly wish to expand foreign trade, make Egypt less arrogantly insular, and improve economic relations with the most powerful kingdom in Asia.'

'You mean . . . the Hittites?'

'We understand each other.'

'Ah. You're spying for them. And your employers like what they see in me?'

Raia nodded.

'What are you proposing?' asked Shaanar, as excited as if he were being offered another rare vase.

'Ramses is rash and war-loving. Like his father, he wants to maintain Egypt's grandeur and supremacy. You, Prince, are a reasonable man, better able to come to terms with foreign powers.'

'If I betray Egypt, Raia, I'm risking my life.'

Shaanar recalled how Tutankhamon's widow had been condemned to death for her dealings with the Hittites, even though she was attempting to protect the throne.

'A certain amount of risk is to be expected on the way to the top.'

Shaanar closed his eyes. The Hittites . . . Naturally, he'd considered using them against Ramses, but that had been no more than idle speculation. Now, suddenly, the idea sprang to life in the form of this ordinary, harmless-looking merchant.

'I love my country . . .'

'No one would doubt it. But you love power more. And only an alliance with the Hittites will guarantee it to you.'

'I need to think this over.'

'I'm afraid I can't indulge you.'

'You want my answer now?'

'My own safety is at stake, now that you know who I am.'

'And if I refuse?'

Raia did not answer, but his expression became fixed and unreadable.

Shaanar had little trouble convincing himself that it was meant to be. He would handle his powerful new partner with the utmost care, exploiting the Hittites without endangering Egypt. Ahsha, of course, would have to be kept in the dark, though he could still be of use.

'I accept, Raia.'

The merchant smiled faintly.

'You live up to your reputation, Prince. I'll be in touch with you every now and again. Now that I'm supplying vases for your collection, no one will be surprised if I visit you. Take this one, please, to seal our bargain.'

Shaanar closed his hands around the silver curves. The future was already looking brighter.

12

Ramses had memorized every parched and rocky inch of the Valley of the Kings, the 'Great Place' he had first visited with his father. Seti had shown him the tomb of his own father, the first Ramses, their dynasty's founder, an elderly vizier selected by a council of wise men to succeed the childless Horemheb. He had reigned for only two years, entrusting to his son the mission of reasserting Egypt's power, a power now invested in Ramses II.

The stifling summer heat felled some of the servants carrying furnishings for Seti's tomb, but it seemed to have no effect on Ramses. Grim-faced, he marched at the head of the procession transporting his father's mummy to its final resting-place.

Ramses felt a rush of hatred for the place that was claiming his father, leaving him so alone. Then the magic of the Valley took hold of him again, a magic that radiated life, not death.

The stony silence rang with the voices of the old ones. They spoke of light, transfiguration, resurrection. They demanded worship and respect for the celestial world that gave birth to all forms of life.

Ramses was the first to set foot inside Seti's vast tomb, the longest and deepest in the Valley. Once he was pharaoh, he planned to decree that no other tomb might surpass it. In the eyes of posterity, Seti would remain without equal.

Twelve priests carried in the mummy. Clad in a panther skin, Ramses was to conduct the rites for Seti's journey into the beyond and rebirth in the land of the gods. Ritual texts on the walls of the tomb would guide his father on the journey and serve his soul through all eternity.

Seti's mummy was a masterpiece of the embalmers' art. He looked perfectly at peace with himself and his life on earth, as if at any minute his eyes might open, his lips might speak . . . The priests placed the lid on the sarcophagus, to be enclosed in a House of Gold where Isis would work her alchemy, making the mortal immortal.

'Seti was a just ruler,' murmured Ramses. 'He upheld the Rule of Ma'at and was beloved of the light. He walks living into the West.'

All over Egypt barbers toiled, shaving off beards now that the official mourning was over. Women pinned up their hair, society ladies summoned their hairdressers.

On the eve of the coronation, Ramses and Nefertari gathered their thoughts in the Temple of Gurnah, where prayers for Seti would henceforth be said every day, maintaining his *ka* – his spiritual essence – and affirming the transfigured pharaoh's presence among the living. Then the couple proceeded to the temple of Karnak to see the High Priest, who welcomed them with cold formality. After a frugal dinner, the Regent and his wife withdrew to the royal quarters within the god Amon's earthly residence. Each of them meditated before a separate throne, symbolizing the primordial mound that emerged from the ocean of chaos at the beginning of time. It figured in the hieroglyph for Ma'at, the timeless Rule, 'That Which Is Right Will Give The Best Direction', the Rule that they must embody and impart to their subjects.

Ramses had the feeling his father was close at hand, seeing

him through these last tense hours before his life changed for ever. As king, his life would no longer be his own. His only care would be for his people's welfare and his nation's prosperity.

Once again, the prospect overwhelmed him.

He wished he could flee this palace, take refuge in his lost youth, in Iset the Fair, and the carefree pleasure they once knew. But now he was Seti's designated successor and Nefertari's husband. He would have to master his fear and ride out this one last night before his coronation.

The shadows parted and dawn came forth, announcing the sun's rebirth. Once more it had won the nightly struggle with the monster from the depths. Two masked priests, one in the guise of a falcon, the other an ibis, stood on either side of Ramses. They symbolized the gods Horus, protector of royalty, and Thoth, master of hieroglyphs and sacred learning. Pouring the contents of two tall vases over the prince's naked body, they cleansed him of his humanity. Then they remade him in the image of the gods, applying from head to toe the nine different unguents that would open his energy centres and give him a perception of reality different from other men's.

The ritual garments also helped construct his new and unique identity. The two priests dressed the prince in a kilt of white and gold, the same as the first pharaohs wore. On the sash, they hung a bull's tail, the emblem of royal potency. Ramses recalled the terrifying encounter with a wild bull his father had arranged as a test of his youthful courage. Now he would embody the bull's power, which he must learn to exercise wisely.

Then the ritualists fastened a large jewelled collar, with seven rows of coloured beads, round his neck, placed copper bracelets on his wrists and upper arms, and shod him in white sandals. They presented him with the white club he would use to strike down his enemies and make the darkness into light. Around his forehead they tied the golden band called *sia*, meaning 'intuitive seeing'.

'Do you accept the ordeal of power?' asked the Horus priest.

'I do.'

Horus and Thoth took Ramses by the hands and led him into another room. On a throne were the crowns of the Two Lands. Protecting them was a priest wearing the mask of the god Set.

Thoth stepped aside as the brothers Horus and Set embraced. Despite their eternal rivalry, they were obliged to be reunited in one being: Pharaoh.

Horus lifted the Red Crown of Lower Egypt, basket-shaped and surmounted by a spiral, and placed it on Ramses' head. On top of it, Set placed the White Crown of Upper Egypt whose oval form tapered up into the shape of a lotus bulb.

'The Two Powers are united in you,' declared Thoth. 'You govern and unify the black land and the red land, you are the rushes of the South and the beehive of the North, you make both lands green.'

'You alone will be able to lay a hand on these two crowns,' revealed Set. 'Within them is thunder to strike down any usurper.'

Horus gave the pharaoh two sceptres. The first was called 'Mastery of Power' and was used to bless offerings. The other, 'Magic', was a shepherd's crook serving to keep his people together.

'The time has come to appear in glory,' Thoth decreed.

Preceded by the three god-priests, Pharaoh left the temple's hidden rooms, heading for the huge inner courtyard where the privileged few allowed within the temple gates had gathered.

On a platform, beneath a dais, was a gilded wooden throne, rather modest and squarely built: Seti's throne, the one he had used for official ceremonies.

Sensing her son's hesitation, Tuya took three steps in his direction and bowed low.

'May Your Majesty rise like a new sun and take his place on the throne of the living.'

Ramses was deeply moved by this welcome from the pharaoh's widow, the mother he would venerate until the end of his days.

'This is the testament of the gods that Seti left you. As it legitimized his reign, so will it yours, so will it your successor's.' Tuya handed Ramses a leather case containing a papyrus written in Thoth's own hand, at the dawn of civilization, declaring Pharaoh the heir to Egypt.

'Here are your five royal names,' continued Tuya in her clear, steady voice. 'Strong Bull, Beloved of Ma'at. Protector of Egypt, Who Binds Foreign Countries. Rich in Armies, He of Stupendous Victories. Chosen of the God of Light, Powerful in His Rule. Ra-Begot-Him: Son of the Light.'

Total silence greeted these words. Even Shaanar felt the poison of ambition drain from him as he surrendered to the magic of the moment.

'A royal couple rules the Two Lands,' continued Tuya. 'Step forward, Nefertari, and take your place beside the king as his Great Royal Wife and Queen of Egypt.'

Despite the solemnity of the occasion, Ramses was so entranced by his bride's fresh beauty that he wished he could take her in his arms. In a long linen gown, with a golden collar, amethyst earrings and jasper bracelets, she gazed at the king and repeated the time-honoured formula:

'I recognize Horus and Set united in one being. I sing your name, Pharaoh: you are yesterday, today, and tomorrow. I live through your word and will keep you from evil and danger.'

'I recognize you as Queen of the North and South and of all lands, lady of utmost sweetness who pleases the gods, who is mother and wife of the god, who has my love.'

Ramses set a crown on Nefertari's head. Its two tall plumes declared her Great Royal Wife and associate ruler.

Like a blot on the sun, a falcon spread its great wings, circling above the new king and queen, then dived for them so suddenly that no royal archer had time to react.

A cry of horror and disbelief rose from the onlookers as the raptor landed on the new king's back, digging its claws into his shoulders. Ramses stood absolutely still; Nefertari stared.

Time stood still as the awe-struck courtiers registered the miracle. The falcon was Horus, protector of the monarchy. This man was truly chosen to govern Egypt!

The falcon flew back towards the sun, strong and serene.

A single cheer proclaimed Ramses' accession to the throne, on this twenty-seventh day of the third month of summer.*

---

* Early June, 1279 BC, according to one of the most commonly used estimates.

13

As soon as the ceremony was over, Ramses was swept up in a whirlwind of activity.

The head steward of the pharaoh's household had him inspect his palace at Thebes, both public rooms and private quarters. As head of state, he toured the pillared grand reception room whose floor and walls were adorned with mosaics and paintings of lotus, papyrus, fish and birds; the smaller private audience chambers; the scribes' offices; the balcony for official appearances, a winged solar disc above its window; the dining room with a table in the middle laden night and day with baskets of fruit and flower arrangements; the bedchamber with coloured pillows piled high on the bed; the tiled bathing room.

Ramses was introduced to the members of his household: the priests in charge of secret rituals, the scribes of the House of Life, the physicians, the chamberlain who superintended the private quarters, the heads of the royal messenger service, the royal treasury, the granary, livestock, and so on, all eager to meet their brand-new pharaoh and assure him of their undying devotion.

'And this is—'

Ramses got to his feet. 'That's enough.'

'Majesty, please!' the head steward spluttered. 'So many important people . . .'

'More important than I am?'

'Forgive me, I didn't mean—'

'Take me to the kitchens.'

'That's no place for you!'

'Who would know better than I where I belong?'

'Forgive me, I—'

'Let's not waste any more time on excuses. I'd rather hear why the vizier and the High Priest of Amon weren't here to pay their respects to me.'

'I have no idea, Majesty. That's completely beyond the scope of my authority.'

'To the kitchens, then.'

Butchers, bakers, pastry chefs, brewers, vegetable peelers, makers of preserved foods – Remet, the palace cook, commanded a small army of specialized workers, jealously guarding their prerogatives and as pernickety about their hours of work as about their days off. Jolly, round-cheeked, slow-moving Remet never worried about his triple chin and bulging belly. He'd do something about his weight when he retired. For now, he concentrated on ruling his domain with an iron fist, preparing delicious and flawless meals, keeping the peace among his staff of prima donnas. A stickler for cleanliness and fresh ingredients, Remet personally tasted each dish that left his kitchens. Whether or not Pharaoh and the members of his court were in Thebes, the cook never settled for less than perfection.

When the head steward appeared with a young man in tow, impressively built and dressed in an immaculate white kilt, Remet groaned inwardly. The head steward must be planning to saddle him with yet another useless worker in exchange for some favour from the boy's family.

'Greetings, Remet! I want to introduce you—'

'I can guess who he is.'

'Then bow, as is fitting.'

'That's rich!' guffawed Remet, hands on ample hips. 'Why should I bow to this young buck? First let's find out if he can even wash dishes.'

Scarlet with embarrassment, the steward turned to the king. 'I *beg* your forgiveness . . .'

'I can wash dishes,' Ramses said. 'Do you know how to cook?'

'Who do you think you are, questioning my expertise like that?'

'Ramses, Pharaoh of Egypt.'

Remet froze, convinced his career was over. Then he crisply removed his leather apron, folded it, and laid it on a low table. An insult to the king, confirmed as such by the vizier's court, carried a heavy penalty.

'What's on the menu for lunch?' asked Ramses.

'Quail,' Remet managed. 'Roast quail, nile perch with herb sauce, fig purée, honey cakes.'

'Tempting, but will it taste as good as it sounds?'

'I stake my reputation on it Majesty!' Remet protested.

'Your reputation means nothing to me. Let me try some food.'

'I'll have the staff prepare the dining room,' the steward said unctuously.

'Don't bother. I'll eat right here.'

Ramses lunched heartily under the steward's anxious gaze.

'Excellent,' he pronounced. 'What is your name, cook?'

'Remet, Majesty.'

'Remet. *Man*. It fits. All right, Remet, you're my new head steward, cup-bearer, and director of royal kitchens throughout the land. Follow me. I have a few questions for you.'

Stunned, the former chief steward stammered, 'Majesty? Pardon me, but where will I—'

'I have no use for inefficiency and meanness. There's always a shortage of dishwashers, though.'

The king and Remet strolled together in the shade of a covered portico.

'You'll report to my private secretary, Ahmeni. He looks frail and doesn't much care what he eats, but he's a tireless worker. Above all, he honours me with his friendship.'

'That's a huge responsibility for a mere cook,' said Remet in astonishment.

'My father taught me to judge men according to my instincts. If I'm wrong, that's just too bad. To govern, I shall need loyal followers. Do you think I'll find them at court?'

'To tell the truth—'

'Do, Remet. That's all I ask.'

'Then I can say that Your Majesty's court is the biggest collection of hypocrites and self-seekers in the entire kingdom. In fact, they seem to think they own the place. Your father kept them in line, but as soon as he was gone they started showing their true colours, like desert flowers after a rainstorm.'

'They hate me, don't they?'

'That's an understatement.'

'What do they hope will happen?'

'That you'll trip yourself up before long.'

'If you're with me, Remet, I demand your total loyalty.'

'Do you think I'm up to it?'

'A good cook isn't thin. A talented cook has everyone trying to steal his recipes. Rumours fly through his kitchen and he has to sort through them with the same care he takes in selecting ingredients. What are the main factions against me?'

'Almost the whole court is against you. The general opinion is that *anyone* would be ineffectual in comparison to a pharaoh of Seti's stature. They see you as a transitional figure until a serious contender appears.'

'Will you risk leaving your own little kingdom here in Thebes to run my households?'

Remet smiled broadly. 'Safety has both good and bad sides. As long as I can still cook good food, I'm willing to try. But I do have one reservation.'

'Tell me.'

'With all due respect, Majesty, you don't stand a chance.'

'Why this pessimism?'

'You're young and inexperienced. You don't intend to play a bit part in an administration run by the High Priest of Amon and dozens of experienced officials who know all the tricks of government. The balance of power is too unequal.'

'A pharaoh doesn't wield much power, according to you.'

'Of course he does. That's why everyone wants to take a shot at him. What chance does one man have against an army?'

'Pharaoh is supposed to be endowed with the might of the bull.'

'Not even a wild bull can move mountains, Majesty.'

'Am I to understand that you're advising me to abdicate, on the day of my coronation?'

'If you let the powers that be take charge, who will even notice, and who would blame you?'

'You, Remet?'

'I'm only the best cook in the country. What I think isn't important.'

'You're chief steward now, aren't you?'

'Would you listen, Majesty, if I offered some advice?'

'It all depends on what it is.'

'Never let yourself be served food or drink that's less than the best. It's the beginning of the end. Now, if you don't mind, I think I should get to work. Starting here in Thebes, there's a great deal to be done.'

Ramses had made no mistake. Remet was the man for the job.

Relieved, he headed for the palace garden.

14

Nefertari tried her hardest not to cry.

What she most feared had finally come to pass. She had dreamed of a quiet, cloistered life; now she felt as if she'd been swept away by a monstrous wave. Immediately after the coronation, she had been separated from Ramses to begin fulfilling her duties as Great Royal Wife, visiting the temples, schools, and weavers' guilds she officially sponsored.

Tuya introduced Nefertari to the managers of the queen's various estates, directors of harems where young women were educated, scribes in charge of administering her affairs, tax-collectors, priests and priestesses who would perform in her name the rites of 'the Wife of God', which were intended to preserve the creative force on earth.

For several days, Nefertari kept up a gruelling pace, meeting hundreds of people, finding the right thing to say to each of them, smiling constantly, never showing the slightest sign of fatigue.

Each morning a hairdresser, make-up artist, manicurist and pedicurist worked to make her even lovelier than the day before. The good of Egypt depended as much on her charm as on her husband's power. No queen could be more beautiful than Nefertari in her elegant, red-belted linen gown.

She lay exhausted on a narrow bed, unable to face the

evening's banquet or the thought of being presented with more jars of perfumed unguents.

Tuya's slight figure moved towards her through the gathering dusk.

'Are you ill, Nefertari?'

'I haven't the strength to go on.'

Seti's widow sat on the edge of the bed and took the young queen's right hand in her own hands.

'I know what you're going through. It was the same for me. Two things will help: a special tonic and the magnetizing force Ramses inherited from his father.'

'I wasn't meant to be queen.'

'Do you love Ramses?'

'More than myself.'

'Then you'll stand by him. He wed a queen, and a queen will fight at his side.'

'What if he chose the wrong woman?'

'He didn't. Don't you think there were times when I felt as tired and discouraged as you are now? The demands placed on a Great Royal Wife are beyond any woman. So it has been since the creation of Egypt, and it cannot be otherwise.'

'Didn't you want to give up?'

'A dozen times, a hundred times a day, at first. I begged Seti to take someone else as his chief consort and let me become his lesser wife. His answer was always the same: he took me in his arms and comforted me, yet did nothing to ease my burden of work.'

'If I can't perform my duties, aren't I unworthy of Ramses' faith in me?'

'Good, Nefertari. You take nothing for granted. Now listen. I'm not going to say this twice.'

The young queen's eyes filled with uncertainty. Tuya's clear gaze locked on hers.

'You're condemned to reign, Nefertari. Don't fight your

destiny. Let yourself glide with it, like a swimmer in the river.'

In less than three days, Ahmeni and Remet had begun a far-reaching reform of the government of Thebes, following Ramses' directives. He had met a wide range of officials, from the mayor to the head ferryman. Owing to its distance from Memphis and the fact that Seti had taken up near-permanent residence in the North, the Southern capital had grown increasingly independent. The High Priest of Amon, with the force of his temple's immense wealth behind him, was beginning to consider himself a kind of monarch, whose decrees took precedence over the king's. Ramses' meetings with local officials made him aware of how dangerous the situation was. Unless he acted quickly, Upper and Lower Egypt might split into two different, even opposing, countries, and the division would lead to disaster.

From the beginning, Ahmeni and Remet worked well together. Physical and mental opposites, they complemented each other *because* of their differences. They shared a deep respect for Ramses as well as the conviction that he was heading in the right direction. Turning a deaf ear to hidebound courtiers, they forged ahead with their sweeping reforms, making a number of unexpected appointments with the king's approval.

Two weeks after the coronation, Thebes was in turmoil. Some officials had predicted that the new pharaoh would prove incompetent. Others saw him as an adolescent, in love with hunting and sporting exploits. Yet Ramses had spent his days in the palace, holding meetings and issuing decrees with a vigour and authority worthy of Seti.

Ramses waited for the inevitable reaction, but it never came. Thebes seemed stunned into inertia.

Summoned by the king, the Vizier of the South was

deferential, noting His Majesty's directives with assurances that they would be carried out at once.

Ramses did not share in Ahmeni's boyish excitement or Remet's amused satisfaction. His enemies might have been taken by surprise, but they were far from defeated. They would regroup and come back at him stronger than ever. The king would have preferred an open fight to their insidious plotting in the shadows, but that was a childish wish, he knew.

Just before sunset he always walked the paths of the palace garden, as twenty-odd workers began watering the trees and flower beds in the cool of the evening. On his left trotted Wideawake, the yellow dog, wearing a collar of blue flowers; on his right loped Invincible, the gigantic lion. And at the entrance to the garden was Serramanna, the Sardinian captain of the Royal Bodyguard, sitting beneath an arbour, alert and ready to act at the smallest sign of danger.

Ramses felt an intense affection for the sycamores, pomegranates, perseas, figs, and other trees that made the garden a paradise and a comfort to his soul. He wished all of Egypt could be like this haven where a wealth of essences lived in harmony.

One evening, Ramses was planting a tiny sycamore, mounding soil around the seedling and watering it carefully.

'Your Majesty should wait half an hour, then give it another jug of water, almost drop by drop.'

He looked up to see a gardener of indeterminate age. The back of his neck showed a healing ulcer where the weight of his yoke rested. Two heavy earthenware water jugs hung from it – one at either end.

'Wise advice,' Ramses told him. 'What's your name, gardener?'

'Nedjem.'

'"The mild one." Tell me, Nedjem, are you married?'

'Married to this garden, you might say. The trees, plants, and flowers are my family, my ancestors and descendants. The sycamore you just planted will outlive you, even if you spend a hundred and ten years on earth like the wise men.'

'You can be sure of that,' said Ramses with a smile.

'It can't be easy to be a king and be wise. The human race are too perverse and devious.'

'You're a member of it. Don't you share those faults?'

'I dare not say, Majesty.'

'Have you trained any of the younger men?'

'That's up to the superintendent, not me.'

'Is he a better gardener than you?'

'How would I know? He never comes here.'

'Do you think the tree population is adequate in Egypt?'

'It's the only population that can never be too large.'

'I agree.'

'A tree is a gift,' the gardener said emphatically. 'During its lifetime, it offers us shade, flowers, and fruit; after its death comes wood. Thanks to trees, we eat, we build, we feel blessed when the soft north wind fans us through the branches. I dream of a country of trees where the only other inhabitants are birds and the souls of the dead.'

'I intend to have trees planted in every province,' revealed Ramses. 'Every village square will have a patch of shade where the generations can meet and the young can listen to the wisdom of their elders.'

'May the gods smile upon your work, Majesty. No government programme could be more useful.'

'Will you help me make it a reality?'

'How could I?'

'The Agriculture secretariat is full of hard-working, competent scribes. But to steer them in the right direction, I need a man who loves nature and knows its secrets.'

'I'm only a gardener, Majesty, a—'

'You have the makings of an excellent minister for

agriculture. Come to the palace tomorrow and ask to see Ahmeni. He'll know what I want you to do and help you get started.'

Ramses went on his way, leaving Nedjem amazed and stunned. At the edge of the huge garden, between two fig trees, the king thought he saw a slim, white figure. Had a goddess just appeared in this magical spot?

He hurried towards the apparition, which hadn't moved.

In the soft glow of sunset he made out shining dark hair and a long white gown. How could a woman be so beautiful, at once aloof and enticing?

'Nefertari . . .'

She ran into his arms. 'I managed to slip away,' she confessed. 'Your mother agreed to stand in for me at the lute concert tonight. Have you forgotten me yet?'

'Your mouth is a lotus bud and your lips cast magic spells, but all I want to do right now is kiss you.'

Their kiss renewed them. As they clung together, their devotion to each other was reborn.

'I'm a wild bird you've trapped in the net of your hair,' said Ramses. 'You're a garden of a thousand different flowers, whose perfumes intoxicate me.'

Nefertari let down her hair, Ramses slipped the straps of her linen dress off her shoulders. In the warmth of a peaceful, sweet-smelling summer night, they came together.

15

The first ray of sunlight woke Ramses. He stroked his sleeping wife's delicious back and kissed her on the neck. Without opening her eyes, she twined round him, fitting her body to his powerful frame.

'I'm so happy.'

'Happiness is what you are, Nefertari.'

'Let's never stay apart so long again.'

'Neither of us has any choice in the matter.'

'Won't our lives ever be our own?' Ramses held her tight. 'You aren't answering,' she said.

'Because you know the answer, Nefertari. You're the Great Royal Wife, and I'm Pharaoh. We can't escape the fact, even in our dreams.'

Ramses rose and walked to the window, looking out over the Theban countryside, lush green in the summer sun.

'I love you, Nefertari, but I'm wed to my country as well. I have to keep this land fertile and prosperous. When Egypt calls, I must not ignore it.'

'Is there so much left to do?'

'I thought I'd be ruling a peaceful country, and I forgot that it's inhabited by men. A few weeks is all it would take to overturn the rule of Ma'at and undo the work of Seti and all our ancestors. Harmony is the most fragile of treasures. If I

79

relax my vigilance, Egypt will soon be conquered by evil and darkness.'

Nefertari crossed to meet him, pressing her naked body to his. The merest touch of her scented skin told him their understanding was complete.

Someone knocked urgently at the bedchamber door. Before they answered, it flew open, and a wild-eyed Ahmeni entered. As soon as he noticed the queen, he looked away.

'It's serious, Ramses, very serious.'

'Isn't it a bit early to come bursting in like this?'

'Come with me. There isn't a moment to lose.'

'No time to wash and have some breakfast?'

'Not this morning.'

Ramses could not ignore Ahmeni's warning, especially when the young scribe, usually so imperturbable, had lost his self-possession.

The king drove his own two-horse chariot. The one behind him carried Serramanna and an archer. The ride made Ahmeni queasy, but he was glad Ramses drove so fast. They came to a halt in front of one of the gates to the temple of Karnak, jumped down and studied the stele covered with hieroglyph inscriptions any literate passer-by would be able to read.

'Look,' said Ahmeni. 'There, the third line down.'

The drawing of three animal pelts, signifying 'Birth' and designating Ramses as the 'Son' of the Light, was incorrect. The error robbed the inscription of its protective magic and damaged the Pharaoh's secret identity.

'I checked,' a shattered Ahmeni informed them, 'and the same mistake is on statue pedestals, and steles like this one, which can be seen by all and sundry. It's deliberate malice, Ramses!'

'Who could have done such a thing?'

'The High Priest of Amon and his sculptors. They carved

all the inscriptions proclaiming your coronation. If you hadn't seen for yourself, you'd never have believed me.'

Although the general meaning of the proclamations was unchanged, the altered royal name was definitely a serious matter.

'Call in the sculptors,' ordered Ramses, 'and have the inscriptions put right.'

'Aren't you going to prosecute the culprits?'

'They were only following orders.'

'The High Priest of Amon is ill; that's why he hasn't come to pay his respects to you.'

'Have you any proof that he's behind this? He's an important religious leader.'

'His guilt is obvious!'

'Don't trust in the obvious, Ahmeni.'

'Is he to go unpunished? No matter how rich and powerful he is, he's still your servant.'

'Compile a list of his possessions for me, will you?'

Remet had no complaints about his new duties. After appointing strict, diligent men to oversee sanitation, to ensure the palace's cleanliness, he turned his attention to the royal menagerie, consisting of three wild cats, two gazelles, a hyena and two grey cranes.

One animal remained beyond his control, however. Wide-awake, the pharaoh's yellow-gold dog, was in the annoying habit of snacking on fish from the royal pond. Since the king's pet lion was his partner in crime, there was no way of stopping him.

Early in the morning, Remet had helped Ahmeni haul in a heavy crate of papyrus. He wondered where the puny young scribe, who barely ate and slept only three or four hours a night, found so much energy. He spent the greater part of his days at his desk poring over papers, never showing the slightest sign of fatigue.

Ahmeni conferred with Ramses while Remet made his

daily inspection of the kitchen. Pharaoh's health, and therefore the health of the entire nation, depended on the quality
of his food, he maintained.

Ahmeni unrolled several papyrus scrolls on low tables.

'Here's the information on Karnak,' he said with a hint
of pride.

'Was it hard to gather?'

'Yes and no. The temple administrators weren't particularly happy to see me or answer my questions, but they didn't
dare stop me checking their figures.'

'And is Karnak as rich as we thought?'

'Richer. Eighty thousand employees, forty-six building
sites on its outlying properties, four hundred and fifty gardens,
orchards and vineyards, four hundred and twenty thousand
head of livestock, ninety boats, and sixty-five settlements
of various sizes directly dependent on the largest religious
establishment in Egypt. The High Priest commands a veritable army of scribes and farm workers. Add to all this
the property belonging to the god Amon, which the clergy
controls, and the total is six million head of cattle and as
many goats, twelve million donkeys, eight million mules,
and several million fowl.'

'Amon is the god of victory and the protector of the
empire,' said Ramses.

'No one's denying that, but his priests are only men. Man-
aging such enormous wealth exposes them to overwhelming
temptations. I didn't have time to investigate any further, but
the situation worries me.'

'Anything specific?'

'The Theban authorities are anxious for Your Majesty to
go north again. You're disrupting their peace and upsetting
their routine. All they want is to fatten Karnak's coffers and
keep it growing like a state within a state, until the day the
High Priest of Amon proclaims himself King of the South
and secedes from the union.'

'That would mean the death of Egypt, Ahmeni.'

'And misery for the people.'

'I'd need solid proof that there's been corruption. If I'm to move against the High Priest of Amon, I can't afford any mistakes.'

'Leave it to me, Ramses.'

Serramanna was uneasy. Ever since Menelaus' bungled coup, he was aware that Ramses' life was in danger. The Greeks might have left the country, but the threat remained.

He kept a close eye on what he considered the trouble spots in Thebes: the military base, palace police headquarters, the barracks for the guard detachment. If a revolt was in the making, it would come from one of those places. The Sard trusted his pirate's instincts, remaining wary of enlisted men and officers alike. In a number of instances, he had survived only by striking the first blow against an enemy who'd pretended to be a friend.

Despite his huge size, Serramanna moved like a cat. He liked to eavesdrop and observe from the shadows. No matter how hot it was, he wore a metal breastplate. In his belt he carried a dagger and a short, sharp-tipped sword. A frizzy moustache and side-whiskers made his massive face even more frightening; he used this to his advantage.

Career army officers, most of whom came from a wealthy background, hated Serramanna and wondered why Ramses had put such a lout in charge of his personal bodyguard. The Sard blithely ignored them. He didn't care about popularity. It wouldn't help him be the best fighter serving a good leader.

And Ramses was a good leader, captain of an enormous ship on a treacherous and adventure-filled course.

In short, his job was everything a Sardinian pirate could have wished for, and he was determined to keep it. He enjoyed his villa, fine food, Egyptian beauties with breasts round as love-apples, but these were not enough to satisfy him. Nothing could replace the thrill of proving himself in combat.

The palace guard was changed on the first, eleventh, and twenty-first of each month. The men received their food and wine rations and were paid in grain. Each time the troops were relieved, Serramanna looked the new men over carefully before he assigned them. Any lapse in discipline, any slackening, resulted in a flogging and immediate dismissal.

The Sard walked slowly down the single row of soldiers. He stopped in front of a fair-haired boy who seemed slightly nervous.

'Where do you come from?'

'A village in the Delta, sir.'

'Your favourite weapon?'

'The sword.'

'Have a drink, soldier. You look thirsty.'

Serramanna handed the fair-haired boy a flask of anise-flavoured wine. He took two quick swallows.

'I'll post you in the hallway to the royal office. Your job is keeping everyone out of there during the last watch of the night.'

'Yes, sir.'

Serramanna had the men present arms, checked their uniforms, exchanged a few words with other soldiers, then sent them on their way.

The palace architects had set windows high in the walls so that cool air could circulate through the corridors on hot summer nights.

Everything was quiet. Outside, the frogs sang their mating songs.

Serramanna crept soundlessly down the tiled hallway leading to Ramses's office.

As he had suspected, the boy from the Delta was not at his post. Instead, he was fiddling with the latch on the office door. The Sard reached out one broad hand and lifted him by the scruff of the neck.

'A Greek, eh? Only a Greek could drink anise wine without flinching. Which faction do you belong to, my lad? One of Menelaus' leftovers, or part of some new plot? Answer me!'

The fair-haired boy twitched briefly, but made no sound.

Feeling the Greek go limp, Serramanna put him down on the floor, where he sprawled like a rag doll. Without meaning to, he had broken the boy's neck.

16

Written reports were not Serramanna's province. He simply stated the facts to Ahmeni, who put them down on papyrus and alerted Ramses. No one knew anything about the young Greek, who had been recruited on the strength of his skill with a sword. His brutal death made it impossible to trace the real instigator, but the king, more grateful than ever for Serramanna's vigilance, refrained from reprimanding his bodyguard.

This time, the object of the break-in was not the pharaoh but his office, meaning affairs of state. Someone wanted confidential documents and information about the new king's future policies.

Menelaus' attack had been motivated by revenge; this incident was far murkier. Who had hired the young Greek to slink through the shadows and compromise Ramses at the beginning of his reign? Of course, there was Shaanar, the embittered brother, strangely inactive and quiet since the coronation. Could he be working behind the scenes, much more effectively than in the past?

Remet bowed to the king. 'Majesty, your visitor has arrived.'

'Show him to the garden pavilion.'

Ramses wore only a simple white kilt and a single piece of jewellery, a gold bracelet on his right wrist. He collected his thoughts for a few moments, aware that the fate of Egypt would hinge on the interview he was about to conduct.

The king had had an elegant wooden pavilion put up in the garden, in the shade of a willow tree. A low table was spread with silvery green grapes and fresh figs. Cups of light, refreshing beer would be ideal in the summer heat.

The High Priest of Amon sat in an armchair with plump cushions and a matching footstool. He was resplendent in his wig, linen robe, bib necklace of pearls and lapis lazuli, and his silver bracelets.

As soon as he saw his sovereign, the High Priest rose and bowed to him.

'I trust this place is to your liking,' Ramses said.

'Majesty, I thank you for considering an old man's health.'

'You're not feeling well?'

'I'm no longer a young man. It's very hard to accept.'

'I was beginning to think we'd never meet.'

'Heavens, no, Majesty. For one thing, I was confined to my bed for a time. For another, I hoped to bring the Viziers of the North and the South along with me, and the Viceroy of Nubia.'

'What a delegation! Did they reject your proposal?'

'At first, no; later they did.'

'What made them change their minds?'

'They're high-ranking officials – they did not wish to displease Your Majesty. Still, their presence would have given my words added weight.'

'If your cause is just, you have nothing to fear.'

'Do you think it is?'

'Let me decide that, with Ma'at to guide me.'

'I'm worried, Majesty.'

'What can I do to ease your mind?'

'You asked for an accounting of Karnak's riches.'

'And I got it.'

'What do you conclude?'

'That you're a remarkable administrator.'

'Should I take that as criticism?'

'Certainly not. Our ancestors taught, did they not, that spiritual and material welfare go hand in hand. Pharaoh endows Karnak, and you make it prosper.'

'I still sense criticism in your tone, Majesty.'

'Puzzlement, nothing more. Why don't we discuss your concerns instead?'

'It's rumoured that Karnak's wealth and glory offend Your Majesty, and you wish to redistribute some of its privileges.'

'Where have you heard this?'

'Here and there.'

'And you believe these rumours?'

'When they are persistent, one cannot ignore them.'

'What do you yourself think?'

'That Your Majesty would be well advised to leave things as they are. That the wisest course would be to follow in your esteemed father's footsteps.'

'Unfortunately, his reign was cut short before he had time to enact a great many necessary reforms.'

'Karnak needs no reforms.'

'That's not what I think.'

'Then my worries were justified.'

'Perhaps mine are, too.'

'Majesty, I don't understand.'

'Is the High Priest of Amon still Pharaoh's faithful servant?'

The prelate averted his eyes. To regain his composure, he ate a fig and drank some beer. The king was as direct in his questioning as he was unpretentious in dress, and the priest had not been prepared for either. However, the young pharaoh was careful not to push him, allowing him time to gather his wits.

'How can you doubt my loyalty, Majesty?' he said at length.

'Because of Ahmeni's investigation.'

The High Priest reddened. 'That snivelling little scribe, that sneak, that rat, that—'

'Ahmeni is my friend, and his only ambition is to serve Egypt. I will not tolerate any insult to him, no matter who utters it.'

'Forgive me, Majesty,' stammered the priest. 'But his methods . . .'

'Did he use undue force?'

'No, but he was more relentless than a jackal devouring its kill!'

'He's conscientious and thorough.'

'For what are you criticizing me?'

Ramses looked the High Priest square in the face. 'Don't you know?'

Again, the prelate looked away.

'Egypt and everything in it belongs to the pharaoh, does it not?' asked Ramses.

'According to the testament of the gods.'

'But the pharaoh may grant land to men who have proved themselves worthy.'

'According to custom.'

'Is the High Priest of Amon authorized to act in Pharaoh's stead?'

'The High Priest is his delegate and his representative at Karnak.'

'Haven't you taken being his delegate too far?'

'I don't see—'

'You've deeded land to secular individuals, putting them in your debt. Military officers, for instance, whose loyalty to me might then be compromised. Perhaps you need an army to defend your private domain?'

'Mere circumstance, Majesty! You can't be thinking—'

'There are three major centres of worship in Egypt. Heliopolis is the holy city of Ra, the God of Light. Memphis worships Ptah, who created the Word, and inspires the work of craftsmen. Thebes is the home of Amon, the hidden god, whose true form no one knows. My father strove to maintain these three cities in harmony. Your policies, however, have thrown them out of balance, giving Thebes a disproportionate importance.'

'Majesty! Would you see Amon slighted?'

'Never. Amon's worldly representative is the one I question. As of today, I suspend you from your administrative responsibilities so that you may concentrate on religious devotions.'

The prelate struggled to his feet. 'You know very well I can't do that.'

'Why not?'

'Because my duties are both spiritual and administrative, exactly like yours.'

'Karnak belongs to Pharaoh.'

'No one would deny that, but who will manage its affairs.'

'I'll appoint an administrator.'

'That would destroy our whole priestly order. Majesty, I beg you to reconsider. Turning the priesthood of Amon against you would be most unwise.'

'Is that a threat?'

'The advice of an experienced man to a young monarch.'

'Do you think I'll follow it?'

'Ruling is a difficult art which requires a number of alliances, including that with the priests of Amon. Of course, as your faithful servant I shall follow your orders, whatever they may be.'

Though visibly weary, the High Priest had regained his confidence.

'Don't fight a pointless battle, Majesty. You could lose much by doing so. When the excitement of coming to power has passed, come to your senses again and don't turn everything upside-down. The gods abhor excess – remember Akhenaton's appalling conduct towards Thebes.'

'Your net is tightly woven,' Ramses told him, 'but a falcon's beak can tear holes in it.'

'Such a waste of energy! You belong in Memphis, not here. Egypt needs your strength to push back the barbarians who long to invade us. Let me take care of Thebes, and I'll support you.'

'I'll think it over.'

The High Priest smiled. 'You have intelligence to match your spirit: you'll be a great pharaoh, Ramses.'

17

Each and every Theban notable had only one thing in mind: pleading his cause with the new king in order to retain existing privileges. Ramses was an unknown quantity, aligned with no particular faction. Who knew what unpleasant surprises he might have in store for even the best-connected courtiers? But to meet with the pharaoh one had to get past Ahmeni, who refused to let anyone waste his own time, much less Ramses'. Then there was the little matter of Serramanna's insistence on searching each visitor for hidden weapons.

Ramses cancelled the rest of the morning's appointments, including one with the dykes inspector Ahmeni had recommended. Well, let Ahmeni take care of him. The king needed the advice of the Great Royal Wife.

After a refreshing dip, they sat on the edge of the pool, their naked bodies basking in the sun that filtered through the sycamores. The palace gardens were more beautiful than ever since Nedjem had been made minister for agriculture.

'I finally met the High Priest of Amon this morning,' Ramses confessed.

'Is his hostility implacable?'

'Absolutely. Either I fall in with his wishes or I enforce my own.'

'What does he want you to do?'

'Leave Karnak as the most powerful temple in Egypt. He'll rule the South and let me keep the North.'

'Out of the question.'

Ramses looked at Nefertari in amazement. 'I was certain you'd preach moderation!'

'If moderation leads to the country's ruin, it's no longer a virtue. This priest is trying to impose his rule on Pharaoh, to protect his own interests with no concern for the general welfare. If you give in, the throne will be shaken and everything Seti built will be destroyed.'

Nefertari spoke calmly, in her soft, soothing voice, yet her views were clear and firm.

'Can you imagine the consequences of conflict between the king and the High Priest of Amon?' Ramses asked her.

'If you show weakness at the beginning of your reign, ambitious and unworthy men will rise up against you. The High Priest will head the rebellion and assert his own authority at the expense of Pharaoh's.'

'I'm not afraid to take him on, but—'

'You're afraid it's for selfish reasons. That you have to prove your strength from the beginning.'

Ramses gazed at her reflection in the blue water of the pool. 'Are you a mind-reader?'

'I'm your wife.'

'Tell me what you think, Nefertari.'

'A pharaoh is larger than life. You are all that is generous, eager and strong. You're acting on those qualities – acting as a ruler.'

'But am I choosing the right way?'

'The High Priest wants to divide and conquer. There is no evil greater than civil war. As pharaoh, you must not cede him a single cubit of ground.'

Ramses laid his head on Nefertari's breast. She gently stroked his hair as all around them swallows dived, rustling the silken air.

The sound of a scuffle at the gates to the garden broke the

spell. A woman was arguing with the guards, her voice growing ever louder.

Ramses threw on his kilt and headed towards the group.

'What's going on here?'

The guards stepped aside and there stood Iset the Fair, blooming and vivacious as ever.

'Majesty!' she exclaimed. 'Let me speak to you, I beg of you.'

'Who's stopping you?'

'Your police, your army, your secretary, your—'

'Come with me, Iset.'

A small boy stepped out from behind her.

'Here's our son, Ramses.'

'Kha!' Ramses picked him up and lifted him over his head. The frightened child burst into tears.

'He's very shy,' said Iset.

The king sat the boy astride his shoulders. Soon Kha forgot his fear and began to laugh.

'Four years old . . . He's getting to be a big boy! What does his tutor say?'

'That he's too serious. Kha doesn't play much; he'd rather be reading. He already knows a lot of hieroglyphs; he can even write a few.'

'He'll catch up with me before long! Come and sit by the pool. I'm going to teach Kha to swim.'

'Is she . . . is Nefertari with you?'

'Of course.'

'Why have I had so much trouble getting in to see you? You shouldn't treat me like a stranger. You'd be dead if it weren't for me.'

'What do you mean?'

'I sent that letter to warn you about the coup.'

'What are you talking about?'

Iset hung her head. 'All right, I admit there was a time when I resented being left in Thebes. I was so alone. But I never stopped loving you, and I refused to join forces with the members of your own family working against you.'

'I never got your letter.'

Iset turned white. 'Then you thought I was against you, too?'

'Was I wrong?'

'Yes, you were! By the name of Pharaoh, I swear I never betrayed you!'

'Why should I believe you?'

Iset took Ramses's arm. 'How could I lie to you?'

Now they approached Nefertari, and her beauty took Iset's breath away. It was not so much her outward perfection as her true radiance that disarmed and conquered everyone around her. Nefertari was truly a Great Royal Wife. No one could touch her.

Iset was untroubled by jealousy. Nefertari shone like the summer sky; her nobility inspired only respect.

'Iset! I'm so happy to see you.' As lesser wife, Iset bowed to her. 'Please don't. Come, Iset, have a swim. It's so hot today.'

Iset had not expected such a welcome. Without a word, she acquiesced, removing her clothes. Naked as Nefertari, she dived into the blue water.

As they swam, Ramses watched the two women he loved. How could his feelings for them be so different, yet so intense and sincere? Nefertari was the great love of his life, an exceptional person, a queen. Neither adversity nor the ravages of time could weaken the passion that illuminated their lives. Iset the Fair was his carefree youth – desire, sensuality, passion. Still, she had lied and plotted against him; he had no choice but to punish her.

'Is it true I'm your son?' piped Kha.

'Yes, it is.'

'The hieroglyph for "son" has a duck in it.' The little boy carefully drew a duck in the sand with his finger.

'Do you know the one for "pharaoh"?'

Kha drew a house, then a column.

'The house means protection, the column means greatness. *Per-ah*, great house – that's the real meaning of the word. Do you know why they call me Pharaoh?'

'Because you're taller than everybody and you live in a great big house.'

'That's right, my son, but the house is all Egypt, and each person must find a home in it.'

'Will you teach me some more hieroglyphs?'

'Wouldn't you like to play another game?'

Kha pouted.

'All right then,' Ramses told him, and the boy brightened. The king traced a circle with a dot in its centre.

'The sun,' he explained. 'The sun is called Ra. His name is made of a mouth and an arm, because he's both word and deed. Now you draw it.'

The child drew a series of suns, each one closer to a perfect circle. Fresh from their swim, Iset and Nefertari inspected Kha's hieroglyphs and were astonished.

'He's very advanced for his age,' said the queen.

'It almost frightens me sometimes,' said Iset. 'His tutor doesn't know what to do with him.'

'Then he needs another tutor,' said Ramses. 'My son should develop his talents, no matter what other children his age do. His ability is a gift from the gods. We mustn't hold him back. Wait here.'

The king left the garden and went into the palace.

Kha began to cry; his finger was sore. 'May I pick him up?' Nefertari asked Iset.

'Yes. Yes, of course.'

The boy quietened almost at once. Nefertari's eyes were full of tenderness. Iset felt bold enough to ask the question tormenting her.

'Despite the loss of your daughter, are you planning to have more children?'

'In fact, I've just begun to suspect I'm pregnant again.'

'Ah . . . may the gods of childbirth smile upon you.'

'Thank you, Iset. Your kind words will help me when my time comes.'

Iset hid her dismay. She did not dispute that Nefertari was Ramses' queen and hardly envied her the crushing responsibilities that came with the position of Great Royal Wife. What she did want was more children with Ramses, many more, and the honour attached to being their mother. For the time being, she remained the mother of his firstborn son, but, if Nefertari gave birth to a boy, he would probably be given precedence over Kha.

Ramses returned with a miniature scribe's palette, complete with two tiny cakes of ink, one red, the other black, and three miniature brushes. When he handed it to his son, Kha's face lit up and he clutched the precious things to his heart.

'Thank you, Daddy!'

Once Iset and Kha had gone, Ramses again spoke his mind to Nefertari.

'I'm convinced she had something to do with the coup.'

'Did you question her?'

'She admits she was upset with me, but she claims she tried to warn me that an attack was being planned. If she did, I never got her message.'

'Why don't you believe her?'

'I think she is lying, and that she hasn't forgiven me for making you my consort.'

'You're wrong.'

'Her offence should be punished.'

'What offence? A pharaoh can't hand out punishments based on fleeting impressions. Iset has given you a fine son. She wishes you no harm. Forgive the offence, if she ever committed one, and forget the punishment.'

18

Setau's outfit stood out from those of the palace courtiers and scribes. His thick antelope-skin garment, cut like a winter tunic, had been treated with antivenom preparations. In an emergency, Setau could whip off his tunic, soak it in water, and produce a satisfactory snakebite remedy.

'This isn't the desert,' Ramses told him. 'You hardly need that portable pharmacy in Memphis.'

'It's more dangerous here than in deepest Nubia. Snakes and scorpions everywhere, though you might not recognize them at first glance. Are you ready?'

'I fasted, just as you told me to.'

'The treatments have gone well so far. You've built up an immunity to most kinds of snakebite, even certain cobras. Do you really want this added protection?'

'I gave you my consent.'

'It's not without risk.'

'Let's get on with it.'

'Did you ask Nefertari about it?'

'Did you ask Lotus?'

'She says I'm slightly mad, but we see eye to eye.'

Unshaven, square-jawed, refusing to wear a wig, Setau would have sent an ordinary patient running.

'If I've got the dose wrong,' he warned his friend, 'you could end up an imbecile.'

'No use trying to scare me off.'

'Drink this, then.'

Ramses drank the potion.

'What do you think?'

'Tastes good.'

'That's because of the carob juice. The other ingredients are less appetizing: extracts of several different stinging plants and diluted cobra blood. Now you're protected against any bite there is. You'll only need to take this mixture every six months to keep up that defence.'

'Setau, when will you come to work for me?'

'Never. And when will you stop being so naive? I could have poisoned you, just now.'

'You're not a murderer.'

'As if you'd know!'

'I learned a few things from Menelaus. What's more, you've been screened by Serramanna, my lion and my dog.'

'What a threesome. But are you forgetting that Thebes can't wait to see you leave and most of the notables hope to see you fail?'

'Nature has endowed me with a good memory.'

'Men are a far more dangerous species than snakes, Ramses.'

'Yes, but men are what a pharaoh has to work with, if his goal is to build a just and harmonious world.'

'Humph! You must be living in a dream world. Beware, my friend. You're surrounded by schemers and villains. Still, you have one advantage: you feel the same mysterious force I do when I work with cobras. It brought you Nefertari, the most wonderful partner any king could have. I think you'll make it.'

'It will be harder without your help.'

'Flattery didn't use to be one of your faults. I'm heading north now, with a load of venom. Take care, Ramses.'

Despite his brother's early show of strength, Shaanar was not discouraged. Who could tell what would happen when the young pharaoh locked horns with the High Priest of Amon? It would probably end in a stalemate, undermining Ramses' authority. His word was far from carrying the weight of Seti's.

Shaanar was beginning to get the measure of his brother.

A frontal attack was certain to fail, since Ramses would defend himself so forcefully that he would turn the situation to his advantage. It would be better to lay a series of traps, using trickery, lies and betrayal. As long as Ramses could not identify his enemies, he would waste his energy flailing at shadows. Once he was exhausted, it would be easy to finish him off.

While the new king was busy forming his government and bringing Thebes to heel, his brother had been quiet and discreet as if these events were nothing to do with him. Soon he would have to make himself heard, or else be suspected of plotting in the background.

After much thought, Shaanar had concluded that his best course was to play an apparently crude game, blatantly exploiting Ramses, who would react in his usual hot-headed way, without realizing that it was exactly the reaction his brother wanted. If his little experiment worked, Shaanar would know that Ramses could be manipulated.

In that case, the future would be bright.

For the tenth time, Ramses was lecturing Wideawake about his fishing expeditions. It wasn't nice to steal from the palace ponds. It *was* nice to share his catch with Invincible, but didn't they both get enough to eat as it was? The yellow-gold dog listened attentively, yet his expression told the king he was wasting his breath. With the lion as his accomplice, Wideawake knew he could get away with murder.

The towering figure of Serramanna appeared in the doorway of Ramses' office.

'Your brother wants to see you, but he refuses to be searched.'

'Let him in.'

Serramanna stepped aside. Shaanar shot him an icy look in passing.

'Would Your Majesty be so good as to grant me a private interview?'

The yellow dog tagged after Serramanna, who always had a treat for him.

'It's a long time since we talked, Shaanar.'

'You have so much to do. I didn't want to be a nuisance.'

Ramses circled his brother, inspecting him.

'Why are you looking at me like that?' Shaanar said anxiously.

'You're thinner, dear brother.'

'I've been trying to cut back these last few weeks.'

Despite his dieting, Shaanar was still plump. His small dark eyes shone in a moon face with the pudgy cheeks and the full lips of a true food-lover.

'Why have you kept your beard?'

'I'll never stop mourning Seti,' he said. 'How could I ever forget our father?'

'I sympathize,' Ramses said feelingly.

'I'm sure you do, but your duties leave you little time to dwell on it. It's not the same for me.'

'What brings you here today?'

'You've been expecting me, haven't you?'

The king made no comment.

'I'm your elder brother and my reputation is excellent. I've put our differences behind me; I can live with the fact that I was passed over for the throne. But I can't resign myself to being a rich, idle courtier, of no real use to my country.'

'I understand how you feel.'

'My work as Head of Protocol is no longer enough for me, especially since Remet, the new head steward, has been handling most of it.'

'What do you want, Shaanar?'

'I've thought long and hard before approaching you. I had to swallow my pride.'

'There should be no question of such a thing between brothers.'

'Will you meet my demands?'

'Not when I have no idea what they are.'

'Will you hear me out?'

'Please go ahead.'

Shaanar began to pace. 'Could I ask to become vizier? Impossible. You'd be accused of favouritism. Head of the police? The bureaucracy is too complicated. Head royal scribe? Too demanding – not enough rest and leisure time. What about overseeing your construction projects? No, I have no experience. Agriculture? You've already filled the position. Finance? You kept the incumbent. You plan to reform the temples, but I have no taste for the religious life.'

'What does that leave?'

'The one job I'm suited for: minister for foreign affairs. You're aware of my interest in trade relations. Instead of concentrating on negotiations for my personal gain, I want to work towards strengthening diplomatic ties with our neighbours, as well as within our dependent territories.' Shaanar finally came to a halt, asking, 'Does my proposal shock you?'

'It's a tremendous responsibility.'

'Would you authorise me to do everything possible to prevent war with the Hittites? No one wants bloodshed. If Pharaoh appoints his elder brother minister for foreign affairs, it will show just how important peace is to him.'

Ramses pondered. 'I'll grant your request, Shanaar, but you'll need help.'

'I know. Who do you have in mind?'

'My friend Ahsha, a professional diplomat.'

'A supervisor?'

'A partner, I hope.'

'As Your Majesty wishes.'

'Meet him as soon as possible, then let me have details of your plans.'

On his way out of the palace, Shaanar could barely contain a whoop of joy.

Ramses had reacted just as he'd hoped.

19

Dolora prostrated herself and kissed her brother's feet.

'Forgive me, I beg of you,' she sobbed. 'Forgive my husband and me!'

'Get up, Dolora. Don't make a spectacle of yourself.'

Dolora let Ramses help her to her feet, but was still afraid to look at him. Tall and listless, she seemed about to swoon.

'Forgive us, Ramses. We didn't know what we were doing!'

'You wanted me dead. Twice your husband tried to have me killed. Sary, who practically raised me!'

'It was wrong of him, very wrong, and I was just as bad. But we were used as catspaws.'

'By whom, dear sister?'

'The High Priest at Karnak. He convinced us you'd be a bad king, that you'd lead the country into a civil war.'

'You didn't have much faith in me at all.'

'My husband knew you as an impetuous boy, always itching for a fight. Now he sees the error of his ways – if you only knew how truly sorry he is!'

'And did our dear brother also try to convince you?'

'No,' lied Dolora. 'He's the one we should have listened to. Once he was reconciled to our father's decision to name you as his successor, Shaanar became one of your staunchest supporters. His only thought now is of serving Egypt in a position worthy of his talents.'

'Why didn't Sary come with you?'

Dolora hung her head. 'He fears the wrath of Pharaoh.'

'You're very lucky, sister. Our mother and Nefertari have pleaded fervently that you shouldn't be punished harshly. They want to keep peace in the family, out of respect for Seti's memory.'

'Are you pardoning me?'

'I'm appointing you honorary superior of the harem at Thebes. A grand title, but not too tiring for you. Just make sure you behave yourself, Dolora.'

'And . . . my husband?'

'He's going to head the brickyard at Karnak. He'll be doing something useful, and can learn how to build instead of destroy.'

'But Sary has always been a scribe, an academic. He can't do manual labour!'

'Remember the teachings of the sages, Dolora. The hand and the mind must work together, or men turn to evil. Now hurry and take up your new posts, both of you. There's work to be done.'

Leaving the palace, Dolora breathed a sigh of relief. Just as Shaanar had predicted, she and Sary had escaped the worst. Having just come to power, still under the influence of his mother and his wife, Ramses was inclined to be merciful.

Being forced to work was a real punishment to her, but less harsh than house arrest in some desert outpost or exile in the wilds of Nubia. As for Sary, his pride would suffer, but, considering he could have been sentenced to death for treason, becoming a brickmaker was better than the alternative.

Their disgrace would be short-lived. Dolora's lies had enhanced Shaanar's credibility as a supportive and respectful brother to the king. Ramses, preoccupied with his new responsibilities, would believe that his old enemies, including his brother and sister, had finally fallen in line.

Moses was overjoyed to be back in Karnak at the works where bricks were being made for the great Hall of Pillars. Once the period of mourning for Seti was over, Ramses had decided to continue work on his father's great project. The young Hebrew had a powerful build, broad shoulders, flowing hair, a full beard on his craggy face. He also had the respect and affection of his crew of stone-cutters and hieroglyph-carvers.

Moses had refused the post of masterbuilder that Ramses had offered him, feeling unequal to such responsibility. He could coordinate the work of experts and motivate workers, yes, but draw architectural plans like the brotherhood at Deir el-Medina, no. By gaining practical experience, listening to those more knowledgeable than himself and becoming familiar with the qualities of different building materials, the young Hebrew would become a skilled builder.

The rough working conditions and hard physical labour helped calm his soul. Every night, tossing in bed as sleep refused to come, Moses tried to understand why his mind was so troubled. He was living in a prosperous country, had a promising career, and was one of Pharaoh's closest friends. He could have any woman he wanted, earned a good living . . . No matter how many blessings he counted, it was no use. Why did he always feel incomplete? Why this unwarranted internal torment?

In the morning, he found relief in the bustle of the work site, the clang of mallet and chisel, the sight of huge blocks of stone sliding along a moistened track on wooden sledges, the constant alertness to danger, the slow satisfaction of raising a column.

Work was usually halted in the hot summer months, but Seti's death and Ramses's coronation had changed that.

Moses had come up with a plan after consulting with the leaders of the various work gangs from Deir el-Medina, as well as the Karnak masterbuilder, who explained his drawings in detail. Each day two sessions would be scheduled, the first from dawn to mid-morning, the second from late afternoon to nightfall, to keep the men out of the heat of day and allow them to rest. Furthermore, awnings would be rigged to provide some shade.

Moses had just passed the guardpost at the entry to the hall of pillars when the head stone-cutter approached him.

'No one can work under these conditions,' the man said flatly.

'Come on, the heat isn't that bad yet.'

'It's not the heat. I'm talking about the brickmakers building the scaffolding for us. It's their new head man.'

'Do I know him?'

'His name is Sary. Married to the pharaoh's sister, Dolora. That's why he thinks he can do as he pleases!'

'What's the problem?'

'It's too rough for him out here, so he only wants his gang to work every other day, but without the afternoon break or any extra water. Does he think he can treat his men like slaves? This is Egypt, not somewhere in Greece or Hittite territory. I stand by the brickmakers!'

'I don't blame you! Where can I find this Sary?'

'Sitting in the shade,' the man said, gesturing towards the foremen's tent.

Sary seemed a different man. The affable, portly tutor he had known was now almost gaunt, sharp-featured, jumpy. He alternately fiddled with a copper band on his left wrist, almost falling off now, and rubbed ointment into the big toe of his right foot, which was gnarled with arthritis. The only sign of his former station in life was an elegant white linen robe, the customary dress of successful scribes.

Reclining against a pile of cushions, Sary was sipping

cool beer. He glanced up absently when Moses entered the tent.

'Why, hello, Sary! Do you remember me?'

'How could I forget Moses, Ramses' brilliant fellow student? So you too are condemned to sweat it out in this brickyard. I thought he'd do better by his old friends.'

'I have no complaints.'

'You ought to try for something better.'

'What could be better than helping to build a monument like this? It's like a wonderful dream.'

'A dream? The heat, the dust, the sweat and toil, the awful noise, and even worse, rubbing elbows with illiterate labourers. A nightmare more like! You're wasting your talents, Moses.'

'Seti entrusted me with a mission. I plan to accomplish it.'

'A noble attitude. But when you get fed up, you'll change your tune.'

'And what is your mission at Karnak?'

A scowl darkened Sary's face.

'Running the brickyard – now there's a plum assignment.'

'The brickmakers are solid, respectable men. I'd take them over a bunch of self-indulgent scribes any day!'

'That's an odd thing to say, Moses. Are you rebelling agains the social order?'

'Against your contempt for other people.'

'Are you lecturing me, by any chance?'

'Look, Sary, I set the schedule here. It's the same in the brickyard as anywhere else, and I want you to follow it.'

'I have made my decision.'

'It doesn't tally with mine. You'll have to give way, Sary.'

'I shan't.'

'As you like. I'll pass on your refusal to the master builder, who'll take it up with the vizier, and he'll go to Ramses.'

'Is that a threat?'

'The usual procedure in a case of insubordination at a royal construction site.'

'You like humiliating me, don't you?'

'All I want is to be part of building this temple, and to see that nothing hinders it.'

'Don't make me laugh,' sneered Sary.

'We're colleagues,' Moses told him. 'Cooperation is the best answer.'

'Ramses will drop you, just like me.'

'Listen, Sary. Get your brickmakers to work on the scaffolding, give them the midday break they're entitled to, and make sure they have all the water they want.'

20

The wine was exceptional, the beef tasty, the bean purée pleasantly spicy. Say what you will about Shaanar, thought Meba, he certainly knows how to entertain.

'Is everything to your liking?' asked Ramses' elder brother.

'Simply wonderful! My dear fellow, your cooks are the finest in Egypt.'

Despite his long years in charge of the Foreign secretariat, Meba was not merely being diplomatic. Shaanar treated his guests to the very best.

'Don't the king's politics strike you as inconsistent?' asked Meba.

'He's not an easy man to understand.'

This veiled criticism satisfied Meba. His broad, kindly face had begun to show rare signs of strain. How could he be sure that Shaanar had not gone over to Ramses' side in order to live in peace and safeguard his own privileges? Still, the words he had just spoken seemed to prove the opposite.

'I can hardly approve of this new rash of ill-timed appointments, turning excellent state officials out of their offices and relegating them to lesser positions.'

'I quite agree, Meba.'

'Naming a gardener to the Agriculture secretariat – what a farce! It makes me wonder what on earth Ramses plans to do with *my* secretariat.'

'That's exactly what I wanted to discuss with you today.'

Meba squared his shoulders and adjusted the costly wig he wore year-round, even in the hottest weather.

'Are you trying to tell me something?'

'Let me give you all the details so that you can fully appreciate the situation. Yesterday, Ramses sent for me, out of the blue. I had to drop everything and go to the palace, where I was made to wait for over an hour.'

'Weren't you . . . concerned?'

'I admit I was. His Sardinian even searched me, despite my protest.'

'You, the king's brother! Has it come to that?'

'I'm afraid so, Meba.'

'Did you complain to the king?'

'He wouldn't let me. Apparently his security takes precedence over family feeling.'

'Seti would never have stood for it!'

'Unfortunately, Seti is no longer with us.'

'Men come and go, institutions remain. A prince of your stature must one day rise to the highest office.'

'It's in the hands of the gods, Meba.'

'Weren't you going to tell me about my secretariat?'

'I'm coming to that. Now there I was, trembling with shame and indignation after the bodyguard searched me, when in walked Ramses, telling me he was making me minister for foreign affairs!'

Meba blanched. 'You, in my job? It's beyond comprehension!'

'You'll understand better when you hear that he plans to monitor my every move. He wouldn't be able to control you, Meba, but I'll make a perfect figurehead. Our allies will be honoured that Ramses cares enough about foreign policy to appoint his own brother to the Foreign Affairs secretariat. They won't realize I'm tied hand and foot.'

Meba was crestfallen. 'So much for me . . .'

'And for me, despite appearances.'

'This king is a monster.'

'As other men of rank will soon discover. That's why we mustn't allow ourselves to be too discouraged.'

'What are you suggesting?'

'What would you rather do, retire or help me keep fighting?'

'I can make trouble for Ramses.'

'Pretend to step aside gracefully and wait for my instructions.'

Meba smiled. 'Ramses may have made a mistake in underestimating you. Heading that secretariat will give you plenty of opportunities, even with his supporters around you.'

'You're still sharp, old friend. Now why don't you explain how you've kept the secretariat running so smoothly all these years?'

Meba was more than willing. Shaanar did not mention that he had an invaluable ally, affording him control of the situation. Ahsha's treachery must remain his most closely guarded secret.

Holding Lita by the hand, the sorcerer Ofir walked slowly down the main street of the city of the Horizon of Aton, the abandoned capital where the heretic pharaoh Akhenaton had reigned with his wife Nefertiti. The buildings were intact but, through the open doors and windows, sand blew in from the desert.

The Horizon of Aton, situated many leagues to the north of Thebes, had been deserted for more than fifty years. After Akhenaton's death, the court had abandoned his grandiose Middle Egyptian capital and returned to Thebes, centre of the worship of Amon some three hundred miles to the south. Akhenaton's cult of the One God Aton, the golden orb, was repudiated in favour of worship of the old gods.

In Ofir's opinion, Akhenaton had not gone far enough. Sun-worship was a travesty: God was beyond any representation, any symbol. God dwelt in the heavens, man on earth. Egyptians believed that their gods walked the earth; they rejected the notion of a single god. Therefore Egypt must be destroyed.

Ofir was descended from one of Akhenaton's advisers, a Libyan who had spent countless hours with the king, transcribing his mystic poems. He had later circulated them throughout the Near East, even among the tribes of Sinai, particularly the Hebrews.

General Horemheb – the true founder of the dynasty to which Seti and Ramses belonged – had ordered the execution of Ofir's great-grandfather, branding him a dangerous agitator and practitioner of black magic who had led Akhenaton astray and distracted him from kingly duties.

That was indeed what the Libyan intended: to avenge the humiliation his people had suffered, to undermine Egypt, to take advantage of Akhenaton's failing health, persuading him to abandon any semblance of a defence policy. And he had very nearly succeeded.

Today, Ofir had taken up his great-grandfather's torch. He had inherited his forebear's magical lore and talent for sorcery, as well as the hatred for Egypt that fuelled his destructive fury. Bringing Egypt to its knees meant defeating the pharaoh – defeating Ramses.

Lita stared blankly, yet Ofir continued to describe each public building, each private residence, the shops and craft establishments, the menagerie where Akhenaton had housed his collection of rare animals. They had already spent hours wandering through the empty palace where the king and Nefertiti had played with their six daughters, one of whom was Lita's grandmother.

On this new visit, Ofir noted that Lita was more attentive, as if her interest in the outside world was finally awakening. She lingered in Akhenaton and Nefertiti's bed-chamber, slumped over an empty cradle and wept.

When her tears were spent, Ofir took her by the hand and led her to a sculptor's workshop. In crates lay plaster heads of women, models for more permanent works in stone.

The sorcerer began pulling them out, one after the other.

Suddenly, Lita reached out for a statue, stroking its sub-limely beautiful face. 'Nefertiti,' she murmured.

Then her hand darted towards another, smaller head, with remarkably delicate features.

'Meritaton, "Beloved of Aton", my grandmother. And her sister . . . and her other sisters . . . my lost family! I've finally found my family.'

Lita clutched the plaster heads to her chest. One tumbled out of her grip and shattered on the floor.

Ofir braced himself for an outburst, but Lita stood mute and rigid. Then she dashed the rest of the heads against a wall and ground the pieces beneath her feet.

'The past is past. Let me kill it dead,' she said with her vacant stare.

'No,' objected the sorcerer, 'the past never dies. Your grand-mother and mother were persecuted because they believed in Aton. But I found you, Lita. I rescued you from exile and certain death.'

'It's true, I remember now. My grandmother and mother are buried out there in the hills, and I should have joined them long ago. But you've been like a father to me.'

'The time for revenge is at hand, Lita. What you suffered as a child was caused by Seti. Seti is dead, but he left his son to oppress us. Ramses must be humbled. You must punish him.'

'I want to walk through my city,' said Lita.

This time she was eager to touch the gates of temples, the doors of houses, as if taking possession of the empty town. At sunset, she climbed on to the terrace of Nefertiti's palace and contemplated her ghostly domain.

'My soul is empty, Ofir. Your thoughts will fill it.'

'I want you to be queen, Lita, so that you can impose worship of the One God.'

'Words, Ofir. Only words. Hatred is what drives you. I can feel it. You're evil inside.'

'Are you refusing to help me?'

'My soul is empty. You've filled it with your desire to do harm. You've patiently moulded me into an avenger. Now I'm ready to fight for your revenge and mine, to cut like a sword.'

Ofir knelt and gave thanks to God. His prayers would be answered.

21

There was entertainment in the Theban tavern: a troupe of dancers, enticing Egyptian girls from the Delta and lissome, ebony-skinned Nubians. Moses looked on in fascination from his table at the back of the room, sipping a cup of palm wine. After a hard day's work, marked by two near-accidents, he felt the need to be alone in a noisy crowd, to be surrounded by people yet remain aloof.

Not far away sat an unusual couple.

The young woman was blonde, full-figured, attractive. The man, much older, had a disturbing countenance: gaunt, with jutting cheekbones, a prominent nose, very thin lips, a strong chin, he looked like a bird of prey. In the din, Moses could not overhear their conversation. He heard only meaningless snatches of the man's droning bass.

The Nubians were pulling patrons in to join in the fun. A tipsy middle-aged man laid a hand on the blonde's right shoulder, asking her to dance. Startled, she pushed him away. When the man persisted, her hawk-faced companion extended his right arm and the drunk was instantly blasted back a good five paces, as if he'd been punched. Muttering an apology, he slunk away.

The gesture had been swift and unobtrusive, but Moses knew he'd seen correctly. This remarkable-looking character seemed to be gifted with extraordinary powers.

When the pair left the tavern, Moses followed them. They walked towards the southern edge of Thebes, disappearing among the workmen's hovels, cramped lanes of single-storey dwellings. For a moment he thought he'd lost them. Then he heard the man's firm footsteps.

This late at night, the streets were deserted. A dog barked. Bats swooped. The farther Moses went, the more curious he grew. He glimpsed the couple threading their way through hovels that would soon be pulled down to make way for new construction. No one lived here.

The woman opened a door with a loud creak, rending the still of the night. The man was nowhere in sight.

Moses hesitated.

Should he go in and question her, ask who they were, what they were doing here? He realized how ludicrous he would seem, with no connection to the police and no business mixing in other people's private lives. What evil genius had inspired him to shadow them? Furious with himself, he wheeled – to find the hawk-faced man directly in his path.

'Were you following us, Moses?'

'How do you know my name?'

'I only had to inquire at the tavern. You're a well-known figure, friend of the pharaoh's and all.'

'And who might you be?'

'First tell me why you were following us.'

'An impulse, nothing more.'

'That's a feeble explanation.'

'Perhaps, but it's the truth.'

'I don't believe you.'

'Let me pass.'

The man held out his hand.

In front of Moses, the dusty street quaked. A horned viper slithered out, its tongue darting furiously.

'A magic trick!' protested Moses.

117

'Don't go near it. It's real enough; I merely roused it.' The Hebrew turned round. Another snake was behind him.

'If you value your life, go into the house.'

The creaking door opened.

In the narrow street, there was no escaping the reptiles. Where was Setau when he needed him? Moses entered a room with a low ceiling and a floor of beaten earth. The man followed and shut the door behind him.

'Don't try to run. The vipers will get you. When I decide it's time, I'll send them back to sleep.'

'What do you want?'

'To talk.'

'I could flatten you with one punch.'

The man smiled. 'I wouldn't try it if I were you. Remember what happened in the tavern.'

The young blonde woman was huddled in a corner of the room, a cloth covering her face.

'Is she sick?' Moses asked.

'She can't bear the darkness. Once the sun comes up, she'll feel better.'

'Are you ever going to tell me what you expect of me?'

'My name is Ofir. I was born in Libya, and I practise magic.'

'At which temple?'

'None.'

'You're outside the law, then.'

'My young companion and I live in hiding, always on the move.'

'What other offence have you committed?'

'Not sharing the faith of Seti and Ramses.'

Moses was bewildered. 'I don't understand . . .'

'This fragile and wounded young woman is named Lita. She's the granddaughter of Meritaton, one of the great Akhenaton's six daughters. He's been dead these fifty years, his royal city abandoned, his name expunged from the annals

– all because he tried to make Egypt worship Aton as the One True God.'

'None of his followers was persecuted!'

'No, only forgotten, which is far worse. Queen Ankhesenamon, Tutankhamon's widow and heir to the throne of Egypt, was unjustly sentenced to death. Then Horemheb and his impious successors gained control of the Two Lands. If there were any justice, Lita would be Queen of Egypt.'

'You want to overthrow Ramses?'

Ofir smiled again. 'I'm only an ageing sorcerer, Lita is weak and despairing; the powerful Pharaoh of Egypt has nothing to fear from us. But there is one force that can topple him and impose its own law.'

'What force is that?'

'The true God, Moses, the one true God whose wrath will soon be felt by all those who fail to bow down before him!'

Ofir's deep, rumbling voice shook the walls of the hovel. Moses was filled with an uneasy mixture of dread and fascination.

'You're a Hebrew, Moses.'

'I was born in Egypt.'

'You and I are alike: both exiles. We're looking for a purer land, untainted by crowds of gods. You're a Hebrew, Moses. Your people suffer. They wish to revive the faith of their fathers, to revive Akhenaton's grand design.'

'The Hebrews are happy in Egypt. They are well-paid and well-fed.'

'Their material needs are being met, perhaps, but that's no longer enough for them.'

'If you're so sure, why don't you become their prophet?'

'I'm only a Libyan, with neither your credentials nor your influence.'

'You're nothing but a madman, Ofir! Turning the Hebrew community against Ramses would end in their utter ruin. They have no desire to rebel and leave the country. As for

119

me, I'm the friend of a pharaoh whose reign promises great things.'

'A fire burns within you, Moses, as it burned in the heart of Akhenaton. He still has followers. We're beginning to find one another.'

'So you and Lita aren't alone?'

'We have to be very careful, but our movement is growing day by day. Akhenaton's way is the religion of the future.'

'I doubt that Ramses would agree.'

'You're his friend, Moses. You can make him see the light.'

'Have *I* seen it?'

'The Hebrews will impose their belief in the One God throughout the world, and you will become their leader.'

'Your prophecy is absurd!'

'It will come true.'

'I have no intention whatsoever of opposing the king.'

'Let him stay out of our way, and no harm will come to him.'

'Stop your raving and go back to Libya, Ofir.'

'The new land I spoke of doesn't exist yet. You'll be its founder.'

'I have other plans.'

'You believe in the One God, don't you?'

Moses was uneasy. 'I don't have to answer that.'

'Don't run away from your destiny.'

'I've had enough of you, Ofir.'

Moses headed for the door. Ofir made no move to stop him.

'The snakes are back underground,' the sorcerer declared.

'Goodbye, Ofir.'

'I'll see you again soon, Moses.'

22

Shortly before dawn, Bakhen left his priest's cell, washed his shaven body, and put on a white kilt. Carrying a water-jug, he walked to the sacred lake, where swallows circling overhead announced the new day. The broad lake, accessible by stone steps at its four corners, contained the water of Nun, the watery chaos from which all life emerged. Bakhen drew off a bit of the precious liquid, which would be used in the many purification rites performed within the sanctuary.

'Bakhen? We meet again.'

The priest turned to the man who had greeted him, dressed as a simple 'pure priest'.

'Ramses . . .'

'When I joined the army and you were my combat instructor, we fought. More or less to a draw, as I recall.'

Bakhen bowed. 'My past is dead, Majesty. Today I belong to Karnak.'

The former supervisor of the royal stables and renowned cavalryman still had his rugged, square-jawed face, harsh voice, and forbidding manner; otherwise, he was very much the priest.

'Does Karnak belong to the crown?' asked Ramses.

'Is someone claiming that it doesn't?'

'I'm sorry to disturb you, Bakhen, but I need to know whether you're a friend or a foe.'

'Why would I oppose Pharaoh?'

'The High Priest of Amon is fighting me, or didn't you know?'

'Quarrels in high places—'

'Don't evade the issue, Bakhen. There isn't room for two masters in this country.'

The ex-supervisor was taken aback. 'I've just finished my novitiate and I—'

'If you're my friend, Bakhen, you must join me in this fight.'

'What can I do?'

'Like every other temple in the land, Karnak should be an example of rectitude. If that were not the case, what would your reaction be?'

'I'd tan the culprits' hides, as sure as I trained my horses!'

'That's how you can help me, Bakhen. Bring me proof that no one here is breaking the law of Ma'at.'

Ramses left him, taking the path round the sacred lake as calmly as the other 'pure priests' who had come to fill their vessels with holy water.

Bakhen was unable to reach an immediate decision. Karnak had become his home, his world. Still, he thought, doing Pharaoh's bidding was the highest calling of all.

In Thebes, the Syrian merchant Raia had acquired three fine market stalls in the centre of town. Cooks from noble families bought his excellent preserved meats, while their mistresses fought over his latest Asian vases, which were exquisite and beautifully made.

Since the end of official mourning, business had picked up again. Courteous, enjoying an excellent reputation, Raia had a faithful and growing clientele. He paid his employees well and praised them lavishly, so they always spoke highly of him.

After seeing his barber out, the merchant stroked his newly

trimmed beard and set to work on his accounts. His staff were instructed not to disturb him for any reason.

Raia mopped his brow. The summer heat was hard on him. Even worse was the setback he had just suffered. The young Greek he had hired had failed to break into Ramses' office and report on which matters were receiving the new king's attention. A predictable enough outcome, however: Raia's main objective had, after all, been to test Ramses and Serramanna's security measures. Unfortunately, they appeared highly effective. Obtaining accurate information would not be easy, although bribery was always a useful weapon.

The merchant pressed an ear to his office door. He heard nothing in the antechamber; no one was spying on him. Just to be sure, he hopped on a stool and peered through a tiny hole in the dividing wall.

Reassured, he entered the storeroom full of small alabaster vases from southern Syria, an ally of Egypt. His ladies were especially fond of these, so Raia displayed only one at a time to whet their appetite. He searched for the one with a tiny red dot beneath the lip. Inside was an oblong fragment of wood with the vase's dimensions and price marked on it.

The code was easy to decipher, and the message from his Hittite employers was clear: oppose Ramses and back Shaanar.

'A beautiful piece,' cooed Shaanar, lovingly stroking the vase that Raia was showing him, in full view of wealthy clients who would never dare outbid the king's elder brother.

'The masterpiece of an old craftsman who'll take his secrets to the grave with him,' said Raia.

'I can offer you six milch-cows, an ebony bed, eight chairs, twenty pairs of sandals and a bronze mirror.'

The merchant bowed. 'A most generous offer, Your Highness. Would you do me the honour of affixing your seal to my accounts scroll?'

Raia steered the prince towards his office at the back of the shop, where they could talk without being overheard.

'I have excellent news,' he said once the door was shut. 'Our foreign friends are most receptive to your plan and would like to back you.'

'What are their conditions?'

'No conditions, no restrictions.'

'It sounds too good to be true.'

'We'll discuss the details later. For the moment, we have an agreement in principle. Consider this an important victory. Congratulations, my lord: I feel as if I'm talking to Egypt's next pharaoh, no matter how long the road we may have to travel.'

For Shaanar, it was a heady sensation. This secret alliance with the Hittites was as effective and dangerous as a deadly poison. He must determine how it could be used to destroy Ramses without harming himself or weakening Egypt too much. It was like walking a tightrope across a precipice. He knew he could do it.

'What is your reply?' asked Raia.

'Send my thanks and tell them I'm hard at work – as the newly appointed minister for foreign affairs.'

'You've been given that position?' said Raia, clearly astonished.

'Under close supervision.'

'My friends and I will count on you to make the most of the situation.'

'What your friends should do is make raids into the weaker Egyptian protectorates, buy up princes and tribes Egypt thinks it controls, and spread as many false rumours as possible.'

'For instance?'

'Oh, suggesting that they plan to expand their borders, annex Syria, invade the ports of Canaan. Say morale is low among Egyptian troops in the territories . . . We must bait Ramses until he loses his head.'

'Allow me to express my admiration.'

'I'm full of ideas, Raia. Your friends won't regret their decision to work with me.'

'Perhaps it's forward of me to hope that my own recommendations may have played some part?'

'On top of the payment you record for the vase, there will be a sack of Nubian gold.'

Shaanar returned to the front of the shop. A man of his rank would never linger in a merchant's office, no matter how well-known his penchant for exotic vases.

Should he tell Ahsha about this secret alliance with Egypt's major enemy? No, that would be a mistake. Shaanar judged it better to keep his networks of supporters strictly apart. That way, he could manipulate them more effectively and compensate for any possible weaknesses.

In the pleasant shade of a sycamore, Queen Tuya was chronicling her late husband's reign, commemorating the essential dates in a blessed era of peace and prosperity for Egypt. Seti's every thought, every deed, was fresh in her mind. She had been attuned to his hopes and fears. She treasured the memory of the intimate moments when their souls had communed.

In this frail woman, Seti lived on.

Watching Ramses come towards her, Tuya saw the stamp of his father's authority. The new pharaoh was all of a piece, without the inconsistencies that plagued most men. Like an obelisk, he seemed able to withstand the strongest tempest. His youth and strength added to the impression of invulnerability.

Ramses kissed his mother's hands and sat down on her right.

'You write all day long.'

'All night, too. Would you forgive me if I left anything out? You look worried, my son.'

Tuya could always read his mood in a minute.

'The High Priest of Amon is challenging my authority.'

'Seti saw it coming. Sooner or later, the clash was inevitable.'

'What would my father have done?'

'You know perfectly well. There's only one possible course of action.'

'Nefertari said as much.'

'She's Queen of Egypt, and, like every queen, is the guardian of the Rule of Ma'at.'

'You don't urge moderation?'

'When it's a matter of preserving the country's unity, there's no room for compromise.'

'Dismissing a High Priest of Amon will have serious repercussions.'

'Who rules Egypt, my son, you or him?'

23

The donkeys followed their grizzled leader through the gates of the temple enclosure. The old one's hooves knew every step from the weaving workshops to the temple warehouses. He held the others to a steady, dignified pace.

It was a full shipment. Bakhen had been sent to help another priest with the receiving. Each length of linen, to be used for vestments, was supposed to be tagged with a number and entered in the accounts with a note on its origin and quality.

'Good stuff,' said Bakhen's colleague, a foxy-looking little man. 'Been here at Karnak long?'

'A few months.'

'You like the life here?'

'It's what I expected.'

'What do you do on the outside?'

'Nothing. I'm a fully fledged priest now.'

'I serve two months at a time here in the warehouses, then go back to town and work as a ferry inspector. It's not too hard. Here, though, we never stop!'

'Then why do you do it?'

'That's my business. Listen, I'll pick out the first-quality material. You record the rest.'

When each donkey was unloaded, warehouse workers carefully laid the linen on a cloth-covered sledge. Bakhen inspected it and made entries on a wooden writing-board, including the date of delivery. It seemed to him that his fellow receiver was not as busy as he claimed. The greater part of his time was spent glancing furtively in all directions.

'I'm thirsty,' he said. 'Care for a drink?'

'Gladly.'

The foxy little lay priest left the storeroom. He'd set his writing-board on the back of the lead donkey, where Bakhen could see it. There were only scribbled approximations of hieroglyphs, nothing to do with shipments of first-quality linen.

When the lay priest returned, carrying a skin of cool water, Bakhen was already back at work.

'Here, have some. Making us work in this heat is inhuman, anyhow.'

'I don't hear the donkeys complaining.'

'Very funny.'

'Almost the end of your shift, isn't it?'

'No such luck! The cloth still has to be routed for shelving.'

'What do we do with our writing-boards?'

'Give me yours, and I'll return it with mine at the main office.'

'Is that far from here?'

'It's some way, but not too bad.'

'You're senior to me. Why not let me do the walking?'

'Oh, no. They wouldn't know you at the office.'

'Then I ought to introduce myself.'

'They have their routine, and they don't like changing it.'

'Isn't that rather a nuisance?'

'Thanks for the offer, but all the same, you'd better leave it to me.'

The man seemed disconcerted. He moved away so that Bakhen couldn't see what he was recording on his board.

'Writer's cramp?' Bakhen inquired.

'No, I'm fine.'

'Just one thing: can you write?'

The lay priest turned indignantly toward Bakhen. 'Why do you ask?'

'I saw your writing-board there, on the donkey's back.'

'Nosy, aren't you?'

'Who wouldn't be, seeing how little work you've been doing? If you want, I'll fill out the records for you. Otherwise, you're going to have trouble at the office.'

'Don't pretend you don't understand, Bakhen.'

'Understand what?'

'Oh, all right. You want me to cut you in. I can understand that, but still, you're quick off the mark.'

'What do you mean?'

The foxy man came closer and spoke in a low voice. 'This temple is rich, the richest in Egypt. Priests are paid nothing. We have to manage. Karnak will never miss a length of linen here and there. Go for the quality, find regular customers, and you do very well. See?'

'Are the office staff in on it, too?'

'Just one scribe and two warehouse foremen. Since the linen we take is never recorded, there's no way of tracing it. A pretty good setup, eh?'

'Aren't you afraid of getting caught?'

'It's foolproof.'

'But the priests . . .'

'They've got other problems. They just turn a blind eye. Now tell me how much of a cut you want.'

'The same as the scribe, or whoever gets the best deal.'

'You've got a nerve! I think we can work together. In a few years we'll both have a nice little nest egg and we won't have to work here any more. How about finishing up this shipment?'

Bakhen nodded and went back to work.

Nefertari laid her head on Ramses' shoulder as the sunrise flooded their bedroom with light. Both of them venerated this daily miracle, this endlessly renewed victory of light over darkness. Celebrating the morning rites, they associated themselves with the solar barque's journey through the realms of darkness, the gods' nightly battle with the monster intent on destroying all of creation.

'I need your magic, Nefertari. This won't be an easy day.'

'So your mother agrees with me about Karnak?'

'Sometimes I have the feeling you're in league with her.'

'We see things the same way,' she admitted with a smile.

'The two of you have convinced me. Today I shall dismiss the High Priest of Amon.'

'Why did you wait so long?'

'I needed proof of mismanagement.'

'And you got it?'

'I put Bakhen on the case – my old military instructor, who's become a priest. He uncovered a ring of warehouse workers stealing linen and reselling it. That means the High Priest is corrupt himself or else he no longer knows what goes on at Karnak. In either case, he's not fit to lead the priesthood.'

'Is Bakhen trustworthy?'

'He's young, but devoted to Karnak. What he uncovered disturbed him deeply. He knew he was honour-bound to report the wrongdoing he witnessed, yet I practically had to drag it out of him. Bakhen is neither ambitious nor an informer.'

'When will you be seeing the High Priest?'

'This morning. I'm sure he'll deny any involvement and claim I'm accusing him falsely.'

'Why are you so hesitant?'

'I'm afraid he'll retaliate by crippling the temple's economic activities and interfering with food distribution, for a time at least. That's the price I'll have to pay for avoiding civil war.'

Her husband's grave tone impressed Nefertari. This was no tyrant locked in a power struggle with a rival, but a pharaoh willing to take huge risks to preserve the unity of the Two Lands.

'I have a confession to make,' she said dreamily.

'Have you been making your own inquiries about Karnak?'

'No, it's nothing like that.'

'Then my mother is using you as her messenger.'

'Wrong again.'

'Is it anything to do with the High Priest's dismissal?'

'No, though it may affect the future of the kingdom.'

'How long are you going to keep me in suspense?'

'A few more months. Ramses, I'm pregnant.'

He took Nefertari gently in his strong arms. 'The best doctors in the country will be at your side every moment.'

'Don't worry.'

'How can I not worry? I hope our child will be strong and healthy, but your life and health mean even more to me.'

'I'll have the best possible care.'

'Suppose I order you to cut back on your public appearances?'

'Would you tolerate a lazy queen?'

Ramses was growing restless. The High Priest's lateness was an insult. What possible excuse could he offer? If he'd got wind of Bakhen's revelations, he was probably trying to stall the investigation, destroying evidence and discharging ringleaders and witnesses – tactics that would ultimately backfire.

As the sun reached its zenith, the Fourth Prophet of Amon requested an audience. The king admitted him at once.

'Where is the First Prophet and High Priest of Amon?' he demanded.

'He is dead, Majesty.'

24

A conclave was held by order of the pharaoh. In attendance were the Second, Third, and Fourth Prophets of Amon at Karnak, as well as the High Priests and Priestesses of the nation's other major temples. The only ones who did not attend were the prelates of Dendera and Athribis, the former being too old and infirm to travel, the latter too ill to leave his residence in the Delta. They were represented by two delegates with full voting powers.

This distinguished company met in a hall in the temple of Tuthmosis III, the pharaoh of whom it was said 'His Monument Shines like the Sun'. Here the High Priests of Amon were ordained, here they received instruction in their duties.

'I need to consult you,' declared Ramses, 'to choose the new head of this great institution.'

There was a murmur of approval. Perhaps this young pharaoh was not as impulsive as some claimed!

'I thought by rights the Second Prophet assumed his functions,' offered the High Priest of Memphis.

'I don't consider seniority a sufficient criterion.'

'May I encourage Your Majesty not to rule seniority out entirely?' chimed in the Third Prophet of Amon. 'In the secular domain, it is no doubt possible to fill high positions from the outside, but that would be a mistake where Karnak is concerned. A man of experience, a man of honour—'

'Honour! Since you bring it up, were you aware that employees have been stealing first-quality linen within these very walls?' An astonished rumble greeted the king's revelation. 'The culprits have been arrested and sentenced to work as weavers. They will never again set foot inside a temple.'

'Our late prelate . . . was he implicated in the affair?'

'Apparently not, but you can understand why I'm reluctant to choose his successor from within the temple priesthood.'

A long silence greeted Pharaoh's remarks.

'Has Your Majesty a name in mind?' asked the High Priest of Heliopolis.

'I expect this conclave to propose a serious candidate.'

'How much time do we have?'

'According to custom, it is now my duty to visit a certain number of towns and temples, accompanied by the queen and select members of the court. Upon my return, you will inform me of the outcome of your deliberations.'

Before leaving on the tour of Egypt that was a traditional part of the first year of a pharaoh's reign, Ramses visited the temple of Gurnah, on the west bank of Thebes. Here Seti's *ka* was maintained in perpetuity. Each day, specially trained mortuary priests placed offerings of meat, bread, fruit, and vegetables on the altars and recited rites to safeguard the immortal presence of the late king's soul.

The king contemplated one of the reliefs that depicted his father, for ever young, addressing the gods. Ramses implored Seti's spirit to come out of the stone, burst forth from the walls, and surround him with the power of a king who now dwelt among the stars.

With each passing day, Ramses had grown more acutely aware of Seti's absence, until it became both a trial and a summons. A trial, because he could no longer seek the advice of a trusted, generous mentor; a summons, because his dead father's voice unceasingly urged him to forge ahead, no matter what obstacles lay in his path.

In plush Theban villas, under shopkeepers' awnings, on doorsteps where mothers sat nursing babies, the topic of conversation was the same: which members of the court would Ramses and Nefertari take with them as they toured the Two Lands, as the new pharaoh sealed his alliance with the pantheon of gods?

Everyone knew someone who had confidential information from someone in authority or from a palace employee. It was widely held that the royal fleet would first head south, to Aswan, then turn round and sail down the Nile to the Delta. The crews had been warned that speed was of the essence: they would have to work hard, with only short stops. There was general rejoicing that this rite of passage would be accomplished in good time, that the new king and queen would maintain harmony with Ma'at, the Eternal Rule.

As soon as the fleet was under way, Ahmeni buried Ramses in a pile of documents he was supposed to study before meeting the governors of the provinces, the temple administrators, the mayors of the major population centres. The king's private secretary provided him with a biography of each important person he would meet, outlining career, family situation, avowed ambitions, and relations with other political leaders. When the information was less than solid or had not been verified, Ahmeni pointed it out.

'This is a gold mine!' Ramses exclaimed. 'How many days and nights have you spent putting it together?'

'I don't keep track. My only concern is for accurate information. Without it, how can one govern?'

'Just skimming your masterpiece, I see that Shaanar has a network of rich, influential supporters.'

'Does that come as a surprise?'

'At this stage, yes.'

'More hearts and minds for you to win over.'

'You're an optimist.'

'You're the king and you're meant to reign. Everything else is beside the point.'

'Don't you ever rest?'

'I can rest when I'm dead. As long as I'm your sandal-bearer, it's my job to smooth the way for you. Is your chair comfortable?'

The pharaoh's folding chair consisted of a leather seat on a sturdy frame. The legs broadened into ducks' heads, encrusted with ivory. The king would be glad of it's convenience during official ceremonies and audiences.

'I've drilled your entourage,' Ahmeni assured him. 'Everything will be taken care of along the way. Your meals will be up to palace standards.'

'You're even serious about food,' teased Ramses.

'First of all, good food guarantees long life. Second, moderation in food and drink preserves energy and concentration. I've sent couriers ahead instructing the mayors and high priests in the cities where we'll be stopping to find lodging for all the members of our group. You and the queen, of course, will stay in the palaces.'

'Have you made arrangements for Nefertari?'

'Of course I have. Your wife's condition is of national concern. Her cabin is well ventilated and as quiet as we can make it. Five physicians will be on call and you'll receive daily updates. Just one small problem . . .'

'About Nefertari?'

'No, about the landing stages. I've had alarming reports that some of them are in poor condition, but I'm sceptical. I think the provincial governors are simply looking for extra money for their upkeep. Fair enough, in view of your tour, but you mustn't let them affect your judgment. You'll have to decide each case as you see it.'

135

'How are our relations with the two viziers?'

'Terrible, from their point of view, but excellent from ours. The Viziers of the North and South are solid public servants, but overcautious. They live in fear of being dismissed. Keep them on. They'd never dare betray you.'

'I was thinking—'

'Of appointing me vizier? I hope not. I'm of far more use to you in my present capacity. I can work behind the scenes, without a huge bureaucracy to stifle me.'

'Tell me how the courtiers feel about being invited.'

'Thrilled to be included, not too happy about Serramanna's security checks and searches. He views every one of them as a potential criminal. I listen to their complaints, then forget them straight away. Your Sard is doing an excellent job.'

'You're forgetting my dog and my lion.'

'Don't worry. They're being well looked after, and they're the best guards you could have.'

'How is Remet working out?'

'I've had glowing reports. You'd think he'd been your head steward for ages. Your household has never run more smoothly. Your instinct didn't fail you.'

'Is Nedjem having as much success?'

'He takes his role as head of the Agriculture secretariat very seriously. Spends a couple of hours every day quizzing me on administrative matters, then confers with his predecessor's technical advisers, who are helping him learn the job. He won't see much of the scenery on this trip!'

'And my beloved brother?'

'Shaanar's ship is a floating palace. He's been hosting receptions right and left, proclaiming the future glories of Ramses' Egypt.'

'Does he think I'm a naive fool?'

'It's not as simple as that,' said Ahmeni thoughtfully. 'He really seems excited about the appointment.'

'Are you saying that Shaanar is becoming an ally?'

'In his heart of hearts, of course not. But the man is clever and knows how far he can go. You had the foresight to indulge his taste for power and keep him in the public eye. Let's hope he enjoys it too much to make any trouble.'

'Let's *pray* he does.'

'Time for bed now. Tomorrow will be a long day: at least ten audiences and three receptions. Will your bunk be comfortable?'

Bunk? thought Ramses. He had a headrest, a mattress of plaited skeins of hemp attached to a mortise-and-tenon frame, with lion's feet on the four legs, a footrest decorated with cornflowers, and poppies and lotus blossoms to sweeten his sleep.

'You'll need more pillows,' noted the secretary.

'One is enough.'

'Heavens, no!' Ahmeni protested. 'Look at this paltry excuse for a pillow,' he said, plucking it from the head of the bed.

Then he recoiled, stiff with horror, as the black scorpion he had uncovered stirred and prepared to attack.

25

Ramses himself had to console Serramanna. The guard captain simply couldn't fathom how a scorpion had been sneaked into the pharaoh's cabin. Close questioning of the servants yielded no results.

'They're not involved,' the Sard informed Ramses. 'I need to talk to your chief steward.'

Remet had little use for Serramanna, yet did not protest when the king asked him to answer the Sard's questions frankly.

'How many of your staff have access to the royal bedchamber?'

'Five. Well, five from the permanent staff.'

'What does that mean?'

'Occasionally I take on one or two temporary workers.'

'Any at our last stop?'

'I did hire one man to take the bed linens in to the local laundry.'

'What was his name?'

'It's on the payroll register.'

'Don't bother checking,' said the king. 'He would have used an assumed name, and besides, we won't have time to turn back and track him down.'

'No one told me about this outside hiring! You've made a mockery of my security measures!'

'Has something happened?' asked Remet, staring.

'You don't need to know! In future, I want to search every single person boarding His Majesty's ship. I don't care whether it's a general, a priest or a street-sweeper.'

Remet turned to Ramses, who nodded his agreement.

'What about meals?' asked the steward.

'One of your cooks will taste every dish – under my supervision,' said the Sard.

'As you wish.'

Once Remet was out of the cabin, Serramanna slammed his fist into a beam, so hard that the wood creaked. 'That scorpion wouldn't have killed you, Majesty,' he offered, 'but it would have made you very ill.'

'And I'd have had to give up the rest of the tour – a sign of the gods' disapproval. That was the object of the exercise.'

'It won't happen again,' promised the bodyguard.

'I'm afraid it may, as long as we don't know who's behind it.'

Serramanna frowned.

'Do you suspect anyone?' asked the king.

'Men aren't always as grateful as they should be.'

'Out with it, man.'

'Remet . . . What if he lied, and he himself is the culprit?'

'It's your job to find out, isn't it?'

'You can rely on me.'

Stop after stop, the new king and queen's ritual tour was a triumph. Ramses' presence and Nefertari's charm won over every provincial governor, high priest, mayor and other notable. Ramses was careful to show he valued his older brother, in view of Shaanar's extensive contacts and the general relief at his appointment to the Foreign Affairs secretariat. In the first place, it showed that there was no serious division within the royal family; furthermore, the prince's love of country and vision for Egypt would guarantee a strong defence policy, essential for preserving civilization from barbarian attack.

In each new town, the royal pair paid homage to Tuya, who inspired reverence whenever she appeared. Frail, silent and withdrawn, Tuya embodied the continuity and tradition without which her son's reign would have seemed unlawful.

As the fleet neared Abydos, the centre of the worship of Osiris, Ramses summoned his friend Ahsha to the prow of the flagship. No matter what the hour or day, the young diplomat was always unruffled and impeccable.

'Glad you came along, Ahsha?'

'Your Majesty is winning the hearts of his subjects, which is good.'

'There's plenty of hypocrisy in some of those hearts.'

'Even if you're dealing with hypocrites, at least they acknowledge your authority.'

'What do you think of Shaanar's new position?'

'A bit unconventional.'

'In other words, it shocked you.'

'I have no right to question Pharaoh's decisions.'

'Do you consider my brother incompetent?'

'In the present circumstances, diplomacy is a highly skilled profession.'

'Who would dare to challenge Egypt's might?'

'Your personal triumph here at home mustn't blind you to reality. The Hittites realize you're going to take a hard line against them, so they'll dig in. They may even be considering direct aggression.'

'Any hard information?'

'Not yet. Just speculation on my part.'

'You see, Ahsha, my brother is a good representative, the perfect host at receptions and banquets. Foreign ambassadors will be charmed by his speeches. Who knows, he may even begin to believe his own rhetoric! But he may be led astray through malice or scheming. I'm not convinced by his sudden change of heart, and that's where you come in.'

'What do you want me to do?'

'I'm appointing you head of the Secret Service of Upper and Lower Egypt. You'll be in charge of a courier network connecting the entire kingdom, including every document that leaves Shaanar's hands.'

'Are you ordering me to spy on him?'

'That will be one of your duties.'

'Won't he suspect me?'

'I've warned him that his every move will be watched. That may help keep him honest.'

'What if he finds a way round me?'

'You're too good to let that happen, my friend.'

Approaching the sacred site of Abydos, Ramses felt heartsick. Everything here spoke to him of his father, the namesake of Set, incarnation of the might of the heavens, who slew his brother Osiris. As an act of conciliation, Seti had built a magnificent sanctuary where the mysteries of Osiris's death and resurrection were celebrated. Ramses and Nefertari had been initiated into these mysteries, imprinting on their souls the certainty of eternal life, the promise of which they must in turn communicate to their people.

The banks of the canal leading to the temple landing were completely empty. Yes, this was holy ground; yes, Osiris' resurrection was a solemn celebration; all the same, the absence of a welcoming party took the royal entourage by surprise.

Serramanna was the first one off the ship, sword in hand and flanked by his fellow guardsmen. 'I smell trouble,' muttered the Sard.

Ramses was close behind. In the distance, behind a row of tall acacias, stood the Temple of Osiris.

'Careful, now,' warned Serramanna. 'Let me have a look around first.'

Sedition at Abydos? The king could hardly credit such sacrilege.

'The chariots,' he ordered. 'I'll take the lead.'

'But Majesty . . .'

He realized it would be futile to protest. Providing security for such an unreasonable monarch was virtually impossible.

The royal chariot drove briskly towards the temple enclosure. To Ramses' amazement, the outer gateway was open. Alighting, he entered the open-air forecourt.

The temple façade was covered with scaffolding. On the ground lay a statue of his father depicted as Osiris. Here and there, tools lay scattered. Not a workman was in sight.

In shock, the pharaoh entered the sanctuary. No offerings on the altars, no priest reciting the daily rites.

The temple had evidently been abandoned.

Ramses emerged and hailed Serramanna, who was waiting at the entrance gate.

'Go and find the men in charge of the construction.'

Relieved, the Sard sprang into action.

The young pharaoh's anger blazed hot as the bright blue sky over Abydos. Serramanna and his men had rounded up the priests, administrators, ritualists, and artisans who were supposed to keep the temple running and in good order. To a man, they bowed, bent their knees and touched their noses to the ground, terror-stricken by the monarch's ringing voice as he lectured them on their laziness and negligence.

Ramses accepted no excuse. It was no use blaming their scandalous behaviour on the fact that Seti's death had interrupted the temple's normal operation. That excuse would mean every crisis would make them panic and effectively shut down an important religious establishment.

Yet the harsh punishment they feared as he spoke was

not forthcoming. The new ruler merely demanded that they double their offerings to his late father's *ka*. He ordered them to lay out an orchard, plant additional trees, gild the temple doors, return to their construction work and finish the statues, and to resume the daily rites. He announced that a barque would be built for use in the celebration of the mysteries of Osiris. The farmers working on temple lands would no longer pay shares to the government, and the temple itself would receive generous grants, provided that it was never again allowed to fall into such a sorry state.

The men of Abydos filed silently out of the forecourt, thankful for the king's leniency and vowing not to provoke his anger a second time.

His fury spent, Ramses entered the central shrine, representing the heavens, where a secret light shone in the darkness. He communed with his father's soul, now one with the stars, as the barque of the sun continued its eternal voyage.

26

Shaanar was jubilant in spite of the failure of the business with the scorpion: he had never really expected Sary's latest scheme to work. The king's old tutor was too blind with hatred to think straight. Cutting Ramses down to size would be no easy task. Yet experience showed that even the strictest security measures could be breached.

Shaanar was jubilant because Ahsha, at the end of a very successful dinner party, had just told him a wonderful bit of news. In the stern of Shaanar's ship, they could have a private conversation. The few guests still on deck had been drinking heavily, and the ship's physician was attending a high government official who had become violently sick, as the rest of the party looked on.

'Head of the Secret Service . . . I must be dreaming!'

'Effective immediately.'

'And spying on me is part of your job, I suppose?'

'Exactly.'

'To all appearances, then, I'll have no real freedom of movement and only be nominally in charge.'

'That's the king's wish.'

'Let's grant it, Ahsha! I'll play my role to the hilt. And you, it seems, will become the king's principal source of information on Hittite policy?'

'Probably.'

'Does our agreement still suit you?'

'More than ever. I'm convinced that Ramses will be a tyrant. He mistrusts other people and has faith in no one but himself. His vanity will lead the country to ruin.'

'My sentiments exactly. But are you resolved to risk everything?'

'My position hasn't changed.'

'Why do you hate Ramses so much, Ahsha?'

'Because he's Ramses.'

Set in the lush green countryside, Dendera, the temple of the beautiful smiling goddess Hathor, was a hymn to the harmony of heaven and earth. Tall sycamores planted around the enclosure shaded the main temple and its outbuildings, including the famous school of music and dance. As patroness of Hathor's priestesses, and an iniate of the mysteries of the dance of the stars, Nefertari had looked forward to this stop on the tour, hoping for a few hours of meditation within the closed sanctuary. After the incident at Abydos, the royal fleet had been forced to sail southward, but the queen refused to omit Dendera from the itinerary.

Ramses seemed troubled.

'Is something on your mind?' Nefertari asked.

'I'm thinking about the new High Priest of Amon. Ahmeni prepared files on the likely candidates, but none of them is exactly what I'm looking for.'

'Have you talked to your mother?'

'She agrees with me. Seti passed them over in the first place; they're hoping I'll forget that.'

As Nefertari studied the images of Hathor's face, stunningly beautiful in stone, a strange glow suddenly illuminated her gaze.

'Nefertari . . .'

Lost in her vision, she did not respond. Ramses took her hand, fearing she would leave him for ever, transported to

145

heaven by the sweet-faced goddess of love. But the queen, as if soothed, nestled against him.

'I was far, far away . . . In a sea of light with a voice that sang to me.'

'What did it say?'

'To forget the official candidates. We'll need to find the new High Priest all by ourselves.'

'I scarcely have time for that.'

'Listen for the voices from on high, like every pharaoh since the dawn of time.'

At the concert held in their honour, Nefertari listened blissfully as the women musicians sang and danced in the temple garden. Ramses, however, seethed with impatience. Would he have to wait for another miracle to find a High Priest of Amon untainted by personal ambition?

He wished he could return to the ship to talk it over with Ahmeni, but was obliged to tour the temple complex, workshops and warehouses. Everything was as beautiful as it was orderly.

Ramses finally found solace by the shores of the sacred lake. The serene water, the lovely beds of irises and cornflowers, the soft tread of priestesses coming to carry water for the evening rites, would have soothed the most troubled spirit.

Nearby, an old man was pulling up weeds and tucking them into a sack. His movements were slow but precise. Kneeling on one knee, he kept his back turned to the king and queen. His irreverence could have earned him a reprimand, but so absorbed in his task was he that the king let the old man go about his work.

'Your flowers are wonderful,' Nefertari told the gardener after a while.

'I say nice things to them,' he replied gruffly. 'If I don't, they grow crooked.'

'I've noticed that, too.'

'Oh? A pretty girl like you likes working in the garden?'

'I enjoy it, when I can find the time.'

'Busy, are you?'

'My duties don't allow me much leisure.'

'Are you a priestess?'

'That's part of my work.'

'And you do other work too? Forgive me, madam. I don't mean to pry. You share my love of flowers; that's all I need to know.'

The old man grimaced in pain. 'My bad knee . . . sometimes it's hard for me to get back up.'

Ramses reached out an arm to help him.

'Thank you, Prince. You *are* a prince, aren't you?'

'Is it the High Priest of Dendera who forces a man of your years to do manual labour?'

'Yes, when it comes down to it.'

'They say he's old and cranky, in poor health, unable to travel.'

'So he is. Do you love flowers, like the pretty lady?'

'Planting trees is my favourite pastime. I'd like a word with the High Priest.'

'What about?'

'About why he isn't at the conclave at Karnak that's helping to choose a new High Priest of Amon.' By now Ramses was certain that the High Pries of Dendera was none other than this old gardener. 'I hardly think a bad knee would be enough to stop the head of Dendera from boarding a ship for Thebes.'

'There's also the frozen shoulder, the aching back, the—'

'Is the High Priest of Dendera unhappy with his lot, perchance?'

'On the contrary, Majesty. His only wish is to live out his days in peace within these temple walls.'

'What if Pharaoh asked him personally to attend the

conclave, to give his fellow prelates the benefit of his experience?'

'If our young pharaoh is already wise in the ways of men, he would spare a tired old servant. Now would Ramses be so kind as to hand me that cane on the garden wall?' The king did as he was asked. 'See for yourself, my lord, how lame poor Nebu is. Why force him out of his beautiful garden?'

'As High Priest of Dendera, will you at least consent to give your king some advice?'

'At my age, the less said the better.'

'Not according to the sage Ptah-hotep, whose maxims have guided us since the age of the pyramids. I value your wisdom. Could you please tell me whom you consider most qualified to become the new High Priest of Amon?'

'I've spent my whole life in Dendera and never set foot in Thebes. I'm really in no position to answer. Excuse me, Your Majesty, but it's almost my bedtime.'

Ramses and Nefertari spent part of the night on the flat roof of the temple. Thousands of souls glimmered in the night sky; the undying celestial bodies revolved around the Pole Star, at the axis of the Visible and the Invisible.

Then the royal couple withdrew into a palace with windows overlooking the countryside. Although their rooms were small and the furnishings rustic, for the short space before the first birdsong their chamber was a paradise. Nefertari fell asleep in Ramses' arms. They shared their dream of happiness.

After performing the morning rites, eating an ample breakfast, and bathing in the pool adjoining the palace, Ramses and Nefertari prepared to depart. The assembled clergy saluted them. But all of a sudden, Ramses veered off from the procession and slipped into the garden, skirting the sacred lake.

Nebu was on his knees, casting a critical eye over the marigolds and larkspur he had just planted.

'How did you like the queen, Nebu?'

'What do you expect me to say, Majesty? She's the soul of beauty and intelligence.'

'So her opinion would count with you.'

'Her opinion on what?'

'I hate to take you away from your garden, but you need to come to Thebes with us, at the special request of the queen.'

'But what on earth would I do there, Majesty?'

'Become the High Priest of Karnak.'

27

When the royal fleet docked at Karnak, lighting up the waters of the Nile, all of Thebes was bubbling with excitement. What was the meaning of the pharaoh's early return? Contradictory rumours spread like wildfire. Some were certain the king planned to abolish the priesthood of Amon and reduce Thebes to the rank of a sleepy provincial capital. Others claimed Ramses had fallen sick and was returning to die with his face towards the Mountain of Silence. The young pharaoh's star had risen much too fast. Now the gods were taking their revenge.

Raia, the Hittite agent, fretted and fumed. For once, he had no reliable information. Thanks to his network of trade contacts, including shopkeepers in the major population centres as well as travelling merchants, he had been able to track Ramses's progress along the Nile without ever leaving Thebes. Yet he had no explanation for the king's precipitate return. Ramses had stopped at Abydos according to schedule, but then instead of continuing north he had backtracked, stopping briefly in Dendera.

Ramses was unpredictable. He acted on the spur of the moment, without confiding in advisers whose loose tongues would have provided grist for the Syrian's mill. Raia was furious. Ramses would make a formidable adversary, difficult to control and Shaanar would be hard pressed to outmanoeuvre him. If open conflict ensued, the king might prove much more dangerous than Raia had calculated. He could not afford to wait and see. He must move quickly and decisively to eliminate any weak links in his chain of informants.

In the Blue Crown and a long, pleated linen robe, sceptre in hand, Ramses was truly majestic. A hush fell when he entered the hall where the conclave was in progress.

'Have you a name to propose to me?' he asked.

'Majesty,' declared the High Priest of Heliopolis, 'our deliberations are still in progress.'

'As of this moment, they're finished. Here is the new High Priest of Amon.'

An old man shuffled into the hall, leaning on his cane.

'Nebu!' exclaimed the High Priest of Sais. 'I thought you were too ill to travel!'

'I am, but Ramses performed a miracle.'

'At your age,' protested the Second Prophet of Amon, 'you should be thinking about retirement. The administration of Karnak and Luxor is a daunting responsibility!'

'I quite agree, but the pharaoh's will must be done.'

'My decree is already written in stone,' revealed Ramses. 'Tablets will soon go up proclaiming Nebu's appointment. Do any of you consider him unfit to fill this position?'

There were no objections.

Ramses gave Nebu a golden ring and a staff of electrum, an alloy of gold and silver, as symbols of his office.

'I hereby name you High Priest of Amon. The treasury and granaries of this great domain are now beneath your seal. As guardian of Amon's temples and estates, be scrupulous, honest and vigilant. Work not for your own advancement but to increase the god's *ka*. Amon can fathom the human soul, read each person's mind and heart. If Amon is well satisfied, he will keep you at the head of his clergy, granting you long life and a happy old age. Do you swear to respect the Rule of Ma'at and fulfil your duties?'

'I swear on the pharaoh's life,' declared Nebu, bowing to Ramses.

The Second and Third Prophets of Amon were furious and humiliated. Not only had Ramses saddled them with a prelate who would instantly obey his every command, but he had also named a complete unknown, Bakhen, as Fourth Prophet. This young zealot would back up the doddering High Priest and become the real master of Karnak. The temple's independence would be compromised for years to come.

The two dignitaries now had no hope of one day controlling the richest domain in Egypt. Squeezed between Nebu and Bakhen, they would sooner or later be forced to resign, prematurely ending their careers. In their confusion, they cast about for an ally. Shaanar immediately came to mind, but now that the king's elder brother was a minister, he might be singing a different tune.

Since he had nothing to lose, however, the Second Prophet arranged to meet Shaanar as the representative of all Karnak's clergy members who opposed Ramses' decision. They met by a fish pond in the shade of a large awning slung between two poles. A servant offered the Second Prophet a cup of carob juice and discreetly withdrew. Shaanar rolled up the papyrus he was studying.

'Your face seems familiar.'

'My name is Doki. I'm the Second Prophet of Amon.'

The little man appealed to Shaanar. With his shaven head, narrow forehead, bulging eyes, long nose and pointed chin, he looked rather like a crocodile.

'What can I do for you?'

'You'll probably think me too forward, but I'm not used to polite society.'

'Get on with it, then.'

'An old man named Nebu has just been named High Priest and First Prophet of Amon.'

'A position you hoped would be yours, unless I'm mistaken.'

'The late High Priest made no secret of the fact that I was his chosen successor, but the king passed me over.'

'It's dangerous to question his decisions.'

'Nebu will never be able to manage Karnak.'

'Bakhen, my brother's friend, will be the one really in charge.'

'Forgive me for being blunt, but do you find this arrangement satisfactory?'

'I accept it as the pharaoh's will.'

Doki was disappointed. As he had feared, Shaanar was in Ramses' camp now. He rose to leave. 'I won't take up any more of your time.'

'Just a moment. If I understand you correctly, you refuse to accept the situation.'

'The king is trying to undermine the power of Amon's priesthood.'

'Do you have the means to oppose him?'

'I'm not alone.'

'Whom do you represent?'

'A good many in the administration, and most of the priests.'

'And are you prepared to act?'

'Lord Shanaar! We have no intention of being disloyal.'

'Make up your mind, Doki. You don't seem to know what you want.'

'I need help.'

'First prove to me that you're serious.'

'But how?'

'That's for you to determine.'

'I'm only a priest, a—'

'You're a man of action or you're a nobody. If all you're going to do is bemoan your fate, I'm not interested.'

'What if I managed to discredit the pharaoh's men?'

153

'Do it first, then come and see me. You understand, though, that this conversation never took place.'

Doki's spirits lifted. He left Shaanar's residence with a head full of impossible schemes. Sooner or later, he would hit on one that would work.

Shaanar was sceptical. This Second Prophet had possibilities, but he seemed indecisive and too easily influenced. Once he realized what a serious step he'd taken, he'd probably back off. But no potential ally could be discounted, and this way the prince would find out what the little priest was made of.

Ramses, Moses and Bakhen inspected the construction under way at Karnak, a project Seti had envisaged but left his son to complete: a vast Hall of Pillars. Delivery of the huge stone blocks was on schedule. The various work gangs were coordinating their efforts to raise the towering pillars, which represented papyrus stalks rising from the primordial ooze.

'How are things going with your workmen?' asked the king.

'Sary gave me some trouble, but I think I brought him back in line,' said Moses.

'What sort of trouble?'

'He's too hard on his workers. I suspect that he's also skimping on their rations and pocketing the difference.'

'Let's send him before a tribunal.'

'I don't think that will be necessary,' said Moses with amusement. 'I'd rather be able to keep an eye on him. The moment he goes too far, I'll deal with him.'

'If you press him, he may lodge a formal complaint against you.'

'Never fear, Majesty. Sary's too much of a coward for that.'

'Wasn't he your guardian?' asked Bakhen.

'Yes,' answered Ramses. 'And a good teacher, too. But

something came over him. After what he tried to do to me, most other men would have banished him to the desert. I'm hoping that honest work will bring him to his senses.'

'It hasn't yet,' said Moses, shaking his head.

'I know you'll get results, though it won't be here. In a few days we're leaving for the North, and you're going to come along, Moses.'

His friend looked less than pleased. 'The Hall of Pillars . . . it's not finished!'

'I'm putting Bakhen in charge as Fourth Prophet of Amon. You'll brief him before we go. He'll see to the hall's completion and also oversee my additions to Luxor. Rows of colossal statues in the forecourt, a pylon gateway, obelisks – it will be wonderful! Keep things moving, Bakhen. I may only be granted a short time to live, and I want to dedicate this masterpiece.'

'I'm honoured by the trust you place in me, Majesty.'

'I don't appoint straw men, Bakhen. Old Nebu will do his job well, and so will you. He'll run the temple and the estates, you'll do the building. Both of you will alert me to any difficulties. Now get to work and forget about everything else.'

Pharaoh and Moses left the construction site and walked down a lane of tamarisks towards the shrine of Ma'at, the goddess of truth and justice.

'This is where I come to meditate,' the king confided. 'It calms my spirit and helps me see more clearly. I envy the priests. The soul of the gods is in every stone here. Every shrine reveals their truths.'

'Why are you taking me away from Karnak?'

'You and I have work to do. Remember when we were schoolboys discussing the future with Ahsha, Ahmeni and Setau? I was convinced that only Pharaoh had true power. I was drawn to it like a moth to a flame, and it would have consumed me if my father hadn't taken me in hand.

Even when I'm at rest, that power moves in me, telling me to build.'

'You have a new project?'

'It's on such a gigantic scale that I can't even tell you yet. I'll need to think more during the journey. If it's possible to carry it through, there's a major role for you.'

'I have to admit you surprise me.'

'Why?'

'I was sure that, when you became king, you'd forget your old friends and concentrate on the court, matters of state and the obligations of power.'

'You misjudged me, Moses.'

'But won't power change you?'

'A man changes according to the goals he sets himself. My sole concern is the glory of Egypt, and that will never change.'

28

Sary fumed. The king's brother-in-law and former tutor reduced to being foreman of a sorry bunch of bricklayers, when he had once been head of the royal school! With another of his former students, that bully Moses, always on his back, too! Day after day, Sary found the physical hardship, the taunts, more difficult to bear. He had tried to turn the workers against the Hebrew, but Moses was so popular that the attempt failed miserably.

Yet Moses was only following orders. Sary knew he must start at the top. He wanted revenge, revenge on the cause of his downfall and unhappiness.

'I hate him, too,' admitted Dolora, nestling deeper into her pillows. 'But what you're proposing scares me half to death.'

'What have we got to lose?'

'I'm afraid, darling. Schemes like this have been known to rebound on us.'

'So? Right now you're a social outcast; I'm subjected to unspeakable brutality. How can we go on like this?'

'I understand, Sary, really I do. But would we have to go that far?'

'Are you with me, or will I have to do it alone?'

'I'm your wife.'

He helped her to her feet.

'Have you thought it over carefully?'

'I've thought of nothing else for the last month.'

'What if someone informs on us?'

'Not a chance.'

'How can you be so sure?'

'I've taken precautions.'

'Will that be enough?'

'You have my word.'

'Isn't there any way round—'

'No, Dolora. Now, are you with me?'

'Let's go.'

Inconspicuously dressed, the pair walked down a lane leading to a section of Thebes where many foreigners lived. Dolora clutched her husband's arm nervously, hesitating at every turn.

'Are we lost, Sary?'

'Of course not.'

'Are we almost there?'

'Not much farther now.'

Inquisitive stares greeted them. But Sary marched stubbornly on as his wife grew increasingly apprehensive.

'Here we are.'

He knocked at a low red door with a dead scorpion nailed to it. An old woman answered. The couple went down a wooden stairway leading to a sort of small, damp grotto ablaze with oil lamps.

'He's here,' announced the old woman. 'Sit on these stools and wait.'

Dolora preferred to remain standing. The place gave her the shivers. Black magic was against the law in Egypt, yet certain sorcerers still dared to sell their services at exorbitant prices.

The plump and obsequious Canaanite magician padded towards his clients.

'Everything is ready,' he announced. 'And the necessary consideration?'

Sary emptied a leather pouch into the man's right hand: ten chunks of perfect turquoise.

'The object you are purchasing has been placed within the grotto. Next to it you will find a shark's tooth. Use that to write the name of the person upon whom your spell is cast. Once you smash the charm, that person will fall ill.'

As the magician spoke, Dolora covered her face with her shawl. When he left, she grabbed her husband by the wrists.

'Let's leave. I can't bear it!'

'Steady. It's almost over.'

'Ramses is my brother!'

'You're wrong. He's now our worst enemy. It's up to us to act, without fear or remorse. It's quite safe – he won't even know where the attack's coming from.'

'Couldn't we—'

'It's too late to back out, Dolora.'

Deep in the grotto, on a sort of altar painted with crude designs of grotesque animals and malevolent spirits, sat a thin limestone tablet and a long tooth whittled to form a stylus. The stone was speckled with brown. The magician had probably soaked it in snake's blood to make the spell even deadlier.

Sary picked up the tooth and began to scratch the hieroglyphic symbols for Ramses' name into the limestone. His wife shut her eyes in horror.

'Now you,' he ordered.

'No, I can't.'

'The spell won't work unless it's performed by a married couple.'

'I don't want to kill my brother!'

'He won't die. The magician swears it. He'll become an invalid, Shaanar will become his regent, and we can go back to Memphis.'

'I can't.'

Sary placed the tooth in his wife's right hand and closed her fingers round it.

'Write "Ramses".'

He guided her trembling hand as she completed the crude inscription. Now for the last step: breaking the tablet. Sary picked it up, while Dolora again hid her face. She refused to witness such an atrocity.

Hard as he tried, Sary could not smash the tablet. The thin limestone seemed hard as granite. He groped for a rock on the floor of the grotto and angrily pounded the magic tablet, but could not even chip it.

'I don't understand. It's only limestone, it's thin . . .'

'Ramses is protected,' screamed his wife. 'Nothing can harm him, not even black magic! Let's leave here as fast as we can.'

Sary and Dolora wandered through the unfamiliar streets. With a feeling of panic in the pit of his stomach, Sary was having trouble retracing his steps. Doors slammed in their faces, eyes peered from slits in shutters. Despite the heat, Dolora still hid her face behind her shawl.

A thin man with a hawklike profile approached them, an eerie gleam in his dark green eyes.

'Might you be lost?'

'No,' replied Sary. 'Get out of the way!'

'Just trying to help.'

'We'll manage.'

'These streets can be dangerous.'

'We can take care of ourselves.'

'You wouldn't stand a chance against armed bandits. A man carrying precious stones is asking for trouble in these parts.'

'We haven't got anything like that.'

'You paid the Canaanite magician in turquoise, didn't you?'

Dolora clung more tightly to her husband.

'That's just tittle-tattle,' countered Sary.

'Both of you were careless. I believe you forgot something.' The thin man produced the limestone tablet bearing Ramses' name.

Dolora turned away and buried her head on her husband's shoulder.

'Are you aware that an act of black magic perpetrated against Pharaoh is punishable by death? Rest assured, however, I have no intention of turning you in.'

'What do you want?'

'To help, as I already told you. See the house to your left? Go inside. Your wife needs something to drink.'

The dirt-floored dwelling was humble but clean. A young blonde woman helped Sary ease his wife on to a wooden bench with a reed mat on top of it, then fetched Dolora some water.

'My name is Ofir,' said the thin man. 'And this is Lita, great-granddaughter of Akhenaton and rightful heir to the throne of Egypt.'

Sary was too amazed to speak. Dolora was slowly coming round.

'Is this some kind of joke?'

'It's the truth.'

Sary turned towards the young woman. 'Is this man lying?'

Lita shook her head, and went and sat in a corner of the room, as if uninterested in what was going on.

'Please pardon her,' Ofir advised. 'She's been through so much that the road back to normal life will be long and difficult.'

'What happened to her?'

'As a child, she was threatened with death, beaten, imprisoned, forced to renounce her faith in Aton, the One God, ordered to forget her name and her parents. In other words, they tried to destroy her soul. If I hadn't come along, she'd be no more than a poor madwoman.'

'Why are you helping her?'

161

'Because my own family was persecuted, like hers. We live only to seek our revenge, which will place Lita on the throne of Egypt and banish the false gods from Egypt.'

'Ramses isn't responsible for your suffering!'

'Of course he is. He belongs to an evil dynasty that has deceived and tyrannized the people.'

'How do you manage to live?'

'Aton still has his followers, who give us food and shelter in the hope that our prayers will be answered.'

'There can't be many left.'

'More than you'd imagine, but they have been muzzled. Even if Lita and I were the only two, we'd keep on fighting.'

'All that happened years ago,' protested Ramses' sister. 'No one cares about it any more.'

'*You* should,' Ofir said firmly.

'Let's get out of here, Sary. These people are crazy.'

'I know who you are,' revealed Ofir.

'You don't!'

'Dolora, the pharaoh's sister, and your husband, Sary, who used to be Ramses' tutor. He's mistreated you both and you want revenge.'

'That's our business.'

'I retrieved the fragment of limestone you used to cast a spell on him. If I take it to the vizier's office and testify against you . . .'

'This is blackmail!'

'Join our cause and the evidence disappears.'

'What's in it for us?' asked Sary.

'Using magic against Ramses is a good idea, but you aren't experts. The spell you tried would have made an ordinary mortal ill, but not a king. At his coronation, Pharaoh was surrounded with special protective forces. They need to be destroyed, one by one. Lita and I can see to that.'

'What do you ask in exchange?'

'Bed and board, a place where our followers can meet in secret.'

'Don't listen,' Dolora whispered to her husband. 'The man in dangerous. No good will come of this.'

Sary turned to face the sorcerer.

'We have a deal,' he said.

29

Ramses lit the oil lamps to reveal the *naos*, Karnak's innermost sanctuary, which he alone was allowed to enter, or the High Priest as his designate. The shadows parted to reveal the holy of holies, a pink granite shrine containing the earthly image of Amon, the Hidden One, whose true form no human being would ever know. Slow-burning incense tablets perfumed this most sacred of places, where divine energy became incarnate in both the Visible and the Invisible.

The king broke the clay seal affixed to the door of the *naos*, drew the bolt and opened the doors of the reliquary.

'Wake in peace, creator of all life. Look upon your son, whose heart is full of love for you, who comes to seek your counsel so that he may fulfil your purpose. Wake in peace and shine upon this earth, which lives only through your love. Let your divine energy flow through every living thing.'

The king shone the light on the holy statue, unwrapped the coloured bands of linen around it, purified it with water from the sacred lake, anointed it with unguents and rewrapped it with fresh, clean cloth. Then, conjuring them up with his voice, the pharaoh presented the offerings that the priests were at that moment placing on the many altars in the temple – a ritual followed each morning in every temple throughout the land.

At last came the supreme offering, in the name of Ma'at, the immortal Rule of life.

'Through her you live,' the king told Amon. 'Her fragrance invigorates you, her dew nourishes you. Your eyes are the Rule, your whole being is the Rule.'

Leaving the Divine Power with a fraternal embrace, Pharaoh closed the doors of the *naos*, bolted it shut and affixed a clay seal. Tomorrow, High Priest Nebu would perform this rite in Ramses' name.

When Ramses left the *naos*, the entire temple was astir. Priests were clearing the altars of the portion of consecrated food that was designated for human consumption; breads and cakes were coming out of the temple ovens; butchers were cutting meat for the noon meal; craftsmen began their day's work; gardeners cut flowers for the shrines. The day would be peaceful and happy.

Close behind Serramanna, Ramses' chariot headed for the Valley of the Kings. Despite the early hour, the day was already torrid. Nefertari rode serene, though she dreaded the heat. A damp cloth around her neck, as well as a parasol, helped keep her cool in the blazing valley.

Before returning to Memphis, Ramses wished to see his father's tomb once more and pray before the sarcophagus, whose name, 'Master of Life' denoted its function. Within the mystery of the golden chamber, Seti's soul lived on.

The two chariots came to a halt in front of the narrow entry to the Valley. Ramses helped Nefertari down, while Serramanna, despite the fact that the police were present, had a look around. Even here, he did not rest easy. The Sard inspected the guard detachment controlling access to the Valley and noted nothing amiss in their behaviour.

To Nefertari's surprise, Ramses did not head straight for the tombs of Seti and his father, Ramses I, which stood side by side. Instead, he veered to the right, towards a site where workmen hacked at the rock, swept up the chips, and carted them away.

A master builder from the company of Deir el-Medina had his scrolls spread over several blocks of polished stone. He bowed to the royal pair.

'This is where I'm building my tomb,' Ramses informed his wife.

'So soon?'

'In the very first year of his reign, a pharaoh must see work begun on his house of eternity.'

The veil of sadness that had fallen over Nefertari's face lifted. 'Death is our constant companion,' she agreed. 'If we prepare for it, it will be kind.'

'Does this seem like a good spot to you?'

The queen turned slowly round, as if taking possession of the place, sounding out the rock and the depths of the earth. Then she stood very still, eyes shut tight.

'It will be your resting-place,' she predicted.

Ramses held her close.

'Even though the Rule requires that your body must lie in the Valley of the Queens, the two of us will never be separated,' he told her. 'Your tomb will be the most beautiful ever created in this hallowed land. Future generations will remember it and sing of its beauty for centuries.'

The Valley's powerful spell and the solemnity of the moment forged a new link between the king and queen. The stone-carvers, quarrymen, and masterbuilder sensed its luminous intensity. They were a man and a woman in love; above and beyond that, they were a pharaoh and his consort, whose life and death bore the stamp of the eternal.

The day's work had been interrupted; the tools fell silent. Each workman felt part of the mystery of these two beings whose task was to reign, so that heaven rested on its pillars and the earth celebrated. Without them the Nile would stop flowing, no fish would leap in its currents, no birds would fly, the breath of life would desert humanity.

Ramses and Nefertari broke from their embrace, still holding each other's gaze. They had just crossed the threshold into a marriage of true minds.

As the men began to swing their picks once more, Ramses approached the masterbuilder.

'Show me your plans,' the king ordered. He studied the drawings. 'The first corridor needs to be longer. Add a forechamber with four pillars. Go deeper into the rock here and open out the Hall of Ma'at.'

Taking the brush the masterbuilder held out to him, the king sketched his modifications in red, specifying the dimensions he wanted.

'Starting from the Hall of Ma'at, we'll angle right into a short, narrow passageway leading to the House of Gold, with eight pillars. The sarcophagus will lie in the centre. Put in several shrines for the funerary furnishings, leading off it. What do you think?'

'Technically, it's quite feasible, Majesty.'

'Let me know immediately if you run into problems during the construction.'

'My job is to solve them.'

The royal couple and their escort left the Valley of the Kings and turned back towards the Nile. Since the king had not informed Serramanna of their destination, the bodyguard scanned the surrounding hilltops carefully. Ramses was indifferent to danger, so keeping him safe was virtually impossible. One day his luck was bound to run out.

At the edge of the cultivation, the royal chariot turned right, passing in front of the nobility's necropolis and the funerary temple of Tuthmosis III, the illustrious pharaoh who had pacified Asia and spread the Egyptian civilization throughout the Near East and beyond.

Ramses stopped at an empty spot at the edge of the desert, not far from the workmen's settlement. Serramanna immediately ordered his men to fan out; a potential attacker might be lurking in the wheat fields to their rear.

'What do you think of this place, Nefertari?'

The lithe and elegant young queen had taken off her sandals, the better to gauge the energy coming from the earth. Her bare feet trod lightly on the burning sand as she paced, circled and came to rest on a flat stone in the shade of a palm tree.

'Power dwells here, exactly like the power within your heart.'

Ramses knelt and gently massaged his queen's delicate feet.

'Yesterday,' she confessed, 'I had a strange, almost frightening, sensation.'

'Can you describe it?'

'You were lying inside a sort of protective stone shell. Someone was trying to break the stone, to remove the protection and destroy you.'

'Did it work?'

'My spirit fought with the dark force and drove it off. The stone remained intact.'

'A bad dream?'

'No, I was awake. I *saw* it in my mind's eye, far away, but real, so real . . .'

'Are you better now?'

'Not completely. I still feel uneasy, as if someone were hiding in the shadows, out of reach, intent on hurting you.'

'I have countless enemies, Nefertari. Is it any wonder? They'd stoop to anything. My choice is between never doing anything that would put me in danger – meaning nothing at all – and going forward without worrying about them. I choose to go forward.'

'Then it's my duty to protect you.'

'Serramanna takes care of that.'

'He'll counter any physical attacks on you, but what about the invisible ones? That will be my role, Ramses. My love will surround you with a wall the demons cannot climb over. But it's not enough. We need more.'

'What do you have in mind?'

'A being who does not yet exist, and who will preserve your name and your life.'

'It will be born here, on the soil your bare feet have trodden. I know you've seen it, a massive guardian with a body of stone, a soul made of everything that endures. On this spot I'll build my Temple of a Million Years. I want us to conceive it together, like our child.'

30

Serramanna groomed his whiskers, put on perfumed oils, dressed in a purple tunic with a flared collar, and checked his haircut in a mirror. Given what he planned to say to Ramses, he needed to look respectable, like someone whose opinion counted. He had hesitated long enough. His suspicions had grown so strong that he had to get them off his chest.

He approached the king in his dressing-room. Ramses would be receptive when it was bright and early.

'You're looking smart,' said Ramses. 'Don't tell me you're resigning as captain of my bodyguard to become a haber-dasher!'

'I thought—'

'You thought that, in view of delicate nature of your business, you'd better look as sophisticated as possible.'

'Who told you?'

'No one, I promise. Your secret is safe.'

'I'm right, Majesty!' blurted the Sard.

'Well, that's a good start. What about?'

'The scorpion that was supposed to put you out of com-mission – someone planted it in your room.'

'Obviously. Go on.'

'It bothered me to have that happen, so I investigated.'

'And you don't like what you found.'

'Majesty, I . . .'

'Are you afraid, Serramanna?'

The colour drained from the Sard's broad face. Anyone but the Pharaoh of Egypt would have earned a punch in the mouth for such an insult.

'I'm responsible for your security, Majesty. You don't always make it easy.'

'Are you saying I'm unpredictable?'

'If you could slow down a bit . . .'

'You'd be bored.'

'Even though I used to be a pirate, I like to do a good job.'

'What's stopping you?'

'Passive protection is no problem, but am I allowed to go any further?'

'Out with it, man.'

'I suspect someone close to you. Whoever sneaked the scorpion in had to know the location of your cabin.'

'That could be any number of people.'

'Possibly, but my instincts tell me I'm close to identifying the culprit.'

'How?'

'Well, I have my methods.'

'Justice is the basis of Egyptian society, my friend. As the first servant of the Rule of Ma'at, Pharaoh is not above the law.'

'In other words, I'll receive no official order to proceed.'

'Wouldn't it only get in the way?'

'I understand.'

'I'm not sure you do, Serramanna. Follow your instincts, but take care. I won't have you using brute force. Official order or no, I consider myself responsible for your actions.'

'No one will get hurt.'

'Give me your word.'

'Do you trust a pirate?'

'A man of courage knows how to keep his word.'

'When I say "hurt", I mean—'

'Your word, Serramanna.'
'All right, Majesty. You have it.'

A spotless palace was one of Remet's obsessions. As Ramses' new head steward, he was responsible for the king's personal comfort. The sweeps, floor-scrubbers, and other cleaners were busy as bees under the direction of a finicky scribe who hoped to bolster his position by pleasing Remet. He checked every job and was quick to threaten salary cuts for substandard performance.

Night was falling when the scribe left the sparkling clean palace. Tired and thirsty, he made haste towards a tavern where they served his favourite beer. As he passed through a narrow street packed with laden donkeys, strong hands grabbed the collar of his tunic and dragged him backwards into a darkened shop, the door slamming shut behind him. Frightened out of his wits, the scribe did not even cry out.

Two enormous hands gripped his neck.

'You're going to talk, scum!'

'Let go! You're choking me.'

Serramanna loosened his grip. 'You follow the boss's orders, eh?'

'Boss?'

'Remet, the head steward?'

'You can't fault my work.'

'Remet hates Ramses, doesn't he?'

'I don't know. No, no, I don't think so. And I'm the king's faithful servant!'

'Remet is a scorpion-fancier, I hear.'

'Scorpions? He's scared to death of them.'

'You're lying.'

'No, it's the truth, I swear!'

'You've seen him handle scorpions.'

'Never!'

The Sard began to have doubts. Usually, this method

yielded excellent results. The man did appear to be telling the truth.

'Are you looking for someone who likes scorpions?' the scribe ventured.

'You know of someone?'

'A friend of the king's called Setau . . . he lives for his snakes and scorpions. They say he even speaks their language and they obey him.'

'Where can I find this Setau?'

'He has a laboratory in the desert outside Memphis. His wife is a Nubian sorceress, as frightening as he is.'

Serramanna released his captive, who rubbed his neck and breathed deeply.

'Can I go now?'

The Sard shooed him away. 'Wait,' he said suddenly. 'I didn't hurt you, did I?'

'No, not at all.'

'Go, but never tell anyone we spoke. If you do, my arms will turn into snakes and choke you to death.'

The scribe bolted into the darkness. Serramanna walked calmly out of the shop and headed in the opposite direction.

His instincts had pointed towards Remet. After his sudden promotion, the steward was in the ideal position to harm the king. He was also the type of man Serramanna mistrusted; a jovial façade often cloaked ruthless ambition. Still, he might as well admit his mistake – a profitable mistake, though, since the scribe had perhaps put him on to a good trail, one that led to Setau, one of the king's friends.

He grimaced. Ramses held friendship sacred. Going after Setau would be risky, especially considering his daunting defence. Nevertheless, Serramanna was honour-bound to follow every lead. As soon as they returned to Memphis, he would pay very special attention to the unconventional couple who lived on such easy terms with reptiles.

'I've received no complaints about you,' noted Ramses.

'I've kept my promise, Majesty,' Serramanna asserted.

'Are you quite sure?'

'Sure as can be.'

'Any results?'

'Not yet.'

'Nothing at all?'

'Only one false lead.'

'But you haven't given up, I take it.'

'My job is to protect you – within the limits of the law, of course.'

'Are you hiding anything from me, Serramanna?'

'Do you think I'd be able to, Majesty?'

'Who knows what a pirate might do?'

'A *former* pirate. I like my new life too much to take needless risks.'

Ramses' eyes narrowed. 'Your prime suspect wasn't the right one, but you want to keep trying.'

Serramanna nodded evasively.

'For the time being, you'll have to call off the investigation.'

The Sard was crestfallen. 'I was careful, just as I promised . . .'

'Not because of anything you've done – because tomorrow we're leaving for Memphis.'

31

Remet didn't know whether he was coming or going, so fraught with difficulty were the preparations for moving the court from Thebes to Memphis. Not a single society lady must miss her pot of rouge, not a single gentleman must be wanting a comfortable chair. Meals on board ship must be of the same high quality as on land. Ramses' dog and lion must enjoy a plentiful and varied diet. Then there was the cook who had fallen ill, the washerman who was late, the weaver who had mixed up the towel order . . .

But Ramses had spoken, and Remet would obey. He had expected to spend his life refining his prize recipes. Now he was struck with admiration for this demanding and ambitious young pharaoh. Yes, Ramses was hard on his entourage, could appear intolerant, burned with a fire that might singe those who ventured too near. But he was as fascinating as the falcon arching high in the sky. Remet wanted to prove himself to his king, even at the expense of his own peace of mind.

The steward, carrying a basket of fresh figs, arrived at the gangway to the royal flagship.

Serramanna blocked his path. 'Mandatory search.'

'I'm His Majesty's steward!'

'Mandatory search,' repeated the bodyguard.

'Are you trying to cause trouble?'

'Are you trying to hide something?'

Remet looked shaken. 'What do you mean?'

'Are you or aren't you?' growled Serramanna.

'I think you've finally gone mad, Sard. All right, if you're so suspicious, take this basket to the king yourself. I have a thousand other things to do.'

Serramanna lifted the white cloth covering the basket. The figs were gorgeous, but what evil might they conceal? One by one, he gingerly lifted them out and set them aside, fully expecting to see a scorpion's deadly tail menacing him.

When the basket was empty, there was nothing to do but refill it, taking care not to bruise the perfectly ripened fruit.

Iset the Fair was lovelier than ever.

She bowed to Ramses, like a young noblewoman meeting the king for the first time and in danger of fainting.

Firmly and tenderly, he helped her up.

'You weren't always such a fragile flower.'

'No, Majesty,' she acquiesced. Her face was grave, almost anxious, but her eyes were smiling.

'Is something worrying you?'

'May I speak confidentially?'

They sat side by side on low chairs. 'I can spare a few minutes,' said the king.

'That's all?'

'My time is no longer my own, Iset. I have more work than there are hours in the day, which is as it should be.'

'You're moving the court to Memphis.'

'Correct.'

'I've received no instructions. Am I to go with you or stay here in Thebes?'

'Do you understand the reason for my silence?'

'I've been trying to.'

'The decision is up to you, Iset.'

'Why?'

'I love Nefertari.'

'You love me too, don't you?'

'You ought to hate me.'

'You rule an empire, but can you see into a woman's heart? Nefertari is special, unique, and I am not. But no one can stop me loving you – not you, not your wife, not even the gods – no matter what place you give me in your life. Why shouldn't a lesser wife glean every scrap of happiness she can? Seeing you, talking to you, sharing a few stolen moments of your day, are precious joys, which I wouldn't exchange for any others.'

'What is your decision.'

'I'm leaving for Memphis with the court.'

Forty or more boats sailed from Thebes, to the cheers of the huge crowd Ramses and Nefertari attracted. The new High Priest had assumed control without incident, the mayor and vizier remained in their positions. The court had thrown elaborate banquets. The people rejoiced because the Nile had risen sufficiently to guarantee their continued prosperity.

Remet allowed himself a brief rest. Everything on board the flagship was perfectly under control, unless you counted Serramanna. The Sard seemed to have some grudge against him. An unannounced search of every cabin and each crew member was his latest move. Some day the foreigner would be cut down to size, and no one would mind. His lack of respect for eminent persons had already earned him an impressive number of enemies. Only the king's support kept him in his job. But would that last?

The steward smoothed the already perfect bedlinen, steadied the armchairs, rechecked the table settings, and bustled up to the bridge with a skin of cool water for the king's pets to share as they lay on their shaded platform.

From one of the windows of Nefertari's spacious cabin, Ramses observed the steward, amused and pleased.

'I've finally found a steward who's more concerned with his work than with his privileges. A pleasant surprise, isn't it?'

A hint of fatigue dulled his wife's habitual glow. Ramses sat down on the bed and held her to him.

'Serramanna would hardly agree with you,' she said. 'He and Remet have taken a dislike to each other.'

The king was astounded. 'Why on earth—'

'Serramanna is suspicious, always on the alert.'

'Suspecting Remet doesn't make sense.'

'Let's hope not.'

'Don't you trust him, either?'

'He hasn't been with us long,' said Nefertari.

'But I've given him his chance to shine.'

'After a while, he'll forget that.'

'You're pessimistic today,' he told her.

'I hope Remet proves me wrong.'

'Have you any reason to doubt his loyalty?'

'Nothing but Serramanna's animosity.'

'You know how I count on your opinion . . .'

She laid her head on his shoulder. 'No one can be indifferent to you, Ramses. They're either for you or against you. Your power is too much for some people.'

The king stretched out on his back. Nefertari snuggled against him.

'My father's power was greater than mine.'

'You're the same, but different. Seti imposed his authority without having to say a single word. His force was hidden. You're like a fire, a raging river. You blaze a trail without a thought for the difficulties ahead.'

'I have a plan, Nefertari, an important new plan.'

'Only one?'

'This one is truly immense. Ever since the coronation, I've had a vision. It can't be denied, and if my plan succeeds, it will change the face of Egypt.'

Nefertari stroked her husband's forehead. 'Has this project taken shape, or is it still a dream?'

'I can make my dream a reality, but I'm waiting for a sign.'

'Why this hesitation?'

'Because heaven must approve of what I'm doing. No one can break a pact with the gods.'

'Do you want to keep it a secret?'

'Just putting it into words seems daring at this stage, but as Great Royal Wife, you have a right to know everything.'

Ramses explained and Nefertari listened. Yes, the plan was indeed immense.

'You're wise to look for a sign,' she concluded. 'I'll help you look for it.'

'If it doesn't come?'

'A sign will come, if we know how to read it properly.'

Ramses sat up and looked at his queen. 'Fairest of the Fair' was her coronation title, and throughout the land people repeated it. She was the womanly ideal of ancient love songs, with limbs of porcelain and turquoise, her slender body restful and deep as heavenly waters.

The king gently laid his ear on his wife's stomach.

'Do you feel our child growing?'

'This one will be strong, I promise you.'

One of the straps of Nefertari's dress had slipped off a shoulder to reveal the swell of her bosom. Ramses bit the gauzy linen, baring his wife's sublime breasts. In her eyes he saw the flow of the celestial Nile, the well of desire, the magic of two bodies joined in a love without limits.

32

For the first time since his coronation, Ramses set foot in his father's office in Memphis. Bare white walls, three barred windows, one large table, a straight-backed armchair for the king and chairs with woven seats for visitors, a chest for papyrus.

Intense emotion choked him.

Seti's spirit still moved in this austere study where he had spent so many days and nights at work, governing Egypt, keeping his country secure and happy. The room spoke to him not of death, but of an undying, invincible spirit.

Tradition dictated that each new pharaoh should build his own home, create his own surroundings. Ramses was expected to order this building pulled down. And such had been his intention, until he had stepped inside the huge chamber again.

From one of the windows, Ramses could see the inner courtyard where the royal chariot was housed. Then he touched the desk, opened the chest containing blank papyrus, and sat on the straight-backed chair.

Seti's soul did not turn him away.

The son had succeeded the father, the father accepted the son as Lord of the Two Lands. Ramses would keep the office intact and work here whenever he was residing in Memphis. It would stay as plain as he found it; it would be an invaluable help when he had to reach a judgment.

On the table sat two springy twigs from an acacia tree, lashed together at the bottom. This was the diviner's rod Seti had used to find water when their expedition was lost in the desert. It had marked a turning-point in Ramses' education in the art of kingship. Seti had shown him that Pharaoh must master the elements, the very mystery of creation. Pharaoh must go to the heart of all matter and draw on its hidden powers.

For a pharaoh was more than a head of state. He was also a conduit to the Invisible.

With his age-stiffened fingers, Homer packed his mixture of sage leaves into the bowl of his pipe, an oversized snail shell that was finally seasoned to his satisfaction. Between two puffs, he treated himself to a sip of full-bodied wine, flavoured with anise and coriander. Thus was the old Greek poet enjoying the cool of evening, in a comfortable armchair beneath his beloved lemon tree, when the maid announced that the king had come to see him.

As Ramses came closer, Homer was astonished at how regal he had become. The poet struggled to his feet.

'Please don't get up.'

'Majesty, how you've changed!'

'Majesty? Are you becoming reverential?'

'You're a king now. A monarch of your bearing commands respect. I can tell that you're not the hot-headed adolescent I used to lecture – though I hope Pharaoh still listens to me.'

'I'm happy to see that you're well. Is everything to your liking?'

'The maid is finally used to me, the gardener is quiet, the cook is a treasure, and the scribe who takes down my verses seems to approve of them. What more could I ask?'

Hector, the black and white cat, jumped into the poet's lap and began to purr.

As was his habit, Homer had rubbed his whole body with olive oil. Nothing could be more healthy or smell better, according to him.

'Making progress with your poem?'

'I'm not unhappy with the words Zeus addresses to the gods: "Attach a golden cord to the sky. If I pull hard on it, I shall drag up the land and the sea; I shall tie it to Olympus, and this world will remain hanging in the winds."'

'In other words, I'm new on the throne and my kingdom is being buffeted by the wind.'

'How would I know, sitting here in my garden?'

'Your muse and the servants' gossip should keep you well enough informed.'

Homer scratched his white beard. 'Could be . . . The reclusive life is not without its convenient aspects. It was time you returned to Memphis, Ramses.'

'I had a tricky situation to resolve first.'

'Finding a High Priest of Amon who won't work against your interests? Difficult, but you accomplished it. Choosing an old and unworldly man showed unusual political finesse for one so young.'

'I chose him on merit.'

'Why not? The main thing is that he obeys you.'

'If conflict between the North and South broke out, Egypt would be ruined.'

'A strange country, but very endearing. I'm getting so used to your customs I've even started to drink my wine plain on occasion.'

'Are you taking care of yourself?'

'There must be two doctors for every Egyptian, I swear! A dentist, an eye doctor, and a physician have all come to see me. They've given me so many potions that I've given up taking them all. Though I admit the eyedrops have helped a bit with my vision. If I'd had them in Greece, I might not have lost my sight. I won't go home now – too much fighting, too many factions, too many tribal chiefs and princelings mired in their rivalries. To write, I need peace and quiet. Concentrate on building one great nation, Majesty.'

'My father had begun doing so.'

'Here are some words of mine: "What good are tears which shake the soul, since this is the fate the gods have decreed for mortals, condemned to live in sorrow?" You can't escape the common lot, and yet your role is to be placed beyond the suffering mass of humanity. The fact that there is a pharaoh, that there has been for centuries, allows your people to believe in happiness, experience it, even share it.'

Ramses smiled. 'You're beginning to undertand the mysteries of Egypt.'

'Don't waste time pining for your father, and don't try to imitate him. Become what he was: irreplaceable.'

Ramses and Nefertari had celebrated rites in every temple in Memphis and praised the High Priest for his excellent administration of the city's famous art schools, where the finest sculptors in Egypt trained and worked.

The dreaded moment had now arrived when the king and queen must pose for these same sculptors. Enthroned, with their heavy crowns and sceptres, they were required to sit motionless for hours on end while the sculptors 'Those Who Give Life', captured the royal couple in stone, for ever young. Nefertari bore the ordeal with dignity, while Ramses grew increasingly restless. On the second day, unable to spend a moment more away from work, he called for Ahmeni.

'The inundation?'

'Fair,' answered his private secretary. 'The farmers were hoping for more, but the reservoir foremen are hopeful. The water supply will be adequate.'

'How is my agriculture minister getting on?'

'He leaves the administrative details to me and never sets foot in his office. He travels from field to field, farm to farm, solving all kinds of practical problems day in and day out. It's not what you'd expect from the head of a secretariat, but—'

'He's on the right track. Are the farm workers complaining?'

'The harvest was good, the granaries are full.'

'Livestock?'

'Numbers on the rise, according to the latest tallies. No reports from the animal doctors of any new diseases.'

'And my beloved brother?'

'Shaanar is a model of responsibility. He met his staff, praised you to the skies, and told them all to serve Egypt with dedication and efficiency. He's taking his position very seriously, starts early in the morning, consults his advisers, and defers to Ahsha. Your brother is becoming a credit to your government!'

'Are you serious, Ahmeni?'

'The Foreign Affairs secretariat is no laughing matter.'

'Have you talked to him?'

'Of course.'

'How did he treat you?'

'Courteously. He didn't object in the least when I asked him to furnish me with a weekly report on his activities.'

'Surprising. He should have shown you the door.'

'He's putting on an act. But insofar as you control him, don't worry.'

'Keep him in line for me, will you?'

'I've already seen to that, Majesty.'

Ramses got up, set the sceptres and crown on his throne, and dismissed the sculptor in mid-sketch. Relieved, Nefertari followed his lead.

'Posing is torture,' the king confessed. 'If anyone had

told me how awful it was, I would never have consented. Fortunately, this likeness will be the only one we sit for.'

'Every station in life has its share of hardships. Your Majesty must never shirk your duties.'

'Watch out, Ahmeni. They may raise a statue to you if you become a sage.'

'No chance of that, with the life you make me lead.'

Ramses drew closer to his friend. 'What do you think of Remet, my new head steward?'

'A good man, but tormented.'

'Tormented?'

'He's obsessed with the smallest detail in his quest for perfection.'

'He's like you, then.'

Annoyed, Ahmeni crossed his arms. 'Anything wrong with that?'

'I want to know if Remet's behaviour puzzles you.'

'Quite the opposite. If all officials behaved like him, I could rest easy. Is there some problem with him?'

'Not yet.'

'You have nothing to fear from Remet. If Your Majesty is finished with me, I'll go back to my office.'

Nefertari tenderly took her husband's arm. 'Ahmeni is a rock.'

'He's a one-man government.'

'You spoke of a sign. Have you seen it?'

'No, Nefertari.'

'I feel it coming.'

'What form will it take?'

'I'm not sure, but it's heading for us like a horse at full gallop.'

33

In early September, the floodwaters spread until Egypt resembled an immense lake from which the occasional hilltop village emerged. Those who did not seek work on one of Pharaoh's building-sites devoted their time to relaxation and boat travel. Well-sheltered on hillocks, livestock fattened on forage. On estates the labourers fished in the fields they had lately tilled.

At the southern tip of the Delta, just above Memphis, the Nile was so wide that one couldn't see one bank from the other. On the northern fringe, it was ten times wider, pushing out into the sea.

Papyrus and lotus grew dense, as if the country were reverting to primeval times, before man walked the earth. The water's benediction purified the earth, drowned vermin and spread the fertile silt that gave the land its fertility and prosperity.

Every morning since mid-May a technician had descended the stairs to the Memphis river-gauge. The cubit ruler carved into its walls provided accurate records of the yearly inundation and a means of calculating the rate of the river's rise. At this time of year, the waters began to recede almost imperceptibly until the level dropped markedly towards the end of September.

The river-gauge was a kind of square well, built of stone

blocks. The technician climbed down the steps carefully, afraid of slipping. In his left hand, he carried a wooden tablet and the fish bone he used as a writing instrument. With his right, he braced himself against the wall.

His foot touched water.

Amazed, he stopped dead and studied the marks on the wall. His eyes must be playing tricks on him! He checked, checked again, then turned and ran up the steps.

The canal district supervisor for the Memphis region looked at the technician in astonishment. 'These figures can't be right.'

'That's what I thought at first, but I checked again today. There's no doubt about it.'

'Are you sure what date it is?'

'Of course! Early September.'

'You've been a reliable worker, set to move up a grade at your next evaluation. Because of your record, I'll agree to forget this incident, provided that you resubmit the report after correcting your mistake.'

'It isn't a mistake.'

'Are you going to make me take disciplinary measures?'

'Check for yourself, sir, please.'

The technician's steady confidence unnerved his superior. 'You know as well as I do that these measurements are impossible!'

'I don't understand it, but it's true. The same measurement, recorded two days in a row.'

The two men went together to check the gauge.

Afterwards, the district supervisor could no longer deny that something extraordinary was happening: instead of receding, the Nile was rising.

Sixteen cubits, the ideal water level. Sixteen cubits, or 'Perfect Joy'.

The news swept the country as fast as a speeding jackal,

187

causing an uproar. Ramses, in the first year of his reign, had performed a miracle! The reservoirs would be filled to the brim, the next season's crops irrigated throughout the dry months. The Two Lands would know a time of plenty, thanks to this royal magic.

Thus Ramses took Seti's place in his subject's hearts. The new pharaoh was beneficent, endowed with supernatural powers, able to control the inundation, banish the spectre of famine and fill people's bellies.

Shaanar was enraged. How could one deal with a people so stupid that they insisted on attributing a natural phenomenon to magic? This damned return of the inundation, which no river-gauge inspector had ever seen before, was strange, of course, even incredible. But Ramses had nothing to do with it! Even so, in every town and village the new pharaoh was being fêted and his name praised to the heavens. He was destined one day to equal the gods.

The king's elder brother cancelled his appointments and gave his entire secretariat a day off in celebration, following the lead of his fellow ministers. Doing otherwise would be a tactical error.

Why did Ramses have all the luck? In the space of a few hours, his popularity had surpassed Seti's. A number of his adversaries caved in, deciding it would be hopeless to oppose him. Instead of forging ahead, Shaanar must proceed more cautiously than ever, slowly weaving his web.

His persistence would pay off in the long run. Fortune was notoriously fickle, and in the end always deserted her followers. When Ramses' luck ran out, Shaanar would make his move. Until then, he would choose his weapons. He would have to strike accurately and hard.

Cries rose from the street. Shaanar thought there must be a scuffle, but the noise grew louder until it was almost deafening. The whole city was cheering! The minister climbed the few steps to his building's roof terrace.

The spectacle that greeted him, along with thousands of his countrymen, turned him to stone.

A huge blue bird, something like a heron, was circling the skies above Memphis.

The phoenix, thought Shaanar. It can't be . . . The phoenix is back?

He struggled in vain to rid himself of the foolish notion, eyes fixed on the soaring bird. Legend had it that the phoenix returned from the underworld to announce a glorious reign and herald a new era.

A bedtime story, a priestly fantasy, a tall tale for the simple folk! Yet there it was, a splendid blue creature circling wide over Memphis, as if surveying the city before choosing a new direction.

If he'd been an archer, Shaanar would have shot the bird down to prove that it was only a migrating waterfowl, confused and disorientated. Order a soldier to do it? None of them would obey him and people would think he was mad. The entire city breathed as one, watching the phoenix. Suddenly, a hush fell.

Shaanar took heart. They knew, of course! If the blue bird really was the phoenix, it would do more than circle over Memphis. According to legend, it would have a specific destination. When the bird departed, it would take the crowd's delusion along with it. The people would stop believing in his brother's second miracle and perhaps even reassess the first one.

The crowd became even quieter. Hah! Ramses' luck was already deserting him! The odd baby cried. Then there was silence.

The huge blue bird continued to circle. In the clear air, the graceful movement of its wings could be heard, like the rustling of cloth. The people's joy seemed to give way to disappointment. This couldn't after all be the phoenix, which appeared only once every fifteen centuries. It must be some poor dazed heron separated from its flock and hopelessly lost.

Relieved, Shaanar went back to his office. This showed how right he was never to heed old wives' tales designed to addle feeble minds. No bird, no man, could live for thousands of years. No phoenix flew in to mark a pharaoh with greatness. Still, there was a lesson to be learned from the incident: knowing how to manipulate the crowd was crucial. People craved dreams in the same way they needed food. If a ruler wasn't popular, it was advisable to manufacture popularity, using rumour and hearsay.

Shouts rang out once more.

No doubt, thought Shaanar, the anger of a crowd balked of the miracle it had expected. He heard the name of Ramses – whose defeat threatened to be more and more bitter.

He hurried back to the terrace, and was astonished to see the crowd exploding as the huge bird landed on top of the city's greatest monument, the sacred obelisk. It *was* the phoenix!

Insane with rage, Shaanar conceded that the gods were indeed proclaiming a new era: the age of Ramses.

'Not one sign, but two,' Nefertari concluded. 'The second inundation, and now the phoenix. Could there be a better beginning?'

Ramses was reading the stack of reports that had just reached him. The Nile's unprecedented return to the ideal water level was a blessing for Egypt. And the entire population of Memphis had beheld the huge blue bird perching on the tip of the great obelisk at the temple of Heliopolis, a ray of sun preserved in sacred stone. There the phoenix remained, contemplating the land the gods loved.

'You look puzzled,' observed the queen.

'Such powerful omens – it's enough to make anyone wonder.'

'You think they're a warning?'

'No, Nefertari. I think they mean I should go ahead and not concern myself with doubters, hindrances or difficulties.'

'Then it's time to launch your great project.'

He took her in his arms. 'According to the Nile and the phoenix.'

A breathless Ahmeni burst into the audience chamber.

'The superior . . . of the House of Life . . . He wants to talk to you.'

'Show him in.'

'Serramanna is trying to search him . . . he'll cause a scandal!'

Ramses hurried towards the antechamber, where a robust man of sixty, with a priest's shaven head and white robe, was trying to stand up to the colossal Sard decked out in helmet and breastplate, sword in hand.

The superior bowed to Pharaoh. Serramanna noted that Ramses seemed less than pleased.

'No exceptions,' grumbled the giant. 'Otherwise I can't vouch for your security.'

'What brings you here?' the king inquired of the priest.

'An urgent request from the House of Life, Majesty. You're needed there.'

34

When Seti had first brought Ramses to Heliopolis, it was to undergo an ordeal on which his future hinged. Today he entered as a pharaoh, passing through the gateway to the great temple of Ra, as vast as that of Amon at Karnak.

On this holy ground, with its own canal, stood a complex of buildings: the temple of the primordial stone, the sanctuary of Atum, the creator, in the shade of a sycamore; the shrine of the willow with the king list carved into its trunk; the memorial shrine of Djeser, builder of the step pyramid at Saqqara.

Heliopolis was a place of enchantment. Garden paths, lined with wayside stone altars holding statues of the gods, led through stands of acacia, willows, and tamarisks. Orchards and olive groves thrived. Beekeepers harvested rich loads of honey, the cowsheds housed cows with well-filled udders, craftsmen trained in the temple workshops, the estates included a hundred villages contributing to the upkeep of Heliopolis and protected in turn by the temple.

Here the lore of the ancients had been handed down and codified in rituals. A long oral tradition of mythology continued. Scholars, ritualists and magicians transmitted their knowledge in silence and secretly.

The superior of the House of Life at Heliopolis, which served as the model for all other institutions of religious learning in Egypt, had grown unaccustomed to the world outside. Dedicated to meditation and learning, he rarely left his domain.

'Your father often spent time among us,' he revealed to Ramses. 'His fondest wish was to enter a religious order, although he knew it could never come true. You, Majesty, are young, and innumerable plans are jostling in your head and heart. But will you live up to the name you bear?'

Ramses controlled his anger with some difficulty. 'Have you any cause to doubt it?'

'Heaven will answer in my place. Follow me.'

'Is that an order?'

'You're lord of this land, and I am your servant.'

The superior of the House of Life did not lower his eyes. Ramses had faced tough adversaries since becoming pharaoh, but none as formidable as this.

'Follow me, please.'

'Show me the way.'

The superior walked at a measured pace towards the sanctuary of the primordial stone, from which an obelisk covered with hieroglyphs rose. On top of it sat the phoenix, perfectly still.

'If Your Majesty will raise your head and fix your eyes on that bird.'

The midday sun was so dazzling that the phoenix was lost in a blur.

'Is your intention to blind me?'

'That is for you to judge, Majesty.'

'Do you expect a king to act on a dare?'

'If it's in his nature.'

'Explain the reason for your attitude.'

'The name you bear, Majesty, is what gives your reign legitimacy. Until now, it's been only an ideal. Will it remain so, or will you dare to make it a reality, no matter what risk that entails?'

Ramses looked straight at the sun.

The golden disc did not burn his eyes. He saw the phoenix rise, flap its wings, and move heavenward. Still the young monarch's gaze remained fastened on the shining orb that lit up the firmament and created the day.

'You are truly Ramses, Ra-Begot-Him, Son of the Light and Child of the Sun. May your reign proclaim victory over darkness.'

The young king understood that he would never have anything to fear from the sun whose earthly incarnation he was. Communing with it, he would be fed by its energy.

Without another word, the superior made his way towards an oblong building with high, thick walls. Ramses followed him and entered the House of Life. In its centre was the mound where the sacred stone lay hidden, covered with a ram's fleece. Alchemists used it to perform transmutations, and pieces of it were buried with the initiates to aid in their passage from death to resurrection.

The superior showed the king into a huge library where works on astronomy and astrology, prophecies and the royal annals were preserved.

'According to our annals,' declared the superior, 'the phoenix was last seen in Heliopolis fourteen hundred and sixty-one years ago. Its appearance in Year One of your reign coincides with the intersection of two astronomical calendars: the fixed-year calendar, which loses a day every four years, and the real-year calendar, which loses a quarter of a day a year. At the precise moment you ascended the throne, these two cosmic cycles came together. A stele will be erected to mark the event, if you so desire.'

'What lesson am I to draw from your revelations?'

'That chance does not exist, Majesty, and that your destiny belongs to the gods.'

A miraculous inundation, the return of the phoenix, a new era . . . It was all too much for Shaanar. Dazed and forlorn, he put up a brave front at the ceremonies organized in honour of Ramses, whose reign, begun under such auspices, promised to be remarkable. The gods had clearly chosen him to govern the Two Lands, preserve their union and increase their prestige.

Only Serramanna was out of sorts. Maintaining security for the king seemed to get harder every day. Dignitaries travelled in packs to shake his hand, it seemed. Even worse, Pharaoh rode in his open chariot through the main streets of Memphis, to the cheers of his people. Intoxicated by his own popularity, he refused the safety measures his guard captain recommended.

As if exposing himself to urban dangers were not enough, the king also ventured into the countryside, most of which lay under the floodwaters. Peasants repaired their tools and ploughs, and stocked granaries, while children learned to swim using floats. Overhead flew cranes with red and black beaks. Herds of belligerent hippos lazed in the muddy river. Allowing himself only two or three hours of sleep a night, Ramses visited a staggering number of villages. He earned the loyalty of provincial administrators and mayors, and gained the trust of the common folk.

When he returned to Memphis, the inundation was beginning to recede and the farmers were preparing for sowing.

'You don't even look tired,' remarked Nefertari.

'What could be tiring about mingling with my people? But you . . . you don't look very well.'

'There's nothing I can put my finger on . . .'

'What do the doctors say?'

'That I must stay in bed if I want a normal delivery.'

'Then why aren't you in your bed?'

'With you away, I had to—'

'I won't leave Memphis again until you give birth.'

'And your great project?'

Ramses frowned. 'Perhaps just one short trip, with your permission.'

The queen smiled. 'Your wish is my command.'

'Egypt is so beautiful, Nefertari. My travels have made me realize that it is a miracle, the child of water and sunlight, the epitome of Horus' strength and Hathor's beauty. We must devote our every waking moment to this country. You and I are meant not to govern but to serve her.'

'I believed that once.'

'What do you mean?'

'Service is the noblest of human achievements. Only by serving a higher goal can we find fulfilment. *Hem*, "the servant", is such a lovely word. It encompasses everyone from the humblest – the seasonal building worker or toiler in the fields – to Pharoah, the most powerful man in the land, the servant of the gods and of his people. Since the coronation, though, I have come to see things differently. Neither one of us can simply serve. We must also direct, guide, ply the helm that keeps the ship of state on a steady course. No one else can do it for us.'

The king grew sombre.

'I felt the weight of that responsibility when my father died. I was so used to having someone who could guide, give advice and orders. Thanks to him, no difficulty was insurmountable, no misfortune without remedy.'

'And that's what your people expect from you.'

'I have looked into the sun and it didn't burn my eyes.'

'The sun is within you, Ramses. It gives life, it makes plants, animals and people grow, but it can also wither and kill if it's too strong.'

'The desert sun is strong, but there's life in the desert.'

'The desert is the underworld on earth. It's not for human habitation, except for houses of eternity that will outlast the ages. A pharaoh's greatest temptation is to immerse his thought in the desert, and forget the world of men.'

'My father was a man of the desert.'

'Every pharaoh should be, but he must also look towards the Valley and see it flourish.'

Then Ramses and Nefertari fell silent in the still of the evening as the sunset gilded the single obelisk towering over Heliopolis.

35

Once the windows in Ramses' bedchamber went dark, Serramanna left the palace, first making sure that his hand-picked guards were at their posts. Jumping on the back of a superb black horse, he galloped through Memphis in the direction of the desert.

Egyptians did not like to go abroad at night. In the absence of the sun, demons were likely to creep out of their lairs and attack unwary travellers. The huge Sardinian scoffed at these superstitions. He could hold his own against a horde of monsters. When his mind was made up, he was unstoppable.

Serramanna had hoped Setau would come to the court and join in the celebrations in Ramses' honour, but, true to his eccentric reputation, the snake-handler stayed at home. In the course of his continuing investigation of the scorpion incident, the Sard had questioned many people. He had learned that no one liked Setau. They feared his evil spells and loathed his reptilian companions, while forced to acknowledge that he was doing a booming business. By selling venom to people who prepared remedies for use in treating serious illnesses, he was beginning to make his fortune.

Though he was still suspicious of Remet, Serramanna had to admit that Setau made an excellent suspect. Suppose he was staying out of sight because he didn't dare face Ramses since planting the scorpion? His reclusiveness was practically an admission of guilt.

Serramanna needed to face Setau in person. The ex-pirate was used to sizing up his opponents, and owed his survival to his ability to read them. Before he could make his move, he needed a good look at Setau. And, since the man was hiding, he would have to flush him out.

As cropland gave way to desert, Serramanna dismounted and tethered his horse to the trunk of a fig tree, whispering a few words of reassurance in the animal's ear. Then he walked noiselessly towards Setau's laboratory. There was barely a crescent of moon, but the night was clear. The laughter of a hyena troubled him not in the least. He felt much as he had when boarding a ship in a surprise attack.

There were lights on in the laboratory. What if Setau took some extra persuading? He'd promised Ramses that he would not use brute force – but necessity made its own rules . . . He cautiously hunched down, skirted a rise and approached the building from the rear.

His back to the wall, the Sard listened.

Low moans issued from the laboratory. Was the snake-charmer torturing some poor wretch? Serramanna edged along to a slit in the wall and peeked inside. Pots, jars, filters, caged snakes and scorpions, knives of various sizes, baskets – all kinds of equipment littered the shelves and workbenches.

On the floor lay a man and a woman, naked and intertwined. A beautiful black woman groaned in pleasure, her slender body arching. Her swarthy, square-jawed partner was stocky and virile.

The Sard looked away. While he freely indulged his own taste for women, he was no voyeur. Yet this woman's beauty had stirred him. Interrupting such passionate lovemaking would be criminal, so he resigned himself to waiting. Spent, Setau would be easier to interrogate.

He smiled to himself thinking of the Memphis beauty he'd be meeting for dinner the following evening. According to her best friend, she liked big, strong men. Serramanna waited.

There was a strange sound to his left.

The Sard looked round to see a huge cobra, its head raised ready to strike – one opponent he'd rather not face. He backed away, bumped into the wall and froze. A second cobra barred his way.

'Get away, you filthy creatures!'

The giant's dagger didn't frighten the snakes. If he did kill one of them, the other one would attack him.

'What's going on here?'

Naked, carrying a torch, Setau inspected the intruder. 'You came to rob my laboratory. Good thing my watchdogs are always on the alert. Unfortunately for you, their bite is definitely worse than my bark.'

'You're not going to commit murder, Setau!'

'So you know my name. No matter, you're a burglar caught red-handed, waving a dagger. The judge will rule that it was self-defence.'

'I'm Serramanna, the captain of Ramses' bodyguard.'

'I thought I recognized you. Why are you trying to rob me?'

'I wanted to see you, have a look at your place, that's all.'

'At this time of night? Not only are you stopping me making love to Lotus, but you're lying through your teeth.'

'It's the truth.'

'Why this sudden wish to see me?'

'Security reasons.'

'What does that mean?'

'My job is to protect the king.'

'You think I'm a threat to Ramses?'

'I didn't say that.'

'But you think it – why else spy on me?'

'I can't afford to make a mistake.'

The two cobras inched closer to the Sard. Setau's eyes blazed with fury.

'Are pirates afraid to die?'

'That way, yes.'

'Get away from here, Serramanna, and don't ever bother me again. Next time I'll let them at you.'

At a signal from Setau, the cobras wriggled aside. The Sard, drenched in sweat, walked straight between them, heading back to his horse.

One thing was clear in his mind: Setau had the soul of a criminal.

'What are they doing?' asked little Kha, watching some peasants herd a flock of sheep through a sodden field.

'After the sowing, the sheep help work the seeds into the soil,' explained Nedjem, the agriculture minister. 'The inundation leaves a huge amount of silt on the banks and fields. That helps us grow strong, plentiful wheat.'

'And the sheep are helpers?'

'Just like cows and every other animal in creation.'

The inundation had begun to recede, and the sowers were out in the fields, glad to trample in the fertile mud that the river had brought in abundance. They began early in the morning, having only a limited number of days while the soil was moist and easily worked. After hoeing to break up the waterlogged clumps of soil, they scattered the seeds and covered the furrows. Livestock followed to help pack down the soil.

'The country is nice,' said Kha, 'but I still like my scrolls and hieroglyphs better.'

'Would you like to visit a farm?'

'All right.'

Nedjem took the little boy by the hand. Even his walk was serious, extraordinary for his age, like his academic gifts. Kind-hearted Nedjem was so concerned for the child, with his lack of interest in toys and playmates, that he'd begged Iset the Fair to let him act as Kha's tutor. He thought it essential to take the little prince outside his gilded cage and introduce him to the wonders of nature.

Kha took in everything around him – not as a surprised and delighted child, however, but as a fully fledged scribe mentally compiling a report.

The farm had granaries, barns, cowsheds, a farmyard, bread ovens and a kitchen garden. At the gate, Nedjem and Kha were invited to wash their hands and feet. Then the owner welcomed them, delighted to have such important visitors. He showed off his best milch-cows, which were fed and tendered with loving care.

'My secret,' he confessed, 'is finding the right pasture, where they don't get too hot and have plenty of grass.'

'The cow is the animal of the goddess Hathor,' ventured the little boy. 'That's why cows are kind and gentle.'

The farmer's eyes widened. 'How do you know that, Prince?'

'I read it in a story.'

'You can already read?'

'Will you do something for me?'

'Anything.'

'Bring me a piece of limestone and a reed-tip.'

'Yes, right away.'

The farmer glanced at Nedjem, who winked his approval. Writing implements in hand, the little boy began to walk round the farmyard, then the cowsheds, much to the farmhands' astonishment.

An hour later, when he returned it to his host, the slab of limestone was covered with writing.

'I've counted carefully,' Kha told him. 'You own a hundred and twelve cows.'

The child rubbed his eyes and clung to Nedjem.

'Now I'm sleepy,' he confessed.

By the time the old man had settled Kha in his arms, the boy was asleep. 'Another of Ramses' miracles,' Nedjem said to himself.

36

Athletic as Ramses, broad-shouldered, with a high forehead, flowing dark hair, and bearded, weather-beaten face, Moses walked casually into the King of Egypt's office.

Ramses rose and the two men embraced.

'This is where Seti worked, isn't it?'

'Yes. I haven't changed a thing. His thought lives on in these walls. I want it to be my inspiration.'

Light filtered through the three barred windows designed to keep air circulating through the room. The late-summer heat was agreeable.

Ramses abandoned his straight-backed royal armchair and sat on a plain seat of woven straw, facing his friend.

'How are you, Moses?'

'Fine, but I don't have enough to do.'

'We never see each other these days. I'm afraid that's my fault.'

'You know that being idle, even in luxury, gets on my nerves. Why did you bring me to Memphis? I was better off working at Karnak.'

'You're not enjoying high society?'

'The courtiers bore me. They never stop singing your praises. They'll be making a god of you soon. It's stupid and pointless.'

'Have I done something wrong?'

'The miraculous inundation, the phoenix, the new era . . . The facts are undeniable, and they explain your popularity. Have you got supernatural powers? Are you one of the Predestined? The people think so.'

'And you don't agree?'

'It may be true. But you're not the True God.'

'Have I ever claimed to be?'

'Be careful, Ramses, or your courtiers' flattery may make you abominably vain.'

'You don't seem to understand the role and the function of a pharaoh. You don't give me much credit, either!'

'I'm only trying to help you.'

'I'm going to give you the chance to do that.'

Moses' eyes shone with curiosity. 'You're sending me back to Karnak?'

'I have a much more important undertaking to entrust to you, if you accept.'

'More important than Karnak?'

The king rose and leaned his back against the window frame.

'I have a tremendous project. So far I've shared it only with Nefertari. We agreed it would be best to look for a sign before I went ahead. The second inundation and the phoenix – in the end the gods gave me two signs. The House of Life confirmed that a new era really has begun, according to the laws of astronomy. Of course I'll continue the work my father began, in Karnak, in Abydos and elsewhere. But this new era should be marked with new creations. Is that vanity, Moses?'

'Every pharaoh must build, according to tradition.'

Ramses looked concerned. 'The world is changing. The Hittites constitute a permanent threat; Egypt is a rich and coveted prize. Those are the truths that led me to conceive my project.'

'To increase your military strength?'

'No, Moses. To move the strategic centre of the country.'

'Do you mean—'

'To build a new capital.'

The Hebrew was astounded. 'What? How will—'

'The northern border is where Egypt's fate will be decided. Therefore, my government should have its seat in the Delta to keep up with the latest developments in Canaan, Syria and our protectorates under threat from the Hittites. Thebes will remain the city of Amon, the home of great Karnak and wonderful Luxor. I'll make sure they're grander and more beautiful than ever. On the west bank, the Mountain of Silence reigns over the Valley of the Kings, the Valley of the Queens and the mortuary temples on the plain.'

'But what about Memphis?'

'Memphis is the fulcrum of the Two Lands, where the Delta joins the Nile Valley. It will remain our economic and administrative capital. But we must go farther to the north and east, Moses, not believe we exist in splendid isolation, nor forget we've been invaded before. Remember that Egypt is a tempting prey.'

'Isn't the line of fortresses enough of a deterrent?'

'In case of danger, I'll have to move quickly. The closer I am to the northern border, the less time it will take information to reach me.'

'Building a capital is a perilous undertaking. Look what happened to Akhenaton.'

'Akhenaton made some unforgivable errors. The site he chose, in Middle Egypt, was doomed from the start. He forgot about the good of his people and pursued his mystical fantasies.'

'He challenged the priesthood of Amon, and so have you.'

'If the High Priest of Amon is faithful to the Rule and loyal to the king, I'll have no quarrel with him.'

'Akhenaton believed in a single god and built a new city to glorify him.'

'His father, the great Amenhotep, left him a prosperous country. He almost ruined it. Akhenaton was weak and indecisive, lost in his prayers. Under his reign, hostile powers seized Egyptian territory. Are you trying to defend him?'

Moses hesitated. 'Today his capital lies abandoned.'

'Mine will be built to last for generations.'

'You almost frighten me, Ramses.'

'Take heart, my friend.'

'How many years does it take to raise a city starting from nothing?'

Ramses smiled. 'It won't start from nothing.'

'What do you mean?'

'While I was Seti's co-regent, he took me to all the most important places. On each journey, he taught me something – though I didn't always understand it then. Today I'm beginning to make more sense of our travels. One of the places we visited was Avaris.'

'The capital of the Hyskos invaders? But the place is cursed.'

'Seti was the namesake of Set, who murdered his brother Osiris. My father had the strength to dominate the forces of destruction, draw out their hidden light and use it to build.'

'And now you want to make Avaris the city of Ramses?'

'Yes, and that's what I plan to call it. *Pi-Ramses*, "the City of Ramses", the capital of Egypt.'

'It's madness!'

'Pi-Ramses will be magnificent and welcoming. Poets will sing of its beauty.'

'How long will it take to build?'

'I haven't forgotten your question. In fact, it's why I called you here.'

'Does this mean what I'm afraid it does?'

'I need someone I can trust to supervise the work and keep the project on schedule. I need Avaris turned into Pi-Ramses as quickly as possible.'

'How long have you allowed?'

'Less than a year.'

'That's impossible!'

'No, it isn't, thanks to you.'

'You think I can move stone with the speed of a falcon and put blocks together through sheer force of will?'

'Stone, no. Bricks, yes.'

'I'm beginning to see . . .'

'Your fellow Hebrews make up most of the brickmaking companies around the country. If we bring them all together, you'll form a group of highly skilled workmen capable of taking on such a gigantic project.'

'Aren't temples supposed to be made of stone?'

'I'll enlarge the temples already there. That can be done over several years. We'll use brick to build the palaces, government offices, villas for the nobles, and large and small houses. In less than a year, Pi-Ramses will be habitable and become a working capital.'

Moses seemed unconvinced. 'I still say it's impossible. The plans alone—'

'The plans are in my head! I'll sketch them myself on papyrus and you'll take personal charge of their execution.'

'The Hebrews are a fairly unruly lot. Each tribe has its own chief.'

'I'm not asking you to become ruler of a nation, only a project leader.'

'Keeping them in order won't be easy.'

'I have faith in you.'

'As soon as the news is out, other Hebrews will try to take my place.'

'Will they be able to?'

Now Moses smiled. 'No one will be able to meet your deadline.'

'We'll build Pi-Ramses to shine under the Delta sun and cast a glow over all Egypt with its beauty. Get to work, Moses.'

37

Abner the brickmaker could stand it no longer. Just because Sary was Ramses' brother-in-law, he thought he could treat his workers like dirt. He reduced their overtime pay, cut their rations and denied them time off, claiming their work had been done badly.

As long as Moses was in Thebes, he had kept Sary in line. Now that he was gone, the situation was worse than ever. Yesterday evening the foreman had caned a fifteen-year-old boy, accusing him of not getting the bricks to the boat fast enough.

It was the last straw.

When Sary arrived at the brickyard, the Hebrews were seated in a circle. Only Abner was standing in front of the empty baskets.

'Get up and go to work!' snarled Sary, who grew thinner by the day.

'We demand an apology,' Abner said calmly.

'What did you say?'

'The boy you beat last night is confined to bed. He did nothing wrong. You owe him and all of us an apology.'

'Have you lost your mind, Abner?'

'We won't go back to work until you agree.'

'Abner, you're a fool.' Sary laughed fiercely.

'All right. We'll file a complaint instead.'

'You're pathetic as well as a fool. I've already called the police in to investigate. They ruled that the boy was injured in an accident, entirely through his own fault.'

'That's a lie!'

'A scribe took his sworn statement in my presence. If the boy goes back on his word, he'll be accused of perjury.'

'How dare you twist the truth so!'

'If you men don't get back to work at once, you'll face stiff penalties. You're supposed to deliver bricks for the mayor's new mansion, and he doesn't like delays.'

'But the law—'

'Don't talk to me about the law, Hebrew. It's over your head. If you file a complaint, your family and friends will suffer the consequences.'

Abner was afraid of Sary. He and the rest of the brickmakers went back to work.

Dolora was more and more fascinated by the strange personality of Ofir, the Libyan sorcerer. His hawklike face was unsettling, yet his voice mesmerized, and when the subject was Aton, the solar disc, his enthusiasm was catching. A discreet house guest, he had agreed to meet a number of the princess' friends and speak about the unjust persecution Akhenaton had suffered, and the need to promote the cult of a single god.

Ofir cast a spell over people. No one walked away from these sessions unchanged. Some were upset by his views, others persuaded. He slowly entangled some worthwhile connections in his web, attracting more support for Aton – and Lita – with each passing week. Even though the throne of Egypt remained only a remote possibility, a movement was beginning to form.

Lita attended these talks without joining in. The young woman's dignity, bearing and reserve were the deciding factor for quite a few notables. She clearly belonged to a royal line that deserved to be taken into consideration. Sooner or later, she must surely regain her rank at the court.

Ofir never criticized, and made no demands. In a low, persuasive voice, he evoked Akhenaton's profound convictions, the beauty of his poetry in honour of Aton, his love of truth. Love and peace: was that not the message of the persecuted king and his descendant, Lita? And this message heralded a magnificent future, a future worthy of Egypt and her civilization.

When Dolora introduced the sorcerer to the former minister for foreign affairs, Meba, she was proud of herself. Proud that she had snapped out of her habitual apathy, proud to be serving a noble cause. Ramses had abandoned her; the sorcerer gave meaning to her existence.

The old diplomat, with his broad, reassuring face and stately manner, made no attempt to hide his distrust.

'I'm only doing this as a favour to you,' he told Dolora.

'I'm grateful, Meba. You won't regret it.' She led him to where the sorcerer sat beneath a persea tree, weaving two strands of linen into a thin cord that would hold an amulet.

He rose and bowed.

'It's a very great honour for me to receive a minister.'

'I'm nothing now,' Meba said bitterly.

'Injustice can strike anyone at any time.'

'That's small consolation.'

Ramses' sister chimed in: 'I explained everything to our friend Meba. Perhaps he'll agree to help us.'

'Let's not fool ourselves, my dear. Ramses has shut me up in a gilded retirement-cell.'

'You want revenge,' said the sorcerer evenly.

'That's going too far,' protested Meba. 'I still have some influential friends who—'

'They're out to protect their own interests, not yours. I have another goal in mind: proving Lita's legitimacy.'

'You're dreaming. Ramses has an extraordinarily forceful

personality. He's not about to step aside. What's more, the miraculous happenings of late have made him very popular. Believe me, it's a lost cause.'

'It's a challenge. I agree we can't fight him on his own ground.'

'What's your plan, then?'

'Interested?'

'Well . . .' Meba fiddled with the amulet around his neck.

'With that gesture you've just given one of the answers: magic. I know how to break through the spells protecting Ramses. It will be long and difficult, but I can do it.'

The diplomat recoiled. 'I can't offer you my assistance.'

'I'm not asking for it, Meba. But there's another area where we must attack Ramses: ideas.'

'I don't follow you.'

'Aton's believers need a respected and respectable leader. When Aton has destroyed the other gods, that leader will play a leading role in overthrowing a pharaoh who's weakened and unable to act.'

'It's . . . It's very risky!'

'Akhenaton was disgraced, but never Aton. His cult has never been banned, and he has many followers, who are determined to impose his worship. Where Akhenaton failed, we'll succeed.'

Meba's hands trembled. 'I'll have to think about it.'

'Isn't it exciting?' asked Dolora. 'A new world is opening up to us, a world where we'll take our rightful place!'

'Yes, of course. Let me think it over.'

A most satisfactory meeting, Ofir thought afterwards. A cautious, faint-hearted diplomat, Meba did not really have the makings of a leader. But he hated Ramses and dreamed of regaining his former rank. Unable to make up his mind, he would turn to his confidant, Shaanar, the man Ofir really

211

hoped to attract. Dolora had told him a great deal about the new minister for foreign affairs and his old rivalry with Ramses. Unless he'd changed completely, Shaanar was proceeding stealthily, his desire to destroy his brother intact. The sorcerer felt sure that Meba would put him in touch with this powerful figure, who was destined to become their most valuable ally.

After a long and exhausting day of work, Sary's right big toe was red and swollen, twisted with arthritis. Standing on it was so painful that he could barely drive his official chariot. His only satisfaction had been taking disciplinary measures against the Hebrews, who had finally understood that it was useless to challenge his authority. Thanks to his connections in the Theban police and the support of the mayor, he was free to vent his frustrations on the brickyard riffraff.

Having Ofir and his silent muse as house guests was beginning to grate on his nerves. They tried to stay out of his way, of course, but their influence over Dolora was getting out of hand. Her new-found devotion to Aton was exasperating. With all the time she spent in prayer or lapping up the Libyan's words as if they were spring water, she was neglecting her conjugal duties.

Tall, dark and languid, she was waiting for him on the doorstep to their villa.

'Go and get the liniment and rub my feet,' he barked at her. 'The pain is unbearable.'

'A hard day at the brickyard?'

'Don't make fun of me! You can't imagine what it's like. Those Hebrews are hopeless.'

Dolora took his arm and led him gently to their bed-chamber. Sary reclined against a heap of pillows as his wife washed and oiled his feet, massaging liniment into his sore toe.

'Is your sorcerer still hanging around?' he asked irritably.

'Meba called on him today.'

'Your father's minister for foreign affairs?'

'He was interested in what Ofir had to say.'

'Meba, a follower of Aton? He's too craven-hearted.'

'He's still an important and well-respected man. Attracting him would really help our cause.'

'Aren't you attaching too much importance to those two lunatics?'

'Sary! How dare you talk like that!'

'All right, forget it.'

'This is our only chance to reclaim our rank. And then this faith is so pure, so appealing. Aren't you moved when Ofir talks about Aton?'

'Who means more to you, your husband or that Libyan sorcerer?'

'What? There's absolutely no comparison.'

'He's with you all day long, while I have to oversee a bunch of lazy Hebrews. A blonde and a brunette to choose from . . . Your Ofir is one lucky fellow.'

Dolora stopped rubbing his inflamed toe.

'You're raving, Sary! Ofir is a sage and a man of prayer. It must be ages since he's thought of—'

'But I'll bet *you* do.'

'You're disgusting!'

'Take off your dress, Dolora, and keep on massaging me. I don't give a damn for prayers.'

'Wait, I forgot to tell you something.'

'What?'

'A royal courier delivered a letter for you.'

'Let me see it.'

Dolora went to fetch the letter. Sary's toe felt better already. What could this official business be? Perhaps an appointment to an office job, where he wouldn't have any Hebrews to supervise?

His wife returned with the scroll. Sary broke the seal on the papyrus, unrolled it and read.

He winced, the colour draining from his face.

'Bad news?'

'I'm to report to Memphis with my team of brickmakers.'

'That sounds like a promotion!'

'Yes, but the letter is signed by Moses, head of royal construction.'

38

Every Hebrew brickmaker in the country answered the summons. When Moses' letters reached the various work sites, the response was enthusiastic. Moses' reputation had spread throughout the land during his tenure at Karnak. Everyone knew he championed the rights of his fellow Hebrews and permitted no ill-treatment. Being Ramses' friend gave him a remarkable advantage, and now he had been named to oversee all royal construction projects. For many, new hope stirred: surely Moses would improve their salaries and working conditions?

Moses was frankly surprised by this success. A few tribal chiefs were upset, but there was no questioning Pharaoh's orders. They yielded to Moses' authority, welcoming him when he toured the tent city north of Memphis, checking on the workers' comfort and sanitary conditions.

Suddenly Sary barred his way. 'What's the meaning of this summons?'

'You'll soon find out.'

'I'm not one of these Hebrews.'

'There are several other Egyptian foremen.'

'Are you forgetting that my wife is the king's sister?'

'And I am head of his building projects. In other words, you must obey my orders.'

Sary chewed his lips. 'My lot of Hebrews are unruly. I

cane them when I need to, and I don't plan to stop.'

'Judicious use of physical discipline can make men listen with their third ear, the one on their back. But anyone who uses the cane without reason should be punished in kind. In fact, I'll see to it personally.'

'Don't try to bully me.'

'Watch yourself, Sary. I can have you demoted. By now you should be an excellent brickmaker yourself.'

'You wouldn't dare.'

'Ramses has given me full authority. Keep that in mind.'

Moses brushed past Sary, who spat in the young Hebrew's footsteps.

The return to Memphis, about which Dolora had been so happy, threatened to become a nightmare. Ramses had been officially informed of her sister's return, along with her husband, but nothing had come of it. They had taken a modest villa, passing Ofir and Lita off as servants. The trio, despite Sary's half-hearted objections, had every intention of continuing to proselytize as they had in Thebes. Given the number of foreigners living in Memphis, the country's economic capital, their work would be easier here. The South was more traditional and resistant to new religious concepts. Dolora considered the summons to Memphis a favourable sign.

Sary remained sceptical and preoccupied with his own fate, pondering what announcement Moses was about to make to the thousands of excited Hebrews.

Guarding the entrance to the Foreign Affairs secretariat was a statue of the god Thoth in the form of an enormous pink granite baboon. Thoth, the scribe god, had created all the world's languages, and members of the secretariat sought his patronage. Learning several foreign tongues was a requirement for diplomats, since the knowledge of hieroglyphs was not for export. When serving abroad, ambassadors and couriers used the local language.

Like other high-ranking officials in the secretariat, Ahsha often meditated in the shrine to the left of the entrance and laid narcissi on the altar of Thoth. Before addressing delicate issues of national security, it was wise to seek the favour of the scribe god.

His offering made, the rising star of Egyptian diplomacy passed through several busy rooms where officials were hard at work, to Shaanar's spacious upstairs office.

'There you are, Ahsha. What kept you?'

'I'm afraid I overslept; I was making rather merry last night. I do hope I haven't inconvenienced you, sir.'

Shaanar's face was red and puffy; he was obviously worked up about something.

'Tell me,' Ahsha said soothingly.

'Have you heard about the Hebrew brickmakers gathering north of town?'

'Yes, but I didn't take much notice.'

'Neither did I, but we should have!'

'What have these people to do with us?' Ahsha felt nothing but disdain for manual labourers, although he hardly knew any.

'You'll never guess who's behind it. The new head of royal construction – Moses!'

'Is that so surprising? He supervised Seti's additions to Karnak; it's a logical promotion.'

'If only that were all. Yesterday Moses called an assembly and told them about Ramses' project: he's going to build a new capital in the Delta!'

A long silence followed this revelation as Ahsha, ordinarily unflappable, registered the shock.

'Are you quite certain?'

'Absolutely certain. Moses is carrying out my brother's orders.'

'A new capital . . . It's impossible!'

'Not for Ramses!'

'How ambitious a project is it?'

'Pharaoh himself drew the plans and chose the site. And what a site – Avaris, the shameful city of the Hyskos invaders we had so much trouble getting rid of !' Shaanar's moon face suddenly brightened. 'What if Ramses has gone mad? A project on this scale can only lead to ruin. Men of sound mind will have to take over eventually . . .'

'I wouldn't be too optimistic. It's true that Ramses takes enormous risks, but his instinct is solid. It's actually the smartest thing he can do. Moving the capital so far north-east and so close to the border, he's sending the Hittites a clear warning signal. They'll see that Egypt is taking nothing for granted, is aware of the danger and won't give up a single cubit of land. The king will have good access to information about enemy actions and will react quickly.'

Shaanar sat down, disheartened. 'It's a catastrophe. Our strategy is falling apart.'

'I wouldn't be too pessimistic, either,' Ahsha advised. 'On the one hand, Ramses' dream may never become reality, and on the other, why should we change our plans?'

'But my brother is obviously taking foreign policy in hand . . .'

'That comes as no surprise, but his policy will still be based on the intelligence he receives, on the basis of which he'll appraise the situation. We may as well let him think he's in charge.'

Shaanar's confidence returned. 'You're right, Ahsha. We won't let a new capital get in our way.'

Queen Tuya had missed the gardens of her Memphis palace. The times she had strolled there with Seti seemed too few and far between, the years she had spent with him too brief. She remembered his every word, his every glance, and had often imagined a peaceful old age at his side, enjoying shared memories. But now Seti roamed through paradise and she walked alone in this marvellous garden, shaded by pomegranates, tamarisks, jojoba trees. On either side of the path bloomed cornflowers, anemones, lupins, ranunculi. Tuya sat pensively by the lotus pond, beneath a wisteria arbour.

When she saw Ramses approaching, her sadness fled.

In less than a year as Pharaoh, her son had grown so self-assured that it was hard to believe he had ever doubted his capabilities. He ruled with the same vigour his father had, with seemingly inexhaustible reserves of energy.

Tenderly and respectfully, Ramses kissed his mother, then he sat down beside her. 'I need to talk to you.'

'That's what I'm here for, my son.'

'Do you approve of the men I've chosen for my government?'

'Do you recall Seti's advice to you?'

'I did my best to follow it: "Look deep in the souls of men. Look for advisers who are upright and firm, able to give an impartial opinion yet ever mindful of their oath of obedience." Have I succeeded? Only the next few years will tell.'

'Do you fear opposition so soon?'

'It's inevitable, at the rate I've been going. I know I'll run up against proud hearts and vested interests. When the idea for this new capital came to me, it was like a lightning bolt. I saw it and knew it was true.'

'The *sia*,' nodded his mother, 'direct intuition, without reasoning or analysis. It was the source of many of Seti's decisions. He believed it was handed down from pharaoh to pharaoh.'

'Has my new capital your blessing?'

'Since the *sia* spoke your heart, why do you need my approval?'

'Because my father's spirit is in this garden, and both of us hear his voice.'

'The signs are clear, Ramses. Your reign opens a new era, and Pi-Ramses will be your capital.'

The pharaoh took his mother's hands in his own.

'You'll see my city, Mother, and be glad.'

'I'm concerned about your protection.'

'Serramanna is ever watchful.'

'I'm talking about your magical protection. Have you thought about building your Temple of a Million Years?'

'I've picked the site, but for now Pi-Ramses is my priority.'

'Don't forget your temple. If the forces of darkness are unleashed upon you, it will be your strongest ally.'

39

The setting was magnificent.

Fertile land, broad fields, thick grass, flower-lined footpaths, apple orchards full of honeyed fruit, a flourishing olive grove, teeming ponds, salt marshes, dense thickets: here sat Avaris, once so despised, now reduced to a handful of houses and a temple to the god Set.

This was where Seti had taught his son the meaning of true power. This was where Ramses would build his capital.

The Hebrews and their Egyptian foremen were part of the expedition Ramses had led in person, accompanied by his lion and dog. Serramanna, on high alert, had ridden ahead with a scouting party of ten.

The little town of Avaris dozed in the sun. Its only inhabitants were government workers in dead-end jobs, slow-moving peasants and papyrus-gatherers. The place seemed suspended in time.

The expedition had made a stop in Heliopolis, where Ramses made an offering to his protector, Ra, and had then headed towards Bubastis (home to the goddess of gentleness and love, Bastet, who had been incarnated as a cat) and along the Pelusiac branch of the Nile, dubbed 'the Waters of Ra'. Near Lake Menezaleh, Avaris was at the western end of the 'Road of Horus', leading across the Sinai coastline towards Palestine and Syria.

The beauty and lushness of the countryside surprised Moses. 'A strategic location,' he commented, as he studied the map Ramses had shown him.

'Do you understand the reasons for my choice now? With the aid of a canal, the "Waters of Ra" will give us access to the lakes around the isthmus of el-Qantara. In an emergency, we can quickly reach the fortress of Sileh by boat, and the smaller frontier outposts as well. I'll be reinforcing the eastern side of the Delta, which commands the invasion routes, and I'll hear immediately of any trouble in our protectorates. The summers are milder here. Our garrisons won't suffer from the heat and so will remain more alert.'

'You're a man of vision,' said Moses admiringly.

'How are your workers?'

'They seem happy to work under me, but the increased wages you're offering probably have a lot to do with that.'

'If I'm generous, they'll give me their best. I want a splendid city.'

Moses bent to study the map again. Four major temples were planned: to the west, one to Amon, 'The Hidden'; to the south, the temple of Set, the local deity; to the east, a shrine to Astarte, the Syrian goddess; and to the north the temple of Wadjet, 'The Verdant', guarantor of the place's prosperity. Near the temple of Set would be the river port. This was at the meeting point of two broad canals, linking the 'Waters of Ra' and the 'Waters of Avaris', which surrounded the city and supplied drinking water. Close to the port lay warehouses, granaries and workshops. Farther north, in the centre of town, were the palace, government buildings, noblemen's villas, and residential neighbourhoods where grand and humble dwellings stood side by side. The main street led away from the palace towards the temple of Ptah, the Creator, with two side roads leading to the temples of Amon and Ra. Set's temple was set apart, on the opposite side of the canal connecting the 'Ra' and 'Avaris' branches.

There were also four military barracks, one between the Pelusiac branch and the government buildings, the three others along the 'Waters of Avaris' – the first behind the temple of Ptah, the second adjoining the residential neighbourhoods, the last near the temples of Ra and Astarte.

'Production of ceramic tiles is ready to start tomorrow,' revealed Ramses. 'From the smallest house to the palace reception hall, Pi-Ramses will sparkle with colour. But first everything has to be built, and that's where you come in, Moses.'

With his right index finger, Moses indicated where the various buildings in the monarch's plan would be situated.

'It's ambitious. I like the way you think on a grand scale. Still . . .'

'Yes, Moses?'

'No offence, Majesty, but one temple is missing. It could easily go in the space between the temples of Amon and Ptah.'

'Which god would it honour?'

'The god who created the institution of pharaoh. Won't it be in this temple that your rededication is celebrated?'

'For that to happen, a pharaoh must have reigned for thirty years. To build it now would be tempting fate.'

'You've left room for it, though.'

'Leaving it out of my plans would also be tempting fate. If I do reach Year Thirty of my reign, at that celebration you'll be in the first rank of dignitaries, together with our other old friends.'

'Thirty years . . . Who knows what God has in store for us?'

'For the moment, he's telling us to build the capital of Egypt together.'

'I've divided the Hebrews into two groups. The first will transport blocks of stone to the temple sites and work under Egyptian supervisors. The second will manufacture the thousands of bricks to be used in your palace and government buildings. Coordinating the two groups will be awkward; I'm afraid my new-found popularity won't last. Do you know what the men call me? *Masha,* "Rescued from Drowning".'

'Is this some miracle I haven't heard about?'

'No, an old Babylonian legend they're fond of repeating. It's a pun on my name, which means "He Who is Born". In their eyes, the gods have blessed me. A Hebrew, educated at the royal school and friend to Pharaoh! God saved me from drowning in poverty and misfortune. A man with my luck is worth following. That's why the brickmakers trust me.'

'Treat them well. You have my permission to use the royal granaries if you lack provisions.'

'I'll build your capital, Ramses.'

The Hebrew brickmakers tied white headbands around the black wigs that stopped above their ears. Many wore moustaches or short beards. A narrow forehead and a thick lower lip were common features. They also shared a pride in their expertise. Syrian and Egyptian brickmakers tried to compete with them, but the Hebrews remained the best and most sought-after in the trade. The work was hard and closely supervised by Egyptian foremen, but the pay was decent and the leave days liberal. Here in Egypt, the food was good and lodgings fairly easy to find. The hardier souls among them even built themselves comfortable homes with salvaged materials.

Moses had made no secret of the fact that at Pi-Ramses the pace would be hotter than usual, but promised bonuses in compensation. Many a Hebrew would prosper here, provided they spared no effort. Under normal conditions, three workmen could produce eight to nine hundred small bricks a day. At Pi-Ramses, they would have to manufacture different sizes: larger bricks for foundations, then a multitude of smaller ones. Usually foremen and stonemasons were responsible for the foundations.

By the end of the first day, the Hebrews realized that Moses would be as stern a taskmaster as he had promised. Any hope of spending their afternoons asleep in the shade of a tree quickly vanished. Like his co-workers, Abner threw himself into his work: mixing mud from the Nile with chopped straw. Finding the right consistency was the trick. Several huge flat areas had been set aside and trenches dug to a canal for water to moisten the river silt. Then, keeping time to songs, the men worked the mixture with picks and hoes, a technique that resulted in stronger bricks.

Abner performed his tasks quickly and well. As soon as the mixture felt right to him, he loaded it into a basket, which a labourer hauled to the workshop, where it was poured into a rectangular wooden mould. Turning out the moulds was a delicate operation; occasionally Moses supervised it in person. The bricks were left to dry for some four hours, then stacked and transported to the various worksites, beginning with the best-cured and therefore lightest-coloured ones.

Humble as it was, the well-made mud brick proved to be a remarkably solid building material. Correctly laid, it could literally last for ages.

A competitive spirit awakened among the Hebrews. The higher salary and bonuses played a part, of course, but so did their pride in being part of such a colossal undertaking and their determination to rise to the occasion. If their enthusiasm waned, Moses got them fired up again. Thousands of perfect bricks were being produced each day.

Pi-Ramses was coming to life, springing out of the pharaoh's dream to become reality. Foremen and stone-cutters, following the king's plans, laid solid foundations; labourers tirelessly carted load after load of the Hebrews' bricks.

Beneath the Delta sun, a city was taking shape.

At the close of each day, Abner admired Moses more. The Hebrew leader moved from group to group, checking the quality of the food, sending those who were sick or overworked off to rest. Contrary to his expectations, his popularity continued to grow.

Abner had already earned enough bonus money to build his family a fine new house right here in the new capital and—

'Pleased with yourself, Abner?' Sary's hollow face wore an evil grin.

'What do you want with me?'

'I'm your foreman. Have you forgotten that?'

'I do my job.'

'Badly.'

'What?'

'Your bricks are below the standard.'

'That can't be!'

'Two building foremen found bad bricks in the loads you sent them. They've written a report. If I pass it on to Moses, you'll be fired, maybe even put in jail.'

'What's this all about? Why are you lying?'

'You have one alternative: buying my silence. Hand your pay over to me and the report will disappear.'

'You're a jackal, Sary!'

'You have no choice, Abner.'

'Why do you hate me?'

'You're a Hebrew, one among many. Let's say you're paying for all the rest.'

'You have no right!'

'I need an answer. Now.'

Abner hung his head. Sary had beaten him again.

40

In Memphis, Ofir felt more at ease than in Thebes. The northern capital was home to many foreigners, who seemed for the most part to fit in perfectly. Some adhered to Akhenaton's doctrine. The sorcerer revived their flagging faith, promising that it would bring them happiness and prosperity in the near future.

Those who were privileged to see Lita, silent as ever, were greatly impressed. None of them doubted that royal blood flowed in her veins, nor that she was the ill-fated pharaoh's rightful heir. The sorcerer's patient, well-reasoned arguments for the existence of a single god worked wonders, and Dolora's Memphis villa was the setting for productive meetings that netted a daily increase in the number of believers.

Ofir was not the first foreigner to propagate original ideas, but he was the only one to revive the heresy quashed by Akhenaton's successors. His capital and burial place had been abandoned; no person of rank had been entombed nearby in the necropolis. Everyone knew that Ramses, after bringing Karnak under his control, would stand for no religious trouble. Therefore, Ofir took care to be sparing in his criticism of the king and his policies, so as not to invite disapproval.

The sorcerer was finally getting somewhere.

Dolora brought him a drink of cool carob juice.

'You seem tired, Ofir.'

'Our work demands constant effort. How is your husband doing on his project?'

'He's very unhappy. According to his last letter, he spends his days scolding lazy, dishonest Hebrews.'

'I've heard the work is going very quickly, though.'

'Everyone says it will be splendid.'

'But dedicated to Set, the evil lord of the powers of darkness! Ramses wants to snuff out the light and hide the sun. We must stop him.'

'I'm convinced of it, Ofir.'

'Your support is essential, as you know. Will you consent to let me use all the resources of my art to keep the pharaoh from destroying Egypt?'

The tall, languid woman bit her lips. 'Ramses is my brother!'

Ofir gently took Dolora's hands.

'He's already done us so much harm. Of course, I'll abide by your decision, but why wait any longer? Ramses isn't waiting for anything! And the further he goes, the stronger his magical defences become. I'm not sure I'll be able to break through them if we delay much longer.'

'It's such a big step . . .'

'Be aware of your responsibilities, Dolora. I can still act, but soon it will be too late.'

Dolora was still unwilling to attack her brother. Ofir let go of her hands.

'There may be another way,' he said after a moment's pause.

'What are you thinking?'

'Queen Nefertari is rumoured to be pregnant.'

'It's no rumour. You've only to look at her.'

'Have you any affection for her?'

'Not in the least.'

'I'll ask one of my compatriots to bring what I need tonight.'

'I'll stay in my room!' cried Dolora, retreating hastily.

The man arrived in the middle of the night. The house was quiet; Dolora and Lita were asleep. Ofir opened the door to the merchant, took the sack from him and paid with two linen sheets Dolora had donated.

The transaction took only a few moments.

Ofir shut himself up in a small room to which he had blocked all the openings. A single oil lamp gave off a dim light.

On a low table, the sorcerer laid out the contents of the bundle: a statuette of an ape, an ivory hand, a crude figurine of a naked woman, a miniature pillar, and another figurine of a woman, this one holding snakes in her hands. The ape would supply him with the power of the god Thoth. The hand was for action. The naked woman gave him power over the queen's reproductive organs. The pillar represented the lasting effect of his spell. The snake woman would poison Nefertari's body with black magic.

Ofir's task would not be easy. The queen possessed great personal strength, and, like her husband, had been endowed with protective forces at the time of her coronation. But pregnancy weakened those defences. The new life inside her sapped Nefertari's own life force.

It would take at least three days and nights for the spell to take hold. Ofir was slightly disappointed not to be attacking Ramses directly, but without his sister's consent that would be impossible. When he had Dolora completely in his sway, he would pursue a more ambitious goal. For now, he could begin to weaken the enemy.

Leaving the daily business of governing in the hands of Ahmeni and his ministers, Ramses made frequent visits to

Pi-Ramses. Thanks to Moses' leadership and organization, as well as a strict schedule, the work was progressing by leaps and bounds.

The atmosphere was lively and bustling. The men were happy with the quality and quantity of their rations. On top of that, generous bonuses were paid as promised, on the merit system. The hardest workers would make a tidy packet and be able to set themselves up either in the new capital or in another city, even to buy a plot of land. There was also a well-equipped infirmary to provide free care for the sick and injured. Unlike other construction sites, Pi-Ramses was not plagued with workers feigning illness in order to go on leave.

The king was safety-conscious; several foremen were permanently assigned to site safety. All but a few minor injuries had been avoided when the Temple of Amon's granite blocks were set in place. Thanks to a scrupulously observed rotation of work gangs, the men never reached the point of exhaustion. Two days off after every six working days allowed them to rest and recuperate.

The only person Moses allowed no rest was himself. He checked all work, resolved conflicts, took urgent decisions, reorganized substandard work crews, ordered materials and supplies, wrote reports, slept for an hour after lunch and three hours each night. Their leader's energy impressed the Hebrew brick workers so deeply that they gave him instant, unquestioning obedience. No supervisor in their experience had ever defended their interests as he did.

Abner could have spoken to Moses about Sary's extortion, but he was afraid of how his foreman might retaliate, given his strong police connections. If he was labelled a trouble-maker, Abner would be deported and never see his wife and children again. Once Sary'd started receiving payments, the foreman had stopped harassing him and had been almost pleasant. It seemed the worst was over. The Hebrew retreated into silence and moulded his bricks with the usual care and speed.

That morning, Ramses was touring the worksite. As soon as his visit was announced, the Hebrews washed, trimmed their beards and moustaches, tied fresh white bands round their best wigs and lined up their bricks in perfect order.

The first chariot that stopped in front of the brickyard discharged a glowering giant with sword and shield in hand. Was one of the workers about to be disciplined? The presence of twenty archers did little to lighten the mood.

Serramanna passed silently along the tense and motionless rows of Hebrew brickmakers. When his inspection was finished, the Sard signalled one of the soldiers to let the royal chariot advance.

The brickmakers bowed to Pharaoh, who congratulated them on their work one by one, addressing each man by name. Cheers greeted his announcement that new wigs and white Delta wine were to be distributed; but what touched the men most deeply was the attention the king paid to the freshly moulded bricks. He picked up several, weighing them in his hands.

'Perfect,' he declared. 'Double rations for a week and an extra day off. Where is your foreman?'

Sary stepped forward.

Ramses' old teacher was the only one who was not glad to see the monarch. He was afraid of meeting the king against whom he had plotted.

'Satisfied with your new duties, Sary?'

'I thank Your Majesty for awarding them to me.'

'If my mother and Nefertari hadn't interceded, your punishment would have been much stiffer, believe me.'

'I'm aware of that, Majesty, and hope my new attitude will persuade you to forgive my past transgressions.'

'They're unforgivable, Sary.'

'The remorse that gnaws at my heart is more painful than acid.'

'It can't be too bad; it's quite some time since your crime, and you're still around.'

'Is it too much to hope for Your Majesty's pardon?'

'I am not familiar with that notion, Sary. One lives within or outside the Rule of Ma'at. You've flouted it, and your soul is for ever stained. Make sure you cause Moses no trouble. This is the last chance I'm giving you.'

'I swear to Your Majesty that—'

'Enough said, Sary. Be glad of the chance to take part in creating Pi-Ramses.'

When the king climbed back in his chariot, cheers rose again, even louder this time. Reluctantly, Sary joined in.

41

As planned, work proceeded more slowly on the temples than on secular edifices. Nevertheless, immediate shipments of granite began, and expert stone-haulers, including a number of Hebrews, made regular deliveries to the work site.

Thanks to the brickmakers' industriousness, the royal palace was rising quickly from its stone foundations, and already dominated the centre of the capital. Shipping was under way, the warehouses were open, carpenters were turning out fine furniture, ceramic tiles were being mass-produced. Villa walls seemed to spring up out of the ground, the residential areas of the city took shape, and the barracks would soon be ready to house their first troops.

'The palace lake will be splendid,' announced Moses. 'It ought to be dug by the middle of next month. Your capital is going to be beautiful, Ramses. It's built with love.'

'You can take credit for that, Moses.'

'All I've done is execute your plans.'

The king detected a slight reproach in his friend's tone of voice. Just as he was about to ask why, a courier from Memphis galloped up. Serramanna made him stop at a respectable distance. The messenger jumped down and approached his sovereign, panting.

'Your Majesty's presence is urgently requested in Memphis. The queen has been taken ill.'

Ramses collided with Dr Pariamaku, head of the palace medical staff, a learned and commanding man of fifty with long, expressive hands. An experienced surgeon, he had the reputation of being an excellent doctor, though strict with his patients.

'I want to see the queen,' demanded Ramses. He was cursing himself for not having honoured his promise to Nefertari to be with her until the birth.

'The queen is sleeping, Majesty. The nurses applied a massage oil mixed with a sleeping-draught.'

'What's wrong with her?'

'There are signs of a premature delivery.'

'Isn't that dangerous?'

'Very, I'm afraid.'

'I order you to save Nefertari.'

'I still predict a favourable outcome.'

'What makes you say that?'

'My staff performed the usual tests, Majesty, placing barley and wheat in two cloth sacks that were sprinkled with the queen's urine for several days in a row. Both grains sprouted, indicating she will give birth successfully. Since the wheat sprouted first, she will have a girl.'

'I've heard the opposite.'

Dr Pariamaku gave him an icy stare. 'Your Majesty must be referring to another technique, in which the grains are covered with soil. In any case, we must hope that the seed of your heart, implanted in the queen's heart, is firmly fixed in the infant's spine and bones. High-quality sperm gives an excellent spinal cord and perfect bone marrow. Need I remind you that the bones and tendons come from the father, the flesh and blood from the mother?'

The doctor was rather pleased with his lecture. And to such an illustrious student!

'Need I remind you that I studied anatomy and physiology at the royal school, Doctor?'

234

'Of course not, Majesty.'

'Nothing led you to expect complications?'

'My learning has certain limits, Majesty . . .'

'My power has none, Doctor, and I demand a safe delivery.'

'Majesty . . .'

'Yes, Doctor?'

'Your own health must be closely monitored. I have not yet had the honour of examining you, which is among my foremost responsibilities.'

'No need. I've never had a day's illness in my life. Call me the moment the queen wakes up.'

The sun was low in the sky when Serramanna granted Dr Pariamaku entry into the king's office.

The physician was ill at ease. 'The queen has awakened, Majesty.'

Ramses rose.

'However . . .'

'Out with it, Doctor!'

Pariamaku, who had boasted that he would be able to handle Ramses, was beginning to miss Seti, taciturn and uncooperative though he had been. Ramses was like a raging storm – best to stay out of his way.

'The queen has just been taken to the delivery room.'

'I demanded to see her immediately!'

'The midwives decided there wasn't a second to lose.'

Ramses snapped the reed pen in his hand. If Nefertari died, would he have the strength to go on?

Six midwives from the House of Life, wearing long tunics and turquoise necklaces, helped Nefertari to the delivery room, an airy, flower-filled pavilion. Like all Egyptian women, the queen would give birth naked, straight-backed, squatting over stones with a bed of reeds on top of them. This symbolized each newborn's destiny, its life span determined by Thoth.

The first midwife would support the queen from behind, the second would ease her through each stage of labour, the third would catch the baby, the fourth would attend to its first needs, the fifth was the wet-nurse, and the sixth would hold two *ankh* amulets – the 'Keys of Life' – for the queen until the infant's first cry was heard. Though aware of the dangers facing them, the six women moved serenely.

After thoroughly massaging Nefertari, the head midwife had applied poultices over her lower abdomen. Judging it necessary to hasten what promised to be a painful labour, she inserted a paste of turpentine resin, onion, milk, fennel, and salt into the vagina. To ease the labour pains, she prepared dried earth to be mixed with warm oil and rubbed on the genital area.

The six midwives knew that Nefertari's labour would be long and its outcome uncertain.

'May the goddess Hathor grant the queen a child,' chanted one of the women. 'May no sickness touch it. Begone, demon of darkness, who enters slyly, with your face turned backwards. You will never embrace this infant, put it to sleep, harm it or carry it off. May the spirit move in the child, may no evil spell touch it, may the stars be favourable.'

As night fell, the contractions came closer together. Bean paste was packed around the queen's teeth so that she could clench them without hurting herself.

Professional, focused, reciting ancient incantations to banish pain, the six midwives helped the Queen of Egypt bring forth new life.

Ramses couldn't stand it a moment longer. When Dr Pariamaku reappeared for the tenth time, he thought the king might fly at his throat.

'Is it finally over?'

'Yes, Majesty.'

'Nefertari?'

'The queen is alive and well and you have a daughter.'

'How is the baby?'

'Too soon to tell . . .'

The king pushed past the physician and charged into the delivery room, where one of the midwives was cleaning up.

'Where are they? The queen and my daughter?'

'In a palace bedchamber, Majesty.'

'Tell me the truth!'

'The baby is very weak.'

'I demand to see them.'

Relieved, radiant, but exhausted, Nefertari was asleep. The head midwife had given her a sedative.

The baby was remarkably beautiful. Fresh, her eyes at once astonished and curious, the child of their love greeted life like the miracle it was.

The king held her. 'She's perfect! Why do you think something's wrong?'

'The cord broke on the amulet we were putting around her neck. A bad omen, Majesty, a very bad omen.'

'Have the signs been read?'

'We're waiting for the prophetess.'

The prophetess appeared a few minutes later. With the six midwives, she formed the circle of the seven Hathors, foreseeing the newborn's destiny. Huddled round the infant, they went into a trance.

Their meditation seemed to last longer than usual.

Grim-faced, the prophetess broke away from the circle and approached the king.

'The time isn't propitious, Majesty. We cannot—'

'Don't lie to me.'

'We may be wrong.'

'Just tell me what you see.'

'The child's fate will be decided within the next twenty-four hours. If we don't find a way to dispel the demons eating away at her heart, your daughter won't live until tomorrow night.'

42

The royal infant's blooming wet-nurse had been personally checked by Dr Pariamaku. Her milk had the pleasant odour of carob flour. To ensure a good milk supply, the nurse had been drinking fig sap and eating roasted fish spines ground up in oil.

Much to the distress of the doctor and wet-nurse, the baby would not take the breast. Another nurse was called in, with the same result. The final remedy, a special reserve of milk kept in a hippopotamus-shaped vessel, worked no better. The child would not take the thick milk flowing from the animal's teats.

The doctor moistened his tiny patient's lips and was preparing to wrap her in damp clothes when Ramses took her in his arms.

'She's becoming dehydrated, Majesty!'

'Your science can't help her. My strength will keep her alive.'

Holding his tiny daughter to his chest, the king went to Nefertari's bedside. Despite her exhaustion, the queen was radiant as ever.

'I'm so happy, Ramses! Nothing can harm her now.'

'How do you feel?'

'Don't worry about me. Have you thought of a name for our baby?'

'That's up to the mother.'

'We'll call her Meritamon, "Beloved of Amon". She'll see your Temple of a Million Years finished. While I was in labour, I had the strangest sensation . . . You must start work on it right away. It will be your best defence against the forces of evil and keep us united against adversity.'

'You'll have your wish, I promise.'

'Why are you holding her so tight?'

Nefertari's gaze was so clear, so trusting, that Ramses was unable to keep the truth from her.

'Meritamon isn't well.'

'What's wrong with her?'

'She won't take the breast, but I'll make her better.'

The queen sank back into the bed. 'I've already lost one child, and now death is trying to take our daughter. It's dark, dark . . .'

Nefertari swooned.

'Your diagnosis, Doctor?' asked Ramses.

'The queen is very weak,' Pariamaku replied.

'Can you save her?'

'I don't know, Majesty. If she survives, she mustn't have any more children. Another pregnancy would be fatal.'

'And our daughter?'

'I've never seen anything like it. She seems so peaceful, now that you're holding her. The midwives may be right, although I find their theory absurd.'

'What is it, then?'

'They think she's under some sort of magic spell.'

'A spell, here, in my palace?'

'That's why I didn't take it seriously. Still, it might be a good idea to consult the court magicians.'

'But what if one of them is involved? No, there's only one thing left to do.'

Meritamon slept in her father's powerful arms.

The court buzzed with rumours: Nefertari's child had been stillborn; the queen was near death; Ramses was mad with despair. While not daring to believe them, Shaanar hoped there might be some truth to these excellent reports.

On the way to the palace with Dolora, Shaanar put on a grave and tearful face. His sister seemed genuinely grief-stricken.

'Been taking acting lessons, sister dear?'

'Can't you see that I'm upset?'

'You don't care about Ramses or Nefertari.'

'No, but the baby . . . the baby isn't responsible.'

'So what? I had no idea you were so sentimental. If the rumours are true, things are looking up for us.'

Dolora could never tell Shaanar what was really upsetting her: Ofir's successful spell. To break through the royal couple's defences and shatter their lives, the Libyan must have extraordinary power over the forces of darkness.

Ahmeni, paler than usual, received Dolora and her brother.

'Given the circumstances,' said Shaanar, 'we thought the king might like his family nearby.'

'Sorry, he'd rather be alone.'

'How is Nefertari?'

'The queen is resting.'

'The baby?' asked Dolora.

'Dr Pariamaku is attending her.'

'Can you tell us anything more definite?'

'You'll have to be patient, I'm afraid.'

As Shaanar and Dolora left the palace, they saw Serramanna and his guard detail escorting a scruffy-looking, bare-headed man, dressed in a strange antelope-skin tunic studded with pockets. They were walking briskly towards the royal couple's private apartments.

'Setau! You're my last hope.'

The snake-charmer went up to the king and gazed at the baby in his arms.

'I don't care for babies, but that one's a beauty. The mother's looks, of course.'

'Meet our daughter, Meritamon. She's dying, Setau.'

'She's . . . ?'

'She's under a spell.'

'Has it come from inside the palace?'

'I'm not sure.'

'What has it done to her?'

'She won't take the breast.'

'Nefertari?'

'Sinking fast.'

'I suppose good old Pariamaku has given up?'

'He doesn't know what to do.'

'As usual. Put your daughter in her cradle. Gently, now.'

Ramses did as he was told. The moment he let go of Meritamon, her breathing grew laboured.

'Your strength is all that's keeping her alive. Just as I feared. What's this now? The baby isn't even wearing an amulet! Don't they know anything in this palace?'

Setau dug a scarab amulet out of a pocket, strung it on a fine cord with seven knots, and put it round Meritamon's neck. The scarab bore the inscription: 'Ravenous death will not take me. The divine light will preserve me.'

'Pick her up again,' ordered Setau, 'and show me the palace laboratory.'

'Do you think you'll be able to —'

'We'll discuss it later. Every minute counts now.'

There were several sections to the palace laboratory. Setau shut himself up in the room where male hippopotamus tusks were stored. He selected one over a cubit in length, and carved it into an elongated crescent moon. He smoothed the surface without damaging the ivory, then carved several symbols with the power to repel the forces of darkness that were trying to kill mother and child. A winged griffin with

241

a lion's body and falcon's head, a female hippo brandishing a knife, a frog, a shining sun, a bearded dwarf with his fists full of snakes – these, he considered, were best suited to the situation. Describing his magical helpers aloud as he carved, he ordered them to cut the throats of all demons, male and female, in their path, to trample them underfoot, to lacerate them and put them to flight. Next, he prepared a potion based on viper venom to clear the opening to Meritamon's stomach, though even the minutest of doses might be too much for a newborn.

When Setau emerged, Dr Pariamaku came running frantically towards him.

'Hurry! The baby is almost dead.'

Looking out at the sunset, Ramses held his daughter, trustfully slumbering against him. Despite his magnetism, her breathing was growing ragged. Nefertari's baby, the only child of their union who might survive . . . If Meritamon died, Nefertari would not survive. Anger welled up in the king's heart, an anger that would repel the creeping shadows and save his daughter from their evil spell.

Setau entered the chamber, holding the newly carved tusk.

'It ought to break the spell,' he explained. 'But it's not enough. We can't reverse the damage to her internal organs unless she swallows this potion.'

When he told them what it was made of, Dr Pariamaku said indignantly, 'I can't recommend this, Majesty!'

'Are you sure it will work, Setau?'

'I admit it's dangerous. It's up to you to decide.'

'Let's go ahead,' said Ramses.

43

Setau laid the carved tusk on Meritamon's chest. Snug in the cradle, her huge eyes inquisitive, the infant breathed peacefully.

Ramses, Setau, and Dr Pariamaku remained silent. The talisman seemed to be working, but would it last?

Ten minutes later, Meritamon began to struggle and cry.

'Have them bring a statue of the goddess Opet,' ordered Setau. 'I'm going back to the laboratory. Doctor, moisten the baby's lips, and make sure that's all you do.'

Opet, the female hippopotamus, was the patroness of midwives and wet-nurses. In the heavens, she took the form of a constellation separating the Great Bear (linked to Set, and therefore potentially destructive) from the reborn Osiris. Magicians from the House of Life had charged the statue with positive energy. Filled with mother's milk, it was placed at the head of the cradle.

Meritamon stopped crying and dozed off again.

Setau reappeared, holding a crudely carved tusk in each hand. 'Not pretty,' he said, 'but they ought to do what's necessary.'

He laid one tusk on the baby's stomach and the other at her feet. Meritamon did not stir.

'A field of positive forces is protecting her now. The spell has been broken, the evil undone.'

'Is she out of danger?' asked the king.

'Not unless she takes the breast. The passage to her stomach has to open, or she'll die.'

'Give her your potion.'

'No, you do it.'

Ramses gently parted his sleeping daughter's lips and poured the amber liquid into her tiny mouth. Dr Pariamaku turned his head away.

Moments later, Meritamon opened her eyes and squalled.

'Quick!' said Setau. 'The statue's breast!'

Ramses picked up his daughter, Setau removed the thin metal stopper in the statue's nipple, and the king brought the baby's mouth to meet it.

Meritamon gulped the life-giving liquid, barely stopping to catch her breath, and gurgled with contentment.

'What can I do to thank you, Setau?'

'Nothing, Ramses.'

'I'll appoint you director of the palace magicians.'

'They can get along without me. How's Nefertari doing?'

'She's amazing. She's going to walk in the garden tomorrow.'

'And the baby?'

'She has an unslakable thirst for life.'

'What were the seven Hathors' predictions?'

'The black cloud over Meritamon's destiny has lifted. They saw a priestess' vestments, a woman of great nobility, the stones of a temple.'

'An austere life.'

'You deserve a fortune, Setau.'

'My snakes, my desert creatures and Lotus are enough for me.'

'You'll have unlimited funds for your research. As for your venom production, the palace will pay top price for it and distribute it to the hospitals.'

'I don't want any favours.'

'It's no favour. Since your pharmaceuticals are the best in Egypt, your salary must be raised and your work encouraged.'

'There *is* one thing . . .'

'Anything.'

'Have you still got any of that red Faiyum wine from Year Three of your father's reign?'

'I'll have several jars of it sent your way tomorrow.'

'Let me know how many vials of venom I'll owe you.'

'It's a present.'

'I don't like presents, especially coming from the king.'

'It's your friend, not your king, who asks you to accept it. Tell me, where did you learn the technique you used to save Meritamon?'

'My snakes teach me almost everything, and Lotus knows the rest. Nubian sorcerers are peerless, believe me. The amulet I put around your daughter's neck will do her a world of good, provided you have its magic renewed every year.'

'I'm giving you and Lotus an official residence.'

'In town? You can't be serious. How would we do our work? We need the desert, the darkness and the danger. Speaking of danger, that was an unusual spell they cast on Meritamon.'

'What do you mean?'

'I had to use extreme measures because the spell was so strong. There was some foreign wizardry at work – Syrian, Libyan or Hebrew. Without three magic tusks, I'd never have been able to break the negative forces. Not to mention the fact that it takes an exceptionally twisted mind to go after a newborn baby.'

'A palace magician, do you think?'

'That would surprise me. No, a familiar of the forces of evil.'

'Then he'll try again.'

'Of that you can be sure.'

'How can we find him and put a stop to his wickedness?'

'I've no idea. A fiend that powerful is sure to be a master of deception. It could even be someone you've met, who seemed friendly and harmless. Or he could be hiding in some inaccessible lair.'

'How can I keep my wife and my daughter safe?'

'Stick to the proven methods: amulets and ritual invocations to the forces of good.'

'What if that's not enough?'

'You'll need to surround yourself with energy more power-ful than black magic.'

'A source of such energy,' mused Ramses.

The Temple of a Million Years – that would be his best hope.

Pi-Ramses was growing.

It wasn't a city yet, but buildings and houses were taking shape in the imposing shadow of the palace, whose stone foundations rivalled those of its Thebes or Memphis counter-parts. The work was proceeding at a lightning pace. Moses seemed tireless and continued to run a model worksite. Seeing results so quickly made everyone, from masterbuilders to rough labourers, eager to see the project reach completion. Some planned to live in the capital their own hands were helping to build.

Two Hebrew tribal chiefs, resentful of Moses's growing authority, had tried to challenge him. Before he could even respond, the brickmakers had unanimously demanded that he remain their leader. From that moment on, Moses became the uncrowned king of a people without a homeland. Building the new capital took so much energy that his mental turmoil abated. He no longer wondered about the One God and concentrated only on organising the worksites efficiently.

The announcement that Ramses had arrived made him happy. The sighting of certain birds of ill omen had made the men uneasy about the queen and her baby. For days, their spirits were low. Moses had told them not to worry, predicting that Ramses would be back before they knew it – and Ramses was proving him right.

Try as he might, Serramanna could not stop the workers lining up on both sides of the royal chariot's route through town. The men wanted to touch their pharaoh, so that some of his magic would rub off on them. The Sard muttered curses. What if one of them had a dagger? Why wouldn't Ramses listen?

The king went straight to Moses' temporary quarters. When he alighted, Moses bowed, but once they were inside, out of public view, the friends embraced.

'If we can keep going at this rate, we may just meet your ridiculous deadline.'

'Let me guess: you're ahead of schedule!'

'We certainly are.'

'This time I want to see everything.'

'I think you'll be pleased. May I ask after Nefertari?'

'The queen is very well indeed. So is our daughter. Meritamon will be a beauty, like her mother.'

'I heard that they came within a hair's-breadth of death.'

'Setau saved them.'

'With his snake venom?'

'No, he's become quite adept at magic. He broke an evil spell someone cast on my wife and daughter.'

Moses was aghast. 'Who'd dare try such a thing?'

'We don't know yet.'

'You'd have to be beneath contempt to attack a mother and child. And insane, to make an attempt on the royal family.'

'I wonder if there's a connection between this vile attack and the building of Pi-Ramses. I've ruffled the feathers of a lot of important people.'

'I don't think so. It's too big a jump from discontent to murder.'

'If it turned out a Hebrew was guilty, how would you feel?'

'A criminal is a criminal, no matter what his race. But I think you're on the wrong track.'

'If you learn anything at all, don't keep it from me.'

'What? Don't you trust me?'

'Would I talk to you this way if I didn't?'

'No Hebrew would stoop so low.'

'I have to be away for several weeks, Moses. Take good care of my capital.'

'The next time you come, you'll hardly recognize it. Don't wait too long, though. We wouldn't want to postpone the opening ceremonies.'

44

The beginning of June brought stifling heat and a round of festivities marking the beginning of Ramses' second year on the throne. Already more than a year since Seti's departure for the kingdom of the stars!

The royal couple's boat moored at Gebel el-Silsila, where the great river narrowed. According to tradition, the spirit of the Nile resided here. Pharaoh must reawaken him so that he would become the father of life and make the waters of the inundation rise.

After making the offering of milk and wine and saying the ritual prayers, the royal pair entered a shrine carved into the river bluffs. Inside, it was pleasantly cool.

'Did Dr Pariamaku speak to you?' Ramses asked Nefertari.

'He prescribed something new to give me back my energy.'

'Nothing else?'

'Is he hiding the truth about Meritamon?'

'No, you can rest easy on her account.'

'Then what was he supposed to tell me?'

'Courage is not the good doctor's greatest virtue.'

'What was he afraid of?'

'It's a miracle you survived childbirth this time.'

A shadow passed over Nefertari's face. 'You're telling me I can't have any more children, aren't you? I'll never give you a son.'

'Kha and Meritamon are the legitimate heirs to the throne.'

'Ramses should have more children and more sons. If you want me to step aside, to join a religious order . . .'

The King clasped his wife to him. 'I love you, Nefertari. You're the light of my life. You are Queen of Egypt. Our souls are joined for eternity. Nothing and no one can come between us.'

'Iset will bear you sons.'

'Nefertari . . .'

'It's necessary, Ramses. You're no ordinary man, you're Pharaoh.'

As soon as they arrived in Thebes, the royal couple proceeded to the site where Ramses was to raise his Temple of a Million Years. The location had grandeur and pulsed with the energy that flowed from the looming Peak of the West and the fertile Theban plain.

'I shouldn't have neglected this project for the benefit of Pi-Ramses,' the king admitted. 'My mother's warning and the threat of black magic opened my eyes. Only a Temple of a Million Years can shield us from the forces of darkness.'

Noble and resplendent, Nefertari paced the vast stretch of rock and sand, which looked doomed to barrenness. Like Ramses, she was a child of the sun, her skin never burning, only glowing from its touch. Time froze. She was the founding goddess. Each place her feet touched became holy ground.

The Great Royal Wife sprang from eternity, and she etched it into this sun-baked land, which was already marked with Ramses' seal.

The two men collided on the gangway to the pharaoh's ship and stopped dead, face to face. Setau was shorter than Serramanna but just as broad of shoulder. Their eyes locked.

'I was hoping not to find you anywhere near the king, Setau.'

'I'm not sorry to disappoint you.'

'There's talk of black magic nearly killing the queen and her baby.'

'Still no idea who was behind it? Some security Ramses has here.'

'Do you want me to shut your mouth?' the Sard growled.

'You're welcome to try. But watch out for my snakes.'

'Is that a threat?'

'Take it any way you want. To me, a pirate is a pirate, no matter how you dress him up.'

'It would save me a lot of time if you'd just confess.'

'For someone in your position, you're not very well informed. Haven't you heard that I saved the princess' life?'

'To cover your tracks. You're a sly bastard, Setau.'

'You've got a warped mind.'

'Make the slightest move in the king's direction and I'll crush you skull.'

'You talk big, Serramanna.'

'Try me.'

'An unprovoked attack on a friend of the king's would land you in jail.'

'That's where you'll end up.'

'You'll beat me to it, Sard. Now get out of my way.'

'Where are you going?'

'To meet Ramses and, at his request, drive the snakes away from his future temple.'

'I'm watching you, sorcerer.'

Setau shoved past Serramanna. 'Stop spouting foolishness and get back to guarding the king.'

Ramses spent several hours at the Temple of Gurnah, on the west bank of Thebes, meditating in the shrine dedicated to his father's perpetual memory. He had brought an offering of grapes, figs, juniper berries and pine cones. Here Seti's soul could rest in peace, nourished by the subtle essences of the offerings.

It was here that Seti had first announced that Ramses would be his successor. At the time, the young prince had not understood the full import of his father's words. He moved in a dream, safe in his father's giant shadow, lost in admiration of a mind that moved like the divine barque through the celestial reaches.

When the Red Crown and the White Crown had been placed on his head, Ramses had left behind for ever the peaceful life of the heir to the throne, and had been thrust into a world whose harshness he had never suspected. On these temple walls, grave and smiling gods sanctified life. Within these walls, a pharaoh's eternal spirit honoured the gods and communed with the Invisible. On the outside were men. Humanity – courageous and craven, upright and hypocritical, generous and greedy. And caught in the middle of these opposing forces was Ramses, entrusted with maintaining the link between gods and men, no matter what his own desires and failings might be.

He had reigned for only a year, but he had long since ceased to live for himself.

When Ramses climbed into the chariot with Serramanna at the reins, the sun was low in the sky.

'Where to, Majesty?'

'The Valley of the Kings.'

'I had every boat in the fleet searched.'

'Anything suspicious?'

'Nothing.' The Sard was edgy.

'Is that really all you have to report, Serramanna?'

'It is, Majesty.'

'Are you sure?'

'To accuse someone without evidence is a serious offence.'

'Do you think you've identified the sorcerer?'

'What I think isn't important. Only facts count.'

'Let's get moving, then.'

The horses galloped towards the Valley, the entrance to which was guarded night and day. In the late summer afternoon, the rocky walls radiated heat absorbed during the day. It was stifling.

Dripping sweat and red with effort, the ranking officer of the guard detachment bowed to the pharaoh and assured him that no robbers would find their way into Seti's tomb.

Ramses directed the chariot not towards his father's final resting place, but to his own. Their working day finished, the stone-carvers were cleaning their tools and arranging them in their baskets. At the unexpected sight of the sovereign, a hush fell. The workmen huddled together behind their foreman, who was finishing his daily report.

'We've finished the corridor into the Chamber of Ma'at. May I show you, Majesty?'

'I'll go alone.'

Ramses went through the entrance to his tomb and descended a short flight of stairs carved into the rock, symbolizing the sun's nightly descent into the darkness. The walls of the corridor below were carved with vertical columns of hieroglyphs, prayers that a pharaoh, depicted as youthful for all eternity, was addressing to the power of light, whose secret names he was reciting. Next came the hours of darkness, the ordeal of the hidden chamber which the old sun must undergo before it could be reborn with the morning.

Passing through this realm of darkness, Ramses next encountered his likeness worshipping the gods, alive in the next world as they were on earth. Skilfully drawn, brightly painted, these images preserved the king's spirit through all eternity.

On the right was the chariot chamber with its four pillars. The shaft, bodywork, wheels and other parts of Ramses' ritual chariot would be stored here, that it might be reassembled in the other world and enable him to travel about as he did battle with the forces of darkness.

From here, the passage narrowed. The walls were decorated with scenes and texts relating to the ritual opening of the mouth and the eyes, carried out on the statue of the risen, transfigured king.

Then all was rock, rough-hewn by the stone-carvers' chisels. It would take them several more months to finish the Hall of Ma'at and the House of Gold where the sarcophagus would be laid to rest.

Ramses' death rose up before him, calm and mysterious. No word would be missing from the ritual texts, no scene from the tableau of the afterlife. The young king felt himself move beyond his earthly body, into a world whose laws were beyond any human understanding.

When the pharaoh emerged from his tomb, a peaceful night had fallen on the Valley of his ancestors.

45

The Second Prophet of Amon, Doki, hurried from the Temple of Amon to the royal palace. The king was here in Thebes and had summoned Karnak's highest officials. Stunted, with a shaven head, narrow face, pointed nose and jutting chin, Doki looked like a crocodile. He rushed on, cursing his idiot of a secretary. Knee-deep in livestock tallies, the fool had neglected to pass on the pharaoh's message. He'd be sent to a farm, far from the comfort of the temple offices.

Serramanna searched Doki and showed him to the pharaoh's audience chamber. Across from him, in a chair with arm-rests, sat old Nebu, the High Priest and First Prophet of Amon. Wizened and slouching, his bad leg propped on a cushion, Nebu sniffed a bottle of flower essences.

'Please forgive me, Majesty,' panted Doki. 'I'm only late because—'

'Don't fret, Doki. Where's the Third Prophet?'

'He's in charge of the rites of purification at the House of Life and wishes to remain in seclusion.'

'Very well. What about Bakhen, the Fourth Prophet?'

'He's at the Luxor worksite.'

'Surely he could take the afternoon off !'

'They're raising the obelisks, a delicate operation, I understand. If you want me to send to Luxor—'

'No matter. The High Priest is in satisfactory health, I hope?'

'No,' replied Nebu wearily. 'I can barely get around. Most of my time is spent in the archives. My predecessor didn't pay much attention to older rituals, and I hope to revive them.'

'And you, Doki? More concerned with affairs of this world?'

'Someone has to be! Bakhen and I run the temple and its estates – under the guidance of our revered leader, of course.'

'I may be lame, but there's nothing wrong with my eyesight,' barked Nebu. 'My young subordinates have come to understand that. The mission the king has given me will be carried out to the last detail. I'll tolerate no carelessness or laziness.'

The firmness in his voice startled Ramses. Weary as he might seem, Nebu was clearly in firm control.

'We rejoice in your visit, Majesty. It shows that the creation of your new capital doesn't mean you're abandoning Thebes.'

'That was never my intention, Nebu. What pharaoh worthy of the role would turn his back on the city of Amon, god of victories?'

'Then why stay away so long?' he asked, almost accusingly.

'It's not the High Priest of Amon's place to question government policy.'

'I agree completely, Majesty, but it *is* his place, I believe, to concern himself with the future of his temple.'

'Put your mind at ease, Nebu. The Hall of Pillars at Karnak has the biggest and most beautiful colonnade ever built, has it not?'

'And I give thanks to Your Majesty for it; but would you permit an old and unworldly man to inquire as to the true reason for your visit?'

Ramses smiled. 'Which of us is more impatient, Nebu?'

'You feel the fire of youth, I hear the call of heaven. I can't waste what little time I have left in idle chatter.'

The clash left Doki speechless. If Nebu continued to challenge the king like this, Ramses was bound to lose his temper.

'The royal family is in danger,' explained Ramses. 'I've come in search of stronger magic to protect us.'

'Why Thebes?' asked the High Priest.

'Because this is where I'll build my Temple of a Million Years.'

Nebu gripped his cane. 'Excellent. But first I suggest you increase your *ka*, the special power with which you are endowed.'

'How is that?'

'By finishing work on the temple at Luxor, where your *ka* is paramount.'

'Pleading the cause of your own temple, Nebu?'

'Under different circumstances, I might have done so, but not after what you've just told us. Luxor is Karnak's direct connection to divine power and might – the power you need in order to reign.'

'I'll make note of your advice, High Priest. For now, prepare to officiate at the ground-breaking of my Temple of a Million Years on the west bank of Thebes.'

To ease his feverish excitement, Doki downed several cups of strong beer. His hands shook and cold sweat ran down his back. He'd suffered so much injustice, but his luck was finally changing!

He was only Second Prophet of Amon, condemned to grow old in this subordinate position, yet he had just been entrusted with a state secret of the highest importance. Ramses had made a serious error of judgment, and if Doki played his cards right he might become High Priest after all.

The Temple of a Million Years – an unexpected opportunity, the solution he thought he'd never find. But he had to calm himself, move slowly and cautiously, not waste one precious second, know what to say and when to say nothing.

His position at Karnak would allow him to steal goods which he could then turn into money. It was simply a matter of removing a line here and there from the inventories. Since he was in charge of the scribes who kept the records, the risk was negligible.

Perhaps he was being too optimistic. Was he really capable of embezzlement on such a scale? The High Priest and the pharaoh were no fools. One unwise move and he'd be done for. Still, it was the chance of a lifetime. A pharaoh built only one Temple of a Million Years.

From Karnak to Luxor it was half an hour's walk down an avenue of sphinxes. Consulting the archives of the House of Life, where all the secrets of heaven and earth were stored, and reading the books of Thoth, Bakhen had drawn up a plan to enlarge Luxor according to Ramses' wishes. Thanks to Nebu's support, the work had proceeded at a rapid pace. A spacious courtyard adorned with statues of Ramses would be added on to the original temple of Amenhotep III. In front of the elegant pylon gateway, six colossal statues of the new pharaoh would guard the entry to this temple of *ka*, while two towering obelisks rose towards the heavens, warding off evil forces.

The richly coloured sandstone, of matchless beauty, the walls covered with electrum, the silver flooring, would combine to make Luxor the finest achievement of Ramses' reign. The poles with their banners affirming the presence of the gods would reach to the stars.

But the strange events of the last hour had plunged Bakhen into despair. An oversized barge hauling the first obelisk from the Aswan quarries was whirling madly in the middle of the Nile, trapped in an uncharted whirlpool. The captain, busy taking soundings from the bow to check for sandbanks, had seen the danger too late. Panic-stricken, the helmsman had lost his grip and fallen into the water. At that moment, one of the rudders broke. The other jammed and was useless.

The barge's chaotic movements had unbalanced the cargo. The shifting obelisk – two hundred tons of solid pink granite – had already snapped several of the ropes that secured it. Soon the rest would give way and the monolith would be flung into the river.

Bakhen clenched his fists and wept.

The accident would be the end of his career. He would and should be held responsible for the wreck, the loss of the obelisk, the deaths of several men. In his haste to see Luxor finished, he, Bakhen, had ordered the barge to sail north before the inundation, ignoring the danger to the crew. What had made him think he could defy the laws of nature?

The Fourth Prophet of Amon would gladly have given his life to undo this disaster. But the boat spun faster and faster, and ominous creakings showed that the hull could not last much longer. The obelisk was a work of art, complete except for the gilding on the pyramidion, to make it glitter in the sunlight. Now its splendour would vanish at the bottom of the river.

On the far shore, a man was gesticulating – a bewhiskered giant with sword and helmet. His shouts were lost in the whipping wind.

He was yelling at a swimmer, Bakhen realized, begging him to turn back. Instead, the man's rapid strokes brought him closer and closer to the spinning barge. At the risk of drowning in the current or being hit by an oar, the swimmer managed to reach the prow and pull himself along the hull, using a dangling rope.

Then he gripped the jammed rudder, struggling with both hands to free it. With a superhuman effort, braced against his heels, the muscles of his arms and chest popping, he dislodged the huge block of wood.

The boat righted itself and was still for a few seconds, parallel to the shore. Taking advantage of a favourable gust of wind, the helmsman steered it out of the whirlpool. Soon the oarsmen were able to help.

The moment the barge reached the shore dozens of stone-carvers and labourers ran up to unload the giant pillar.

The daring swimmer appeared at the top of the gangway, and Bakhen knew him at once. Ramses, King of Egypt, had risked his life to save the obelisk which would reach to heaven.

46

On six meals a day, Shaanar was getting fatter by the day. Whenever he lost all hope of winning the throne and finally taking revenge on Ramses, he ate. Food made him feel better, helped him forget about his brother's burgeoning new capital and flagrant popularity. Even Ahsha failed to raise his spirits, convincing as his arguments seemed. Power would take its toll on Ramses, he argued; the popularity of the first months of his reign would unravel, and his path would be strewn with obstacles . . . Yet Ahsha had nothing concrete to back up his claims. The Hittites were inactive, daunted by what they'd heard of the young monarch's miracles.

In short, things were going from bad to worse.

Shaanar was gnawing on a plump goose drumstick when his steward announced Meba, the former minister for Foreign Affairs.

'I don't want to see him.'

'He's insisting.'

'Send him away.'

'He claims he has important information concerning you.'

The former minister was not one to exaggerate; his entire career had been built on proceeding with caution.

'All right, then.'

Meba was the same as ever: a broad, reassuring face, a

self-important manner, a droning voice. A high government official who had felt he was set for life and could never understand the real reasons for his dismissal.

'Thank you for seeing me, Shaanar.'

'Always a pleasure, old friend. May I offer you anything to eat or drink?'

'Water would do very nicely.'

'Have you given up wine and beer?'

'Since I lost my job, I've suffered from dreadful headaches.'

'I'm so sorry to have benefited from this injustice to you. Perhaps in time I can find a place for you.'

'Ramses isn't the type to go back on his decisions. And look how far he's come in one short year!'

Shaanar bit into a goose wing.

'I was quite resigned,' the former diplomat admitted, 'until your sister, Dolora, introduced me to a most uncanny man.'

'Do I know him?'

'A Libyan named Ofir.'

'Never heard of the fellow.'

'He's in hiding.'

'Why is that?'

'Because he's protecting a girl by the name of Lita.'

'What sort of squalid story is this?'

'According to Ofir, Lita is a descendant of Akhenaton.'

'But all his descendants are dead!'

'And what if this claim is true?'

'Ramses would banish her on the spot.'

'Your sister has fallen in with them and other believers in Aton, the One God, who will expel all others. In Thebes there is quite an extensive membership.'

'I hope you're not joining! No good can come of this foolishness. Ramses belongs to the dynasty that put an end to Akhenaton's experiment.'

'I'm well aware of that and simply meeting Ofir made me nervous. But on reflection, I think he could be a valuable ally against Ramses.'

'A Libyan who lives in hiding?'

'Ofir has a certain advantage: he's a sorcerer.'

'There are hundreds in Egypt.'

'How many of them could endanger the lives of Nefertari and her baby daughter?'

'Whatever do you mean?'

'Dolora is convinced that Ofir is a wise man and that Lita is destined to be queen. Since she is relying on me to unite the followers of Aton, she tells me everything. Ofir is a master of black magic, determined to break through the royal couple's magical defences.'

'Are you quite certain?'

'Once you've seen him, you'll believe it. But that's not all, Shaanar. Have you given any thought to Moses?'

'No. Why Moses?'

'Akhenaton's beliefs are not that different from those of the Hebrews. I've heard rumours that the pharaoh's oldest friend is tormented by the idea of a single god, and that he's disenchanted with our civilization.'

Shaanar studied Meba attentively. 'What are you getting at?'

'I think you should encourage Ofir to practise his magic, and introduce him to Moses.'

'This girl, Akhenaton's heir, bothers me.'

'Me too, but never mind,' Meba countered. 'Let's convince Ofir that we believe in Aton and back his Lita. Once the sorcerer has undermined Ramses' health and recruited Moses, we'll get rid of the Libyan and his princess.'

'An interesting plan, old friend.'

'I'm counting on you to improve it.'

'What's in this for you?'

'I want my job back. Foreign Affairs was my life. I miss receiving ambassadors, hosting state banquets, holding secret talks with foreign dignitaries, nurturing relationships, setting traps, juggling protocol . . . It's hard to understand unless you've been part of it. When you become king, appoint me to my old position.'

'Your suggestions all deserve serious attention, Meba.'

The old diplomat beamed. 'If it's not too much trouble, I might take some of that wine you offered me. My headache is gone.'

Bakhen, the Fourth Prophet of Amon, prostrated himself before his pharaoh.

'I have no excuse to offer, Majesty. I take complete responsibility for this catastrophe.'

'What catastrophe?'

'The obelisk could have sunk, we almost lost the crew.'

'Your nightmares are foolish, Bakhen. Only reality counts.'

'That doesn't excuse my carelessness.'

'It's not like you, I agree. What were you thinking?'

'I wanted Luxor to be the jewel of your reign.'

'Did you think I'd settle for only one jewel? Rise, Bakhen.'

The former soldier was burly as ever. He looked more like an athlete than a holy man.

'You were fortunate, Bakhen, and I like the men around me to be lucky. There's magic in knowing how to stay out of harm's way.'

'If you hadn't been there . . .'

'You were even able to make Pharaoh appear! Nice trick – in fact, it's one for the royal annals.'

Bakhen was afraid some terrible punishment would be pronounced after these ironic remarks. Instead, Ramses turned his piercing gaze towards the barge. The gigantic pillar was being unloaded without further incident.

'It really is a splendid obelisk. When will the other one be ready?'

'By the end of September, I hope.'

'The hieroglyph-carvers had better get busy!'

'Aswan is hotter than here, and in the quarries—'

'Excuses, excuses! Go to Aswan yourself and see that the work's done on schedule. And what about the colossal statues?'

'The sculptors have found the perfect sandstone at Gebel el-Silsila.'

'Get them moving, too. Send someone today to make sure they're not wasting a minute. Why isn't the courtyard finished?'

'We're going as fast as we can, Majesty!'

'Wrong, Bakhen. When you're building a home for the pharaoh's *ka*, a resting-place for the force that continuously creates the universe, you can't behave like a humble foreman, quibbling over technique, unsure of your materials. Your mind has to meet the stone like a bolt of lightning for the temple to rise from the ground. You've been slow and lazy: that's your real mistake.'

Astonished, Bakhen was unable to protest.

'When Luxor is finished, my *ka* will prosper. I need its energy as soon as possible. Find more workmen – the best available.'

'Some of them were assigned to your House of Eternity in the Valley of the Kings.'

'Bring them back here. My tomb can wait. And there's another urgent matter for you to see to: the building of my Temple of a Million Years on the west bank. Its existence will guard the kingdom against many evils.'

'You're planning—'

'A colossal complex, a temple so powerful that its magic will repel adversity. We'll start on it tomorrow.'

'But there's Luxor, Majesty.'

'There's also Pi-Ramses, an entire new city. Call forth the sculptors from every province and weed out all but the best.'

'Majesty, there are only so many hours in a day!'

'Make time, Bakhen.'

47

Doki met the sculptor in a tavern in Thebes where neither of them was known. They sat in the darkest corner, near a noisy bunch of Libyan labourers.

'I got your message and here I am,' said the sculptor. 'Why all the mystery?'

Wearing a wig that came low on his forehead and covered his ears, Doki was unrecognizable.

'Have you mentioned this meeting to anyone?'

'No.'

'Not even your wife?'

'I'm single.'

'Your girlfriend, then?'

'I shan't see her until tomorrow night.'

'Give me back my letter.'

The sculptor handed the papyrus scroll to Doki, who tore it to shreds.

'In case we can't reach an agreement,' he explained, 'there should be no evidence that we were ever in contact.'

The sculptor, a broad-backed and forthright fellow, took a dim view of this.

'I've worked for Karnak before with no complaints, but no one ever made me sneak into a tavern and listen to mumbo-jumbo.'

'I'll get to the point, then. Would you like to be rich?'

'Who wouldn't?'

'I can offer you a quick way to make a fortune, but it does involve risk.'

'What kind of risk?'

'Before I tell you, we have to agree on something.'

'What is it?'

'If you turn me down, you get out of town for good.'

'And if I don't?'

'Perhaps we should leave it at that,' said Doki, rising.

'All right, I agree. Don't go.'

'Do you swear on the pharaoh's life and in the presence of the goddess of silence who strikes down oath-breakers?'

'I do.'

Giving one's word was a magic act, which, committed one's entire being. Breaking it caused a person's *ka* to flee, weakening the spirit.

'All I'm asking is for you to carve hieroglyphs on a stele,' Doki said.

'That's what I do for a living! Why all the mystery?'

'You'll see when the time comes.'

'About the payment . . .'

'Thirty dairy cows, a hundred sheep, ten fattened steers, a light boat, twenty pairs of sandals, furniture and a horse.'

The sculptor was stunned. 'All that for a simple stele?'

'Yes.'

'Only a fool would say no. You're on!' The two men shook hands. 'When do I start?'

'Tomorrow at dawn, on the west bank.'

Meba had invited Shaanar to a country villa belonging to one of his former staff. The two men arrived by different routes, two hours apart. Shaanar had thought it best not to inform Ahsha of the meeting.

'Your sorcerer is late,' complained Shaanar.

'He promised he'd be here.'

'I'm not used to waiting. If he doesn't show up soon . . .'

Ofir made his entrance, accompanied by Lita.

Shaanar's irritation vanished. He stared in fascination at this disturbing stranger. Gaunt, with high cheekbones, a hooked nose, and thin lips, the Libyan was like a vulture about to devour its prey. The girl had a blank, hangdog look about her.

'You do us great honour,' declared Ofir in a deep voice that sent a chill down Shaanar's spine. 'We hardly dared to hope for such a favour.'

'My friend Meba told me about you.'

'Aton will be grateful to him.'

'That's a name I wish you wouldn't mention.'

'I've devoted my life to pursuing Lita's claim to the throne. The fact that you're willing to meet me must mean that you agree with what I'm doing.'

'Quite right, Ofir, but aren't you ignoring one major obstacle – Ramses himself ?'

'On the contrary. The pharaoh is endowed with exceptional calibre and breadth of vision, a formidable adversary. Breaching his defences will be difficult. However, I have a few secret weapons.'

'If you're caught practising black magic, you face the death penalty.'

'Ramses and his dynasty have tried to wipe out the memory of Akhenaton. The fight between him and me will be to the finish.'

'Then it's no use preaching moderation.'

'No,' Ofir said firmly.

'I know my brother well. He's a stubborn, violent man, who will not tolerate any challenge to his authority. If he finds followers of the One God standing in his way, he'll crush them.'

'That's why we need to attack him from behind.'

'A good plan, but hard to execute.'

'My magic will eat away at him like acid.'

'What if we had an ally in his inner circle.'

The sorcerer's eyes narrowed to inscrutable slits, like a cat's.

Yes, thought Shaanar. I've hooked him.

'Who is it?'

'Moses. A boyhood friend of Ramses, a Hebrew he put in charge of building Pi-Ramses. If you can persuade him to help you, I'll join you, too.'

For the commanding general at the southern outpost of Elephantine, it was a good life. Since the raid that Seti had led a few years earlier, the Nubian provinces under Egyptian control were quiet as well as profitable.

The southern frontier of the Two Lands was well guarded. For decades, no Nubian tribe had dreamed of attacking or even protesting against the line of fortifications. Nubia belonged to Egypt for good. Tribal chieftains sent their sons north to be educated, and they returned as loyal subjects of the pharaoh, under the guidance of the Viceroy of Nubia, who was appointed by the king. Although the thought of living abroad was painful to Egyptians, the post was highly sought-after because of the considerable privileges attached to it.

Still, the general wouldn't want to trade places. Elephantine was tranquil, the climate was wonderful and, besides, he'd been born here. The garrison trained at dawn, then reported to the quarry, overseeing the docks where granite was loaded on to northbound barges. His fighting days were far behind him – the farther the better.

Since his appointment, the general had become a customs official. His men inspected shipments from the Far South and levied taxes on a sliding scale worked out by the Finance secretariat. His headquarters were cluttered with government documents, but he'd rather fight documents than a formidable band of Nubian warriors.

270

In a little while he'd take a fast boat down the Nile to check the fortifications from the river. He always enjoyed the soft breeze and feasting his eyes on the beauty of the lush banks and scenic cliffs. Smiling, he thought ahead to his dinner engagement with the young widow he was tenderly consoling.

A strange sound startled him: footsteps, running.

'Urgent message, sir,' panted his orderly.

'Where is it from?'

'Desert patrol in Nubia, sir.'

'The gold mines?'

'Yes, sir.'

'What did the courier say?'

'That it's very serious.'

In other words, the scroll couldn't be tossed into a chest and forgotten. He broke the seal, unrolled it and skimmed it with growing alarm.

'It's a fake. A joke!'

'No, sir. You can talk to the messenger.'

'Attack,' he read, incredulously. 'Nubian rebels have attacked a convoy carrying gold to Egypt!'

48

The new moon had just risen.

Bare-chested, Ramses wore a wig and kilt in the style of those worn by the pharaohs of the Old Kingdom. The queen was dressed in a long, close-fitting white dress. In place of a crown, she wore the seven-pointed star of the goddess Sechat, whom she represented in the evening's ritual. The cornerstone of the pharaoh's Temple of a Million Years, was being laid.

Ramses thought of the time he had spent in the quarries of Gebel el-Silsila, working with mallet and chisel alongside the stone-cutters. He had wanted to stay there, but his father had woken him from that dream.

Twenty ritualists from the temple of Karnak assisted the royal couple, with three of the Four Prophets presiding: Nebu, Doki and Bakhen. The next day two architects would descend on the site with their work gangs.

The complex would be vast – twelve acres, Ramses had decreed. Room for the temple itself, as well as numerous annexes, including a library, storerooms and a garden. This holy city, economically self-sufficient, would be dedicated to the supernatural power present within the pharaoh.

Stunned by the scope of the project, Bakhen refused to dwell on what lay ahead, focusing his attention on the rites performed by the king and queen. After marking the symbolic corners of the future temple, they pounded in stakes and stretched a cord around them, invoking the memory of Imhotep, father of architecture, builder of the first pyramid and exemplar of architects.

Then Pharaoh dug a section of the foundation with a hoe and laid down small bars of gold and silver, amulets and miniature tools, which he covered with sand. With a sure hand, he laid the first cornerstone with a lever, then moulded a brick. His act of creation would make the temple, its floors, walls and ceilings rise fast. Next came the ritual purification: Ramses walked round the temple site scattering incense, whose hieroglyphic name, *sonter*, meant 'That Which Makes Divine'.

Bakhen held up a wooden model of the monumental entrance. In blessing it, the king opened the mouth of his Temple of a Million Years, bringing it to life. Henceforth the Word was in it. Ramses struck the door twelve times with the white club called 'She Who Illuminates', summoning the gods. He lit a lamp, showing the way to the inner sanctuary where the Invisible would reside.

He concluded with the ancient words affirming that this temple was built not for him but for his true master, the Rule – the beginning and end of every temple in Egypt.

Bakhen had the sensation that he was witnessing a miracle. What had happened here, before the eyes of a privileged few, was beyond human understanding. In this empty space, which already belonged to the gods, the power of Ramses' *ka* was beginning to manifest itself.

'The foundation stele is ready,' declared Doki.

'Let it be embedded,' ordered the king.

The sculptor Doki had hired appeared with a small stone tablet covered with hieroglyphs. The text consecrated for ever the site of the temple. The magical symbols transformed the earth into heaven.

Setau came forward, holding a blank papyrus and a flask

of fresh ink. Doki jumped. This rough-looking character had been given no role in the ceremony!

Setau wrote on the papyrus, in horizontal lines from right to left, then read his text aloud.

'May any living mouth be sealed which would speak ill of the pharaoh or so intend, either night or day. May this Temple of a Million Years be the magical haven protecting the royal person and shielding him from evil.'

Doki was sweating profusely. No one had mentioned this magical incantation. Fortunately, it would not affect the working-out of his plan.

Setau rolled up the papyrus and presented the scroll to Ramses. The king affixed his seal to it and placed it at the foot of the stele, where it would be buried. By letting his gaze rest on the hieroglyphs, the king would bring them into existence.

He whirled round. 'Who carved these hieroglyphs?'

The sculptor stepped forward. 'I did, Majesty.'

'Who gave you the text to inscribe on the tablet?'

'The High Priest of Amon himself, Majesty.'

The man prostrated himself, partly out of respect and partly to avoid Ramses' rising fury. The traditional inscription for the foundation of a Temple of a Million Years had been modified and distorted, destroying its protective powers.

Nebu! The High Priest must be in league with the forces of darkness. He'd sold out to Ramses' enemies. The pharaoh felt like smashing the old man's head with the ceremonial mallet. But then a strange force seemed to emanate from the newly consecrated ground, a wave of soothing warmth rising up his spine, the 'tree of life'. A door opened within his heart. Violence was not the answer. Out of the corner of his eye, he saw Nebu make a gesture that confirmed his opinion.

'Rise, sculptor.'

The man obeyed.

'Now go to the High Priest and bring him to me.'

Doki gloated. His plan was working perfectly. The old man's protests would be ineffectual, the punishment merciless, and the office of High Priest vacant. This time, the king would call on a man who knew how to run Karnak. He, Doki, was that man.

The sculptor was well rehearsed. He stopped in front of an old man who held a gilded staff in his right hand and wore a golden ring on his middle finger, the two symbols associated with the High Priest of Amon.

'You're sure that's the man who gave you the text for the stele?'

'I am.'

'Then you're a liar.'

'No, Majesty! I swear it was the High Priest in person who —'

'Sculptor, you've never laid eyes on him.'

Nebu retrieved his cane and staff from the elderly ritualist to whom he had handed them when the sculptor, who had turned away from him, began to make his accusation.

Frantic, the sculptor began to cry out, 'Doki! Where are you, Doki? Help me! It wasn't my idea! You were the one who told me to say the High Priest of Amon wanted to destroy the temple's magic!'

Doki made a run for it.

The sculptor went after him, blind with rage, fists flying.

Doki succumbed to his injuries. The sculptor, accused of a crime of blood, debasing hieroglyphs, bribe-taking and perjury, would appear before the vizier's tribunal and be sentenced either to death by suicide or else to forced labour in a remote desert prison.

The day after the incident, at sunset, Ramses embedded the correctly reworded commemorative stele with his own hands.

The foundation was complete. The Temple of a Million Years was born.

'Did you suspect Doki?' Ramses asked Nebu.

'It's human nature,' replied the High Priest. 'Satisfaction with one's lot in life is the exception, unfortunately, not the rule. As the sages so aptly put it, envy is a fatal disease, which no physician can cure.'

'We'll have to find another Second Prophet.'

'Are you thinking of Bakhen, Majesty?'

'Of course.'

'I won't oppose your decision, but I'm not sure it's time yet. You've put Bakhen in charge of both the renovations at Luxor and the construction of your Temple of a Million Years, and that was wise of you. He's worthy of your trust in him. But don't overburden him, don't pull him in too many directions at once. When the time is right, he can move up through the hierarchy.'

'What do you suggest?'

'Replace Doki with an old man like me, preoccupied with meditation and priestly duties. That way the Temple of Amon at Karnak will no longer be a source of worry for you.'

'Good idea. You can choose him yourself. Have you taken a look at the plans for the temple?'

'My life has been a long and happy one, with only one regret: that I won't live long enough to see your temple finished.'

'Who knows, Nebu?'

'My bones ache, Majesty, my eyes are growing dim, I'm hard of hearing and I have trouble staying awake these days. The end is near – I can feel it.'

'I thought sages lived to be a hundred and ten.'

'I've been blessed in my life. I don't mind if death wants to take me and share my good fortune with others.'

'You see pretty clearly, I'd say. If you hadn't handed

your staff and your ring to the ritualist, what would have happened?'

'Needless to speculate, Majesty. The Rule of Ma'at protected us.'

Ramses looked out over the expanse where his Temple of a Million Years would be built.

'I see a magnificent building, Nebu, a temple of granite, sandstone and basalt. The pylons will reach to the sky. The doors will be gilded bronze. Trees will shade pools of pure water. The granaries will be full of wheat, the treasury full of gold and silver, precious stones and rare vases. Living statues will fill the courtyards and shrines. A rampart will protect all these wonders. At sunrise and sunset, the two of us will go up to the roof terrace and survey this slice of eternity. Three spirits will live for ever in this temple: my father's, my mother's and my wife Nefertari's.'

'You're forgetting the fourth one, which should be the first: yourself, Ramses.'

The Great Royal Wife approached the king, carrying an acacia seedling.

Ramses knelt and planted the seedling, and Nefertari watered it carefully.

'Take care of this tree for us, Nebu. It will grow with my temple. Let us pray that the gods let me come to rest one day in its kindly shade, forgetting the world of men. That the Lady of the West will show herself in its leafy branches, then bend down and take me by the hand.'

49

Moses stretched out on his sycamore bed.

It had been an exhausting day. Fifty minor incidents, two slight injuries at the palace worksite, rations delivered late to the third barracks site, a thousand reject bricks to destroy. Nothing out of the ordinary, just an accumulation of headaches that slowly wore him down.

The old questions began to plague him. Building this new capital was a joy, but wasn't raising temples to several different divinities, including the evil Set, an offence to the One God? His work on Pi-Ramses meant contributing to the greater glory of a pharaoh who was perpetuating the old ways.

In a corner of the room, near the window, someone moved.

'Who's there?'

'A friend.'

A gaunt figure with a hawklike face stepped out of the shadows and moved through the flickering lamplight.

'Ofir!'

'I need to talk to you.'

Moses sat up. 'I'm tired and I want to sleep. Come and see me on the site tomorrow. I'll try to find time for you.'

'I'm in danger, my friend.

'Why?'

'You know why! Because I believe in the One God, the saviour of humanity. The god your people worship in secret, the god who will one day reign supreme, destroying false idols. And his conquest must begin with Egypt.'

'Are you forgetting that Ramses is the pharaoh?'

'Ramses is a tyrant, obsessed with his own power. He cares nothing for religion.'

'You'd better not discount his power. Ramses is my friend, and I'm building his capital.'

'I respect your loyalty, but you're being torn in two, Moses, and you know it. In your heart, you reject this pharaoh's supremacy and long for the rule of the One True God.'

'You're raving, Ofir.'

The Libyan stared hard into his eyes. 'Be honest, Moses. Stop lying to yourself.'

'Do you think you know me better than I know myself?'

'Why not? We reject the same errors and share the same ideal. If we join forces, we can transform this country and the future of its inhabitants. Like it or not, Moses, you've become the leader of the Hebrews. With you in charge, the faction fighting has ceased. Without you realizing it, they've become a people.'

'The Hebrews are subject to Pharaoh's authority, not mine.'

'That tyranny! I reject it, and so do you.'

'You're wrong. I know my place.'

'Your place is at the head of your people, guiding them towards the truth. Mine is to place Lita, the legitimate heir of Akhenaton, on the throne and reinstate the supremacy of the One True God.'

'Stop your ranting, Ofir. Inciting a revolt against Pharaoh will only lead to disaster.'

'Do you know of any other means to our end? Or don't you think the truth is worth fighting for?'

'You and Lita . . . Two lunatics! It's laughable.'

'It's not just the two of us any more.'

Moses raised an eyebrow. 'No?'

'Since the last time we met,' Ofir informed him, 'the situation has changed considerably. The movement is larger and far more determined than you imagine. Ramses' power is nothing but an illusion, which will lead him into a trap of his own making. A good part of the country's elite will follow us once you blaze the trail, Moses.'

'But why me?'

'Because you have the ability to guide us, and to become leader of the movement when the time is ripe. Lita must remain in the background until it's time for her to take the throne. I'm the keeper of the flame, not a man of influence. We need your voice to make our ideas heard.'

'Who are you really, Ofir?'

'A simple believer, like Akhenaton, convinced that the One God will rule all nations, once proud Egypt bends to his will.'

Moses knew he should have shown this madman the door long since, but . . . What he said was compelling. Ofir gave voice to Moses' own repressed and highly subversive thoughts.

'Your plan is crazy. You have no chance of succeeding.'

'Time is on our side,' Ofir reassured him. 'Take charge of the Hebrews, give them a country, let them acknowledge the supreme being. Lita will govern Egypt and we'll be your ally. Our alliance will foster the truth that will sweep the world.'

'It's only a dream.'

'I'm no dreamer, and neither are you.'

'Ramses is my friend, I tell you, and he rules with an iron fist.'

'No, Moses, he's not your friend but your worst enemy – the man who wants to snuff out the truth.'

'Get out, Ofir.'

'Think over what I've said and prepare for action. We'll meet again soon.'

'Don't count on it.'

'I'll be seeing you, Moses.'

The Hebrew spent a sleepless night. Ofir's words swept through his mind like a wave, washing away all his fears and objections.

Whether or not he was ready to admit it, this meeting was what he'd been waiting for.

Side by side, the pharaoh's dog and pet lion were licking chicken carcasses clean as Ramses and Nefertari sat entwined beneath a palm tree, admiring the scenery. With some difficulty, the king had persuaded Serramanna to let them leave Thebes for a day in the country, taking Invincible and Wideawake as bodyguards.

The news from Memphis was excellent. Little Meritamon was thriving on her wet-nurse's milk. Her brother Kha flourished under Nedjem's watchful eye. Iset the Fair had been delighted to learn of the princess' safe birth and sent warm congratulations to Nefertari.

The late-evening sun shone gold on Nefertari's silken skin. A flute tune drifted through the soft air. Cowherds sang as they rounded up their cattle; heavily laden donkeys lumbered homeward. In the west, the sun glowed orange, while above Thebes the Peak turned red.

The hard day gave way to the tender night. How beautiful Egypt was, resplendent in her golds and greens, the silver of the Nile and the blaze of sunset. How beautiful Nefertari was, in her sheer linen dress. An intoxicating scent wafted from her recumbent body. Her expression was grave and peaceful, a noble window on her luminous soul.

'Am I worthy of you?' asked Ramses.

'What a strange question.'

'Sometimes you seem so far from this world and its vileness, from the court and its pettiness, from all the temporal duties we have to carry out.'

'Have I failed in my duties?'

'Quite the contrary: you do everything perfectly, as if you'd been a queen all your life. I love you and admire you, Nefertari.'

Their lips met, warm and vibrant.

'I'd made up my mind not to marry,' she confessed, 'and to live secluded in a temple. It wasn't that I didn't like men, but they all seemed driven by ambition which in the end made them small and weak. But you were beyond ambition, for fate had chosen your path in life. I admire you and love you, Ramses.'

They both knew that they thought as one and that nothing would ever come between them. Conceiving the plan for the Temple of a Million Years had been their first magical act as royal couple, the source of an adventure that only death would end, and then only outwardly.

'But I'll have to keep reminding you of your duty,' she added.

'Which one?'

'To have sons.'

'I already have one.'

'You need more. If your life is long, you may outlive some of them.'

'Why couldn't our daughter succeed me?'

'According to the astrologers, her nature will have a contemplative bent, just like Kha's.'

'That might be a good attribute in a ruler.'

'Depending on circumstances. Tonight our country is perfectly serene, but what will tomorrow bring?'

The sound of a galloping horse shattered the quiet. Serramanna leaped to the ground in a cloud of dust.

'Forgive the disturbance, Majesty. Emergency dispatch.'

Ramses skimmed the papyrus the Sard handed him.

'A report from the commander at Elephantine,' he explained to the queen. 'Nubian rebels have attacked a convoy carrying gold for our principal temples.'

'Any dead?'

'More than twenty, and there are injured.'

'Was it just robbery or the start of an uprising?'

'No one knows yet.'

Shaken, Ramses began to pace. The lion and dog, sensing their master's mood, came and licked his hands.

The king said the words the Great Royal Wife had been dreading: 'I'll leave at once. Pharaoh must set his house in order. In my absence, Nefertari, you will govern Egypt.'

50

Pharaoh's war fleet was made up of roughly twenty boats. Their hulls were crescent-shaped, with bow and stern curving upward from the water. A large sail was rigged on the single sturdy mast. In the centre was a huge cabin for crew and troops. The smaller forward cabin housed the captain.

Aboard the flagship, Ramses had personally checked the port and starboard rudders. A covered pen had been built for his pets. The dog snuggled up between the lion's front paws; both were replete from their daily feed.

As on his previous voyage, Ramses was fascinated by the barren, green-flecked hills, the bright blue sky and the thin band of lush growth the river carved through the desert. It was a land of fire, unforgiving and yet beyond all conflict, like his soul.

Swallows, crested cranes and pink flamingoes flew over the fleet, while high in the palm trees baboons whooped at their passage. The soldiers spent their time gambling, drinking palm wine and dozing in shady corners, as if they were on a pleasure cruise.

Their arrival in the land of Kush, beyond the Second Cataract, was a rude awakening. The boats moored alongside a dreary shore, and the men disembarked in silence. After pitching their tents on the desolate shore and building a palisade, they awaited Pharaoh's orders.

The Temple of a Million Years

A few hours later, the Viceroy of Nubia and his military escort reported to the monarch, who was seated on his travelling throne of gilded cedar.

'What have you to say for yourself?' asked Ramses.

'We have the situation well in hand, Majesty.'

'I asked for an explanation.'

The Viceroy of Nubia had grown very stout. He mopped at his brow with a white cloth. 'A deplorable incident, to be sure, but we mustn't blow things out of proportion.'

'An entire shipment of gold lost, soldiers and miners slaughtered – doesn't that justify the presence of Pharaoh and an armed force?'

'The message that was sent to you may have been somewhat alarmist, but of course we rejoice that Your Majesty has come.'

'My father pacified Nubia and entrusted you with preserving the peace. Now your laxness and dawdling have compromised it once again.'

'It was fate, Majesty, fate!'

'You're the Viceroy of Nubia, royal standard-bearer, superintendent of the southern desert region, head of a royal cavalry division, and you dare speak to me of fate! You are presumptuous!'

'My performance has been flawless, I can assure you, Majesty. But it's too big a job for one man: meeting village mayors, making sure the granaries are stocked, checking the—'

'What about gold production?'

'Mining and shipping are under my close supervision, Majesty.'

'Is that why you let the convoy go unescorted?'

'How could I know that a handful of madmen was on the loose?'

'I thought that was part of your job.'

'Majesty, fate—'

'Take me to the scene of the attack.'

'It's on the gold route, a barren and lonely spot. It won't tell you anything.'

'Who are these rebels?'

'Some miserable tribe. They probably primed themselves with drink.'

'Have you searched for them?'

'Nubia is a very large province, Majesty, and my troop levels have been cut.'

'In other words, no serious investigation has been attempted.'

'Only Your Majesty could order a military sweep.'

'That's all, Viceroy.'

'Shall I help Your Majesty hunt down the rebels?'

'Just tell me the truth: is Nubia prepared to rise up in support of them?'

'Well, it's unlikely, but—'

'Is a rebellion already under way, then?'

'No, Majesty, but there does seem to be some unrest. That's why we were hoping you'd come to help us.'

'Drink up,' Setau told Ramses.

'Can't I get along without it?'

'Yes, but I'd rather err on the side of caution. Serramanna can't guard you from snakes.'

The king drank the dangerous brew made from nettle extracts and diluted cobra blood. Setau gave him regular doses to build up his immunity to snakebite. At least he could eliminate one risk along the gold route.

'Thanks for bringing us along. I love it here, and Lotus is glad to be home. Just imagine the specimens we'll find!'

'It's no holiday, Setau. Nubian warriors have earned their fierce reputation.'

'Why not let the poor devils have their gold, and things will quieten down?'

'They committed robbery and murder. No one can flout the rule of Ma'at with impunity.'

'Nothing can change your mind, I suppose.'

'No, nothing.'

'Have you considered your personal safety?'

'This mission isn't one I can delegate.'

'Tell your men to take special care. Snakes are especially venomous at this time of year. Use asafedita: the odour of the gum resin will repel some reptiles. If anyone is bitten, send for me at once. Lotus and I will be sleeping in our wagon.'

The expeditionary force marched along the rocky trail, led by a scout. Next came Serramanna and Ramses on sure-footed horses, then oxen pulling wagons, donkeys laden with weapons and water gourds, and finally the foot-soldiers.

The Nubian scout was convinced that the rebels were still close by the site of the attack. Nearby was an oasis, the perfect place to stash their booty until they attempted to trade it.

According to the map supplied by the Viceroy, the gold route was studded with wells, and reports from the Nubian mines had indicated no recent problem with the water supply. They could advance without fear through the heart of the desert.

The scout was surprised to encounter a decomposing donkey. Usually the convoy leaders selected only the healthiest animals for their long marches.

As they neared the first well, the men's spirits rose. To quench their thirst, refill their gourds, sleep in the shade of their cloth shelters . . . From the officers down, every soldier was looking forward to the same prospect. Since night would fall in three hours or less, the king would certainly make camp here.

When the scout reached the well, his blood ran cold despite the heat. He ran back to Ramses.

'Majesty! The well is dry.'

The troops did not have enough water to go back the way they had come. The only option was to march forward, in hope of making it to the next well. But since the provincial government's information had proved unreliable, the next well might be just as dry.

'We could leave the main road,' suggested the scout, 'and branch out to the right towards the rebels' oasis. Between here and there is a well they must use on their raids.'

'Rest until dusk,' ordered Ramses. 'Then we'll continue.'

'A night march is dangerous, Majesty! Snakes, the potential for ambush—'

'We have no choice.'

Ramses was reminded of an earlier expedition, with his father. Their soldiers had faced a similar situation – local insurgents had poisoned the wells. In his heart of hearts, he admitted that this time he'd underestimated the danger. He knew from experience that a simple mission to restore order could end in disaster.

The king addressed his men and told them the truth. They were worried, but the more experienced soldiers kept morale high. Pharaoh was their leader, and Pharaoh was a miracle-worker, they told their comrades.

Despite the risks, the foot-soldiers enjoyed the night march. The rearguard, more alert than ever, would counter surprise attacks. In front, the scout advanced cautiously. Thanks to the full moon, he could see far into the distance.

Ramses thought of Nefertari. If he failed to return, the burden of ruling Egypt would fall on her. Kha and Meritamon were too young to take the throne. Faction fighting would resume, more desperate than ever for having been temporarily quelled.

Suddenly Serramanna's horse reared, throwing him to the rocky ground. Half-stunned, he rolled down a sandy slope and came to rest in a crater not visible from the trail.

A curious sound, like heavy breathing, caught his attention.

Just in front of him, a viper rasped, threatening and ready to strike.

Serramanna had lost his sword in the fall. Unarmed, all he could do was back away, avoiding any sudden movements. But the hissing viper, slithering sideways, blocked his path.

He tried to stand, but an excruciating pain in his right ankle stopped him. Unable to run, he'd be easy prey.

'Get away from me, snake! I promised I'd die by the sword!'

The viper inched closer. Serramanna threw sand in its face, making it even more furious. Just as it was about to strike at him, a forked stick pinned it to the ground.

'Nice shot!' Setau said admiringly. 'Only one chance in ten I'd make it.' He grabbed the snake by the neck; its tail thrashed wildly.

'What a beauty. Light blue, dark blue and green — a lovely specimen, don't you agree? Luckily for you, the hissing carries and it's pretty easy to recognize.'

'I suppose I should thank you.'

'Its bite causes local swelling. Then the whole limb is affected and begins to haemorrhage. That's all. Only a small amount of venom, but very toxic. With a strong heart, you might survive it. Honestly, this snake isn't half as dangerous as it looks.'

51

Setau plastered Serramanna's sprained ankle with herbs, then applied linen dressings soaked in salve to reduce the swelling. In a few hours, it would be fine. Ever suspicious, the Sard wondered if the snake-charmer might not have masterminded the whole incident to make himself look like a hero, and to convince Serramanna that he was innocent of any wrongdoing and a true friend to Ramses. However, Setau had made no attempt to capitalize on the rescue, which was a point in his favour.

At dawn, they stopped to rest until mid-afternoon. Then the march resumed. There was still enough water for man and beast, but soon it would have to be rationed. Despite the men's fatigue and anxiety, Ramses stepped up the pace and exhorted the rearguard not to relax their vigilance. The insurgents would never attack head-on: they would try for the advantage of surprise.

In the ranks, there was no more joking or talk of home. In time, the men fell silent.

'There it is,' announced the scout, pointing.

Puny weeds, a circle of parched stones, a wooden frame to hold the weight of a large water-skin hanging from a frayed rope: the well. Their only hope of survival.

The scout and Serramanna ran forward. They peered down for a long moment, then slowly straightened.

The Sard shook his head. 'The place has been dry for ages. We're all going to die of thirst. No one's been able to find a permanent water source. We'll have to fill our skins in the great beyond.'

Ramses called the men together and told them that the situation was serious. By the next day, their water would be gone. They could neither advance nor retreat.

Several soldiers threw down their weapons.

'Pick those up,' ordered Ramses.

'What's the use,' asked an officer, 'if we're going to die of thirst?'

'We've come here to re-establish order, and we won't leave until we've done so.'

'How can our dead bodies fight the Nubians?'

'My father once found himself in a similar situation,' said Ramses, 'and he saved his men.'

'Then you save us, too.'

'Take shelter from the sun and water the animals.'

The king turned his back on his army and faced the desert.

Setau came to join him. 'What do you plan to do?'

'Walk until I find water.'

'That's crazy.'

'I have to do as my father taught me.'

'Stay here with us.'

'A pharaoh doesn't simply give up and wait for death.'

Serramanna approached them. 'Majesty . . .'

'Don't let the men panic, and keep up the watch, day and night. They must remember they're under threat of attack.'

'I can't let you go off alone into this desert. As your head of security—'

Ramses put his hand on the Sard's shoulder. 'Keep my army safe for me.'

'Hurry back. Your troops need a general.'

As the foot-soldiers looked on in horror, the king walked

away from the dried-up well and into the red desert towards a rocky promontory. He scaled it easily, and surveyed the desolate scene from the top.

Like his father, he needed to probe the earth's hidden secrets, find the veins of water that sprang from the ocean of energy, flowed through the rocks, and filled the heart of the mountains. Ramses' solar plexus ached, his vision was blurred, his body burned as if consumed with fever.

He took the divining-rod tied to the sash of his kilt, the same wand his father had used to see into the earth. Its magic, he knew, would still work, but where should he search in all this sand?

A voice spoke within the king's body, a voice from the beyond, a voice as ringing as Seti's. The pain in his solar plexus forced him to move, to climb down from the promontory. He no longer felt the heat that had killed many a traveller. His heartbeat slowed like an oryx's.

The sand and rocks changed shape and colour. Ramses' gaze gradually penetrated deep into the desert sand; his fingers gripped the two pliable acacia branches bound together at the tip with linen thread.

The rod quivered, paused, went dead. He walked on and the voice grew more distant. He retraced his steps, going left, the direction of death. The voice became louder again and the rod twitched. Ramses bumped into a huge pink granite boulder, lost in the sea of stone.

The force from the earth tore the rod out of his hands.

He had found water.

Parched, sunburned and with aching muscles, the soldiers rolled the boulder away and dug where the king told them. Thirty cubits down, they hit a huge pool of water. Their cheers reached the sky.

Ramses had them sink a series of wells, linked by an underground gallery, a technique he had picked up from miners. In this way, he could not only save his army, but provide for future irrigation over a wide area.

'Are you imagining gardens already?' asked Setau.

'Fertility and prosperity are the best footprints we could leave,' answered the king.

'I thought we were here to put down an insurrection,' protested Serramanna.

'We are.'

'Then why are your soldiers digging ditches?'

'It's often part of their mission, according to our custom.'

'Pirates don't try to be fishermen,' he sniffed. 'If we're attacked, will we be able to defend ourselves?'

'I thought I put you in charge of our security.'

While the soldiers completed the wells and gallery, Setau and Lotus were busy trapping snakes, outstanding in both variety and size. They milked a quantity of priceless venom.

Serramanna uneasily stepped up the scheduled watches and also instituted barracks-style training. The men seemed to have forgotten about the stolen gold and the rebel threat. Their pharaoh worked wonders, and soon he'd be leading them home.

Amateurs, thought the ex-pirate. These Egyptian soldiers were temporary recruits who soon reverted to the labourers or peasants they really were. They had never experienced the heat, blood, and death of combat. There was no better training for war than being a pirate, always on the alert and ready to dispatch any enemy with any weapon. Discouraged, Serramanna hadn't even tried to teach the men about vicious attacks and surprise defences. These 'foot-soldiers' would never learn to fight.

Yet he had the feeling that the Nubian rebels were not far off and for the past two days or more had been sneaking up on the Egyptian camp, spying. Ramses's lion and dog also sensed a hostile presence. They grew agitated, slept less and prowled around sniffing the air.

If the Nubians were anything like some of the pirates Serramanna had known, the Egyptian forces were doomed.

The new capital of Egypt was going up at an astonishing rate, but Moses no longer saw it. To him, Pi-Ramses was now a foreign place, full of false gods and men deluded into meaningless beliefs.

Faithful to his promise, he kept the work moving along. Yet everyone noticed how short his temper was becoming, especially when he dealt with the Egyptian foremen; his complaints about their strictness were usually unfounded. He spent more and more time with his Hebrew brethren, discussing their people's future with small groups of men each evening. Many were satisfied with their life in Egypt and felt no urge to go in search of an independent homeland. The risk seemed too great.

Moses persisted, stressing their faith in a single god, their unique culture, the need to throw off the Egyptian yoke and reject false idols. He changed a few minds, but many more remained closed to him. Still, Moses was recognized as a leader who had done them a world of good. No one took his opinion lightly.

Ramses' old friend was sleeping less and less. His waking dream was of a fertile land where the god he cherished would reign supreme, a land the Hebrews would govern on their own, defending its borders as their most prized possession.

At last he understood the nature of the fire that had been consuming his soul for so many years. He could name this unquenchable desire; he could see the truth and lead his people towards it. He knew, and was filled with dread. Would Ramses accept such a defection, such a challenge to his power? Moses would have to convince him, make him see the light.

Memories flooded his mind. Ramses was far more than an old playmate. He was a true friend, who burned with a different version of the fire that consumed Moses. He would never betray Ramses by plotting against him. He would meet him face to face and win him over. No matter how impossible that might seem, Moses was confident.

For God was with him.

52

The Nubian rebels had half-shaved heads, hoop earrings, broad noses, ritual scars on their cheeks, beaded necklaces and panther-skin loincloths. They encircled the Egyptian encampment while most of Ramses' soldiers dozed in the afternoon heat. Their huge acacia bows launched a number of successful hits before the Egyptians could muster a response.

What kept the rebel chief from giving the order to attack was the sight of a small band of men, also armed with sturdy bows, behind a palisade of shields and palm fronds. In the lead was Serramanna, who had been expecting them. His hand-picked archers would have a clear shot into the Nubian ranks, as the Nubian chief could see. The advantage was his, but even so . . .

Time stood still. No one moved a muscle.

The rebel chief's main adviser urged him to start shooting and bring down as many of the enemy as possible, while a few fleet-footed warriors stormed the palisade. But the chief had been in a battle or two, and didn't like the look of Serramanna. The bewhiskered giant might well have a trick or two up his sleeve. He didn't look like the Egyptians they'd killed. The chief's hunter's instincts warned him to be careful.

When Ramses emerged from his tent, all eyes were

upon him. In a close-fitting blue crown which flared out at the back, a short-sleeved, pleated linen tunic and gold-trimmed kilt with a wild bull's tail dangling from the sash, the pharaoh held in his right hand the sceptre 'Magre', shaped like a shepherd's crook. He clutched the end of it to his chest.

Behind him came Setau, bearing the king's white sandals. He thought of Ahmeni, the king's official sandal-bearer, and almost smiled despite the tenseness of the situation. How amazed their friend would be to see Setau decked out in wig and white loincloth, clean-shaven, exactly like a seasoned courtier except for the odd-looking sack suspended from his waist and hanging down behind him.

As the Egyptian soldiers looked on nervously, Pharaoh and Setau walked to the edge of the camp, stopping less than a hundred paces from the Nubians.

'I am Ramses, Pharaoh of Egypt. Who is your chief?'

'I am,' said the Nubian, stepping forward.

Two feathers stuck in his red headband, muscles bulging, the rebel chief held a light spear trimmed with ostrich plumes.

'If you're not a coward, come here.'

The chief's adviser made a sign of disapproval. But neither Ramses nor his sandal-bearer was armed, while he had his spear and his adviser carried a double-edged dagger. The chief glanced over at Serramanna.

'Stay on my left,' he ordered his adviser. If the bewhiskered giant gave the order to shoot, the chief would be protected by a human shield.

'Are you afraid?' asked Ramses.

The two Nubians broke away from the war party and walked towards the king and his sandal-bearer, coming to a halt only ten paces in front of them.

'So you're the pharaoh who oppresses my people.'

'Nubians and Egyptians live in peace. You broke that

peace when you killed the members of the convoy and stole the gold being shipped to our temples.'

'The gold is ours, not yours. You're the one who's a thief.'

'Nubia is an Egyptian province, subject to the Rule of Ma'at. Murder and robbery must be severely punished.'

'Your laws mean nothing to me, Pharaoh. I make my own. Other tribes are prepared to join us. Killing you will make me a hero! Every warrior in Nubia will be at my command, and we'll rid our country of Egyptians once and for all!'

'Kneel down,' ordered the king.

The chief and his adviser looked at each other, bewildered.

'Lay down your arms, kneel, and submit to the Rule.'

The chief grimaced at him. 'If I bow to you, will you grant me your pardon?'

'You've placed yourself outside the Rule. To pardon you would also go against it.'

'You show me no mercy.'

'I know none.'

'Why should I bow to you?'

'Because it's the only freedom permitted you as a rebel.'

The adviser jumped in front of his chief, waving his dagger. 'Let Pharaoh's death set us free, then!'

Setau, who hadn't taken his eyes off the two men, opened the sack at his waist and released a sand viper. Slithering across the sand with deadly speed, it bit the Nubian's foot before he could spear it.

Crying out, he bent over to slash the bite with his dagger and let out the poison.

'He's already colder than water and hotter than flame,' intoned Setau, looking the chief straight in the eye. 'He's sweating, his eyes are glazing over, he's starting to drool. Now his eyes and eyelids are stiffening, his face is swelling, his throat is burning. He's about to die. He can't get up, his skin is turning purple, his whole body is shaking.'

Setau held up his sack full of vipers. The Nubian war party backed away.

'Kneel,' Pharaoh ordered again, 'or prepare to die an awful death.'

'You're the one who's going to die!'

The chief lifted his spear over his head, then froze as a terrible roaring filled his ears. Turning, he barely caught a glimpse of the lion's mane and gaping jaws before it ripped his chest open with it's claws and its jaws closed on his head.

At a signal from Serramanna, the Egyptian bowmen fired at the scattering Nubians. The foot-soldiers advanced and disarmed the war party.

'Tie their hands behind their backs!' shouted the Sard.

As news of Ramses' victory spread, hundreds of Nubians left their hideouts and villages to pay him homage. The king gave a white-haired tribal chief the use of the newly created fertile zone around the water hole, and also put him in charge of the prisoners of war, who were to do farm work under the supervision of the Nubian police. Escapees and repeat offenders would get the death penalty.

Then the Egyptian forces marched to the oasis that had served as the rebel stronghold. They met with only feeble resistance, and took possession of the gold that would one day grace statues and temple doors in the motherland.

At nightfall, Setau found two lengths of well-dried palm rib, held them between his knees, set a piece of dead wood between them and rubbed them together faster and faster until sparks flew. The soldiers on watch would have a fire to keep away cobras, hyenas and other pests.

'Have you collected more snakes?' asked Ramses.

He nodded. 'Lotus is delighted. Tonight we'll rest.'

'It's a wonderful country.'

'You seem to like it as much as we do.'

'It tests me and makes me excel myself. Its power is mine.'

'Without my viper, the rebels would have killed you.'

'But they didn't, did they?'

'It was still a risky plan.'

'It prevented a great deal of bloodshed.'

'Do you ever consider being more cautious?'

'What for?'

'I'm only Setau the snake-charmer. It's all right if I fool around with reptiles. But you, Ramses, are Lord of the Two Lands. Your death would plunge Egypt into disarray.'

'Nefertari would reign wisely.'

'You're only twenty-five, Ramses, I know. But you no longer have the right to behave like a young man. You must consider your safety. You'll have to send others into battle.'

'Is Pharaoh to be a coward?'

'Don't exaggerate. I'm only telling you to be a bit more careful.'

'But I'm protected on all sides: Nefertari's magic, you and your snakes, Serramanna and his Royal Bodyguard, Wideawake and Invincible . . . I'm the luckiest man on earth.'

'Save your luck for when you need it.'

'It'll never run out.'

'Pig-headed as ever, I see. I might as well go to bed.'

Setau turned his back on the king and went and stretched out beside Lotus. Her contented sigh told Ramses that it was time to slip away. His friend might not be allowed to rest for long.

How could he make Setau realize his real place was high in the government? Ramses' failure to recruit him was his first major setback. Should Setau be free to go his own way or be forced into an official position?

The Temple of a Million Years

Ramses spent the night gazing at the starry sky, the luminous home of his father's soul and the souls of all the pharaohs before him. He was proud of having found water in the desert and put down the rebellion, just as his father had done, but he was not content with his victory. The earlier campaign had not had lasting results. This time would be the same. He would have to get to the root of the problem, but how could he determine what it was?

In the first light of dawn, Ramses sensed a presence at his back and slowly, very slowly, turned round.

There stood an enormous elephant. It had come into the oasis as silently as the wind, avoiding the dried palm ribs strewn all around. The lion and watchdog had opened their eyes but sounded no warning, as if they knew their master was safe.

As Ramses looked, he fancied that there was something familiar about the beast. Of course: the big bull elephant with flapping ears and long tusks was his friend. Years earlier, Ramses had saved it, removing a spearhead from its trunk.

The King of Egypt stroked that trunk now, and the lord of the savannahs trumpeted in joy, waking the whole encampment.

The elephant moved away, then turned to look back at the king.

'We must follow him,' said Ramses.

53

Ramses, Serramanna, Setau and a handful of armed soldiers followed the elephant across a strip of arid plain, then up a thorny slope to a plateau topped with a venerable acacia.

The elephant waited for Ramses to catch up.

Following the huge beast's gaze, he discovered a splendid view. The huge spur of rock where they stood, a landmark for navigation, looked down on a vast bend in the Nile. Ramses, spouse of Egypt, contemplated the life-giving waters, the divine river in all its majesty. On the nearby rocks, hieroglyphic inscriptions dedicated the spot to the goddess Hathor, sovereign of the stars and of sailors, who often stopped here.

With its right front foot, the elephant sent a boulder tumbling down the cliff. It landed in a deep sandy ravine between two promontories. To the north, the cliffs were vertical, dropping almost straight down to the water. To the south, they sloped gradually into a vast open stretch, broadening westward.

On the shore below, a boat hollowed out of a palm trunk was moored, with a young boy sleeping inside.

'Go and get him,' the king ordered two of his soldiers.

The young Nubian saw them coming and took to his heels. He would have got away if he hadn't tripped on a rock and sprawled on the riverbank. The Egyptian soldiers twisted the young Nubian's arms behind his back and brought him before the king.

The runaway's eyes rolled in panic: he was afraid his nose would be cut off. 'I'm not a thief,' he cried. 'The boat belongs to me, I swear it, and—'

'Answer my question,' Ramses told him, 'and you'll go free. What do they call this place?'

'Abu Simbel.'

'You may go.'

The boy ran back to his boat and paddled away with all his might.

'We can't stay here long,' advised Serramanna. 'I don't think this spot is safe.'

'No sign of any snakes,' complained Setau. 'Bizarre. Could Hathor have driven them off ?'

'Don't follow me,' the king commanded.

Serramanna stepped forward. 'Majesty!'

'Must I say it again?'

Ramses began the descent towards the river.

Setau restrained the Sard. 'You'd better do as he says.'

Grumbling, Serramanna gave in. The king on his own, in the middle of nowhere, in hostile territory! If danger arose, despite his orders he would step in.

When he reached the riverbank, Ramses turned to face the sandstone cliff.

This was the heart of Nubia, though she didn't know it. He, Ramses, the Son of the Light, would reveal it, make of Abu Simbel a wonder that would outlast time and seal the pact between Egypt and Nubia.

The pharaoh meditated at Abu Simbel for several hours, steeping himself in the purity of the sky, the sparkling of the Nile and the strength of the rocks. The province's main temple would be built here, concentrating divine energy and radiating a protective force so strong that the clash of arms would be for ever stilled.

Ramses observed the sun. Its rays did not merely glance off the cliff, but penetrated to the heart of the rock, lighting it from within. When his architects worked on the site, they must capture this miracle.

By the time the king climbed back to the top of the cliff, Serramanna's nerves were stretched to the limit. He was tempted to quit for good, but the elephant's placid attitude changed his mind. He refused to appear less patient than an animal, even the most majestic of animals.

'We're going back to Egypt,' decreed the king.

After cleansing his mouth with natron, Shaanar surrendered his face to the barber, who was skilled in the painless removal of body hair. He was extremely fond of massage, and particularly liked having his scalp rubbed with perfumed oils before the hairdresser came to do his wig. These small pleasures lightened his days and helped him present his best face to the world. He might not be as handsome or athletic as Ramses, but he could be just as well groomed, if not better so.

His water-clock, a costly piece, told him that the hour of his meeting was near.

His litter, comfortable and roomy, was the finest in Memphis except for the pharaoh's, which he one day planned to occupy. Shaanar had the bearers drop him off at the canal that gave heavy barges passage to the main river landing.

Ofir was sitting in the shade of a willow tree. Shaanar leaned against the trunk and watched a fishing boat go by.

'Any progress, Ofir?'

'Moses is an exceptional man, with a mind of his own.'

'In other words, you can't persuade him.'

'I didn't say that.'

'I need facts, Ofir. Vague impressions won't do.'

'The road to success is often a long and winding one.'

'Spare me the philosophy. Have you succeeded, yes or no?'

'He didn't reject my proposal. That's quite something, isn't it?'

'Interesting, I admit. Did he admit that your plan is feasible?'

'Moses is familiar with Akhenaton's ideas. He knows they helped shape the Hebrew faith and that we could do great things together.'

'And the Hebrews will follow him?'

'He's more popular than ever. Moses is a born leader. Once Pi-Ramses is finished, he'll rally his people.'

'How long will that take?'

'A few more months. He has the brickmakers working at lightning speed.'

'That damned capital! Ramses' fame will spread beyond the northern border, I'm afraid.'

'Where is pharaoh now?'

'In Nubia.'

'A dangerous place.'

'Don't fool yourself, Ofir. The royal couriers have brought excellent news. More miracles for Ramses: he found an underground spring in the desert and opened up new farmland. He's bringing back the stolen gold for the temples. A successful expedition, a signal victory.'

'Moses knows that he'll have to confront the pharaoh.'

'His closest friend . . .'

'His belief in the One God will be stronger than their friendship: a clash is inevitable. When it comes, we must support Moses.'

'That's your role, Ofir. You understand why I have to remain in the background.'

'I'll need your help.'

'What do you need?'

'A place in Memphis, servants, a communication net-work.'

'Granted, on condition that you send me regular reports on your activities.'

'Confidential reports.'

'When are you going back to Pi-Ramses, Ofir?'

'Tomorrow. I plan to tell Moses how our numbers are growing.'

'I'll take care of your everyday routine; you concentrate on persuading Moses to fight for his faith, against Ramses' tyranny.'

Abner the brickmaker hummed to himself. In less than a month, the first Pi-Ramses barracks would be finished and the initial detachment of foot-soldiers transferred from Memphis. The premises were spacious and well ventilated, the fittings remarkable.

Thanks to Moses, who had recognized his talent, Abner now headed a small crew of his fellow craftsmen, as experienced and industrious as himself. Sary's extortion was only a bad memory. Abner would move his family to the new capital and work in public building maintenance. The future was looking bright.

Tonight he would enjoy a meal of Nile perch with his comrades. Then they would play a game of snake, advancing their pieces along the board and trying to avoid various traps marked on the reptile's body. Abner had a feeling it was his lucky night.

Pi-Ramses was coming to life. The construction site was gradually turning into a real city. It didn't seem long now until the time for the dedication, the moment when Pharaoh would bring his capital to life. It had been his special privilege, Abner reflected, to serve a great king's vision and work with Moses.

'How are you, Abner?'

Sary wore a Libyan tunic with wide vertical stripes of black and yellow, caught at the waist with a green leather belt. His face had grown even more emaciated.

'What do you want with me?'

'Asking after your health, that's all.'

'Move along.'

'Is that any way to talk to me?'

'I think you've forgotten I was promoted. I don't report to you any more.'

'Proud as a peacock, aren't we, Abner? Now, now, don't get worked up.'

'I'm busy.'

'Too busy to talk to your old friend Sary?'

The Hebrew was growing uneasy, to Sary's amusement.

'You're a reasonable fellow, Abner. You want a nice little life for yourself, but you know that everything has a price. And I'm the one who sets it.'

'Go to hell!'

'Hebrew, you're nothing more than an insect and bugs don't complain when you squash them. I demand half your wages and bonuses. When the work is done here, you'll volunteer to stay on as my servant. Mmm, I'd love to have a Hebrew houseboy. I'll keep you busy, don't worry. You're lucky, Abner. If I hadn't noticed you, you'd have ended up as vermin.'

'You can't make me, I tell you, I—'

'Stop babbling and do as I say,' the foreman snarled in parting.

Abner crouched in a corner, hanging his head. This time Sary had gone too far. This time he'd speak to Moses.

307

54

Peerless Nefertari, her beauty like the morning star at the dawn of a good year, her touch like a lotus flower. Luminous Nefertari, catching him in the dark loops of her fragrant hair.

To love her was to be reborn.

Ramses gently massaged her feet, then kissed her legs, letting his hands wander over her lithe, sun-gilded body. She was the garden where the rarest flowers grew, the pool of clear water, the distant country of frankincense trees. When they came together, their desire was strong as the surge of a wave cresting the inundation, tender as a flute tune in the twilight.

As soon as the expedition had returned from Nubia, the king had made straight for his wife, ignoring well-wishers and advisers. Nefertari and Ramses had celebrated their reunion beneath the verdant foliage of a sycamore. The refreshing shade of the great tree, its turquoise leaves and notched fruit red as jasper were one of the treasures of the palace at Thebes where they had managed to slip away.

'You were gone for so many, many months . . .'

'The baby?'

'Kha and Meritamon are both doing wonderfully. Your son thinks his little sister is very pretty but a little noisy. He's already trying to teach her to read. His tutor made him stop.'

Ramses took his wife in his arms. 'That's wrong. Why hold him back?'

Before Nefertari could answer, her husband's lips sought hers as the sycamore branches bent discreetly over them in the cool north wind.

Bakhen, carrying a long staff, marched in front of the royal pair. It was the tenth day of the fourth month of the inundation season, Year Three of Ramses' reign, and he was leading them to inspect the newly completed additions to the temple of Luxor. A long procession followed them down the avenue of sphinxes leading from the temple of Karnak.

The new façade of Karnak imposed silence. The two obelisks, the colossal royal statues and the massive yet elegant pylon gateway formed a perfect whole, worthy of the greatest builders of old.

The obelisks repelled negative energy and attracted divine power to the temple, where it would nourish the *ka* produced here. At their bases were carved dog-faced baboons, symbols of the mind of the god Thoth, uttering the sounds that helped bring forth each new dawn. Each element, from hieroglyph to colossal statue, contributed to the daily rebirth of the sun, which now sat in glory above the twin towers of the pylon and central gateway.

Ramses and Nefertari passed through it, entering a great open-air forecourt with huge columns lining the walls, a powerful expression of the *ka*. Between them stood colossal statues of the king, a testimony to his indomitable strength. Leaning lovingly against one of the giant's legs was Nefertari, at once frail and steadfast.

Nebu, the High Priest of Karnak, slowly made his way towards the royal pair, his golden staff tapping. The old man bowed. 'Majesty, here is the home of your *ka*, the endless source of energy for your reign.'

The feast of the dedication of Luxor involved the entire population of Thebes and its environs, from the humblest to the wealthiest. For ten days, there was singing and dancing in the streets; taverns and open-air drinking establishments were crammed. By the grace of Pharaoh, free beer would fill every belly.

The king and queen presided at a banquet recorded in the royal annals. Ramses proclaimed the temple to his *ka* completed, decreeing that no architectural feature would be added in the future. It remained only for him and the queen to choose the themes and symbolic figures that would adorn the façade of the pylon and the walls of the great forecourt. It was generally agreed that the young pharaoh was wise not to make his decision until he had conferred with the ritualists of the House of Life.

Ramses appreciated Bakhen's attitude. The Fourth Prophet of Amon made no mention of his own contributions, but praised the architects who had designed Luxor in accordance with the laws of harmony. When the feasting was over, the king presented the High Priest of Amon with the Nubian gold, which would henceforth be shipped with stringent security measures.

Before departing northward, the royal pair visited the site of the Temple of a Million Years. Bakhen's competence was in evidence there as well. Graders, unskilled labourers, and stone-cutters were hard at work. The temple was beginning to rise from the desert floor.

'Hurry, Bakhen. I want the foundations laid as quickly as possible.'

'The Luxor work gangs will start working here tomorrow. Then we'll have full crews and enough skilled workers.'

Ramses noted that his plan for the complex had been followed to the letter. He could already picture the shrines, the great Hall of Pillars, the offering tables, the laboratory, the library . . . Millions of years would flow through the building's stone veins.

The king toured the holy site with Nefertari, describing his vision as if he were already touching the carved walls and columns covered with hieroglyphs.

'This temple will be your greatest monument.'

'Perhaps.'

'Why do you doubt it?'

'Because I hope to build temples all over the country, make hundreds of homes for the gods. I want my country drenched with their energy. I want the land of Egypt to be heaven on earth.'

'What could surpass your Temple of a Million Years?'

'In Nubia I met an old friend, an elephant. He led me to an extraordinary place.'

'Does it have a name?'

'Abu Simbel. A stopping place for sailors, protected by Hathor, where the Nile is at its most beautiful. The river blends with the rock, the sandstone cliffs seem ripe to give birth to a temple.'

'But so far south . . . Won't the technical difficulties be overwhelming?'

'We won't let them overwhelm us.'

'No pharaoh before you has attempted such a thing.'

'True, but I'll succeed. From the moment I first saw Abu Simbel, I haven't been able to get it out of my mind. The elephant was a messenger from the gods, I'm sure of it. Abu stands for elephant, and as you know its hieroglyph can also be read as 'start' or 'beginning'. A new start for Egypt, the beginning of her territory, must be there in the heart of Nubia, at Abu Simbel. It's the only way to assure a lasting peace.'

'It's a wild idea.'

'Of course it is! But it's also an expression of my *ka* – the fire within me captured for ever in stone. Luxor, Pi-Ramses and Abu Simbel are each my desire and my brainchild. If I spent my time on day-to-day matters, I wouldn't be acting like a pharaoh.'

'My head rests on your shoulder and I feel secure in your

love. But you can also rest on me, like a colossal statue on its pedestal.'

'Do you approve of my Abu Simbel project?'

'Think more about it. Let it grow inside you until your vision is dazzling and imperious. Then act upon it.'

Within the enclosure of the Temple of a Million Years, Ramses and Nefertari felt a strange force move within them, making them invulnerable.

Workshops, warehouses, barracks – all were ready to be occupied. The main streets led through residential neighbourhoods and ended at the major temples, still under construction but with each inner sanctum in usable condition.

The brickmakers' work was finished, and an army of landscapers and painters took their place, not to mention the decorative artists who would give Pi-Ramses its outward face. But would Ramses smile on it?

Moses climbed to the roof of the palace and contemplated the city. Like Pharaoh, he had worked miracles. The men's physical labour and his own careful organization had not been enough. The spark had come from enthusiasm, not human but divine in origin, the sign of God's love for his creation. And Moses longed to offer this city to God, not leave it to Amon, Set and the like. Such an outpouring of talent wasted on those mute idols . . .

His next city would be built to the glory of the One God, in his own country, on holy ground. If Ramses was truly his soulmate, he would understand.

Moses pounded his fist on the edge of the balcony.

The King of Egypt would never tolerate a minority revolt, never let a descendant of Akhenaton take over the throne. To believe otherwise was, at best, an impossible dream.

Below, near one of the side entries to the palace, stood Ofir. 'May I speak to you?' he called.

'Come up.'

Ofir had learned to blend in wherever he went. At Pi-Ramses he could pass for an architect coming to offer Moses valuable advice.

'I'm giving up,' declared Moses. 'It's no use arguing any more.'

The sorcerer eyed him coolly. 'Has something happened to change your mind?'

'I've thought it over, that's all. Our plans are crazy.'

'I came to tell you that our ranks have been growing steadily. There are influential people who believe Lita will take the throne with the blessing of the One God. In that case, the Hebrews will be free.'

'You mean to overthrow Ramses? Are you mad?'

'Our convictions are firm.'

'Do you think your sermons will sway the king?'

'Who said we'll stop at sermons?'

Moses stared at Ofir as if he were meeting a stranger. 'You can't mean—'

'Of course I can, Moses. You've reached the same conclusion I have, and that's what alarms you. Akhenaton was defeated and persecuted only because he refused to use force against his enemies. No fight can be won without bloodshed. Ramses will never give up a single morsel of his power. We'll have to fight him from within. And you will lead the Hebrews in their revolt.'

'The dead will number in the hundreds, even thousands. Is carnage what you want?'

'If you prepare your people, they'll win. God is with us.'

'I won't listen to another word. Get out of here, Ofir.'

'I can see you in Memphis as well as here.'

'Don't count on it.'

'There's no other way, and you know it. Don't try to ignore the voice inside you. We'll fight the good fight together, and God will triumph.'

55

Raia, the Syrian merchant, fingered his beard. Business was booming. The quality of his preserved meats and Asian vases attracted an ever-growing clientele among the upper classes of Memphis and Thebes. The creation of the new capital, Pi-Ramses, meant yet another market would open up. Raia had already secured a permit to open a large shop in the heart of the commercial district and was training the sales force to deal with demanding customers.

In preparation, he had ordered a hundred precious vases, all new designs, from his Syrian sources. Each piece was unique and would be priced accordingly. Raia's personal opinion was that Egyptian craftsmen did better work, but the buying public's taste for the exotic (not to mention its rampant snobbery) was lining his pockets.

Although the Hittites had ordered their spy to back Shaanar and oppose Ramses, after a single unsuccessful attempt on the king Raia had given up trying. Pharaoh was too well protected and a second unsuccessful attempt might lead the investigators to him.

Over the last three years, Ramses had proved as strong a ruler as his father, with the added energy of youth. He was like a raging torrent, sweeping all obstacles out of his way. No one had the authority to oppose him, even if the number of building projects he had undertaken was sheer madness. The court and the people were at once enthralled and subjugated.

Raia checked his shipment. Among the new pieces were two alabaster vases.

He shut the storeroom door, then put his ear to it for several moments. Satisfied that he was alone, he stuck his hand inside the vase with the small, distinctive red mark under the rim and pulled out a pine tablet inscribed with the vase's dimensions and origin.

Raia knew the code by heart and easily worked out the message his contact in southern Syria had forwarded from the Hittites.

Stunned, the secret agent destroyed the message and went running out of the shop.

'Superb,' said Shaanar, admiring the blue swan-necked vase Raia had just unpacked for him. 'The price?'

'Rather high, I'm afraid, Your Highness. But it's a unique piece.'

'Let's discuss it, shall we?'

Clutching the vase to his chest, Raia followed Shanaar to one of his villa's roofed terraces, where they could speak without fear of being overheard.

'If I'm not mistaken, Raia, you're following emergency procedure.'

'Correct.'

'Why?'

'The Hittites have decided to take action.'

It was the news Shaanar had hoped for, but also dreaded. If he were Pharaoh, he would put Egyptian troops on high alert and reinforce the border defences. But Egypt's most dangerous enemy was offering him a way to win the throne. He would have to use this vital secret to his sole advantage.

'Could you be more specific, Raia?'

'You look disturbed.'

'Who wouldn't be?'

'It's true, Your Highness. I'm still in shock myself. This decision will shatter the existing state of affairs.'

'More than that, Raia, much more. The fate of the whole world hangs on it. You and I will be major players in the drama that unfolds.'

'But I'm only a humble information-gatherer.'

'You'll be my contact with the Hittites. A good part of my strategy depends on the accuracy of the information you provide.'

'You make it sound so important.'

'Do you hope to stay in Egypt, once we win?'

'I'm at home here.'

'You'll be rich, Raia, very rich. I shan't be ungrateful to the people who help me to power.'

The merchant bowed. 'Your humble servant, Prince.'

'Do you have any details?'

'Not yet.'

Shaanar took a few steps, leaned over the balustrade, and looked towards the north.

'This is a great day, Raia. One day we'll tell ourselves it marked the beginning of the end of Ramses.'

Ahsha's Egyptian mistress was a marvel. Playful, inventive and insatiable, she had elicited from him new and subtle responses. She was a definite improvement over her pretty but boring predecessors, two Libyan girls and three Syrians. Ahsha demanded imagination in his lovemaking. That alone could release the unexpected melodies straining within the body. He was just getting round to sucking his lady love's sweet little toes when he heard his steward hammering at the door, despite strict orders.

Outraged, Ahsha flung the door open without thinking to cover himself.

'Forgive me, sir. An urgent message from your office.'

Ahsha consulted the wooden tablet. Just two words: 'Report immediately.'

At two in the morning, the streets of Memphis were deserted. Ahsha's horse quickly covered the distance between his house and the secretariat. Not stopping to make the customary offering to Thoth, Ahsha took the stairs four at a time and sped to his office. He found his secretary waiting.

'I thought I should let you know immediately.'

'About what?'

'A dispatch from one of our agents in northern Syria.'

'If it's another false alarm, I'll deal with him.'

The bottom of the papyrus scroll looked blank, but when heated over the flame of an oil lamp, hieratic characters appeared. This shorthand method of writing hieroglyphs sometimes made them almost illegible. The hand of the Egyptian spy on their payroll in northern Syria was unmistakable.

Ahsha read and reread the message.

'Glad I sent for you?' asked the secretary.

'Please leave.'

Ahsha spread out a map and checked the information against it. If his calculations were correct, the worst was in store.

'The sun hasn't even risen,' grunted Shaanar, yawning.

'Read this,' advised Ahsha, handing his minister the secret message.

Shaanar's eyes opened wide. 'What? The Hittites have taken control of several villages in central Syria, well outside the zone of influence acceptable to Egypt . . .'

'He's categorical.'

'No one killed or wounded. They could just be testing the waters.'

'It wouldn't be the first time. But the Hittites have never gone so far south.'

'What do you make of it?'

'They're preparing a fully fledged campaign in southern Syria.'

'Is that a statement or a guess?'

'A guess.'

'How can we find out for sure?'

'In the light of the situation, I assume more messages will soon follow.'

'Whatever the case, let's keep this quiet as long as possible.'

'We're taking quite a risk.'

'I know we are, Ahsha. But that's what we have to do. We were trying to coax Ramses into making mistakes that would cost him dearly, but it seems the Hittites are restless. We'll have to delay the mobilization of the Egyptian army as long as we can.'

'I'm not so sure,' objected Ahsha.

'Why?'

'On one hand, that would only buy us a few more days, hardly enough time to stop a counteroffensive. On the other, my secretary knows I received an urgent message. Any delay in informing the king will look suspicious.'

'Then having advance information does us no good at all!'

'Wrong, Shaanar. Ramses appointed me head of the Secret Service. He trusts me. In other words, he'll believe what I tell him.'

Shaanar smiled. 'A very dangerous tactic. They say Ramses is a mind-reader.'

'A diplomat's thoughts are unreadable. What I want you to do is tell him your concerns, once I've alerted him. That will make you look honest and credible.'

Shaanar settled into an armchair. 'Damnably intelligent, Ahsha.'

'I know Ramses. Underestimating his insight would be a fatal error.'

'I agree. We'll follow your plan.'

'Just one more problem: being sure of the Hittites' real intentions.'

Shaanar knew what those intentions were. But he judged it wiser not to reveal his sources to Ahsha, whom he might be forced to sacrifice to his Hittite friends as the situation evolved.

56

Moses raced from building to building, checking the walls and windows. He drove his chariot all the way across town, urging the painters to hurry and finish their work. It was only a matter of days until the king and queen arrived for the official dedication of Pi-Ramses.

A thousand flaws jumped out at him, but how could they be fixed in so short a time? The brickmakers had agreed to lend a hand to the frantic workmen finishing the site. In the final rush, Moses' popularity remained intact. His enthusiasm was catching, even more so as the dream was transformed into reality.

Despite his exhaustion, Moses had spent long evenings with his Hebrew brethren, listening to their grievances and hopes. He had grown comfortable in his role as leader of a people in search of its identity. His ideas frightened most of the men, yet they were drawn to him. When the grand adventure of Pi-Ramses was finished, would Moses be taking his fellow Hebrews in a new direction?

Overtired, the young supervisor slept only fitfully. In his dreams, Ofir's gaunt face loomed. The worshipper of Aton had spoken the truth: in a crisis sermons and speeches were not enough. They would have to act, and action often meant violence.

Moses had fulfilled the mission Ramses had entrusted

to him, thus discharging any obligation to the King of Egypt. Yet he still owed loyalty to his oldest friend and vowed to warn him of the dangers facing him. Once his conscience was eased on that score, Moses would be free – completely free.

According to the royal courier, the pharaoh and his wife would arrive around noon the following day. The population of the surrounding towns and villages had flocked to the outskirts of the new capital so as not to miss the event. Overwhelmed, the security forces could not stop the curious from spilling in.

Moses was hoping to spend his last few hours as construction supervisor outside the city, strolling in the countryside. Just as he reached the edge of town, however, an architect ran up to him.

'The statue is breaking loose! The giant statue!'

'At the Temple of Amon?'

'We can't stop it.'

'I told you not to touch it!'

'We thought—'

Moses' chariot sped like the wind through the city. The scene in front of the Temple of Amon was chaotic. A two-hundred-ton statue of the king seated on his throne was slowly slipping towards the façade. It could either collide with the building, causing enormous damage, or fall from its sledge and shatter. What a sight to greet Ramses at the dedication!

Fifty or more men strained desperately, holding the ropes that secured the giant sculpture to a wooden sledge. Where rope touched stone, several leather pads had already split.

'What happened?' asked Moses.

'The foreman climbed up on the statue to help guide it into place. He fell, and to avoid crushing him the men pulled the wooden brakes to stop the sledge. It jumped the track and kept going. There was dew on the ground, the runners were already wet . . .'

'You should have had at least a hundred and fifty men!'

'There isn't a hand to spare.'

'Bring me jugs of milk.'

'How many?'

'Thousands! And get more men here as fast as you can.'

Heartened by Moses' arrival, the struggling workers quieted. When he climbed along the right side of the statue, perched on its granite apron and poured milk in front of the sledge to lay a new track, they took hope. A chain formed to pass jugs to Moses. Following his directives, the first spare hands to arrive on the scene tied long ropes to the sides and back of the sledge, slowing the statue's momentum.

Little by little, the colossus moved back on track.

'The braking beam!' shouted Moses.

Thirty men sprang into action, hauling the notched log into place. It would halt the sledge at the spot where Ramses' statue would sit, in front of the Temple of Amon.

The colossus, righted and slowed, slid easily into place.

Dripping with sweat, Moses hopped down, glowering. The men feared the punishment that was sure to come.

'Bring me the man responsible for this fiasco, the man who fell off the statue.'

'Here he is.'

Two workmen pushed Abner forward. He fell to his knees in front of Moses.

'Forgive me,' he groaned, 'I had a dizzy spell, I—'

'Aren't you one of my brickmakers?'

'Yes. My name is Abner.'

'Why were you working here?'

'I . . . I'm in hiding,' he gulped.

'Have you lost your mind?'

'I can explain.'

Abner was a Hebrew: he deserved a hearing before being punished. Moses could see that the man was distraught and would talk to him only if they were alone.

'Come with me, Abner.'

An Egyptian architect stepped forward. 'This man is responsible for a serious incident. Letting him off would be an insult to his co-workers.'

'I'll question him and then decide what to do.'

The architect bowed to the project supervisor. If Abner had been an Egyptian, Moses would surely have shown less consideration. Lately he had shown a favouritism towards his fellow Hebrews that was bound to rebound on him.

Moses helped Abner into his chariot and fastened a leather strap round him.

'Enough falls for one day, don't you think?'

'Please, Moses, forgive me!'

'Stop whining, man, and tell me what happened.'

In front of Moses' house, there was a small courtyard sheltered from the wind. The two men got down from the chariot and went inside. Moses took off his wig and kilt, and gestured towards a large jug.

'Get up on the ledge,' he ordered Abner, 'and pour that water slowly over my shoulders.'

As Moses briskly rubbed his skin with herbs, the brick-maker emptied the heavy jug.

'Cat got your tongue, Abner?'

'I'm afraid.'

'Why?'

'Someone's after me.'

'Who?'

'I can't say.'

'If you won't tell me, I'll turn you over to the tribunal for disciplinary action.'

'No! I'll never work again.'

'Wouldn't that be fair?'

'No! I swear it.'

'Then talk.'

'I've been the victim of extortion,' Abner sighed.

'Who's doing this to you?'

'An Egyptian.'

'What's his name?'

'I can't tell you! He has connections.'

'Then I can't help you.'

'If I tell you, he'll kill me!'

'Don't you trust me?'

'I wanted to tell you, but I was too scared.'

'Stop shaking and give me a name. I'll take care of him for you.'

Abner trembled so violently that the jug slipped from his hands and shattered.

'Sary,' he said. 'It's Sary.'

The royal fleet entered the grand canal leading to Pi-Ramses. Every member of the court, it seemed, was accompanying Pharaoh and the Great Royal Wife. No one could wait to see the new capital, which would be the place to live if you sought the king's favour. There was a great deal of negative speculation, bordering on criticism: how could a city built so quickly be any match for Memphis? It would be a major setback for Ramses, and sooner or later he'd be forced to abandon his new capital.

In the prow, the pharaoh was watching the Nile fan into its Delta when the boat tacked towards the canal.

Shaanar sidled up to his brother. 'I know this is hardly the time, but I have a serious matter to discuss with you.'

'Can't it wait?'

'I'm afraid not. If I'd been able to speak to you sooner, I wouldn't have intruded on this happy occasion. But you were out of reach.'

'I'm listening, Shaanar.'

'You did me a favour appointing me minister for foreign affairs, and I wish I could repay you with nothing but the best of news.'

'And that's not the case?'

'If reports reaching me are to be believed, the international situation leaves something to be desired.'

'Get to the point.'

'The Hittites seem to have gone beyond the limits our late father established and invaded central Syria.'

'Is that fact or hearsay?'

'It's too early to tell, but I wanted to be the first to warn you. In the recent past, the Hittites have tended to engage in provocation, then back away. We can hope that this is simply another bluff. Still, it would be wise to take certain precautions.'

'I'll consider it.'

'Are you sceptical?'

'You said yourself that the reports haven't been verified. Once you have solid information, let me know.'

'At your service, Majesty.'

The current was strong, there was a good following wind, and the boat sailed briskly. Shaanar's announcement left Ramses thoughtful. Did his elder brother really take his new position seriously? He was capable of inventing reports of a Hittite invasion, just to show how well he was running his secretariat.

Central Syria was a neutral zone where neither nation maintained a military presence, relying on a patchy intelligence network. Since Seti had refrained from taking the Hittite stronghold of Kadesh, the fighting had been small-scale and intermittent.

Perhaps the creation of Pi-Ramses, which occupied a strategic position, had roused the Hittites to action. They might have decided the young pharaoh was looking toward Asia and their empire. Only one man could sort out the truth for him: his friend Ahsha, head of the Secret Service. The official reports that reached Shaanar would be fragmentary, while Ahsha's sources would reveal the enemy's real intentions.

A sailor who had climbed to the top of the mast began to cheer.

'Ahoy! There it is, the port, the town – Pi-Ramses!'

57

Alone in a golden chariot, the Son of the Light rode down the main thoroughfare of Pi-Ramses, towards the Temple of Amon. At high noon, he shone like the sun that had given life to the city. Alongside his two plumed horses marched his lion, head high, mane blowing in the wind.

Stunned by the power their monarch radiated, and by the magic that permitted him to have the king of beasts as a bodyguard, at first the crowd was silent. Then a voice shouted, 'Long live Ramses!' Then another, ten more, a hundred, a thousand took up the chant . . . The jubilation was passionate and clamorous as the king made his slow and majestic way down the avenue.

Nobles, tradesmen and country folk were all dressed for a feast day. Their hair shone with moringa oil, the women wore their best wigs, children and servants threw armfuls of flowers and greenery in the royal chariot's path.

An open-air banquet was being prepared. The steward of the new palace had ordered a thousand loaves of the whitest bread, two thousand rolls, ten thousand pastries, mounds of dried meat, milk, bowls of carob, grapes, figs, pomegranates. Roast goose, game, fish, cucumbers and leeks would also be on the menu, not to mention thousands of jars of wine from the royal cellars and vats of beer brewed for the noble occasion.

The king had invited all his people to celebrate his capital's birthday.

No little girl was without a colourful new dress, no horse without bright bands of cloth and copper rosettes, no donkey without a garland of flowers around its neck. Pet dogs, cats, and monkeys would have an extra feed. Elders, no matter what their station in life, would be served first, seated in comfort beneath sycamore and persea trees. Petitions would be collected – for a house, a job, a plot of land, a cow – and carefully examined by Ahmeni. Generosity and indulgence were the order of the day.

The Hebrews joined in the festivities. Their labours had earned them a long well-paid rest, as well as the satisfaction of having built the new capital of the Kingdom of Egypt with their own hands. Their accomplishments would go down in history.

A hush fell over the assembled crowd as the chariot drew to a halt before the colossal statue of the pharaoh that had come so close to causing a disaster the day before.

Ramses looked up, meeting the giant's stony stare. On its forehead the statue wore the uraeus, the figure of a spitting-cobra, whose venom would blind the king's enemies. On its head were the 'Two Powers', the White Crown of Upper Egypt and the Red Crown of Lower Egypt. Seated on his throne, his hands placed flat on his kilt, the granite pharaoh gazed out over his city.

Ramses stepped down from his chariot. He, too, wore the double crown, and was dressed in a billowing full-sleeved robe of gauzy linen; beneath it shone a gilded linen kilt held in place by a belt of silver. A broad gold collar covered his chest.

He addressed the statue. 'You are my *ka* incarnate, the spirit of my reign and my city. I open your mouth, your eyes, your ears. I pronounce you a living being. Anyone who dares attack you will be punished by death.'

The sun was at its zenith, directly above the pharaoh. He turned to his people.

'Pi-Ramses is born, Pi-Ramses is our capital!'

Thousands of enthusiastic voices took up the chorus.

All day long, Ramses and Nefertari had travelled broad avenues, streets and alleys, visiting each section of Pi-Ramses. Dazzled, the Great Royal Wife dubbed it 'the Turquoise City', a phrase that was instantly on everyone's lips. That was Moses' final surprise for the king: the façades of villas, houses and modest dwellings had been covered with blue-glazed tiles of exceptional luminosity. The faience workshop had been Ramses' idea, but he had never imagined that so many tiles could be produced in so short a time, providing the city with a visual unity.

A dashing Moses served as master of ceremonies. There was no doubt now that Ramses would name his old friend vizier and first minister of the country. It was obvious how well they understood each other and how perfectly Moses had realized the pharaoh's plans and wishes for his new capital.

Shaanar was furious. Ofir had either lied about his influence over the Hebrew, or grossly miscalculated. Moses was poised to become a rich man, a devoted courtier. Confronting Ramses over religious differences would be suicide. Besides, his people were so well assimilated that they had no desire to change things. Shaanar's only true allies remained the Hittites. Dangerous as vipers, but allies.

A reception was held in the royal palace, its great columned hall adorned with peaceful, ordered scenes from nature. In this enchanted setting, Nefertari appeared lovelier and more charming than ever. The king's consort, magical protectress of the royal residence, found the right thing to say to each courtier.

Everyone admired the painted-tile flooring, in delightful patterns evoking garden ponds, flowers in bloom, ducks flying in a veritable forest of papyrus, lotuses in full bloom, darting fish. Pale green, light blue, off-white, golden yellow and deep purple blended in a song of colour, praising the perfection of creation.

Scoffers and nay-sayers were reduced to silence. Pi-Ramses' temples were still far from completion, but in terms of luxury and refinement the palace was in every way the equal of Memphis and Thebes. The court could feel quite at home. The aristocracy and government officials were already planning their villas in Pi-Ramses.

Another miracle for Ramses – an incredible string of miracles.

'Nothing you see would exist without this man,' declared Pharaoh, laying a hand on Moses' shoulder. Conversations broke off.

'Protocol dictates that I should sit upon my throne, Moses should prostrate himself before me and I should reward him for his faithful service with collars of gold. But he is my friend, my friend since childhood, and we have worked side by side. I conceived the idea for this capital; he carried out my plans.'

Ramses took Moses in a solemn embrace, the highest accolade a pharaoh could bestow.

'Moses will remain a few more months as head of construction, until his replacement is trained. Then he will come to work at my side for the greater glory of Egypt.'

Shaanar's worst fears were realized. The two of them combined would be harder to deal with than an entire army.

Ahmeni and Setau congratulated Moses and were surprised to note his nervousness. They put it down to the emotion of the moment.

'Ramses is mistaken,' said the Hebrew. 'He's crediting me with qualities I don't possess.'

'You'll make an excellent vizier,' Ahmeni said firmly.

'But you'll have to answer to this wretched little scribe,' teased Setau. 'He's the one who really gives the orders.'

'Watch it, snake man!'

'The food is wonderful. If Lotus and I can unearth some lovely new snakes, we may find a place nearby. Has anyone seen Ahsha? Why isn't he here?'

'No idea,' said Ahmeni.

'You'd think he'd be more diplomatic.'

The three friends saw Ramses walk up to his mother, Tuya, and kiss her on the forehead. Despite the hint of sadness that would never leave her grave and lovely face, Seti's widow shone with pride. When she had announced she was moving her household to the palace for an extended stay at Pi-Ramses, her son's triumph had been complete.

The palace aviary was finished but not yet stocked with the exotic birds that would delight both the ear and the eye. Leaning against a pillar, arms crossed, features drawn and tense, Moses avoided looking Ramses in the eye. He had to forget the man and address an adversary, the Pharaoh of Egypt.

'Everyone is sleeping, except you and me.'

'You look exhausted, Moses. Can't this talk wait until tomorrow?'

'No. I have to stop pretending.'

'Pretending what?'

'I'm a Hebrew. I believe in the One True God. You're an Egyptian and you worship idols.'

'Not this childish nonsense again.'

'It disturbs you because it's the truth.'

'You've been instructed in the wisdom of the Egyptians, Moses. Your One God, shapeless and unknowable, is the hidden power within each speck of life.'

'He isn't incarnated in a sheep!'

331

'Amon is the secret of life, revealing himself in the gust of invisible wind that fills the sails of the barque, in the ram's horns whose spiral traces the harmonious development of all creation, in the stone that gives shape to our temples. He is all that and none of that. You know these ancient teachings as well as I do.'

'It's all an illusion. There's only one God.'

'Does that prevent him from taking the form of his many creatures, while remaining One?'

'He doesn't need your temples and your statues.'

'I'm telling you again, Moses, you've been under too much strain.'

'I know what I believe. Even you can't change that.'

'If your god makes you intolerant, be careful. He'll turn you into a fanatic.'

'You're the one who ought to be careful, Ramses! A movement is gathering strength in this country, still tentative, but a force for the truth.'

'What do you mean?'

'Do you remember Akhenaton and his belief in One God. He blazed the trail. Listen to his voice, Ramses. Listen to me. Or else your empire will crumble.'

58

For Moses, the situation was clear. He hadn't betrayed Ramses' trust and had even warned him of the peril that lay ahead. He could proceed with an easy conscience, following his destiny and unleashing the fire in his heart.

The One God, Yahweh, lived on a mountain. He would go in search of it, no matter how difficult the journey might prove. A few other Hebrews had decided to risk losing everything and leave Egypt with him. As he finished packing, Moses remembered the one pressing matter he should resolve before he said goodbye to his native land.

It was only a short distance to Sary's estate on the west of the city. The house was set in an old and thriving palm grove. He found his old teacher drinking cool beer by a fish pond.

'Moses! What a pleasure to see the real power behind Pi-Ramses! To what do I owe this honour?'

'The pleasure is all yours, and it certainly isn't an honour.'

Sary rose, insulted. 'You may be the man of the hour, but you have no right to be rude. Remember who you're talking to.'

'To a scoundrel.'

Sary struck out at Moses, but the Hebrew caught his wrist. He crumpled and fell to his knees.

'You've been hounding a fellow by the name of Abner.'

'Never heard of him.'

'You're lying, Sary. You stole from him and blackmailed him.'

'He's only a Hebrew brickmaker.'

Moses tightened his grip. Sary groaned.

'I'm only a Hebrew, too,' said Moses, 'but I could break your arm and cripple you.'

'You wouldn't dare.'

'My patience is wearing thin, I warn you. Stop bothering Abner or I'll drag you into court by the scruff of your neck. Now swear it!'

'I . . . I swear not to bother him again.'

'In the name of Pharaoh?'

'The name of Pharaoh.'

'Break your oath and a curse will fall on you.' Moses released him. 'You're getting off easy, old man.'

If he hadn't been in such a hurry to leave the country, he'd have initiated formal proceedings. He hoped a warning would be sufficient, but as he left the house, his mind was not at ease. He had read hatred, not submission, in Sary's eyes.

Moses hid behind a palm tree. He didn't have to wait long.

Carrying a cudgel, Sary slipped out of the house and headed south towards the brickmakers' quarters.

Moses kept a good distance between them until he saw him go through the open door of Abner's house. Almost at once, he heard cries of pain.

He ran into the house and in the semi-darkness saw Sary clubbing Abner, who crouched on the dirt floor, shielding his face with his hands. Moses grabbed the cudgel from Sary and whacked him on the back of the skull. The Egyptian collapsed, blood streaming down his neck.

'Get up, Sary, and get out!'

But Sary lay still.

Abner crept closer. 'Moses . . . it looks like . . . he's dead!'

'He can't be. I didn't hit him that hard!'

'He isn't breathing.'

Moses bent over and touched the body – the corpse?

He had just killed a man.

In the street outside it was quiet.

'Run for it,' said Abner. 'If they arrest you . . .'

'You'll defend me, Abner. You'll explain I was saving your life!'

'Who'd believe me? They'd say it was a cover-up. Go, Moses, go quickly!'

'Have you got a big sack?'

'Yes, for my tools.'

'Let me have it.'

Moses stuffed Sary's body inside and hoisted the sack over his shoulder. He'd find some sandy spot where he could dig a shallow grave, then hide in an unoccupied villa until he could gather his wits.

The police dog let out a high-pitched whine and strained on his leash, which was most unusual for him. When the patrolling guard released him, the hound bolted towards a piece of sand-strewn vacant land.

The dog was digging fast. By the time the patrol caught up, they saw him unearth an arm, then a shoulder, then the face of a dead man.

'I know him,' said one of the policemen. 'It's Sary.'

'The king's brother-in-law?'

'That's the one. Look, there's dried blood on his neck!'

They uncovered the body. There could be no doubt: Sary had been killed by a blow to the back of the head.

All night long, Moses paced like a Syrian bear in its cage. What he'd done was wrong, trying to hide the body of a villain like Sary, fleeing justice when it would have absolved him. But there had been Abner, his fear, his hesitation – and they were both Hebrews. Moses' enemies would be sure to use the incident to bring about his downfall. Even Ramses would side with them and punish him harshly.

Someone had just entered the half-finished villa. The police, so soon? He would put up a fight. He would never surrender.

'Moses, Moses, it's me, Abner! Come out if you're hiding here!'

He stepped from the shadows. 'Will you testify in my favour, Abner?'

'The police have discovered Sary's body. You're accused of murder.'

'But who—'

'My neighbours. They saw you.'

'But they're Hebrews, like us!'

Abner hung his head. 'They don't want trouble with the law. I know how they feel. Run, Moses. You have no future here in Egypt.'

Moses was appalled. The king's construction supervisor and potential first minister reduced to being a fugitive from justice! In the space of a few hours, to fall from the pinnacle into the abyss . . . God must have sent him this suffering to try his faith. Instead of a comfortable but empty life in a heathen country, God was offering him freedom.

'I'll leave at dark. Farewell, Abner.'

Moses passed through the brickmakers' quarters. He hoped to persuade a handful of followers to leave with him and form a sect that would eventually attract other Hebrews, even if their first homeland was only an isolated desert region. He had to set an example, no matter what the cost.

A few lamps shone. Children slept, housewives chatted on doorsteps. Beneath the awnings, their husbands drank herb tea before going off to bed.

In the street where his closest followers lived, two men

were fighting. As he drew near, he could see that it was his two most vocal supporters, quarrelling over a stepladder one had supposedly stolen from the other.

Moses broke up the fight.

'You!' they exclaimed, almost in unison.

'Stop fighting over a trifle and come with me. Let's leave Egypt and go in search of our true homeland.'

The older man eyed Moses with disdain. 'Who made you our prince and our guide? If we don't obey you, will you kill us, as you murdered the Egyptian?'

Stricken, Moses found no answer. A grandiose dream shattered inside him. He was no better than a criminal on the run, utterly abandoned.

59

Ramses insisted on viewing Sary's body. This was the first death in Pi-Ramses since its dedication.

'It was murder, Majesty,' confirmed Serramanna. 'A violent blow to the back of the head with some kind of club.'

'Does my sister know yet?'

'Ahmeni saw to it.'

'Is the suspect in custody?'

'Majesty . . .'

'What aren't you telling me? No matter who it is, he'll be tried and sentenced.'

'Majesty . . . there's a warrant out for Moses.'

'That's absurd.'

'The police have witnesses.'

'Reliable witnesses?'

'All Hebrews. The main accuser is a brickmaker named Abner. He saw it happen.'

'What does he say?'

'That they scuffled and it got out of hand. Moses and Sary were not on the best of terms. My sources tell me they'd already quarrelled in Thebes.'

'What if all the witnesses are wrong? Moses can't be a murderer.'

'Police scribes have recorded sworn statements from all the brickmakers.'

'Moses will explain.'

'No, Majesty. He's fled.'

The pharaoh ordered a search of every house and building in Pi-Ramses, but nothing came of it. Mounted policemen combed the Delta, questioning villagers, but found no trace of Moses. The north-eastern border patrol received strict orders, but they were probably too late.

Ramses was frustrated to find that his daily updates gave no clue as to which route Moses had taken. Was he hiding in a fishing village along the Mediterranean? Had he stowed away in a boat heading south, or taken refuge in some remote temple?

'You must eat something,' urged Nefertari. 'Since Moses disappeared, you really haven't had a good meal.'

Ramses gave his wife's hands a tender squeeze. 'Moses was exhausted. Sary must have provoked him. If he were here in front of me, he could explain. The fact that he ran away tells me he was at his wits' end.'

'Will he be able to live with himself ?'

'I'm afraid he won't.'

'Your dog is sad. It thinks you're neglecting it.'

Ramses let Wideawake jump on his lap. Wriggling with joy, the dog licked its master's face, then rested its head on his shoulder.

Ramses' three years on the throne had been wonderful. The additions to Luxor completed, the Temple of a Million Years under way, the new capital dedicated, Nubia under control and now this calamity! Without Moses, the world Ramses had begun to build would begin to crumble.

'You've been neglecting me, too,' said Nefertari in a hushed voice. 'Can't I help you rise above this suffering?'

'Yes. Only you can do it.'

Shaanar and Ofir met by the docks at Pi-Ramses, now bustling with activity. Foodstuffs, furnishings, household goods and countless other supplies needed in the new capital were being unloaded every day. Boats brought in donkeys, horses and cattle. The grain silos filled, cellars were stocked with fine wines. Discussions as heated as any in Memphis or Thebes were heard among the merchants vying to establish trade in the new capital.

'Now Moses is only a wanted killer, Ofir.'

'It doesn't seem to upset you much.'

'You were wrong about him. He would never have changed sides. His rash action has cost Ramses a valued associate.'

'Moses is an honest man. His faith in the One God is no mere whim,' said the sorcerer.

'Let's stick to the facts. Either he'll turn himself in or he'll be arrested and sentenced. We no longer have any hope of using the Hebrews.'

'Those who believe in Amon are no strangers to adversity. We've struggled on for years. This won't stop us. I hope we can count on your help.'

'Don't press me. I need to know about your concrete plans,' said Shaanar.

'Every night I work to undermine the health of the royal couple.'

'He's at the height of his power! Then there's the Temple of a Million Years too.'

'Pi-Ramses is the only one of his projects that Ramses has completed. We'll have to capitalize on the slightest sign of weakness, be ready to rush in when the first breach opens.'

The sorcerer's manner, calm yet firm, impressed Shaanar. If the Hittites succeeded with their plan, Ramses' *ka* would certainly be weakened. Ofir's magical attacks would further sap the king's strength. Resilient as he was, eventually Ramses would falter.

'Keep it up, Ofir. Perhaps you've heard that I never forget a favour.'

Setau and Lotus had decided to set up a new laboratory at Pi-Ramses. Ahmeni, in his smart new offices, worked day and night. Tuya kept the court running smoothly. Nefertari performed her religious and queenly duties. Iset the Fair and Nedjem were busy bringing up Kha. Meritamon was blooming. Remet the steward puffed from palace kitchens to wine cellar, wine cellar to state dining-room. Serramanna tinkered with his security procedures. Life in Pi-Ramses was orderly and peaceful, but for Ramses nothing was the same without Moses.

Despite their differences, his old friend's strength had been a gift that helped Ramses achieve his vision. Moses had put his soul into the city he left behind, and it showed. Their final conversation proved that his friend had fallen victim to evil influences, was caught in invisible bonds.

A spell – someone had cast a spell on him.

Ahmeni, juggling an armload of scrolls, hurried towards the king as he paced his audience chamber.

'Ahsha has just arrived. He wants to see you.'

'Show him in.'

Although suave in his elegant pale-green robe with red trim, the young diplomat looked less stylish than usual.

'It distressed me that you missed the dedication,' Ramses told him.

'The head of the secretariat represented me, Majesty.'

'But where were you?'

'In Memphis, collecting the dispatches from my information network.'

'Shaanar mentioned Hittite troop movements in central Syria.'

'It's more than troop movements, and it goes much farther than Syria,' Ahsha said with uncharacteristic gruffness.

341

'I thought my dear brother might be exaggerating. He likes to make himself look important.'

'If anything, he minimized the danger. Now that I've checked my own sources, I'm convinced that the Hittites have launched a full-scale campaign in Caanan and Syria – all of Syria. Even the ports of Lebanon are under threat.'

'Have there been direct attacks on our garrisons?'

'Not yet, but they've moved into areas we considered neutral and taken villages. Before this it's only been political manoeuvring in our territories, apparently non-violent, but in practice the Hittites have taken control of Egyptian territory – provinces under our jurisdiction and supposedly sending us tributes.'

Ramses bent over the map of the Near East spread out on a low table.

'The Hittites are working their way down a corridor to our north-east. They plan to invade,' the king predicted.

'It's too early to be sure, Majesty.'

'Why else would they be heading in this direction?'

'To extend their territory, cut us off, sow panic in our protectorates, hurt Egypt's reputation, demoralize our army . . . Take your pick.'

'What does it look like to you?'

'Like war.'

Ramses drew a quick slash of red ink across the Anatolian peninsula, home of the Hittites.

'These people love only savagery, blood and violence. Unless we stop them, they will endanger civilization as we know it.'

'Diplomacy . . .'

'Too late for that.'

'Your father negotiated—'

'A buffer zone around Kadesh, I know. But the Hittites won't honour it. They honour nothing. I demand a daily report on their movements.'

Ahsha bowed. Ramses no longer spoke as a friend, but as a commanding pharaoh.

'Have you heard that Moses is a fugitive from justice, wanted for murder?'

'Moses? It's unbelievable.'

'I think he's the victim of a plot. Put out a message through your network, Ahsha, and find him for me.'

Nefertari was playing the lute in the palace garden. To her right lay the cradle where her plump and rosy-cheeked daughter napped; on her left sat Kha, cross-legged, reading a tale full of wizards and demons. Just in front of her was Wideawake, trying to dig up a tamarisk sapling Ramses had planted the day before. Nose in the dirt, front paws flying, he worked so hard that the queen didn't have the heart to scold him.

Suddenly he stopped and ran to the garden gate. His joyful barking and jumping could only mean a visit from his master.

The sound of her husband's footsteps told Nefertari that his heart was heavy. She rose to meet him.

'Is it Moses?'

'No, I'm sure he's all right.'

'Not . . . not Tuya.'

'My mother is fine.'

'Tell me what's wrong.'

'It's Egypt, Nefertari. The dream is over – the dream of a country where peace and prosperity rule, where each day is a blessing.'

The queen shut her eyes. 'War?'

He nodded. 'It's unavoidable.'

'You're leaving, then.'

'Who else should command the army? If we don't stop the Hittites, it's death to Egypt.'

Little Kha glanced up at the embracing couple, then

went back to his story. Meritamon napped. Wideawake kept digging.

In the tranquil garden, Nefertari clung to Ramses. In the distance, a white ibis took flight above the wheat fields.

'War will separate us, Ramses. Where will we find the courage to go on?'

'In the love that unites us and always will, no matter what happens. While I'm gone, you, my Great Royal Wife, will reign in my Turquoise City.'

Nefertari gazed into the distance.

'You're right to go,' she told him. 'Never negotiate with evil.'

The white ibis soared majestically above the royal pair, bathed in the glow of sunset.